**Stephen Bayley Hon FRIBA** was the person for whom the term 'design guru' was coined, something he accepts with what he likes to think of as self-deprecating irony. After a short and blameless period in provincial academe, he joined Terence Conran in an attempt to popularize design. This resulted in the Boilerhouse Project in London's V&A, which became the most successful gallery of the eighties. The Boilerhouse evolved into the unique Design Museum, which Mrs Thatcher opened in 1989, after some finger-wagging and insisting it should not be called a 'museum'. During this period he learnt a lot about the perversity of genius and the absurdity of ambition.

Although Stephen Bayley has written many books and hundreds of articles that have shaped the popular understanding of design, this is his first work of fiction. He is Chairman of the Royal Fine Art Commission Trust, an honorary visiting professor at the University of Liverpool School of Architecture, and a Chevalier de l'Ordre des Arts et des Lettres, France's highest artistic accolade.

*Also by Stephen Bayley*

NON-FICTION

In Good Shape: Style in Industrial Products 1900 to 1960

The Albert Memorial

Harley Earl

The Conran Directory of Design (ed)

Sex, Drink and Fast Cars

Commerce and Culture

Taste: The Secret Meaning of Things

General Knowledge

Design: Intelligence Made Visible

Labour Camp

Sex: A Cultural History

A Dictionary of Idiocy

Life's a Pitch

Work: The Building of the Channel Tunnel Rail Link

Cars

Woman as Design

Liverpool: Shaping the City

La Dolce Vita

Ugly: The Aesthetics of Everything

Taste: An Essay

Death Drive: There Are No Accidents

Signs of Life: Why Brands Matter

How To Steal Fire: The Myths of Creativity Exposed,
the Truths of Creativity Explained

Value: What Money Can't Buy: A Handbook
for Practical Hedonism

Terence: The Man Who Invented Design

# The Art of Living

*The Well-Designed Tragedy of Eustace Dunne*

STEPHEN BAYLEY

PENGUIN BOOKS

TRANSWORLD PUBLISHERS
Penguin Random House, One Embassy Gardens,
8 Viaduct Gardens, London SW11 7BW
www.penguin.co.uk

Transworld is part of the Penguin Random House group of companies
whose addresses can be found at global.penguinrandomhouse.com

Penguin
Random House
UK

First published in Great Britain in 2021 by Doubleday
an imprint of Transworld Publishers
Penguin paperback edition published 2022

A CIP catalogue record for this book
is available from the British Library.

ISBN 9781529176896

Printed and bound in Great Britain by Clays Ltd, Elcograf S.p.A.

The authorized representative in the EEA is Penguin Random House Ireland,
Morrison Chambers, 32 Nassau Street, Dublin D02 YH68.

Penguin Random House is committed to a sustainable
future for our business, our readers and our planet. This book
is made from Forest Stewardship Council® certified paper.

MIX
Paper from
responsible sources
FSC
www.fsc.org    FSC® C018179

1

For Semi-Precious Stone, one of *la famiglia*.
Brian Stone, 1937–2019

# Contents

*Olim dives et potens fecit ille mihi iniustitiam.*


A *PROTECTOR* JOURNALIST:
'What makes you get up in the morning?'

EUSTACE DUNNE:
'It's really all about what I call the art of living. You know,
every little detail of existence matters. Lighting a candle,
for example. Making a decent cup of coffee is as important
as writing a symphony. And you can do it more often.'

## All novels are memoirs, all memoirs are novels: an introduction to Eustace Dunne, the man who designed the world.

My name is Rollo Pinkie. I know, or knew, Eustace Dunne very well. In fact, I think I knew him better than he knew himself. I was his ghost writer, occasional confessor, his voice, prompt, stooge, factotum, intellectual crutch, researcher, test bed, sounding board, flunky, bag-carrier, scapegoat, dining companion and moral conscience. Although the last of these roles was not a demanding one and took very little of my time.

He was one of the most fascinating, yet exasperating, people imaginable. If he was not interested in someone, he might appear very reserved. Some even thought him 'shy'. But this was not a nice, cautious reticence. He was just plain bloody rude. If you were of no use to him, he simply did not care and would not waste his breath. Concepts of 'waste' – and its avoidance – influenced every aspect of his being. Waste of time, waste of space, waste of money: all these were horrible for him.

Following one of many alignments that defined our relationship, our handwriting became identical, even if the purpose of our scribbling remained obstinately different. We had the same tailor, the same shoes. We ate the same food. He sold me a precious vintage car. At least, I thought it was precious because he had once owned it and that made it special to me in my sentimental phase. But Eustace was only inclined to let me buy the car when he decided it was merely tiresomely old and not yet a 'classic'. It was his fifteenth Porsche and my first. Once, we even married the same woman. But not at the same time. We knew the same people, although he had no real friends and I had many. I wrote his books and he paid me to be invisible. Or just about. Ghosts have an indeterminate status in this tale.

Eustace would become very rich and very famous. Prodigally so. In a prolific career, there were as many accidents as there were stellar achievements.

'If everything seems under control, you are simply not going fast enough,' he liked to say. Many bodies had to be buried during his rapid ascent. And I knew where they were.

Every business, romantic, family or personal relationship of Eustace's ended in acrimony and dispute. Towards the end, only his very well-paid banker and lawyer spoke to him. Yet Eustace Dunne received every public honour and the media fawned on him. He had £120 million and no one to talk to.

His life mixed a high purpose visible to the public with unscrupulous manipulation observed more frequently in private. His was a world maybe now past, but it was a world where artists and designers met and miscegenated with money and media. Many fabulous creatures – clever, ruined, showy, desperate – were created from this union.

Was he a creative genius or a villainous conman? A visionary or a swindler? Only experts could say and experts are often fooled. I know I was.

What did Eustace Dunne do?

He made a fortune selling a promise of transcendent perfection through a scented candle.

He spiked Margaret Thatcher's *foie gras*.

Potential critics were tamed by employing them as 'consultants'.

2

He made eating out a national sport and a pastime.

The word 'foodie' was coined for him, but he never actually cooked: just put on a pinafore and picked up a wooden spoon when photographers were present or guests were arriving.

He became Britain's best-known designer, but the complete catalogue of his works is a very thin volume.

He thought the law was for little people.

He forged works of art.

He counterfeited wine.

Krug was his Rohypnol. Every new woman employee did time on his Eames-designed casting couch or in a furtive huddle in a storeroom.

He stole students' drawings.

He found inspiration – some said too much – in other designers.

He betrayed everyone he ever knew.

He never said please or thank you.

He was reluctant to nurture the reputation of others.

Many years ago, I was asked by a national newspaper to write Eustace's obituary. None of the above appeared because there is a convention that obituaries are reverential, up to a point. *De mortuis nil nisi bonum.* At the time, he was quite elderly, but still very busy. Newspapers maintain this macabre anticipatory practice. If someone is over sixty, very famous or known to be unwell, they will have an obituary on file. I imagine they already have my own. Perhaps Eustace wrote it.

3

Eustace's obituary ends with me saying that on the day it is published, I'll lunch at Le Gardian, his famous restaurant. Le Gardian's reputation had been secured when Eustace hired – some might say 'bribed' – Crisp Gascoyne, the restaurant critic, by making her a 'consultant'. Good reviews were the result of a canny £20,000 per annum investment. At the table, I will be alone apart from ghosts and memories and a rather good bottle of Puligny-Montrachet.

And, of course, given Eustace Dunne's history of duplicity, I will be wondering if this great, delicious wine is real or fake.

And here I am today. On my second glass. The obituary is in the paper this morning. Eustace is dead. And I think the wine, while it might be real, is most definitely corked.

But the restaurant has changed. Le Gardian was conceived at the height of the Francophilia rage that Eustace – wearing a bin man's *bleu de travail* and a chef's *toque* for avid *Sunday Times* photographers – promoted with such very un-British *élan*.

French cars lost their character long ago. No one wants a Citroën. Once *le dernier mot* in style, they are now suburban. And now the same is happening with French food. Nowadays, no one wants *bouillabaisse*. Who can be arsed? They don't want viscous white Burgundy or ruby-red Côtes du Rhône, they want cloudy organic wine the colour of a urological specimen from a sickening pet. So Le Gardian is now run by Nuno Camões whose Portuguese-Hawaian 'fusion' food is *à la mode*. Where once there were skillets and whisks, there are now tweezers and blowtorches. No one wants Anjou pigeon cooked pink any more. Everyone seems to want octopus deconstructed into a lollipop with a molecular foam of algae and a gel of seaweed with ponzu.

Yesterday morning, the beginning of the day he died, Eustace was in the Getty villa at Ladispoli, an ochre nightmare south of Rome which he had recently added to his bizarre portfolio of landmark homes. At eight in the morning, the Tyrrhenian Sea gently washing the rocks outside his study, he was poring over his diminishing pile of press cuttings, a cigarillo in hand and a glass of whisky not far away. I used to find this cigarillo thing exasperating. Of course, with his indulgent attitude towards himself and his taste for the very best, Eustace naturally preferred proper Havana cigars. But when someone was looking, he might opt for a proletarian Phillies Mexicali Slim to demonstrate impressive solidarity with ordinary people. Harold Wilson had been the same with his pipe. His pipe was for photo ops alone. Inside Number 10, it was Havanas.

Anyway, he soon flew back to London on a borrowed Bombardier Global Express jet. His battered heart had not given him time to write a memo to the owner, a French handbag billionaire, advising the removal of the vulgar gold taps from the bathroom, before, spilling his second large Scotch of the morning, he died of a heart attack somewhere over the Alps. Only one person was looking.

I think I had better let Eustace Dunne explain.

# 1946 – It was a dark and stormy night

*'All animals are equal, but some animals are more equal than others.'*

George Orwell, *Animal Farm*, 1945

*My teacher was inspired by Eric Gill.*

THEY SAY YOU SHOULD NEVER start a story with an account of the weather. But what do they know?

In 1946, when I was fourteen, Met Office archives confirm that it was a cool, unsettled spring and early summer: unusually drizzly with mist even on May mornings. I was at Fraylings, a school in the West Country, territory that had escaped the recent German bombing, unlike London or the Midlands. 'Progressive' is what we would call this school today.

It was a school for talented misfits, so I felt at home there even if it was a home I did not much like. My father was a financier and a swindler, a one-time Member of Parliament, but a talented and inventive professional liar long before he entered Westminster, where mangling the truth became compulsory.

Claiming a radical past, my father, Eustace Senior, had fantasized freely about his family tree. Were we gentry from Wales? He let people think that. In fact, he had left the bitter austerity and harsh discipline of Josiah Mason's Orphanage in Shoreditch to become a Fleet Street runner. He took a Pitman's shorthand course, unusual for a boy, became a court reporter and, somehow, eventually found himself the proprietor of some minor City trade rags that formed the basis of what became the *Financial Times*.

This made him rich, but an over-ambitious flotation accompanied by some fanciful supporting literature and entirely fictitious accounts found him arraigned for fraud in 1903. He defended himself in court, was acquitted and became that Home Counties MP, featuring often in newspaper diary pages. Soon, another bankruptcy forced his resignation from Parliament. Then, a reckless bond scheme found him guilty of fraud once again and he was sent to Pentonville the very same year he proudly took delivery of a new Bentley Mark VI, the luxury 'sports saloon' which was for so many people a symbol, profound if remote, of national aspirations in the bleak years after Hitler's war.

During the trial, as the newspapers gleefully reported, he won the right to a quarter of an hour's daily adjournment during which time he drank a quart of champagne on what he claimed were medical grounds established by the Surgeon-General, a gentleman of his acquaintance, as he often reminded people. Knowledge of all this paternal success, excess and resonant failure gave me, I think, an enduring caution about money, as well as a puritanical streak a mile wide and an inch deep.

Still, everyone agreed that my father was a man of unusual talent, great application and no morals whatsoever. A man made by effort and imagination, but undone by greed and ambition. A man incapable of being reasonable, with himself or others. Of the more conventional morality, he had little to say. My father could not distinguish fact from fiction, believing something was true if he wanted it to be. But he taught me about charm, persuasion and commitment. He taught me never, ever to give up. To keep on, long after it seemed sensible to quit. 'Coming second is just being first of the losers,' he told me.

His belief was that anything might be achieved by hard work. Perhaps like Picasso, for whose art, being a complete philistine, he had no time at all, my father believed that if you could imagine something, it was already real. It would be harsh and crude to call him a conman, but he taught me that self-invention is an art form. And that people are credulous and their belief in what you tell them can be reinforced by repetition. What I tell you three times is true. And the more so if it is four.

But, most important of all, he taught me, by example, to stay out of jail.

Like many children who have been mistreated or abandoned, I coped with this miscreant, fantasist, but beguiling parent by freezing my own emotions and refusing properly intimate engagement with anyone.

In truth, neither of my parents was able to give me any sense of certainty. My father was erratic and improvident, while, despite her forbidding *hauteuse*, my mother was essentially weak and indecisive. So I had to make my own certainties. And, to be honest, I chose taste and style over morals and ethics.

People who have unhappy childhoods often become adept at inventing themselves. I began my own course of self-invention aged about ten.

## postbellum tristesse

Wrenaissance Fraylings, so called because its architectural references were simultaneously to the Florence of Brunelleschi and to the designer of London's St Paul's, was unmarked by shrapnel. It daringly mixed genders in class, was reluctant to thrash its pupils, adventurous in its curriculum, but gentlemanly in an old-fashioned way, nonetheless.

It stood in its cheerful red brick and Portland stone dressings in a fine park. They always said it was designed by Lutyens, but, really, it was just designed by an architect who liked Lutyens very much. Still, impressive, optimistic and decent, Fraylings was a rebuke to any stubborn remains of postbellum *tristesse*.

The grounds were four hundred lush acres. Indeed, Godfrey Boate, the freethinking headmaster, took an educated interest in avant-garde forestry as well as Austrian dietetics. 'Angst' had not yet become a German loan-word, even if 'Blitz' unfortunately had.

Bombsites were, of course, unknown in the countryside. Sometimes Godfrey Boate took small, mixed groups into the woods to collect berries and prune the crab apple trees.

The early summer that year was characterized by practical promise, if unrealized, of proper sunshine: in my memory, school days were long and brightly lit by cautious optimism, an effect magnified daily as the war passed into history. Realistically, there was no longer any prospect of a bomb being dropped on your head nor of a *Fallschirmjäger* parachuting on to the lawn and massacring your family at a sun-dappled tea and scones event with his FG-42 automatic rifle. In edited recollection, of course, the sun mostly shines. Very few of our most precious memories involve downpours or mist.

But it would be stupid to pretend that in 1946 most of the country was anything but savagely bruised. Yet people were neither deterred nor depressed. Or not yet. Survivors do not capitulate. And they find stratagems for renewal. And, for those seeking symbols, there was symbolism everywhere. Heathrow had just opened: a modern, international airport for the weary, old, sea-borne imperium. You could now fly direct to full-blooded and sunny Buenos Aires, even if at home bread was rationed, meat was grey and your bike had been stolen. On a clear day in Devon, from Fraylings you could see the lofty contrails of a Boeing Stratoliner, Douglas DC-6 or a Lockheed Constellation groaning westward-ho at twenty thousand feet towards the promised land. I can remember now the keen – almost painful – sense of yearning the sight gave me.

Euphoria is not the English way; empirical construction is. In my youth Stevenage was declared a new town with the promise of enlightenment via Scandinavian-style town planning, modernist lamp posts with clean lines, and semi-automatic garbage disposal. The Bank of England was nationalized and Bentley introduced that handsome and powerful Mark VI saloon, as fine a car as you could buy in all of Europe. My father's was gun-metal grey. Now he was in Pentonville and the car sat forlorn in a U-shaped gravel drive on a Surrey private estate, sticky pine needles coagulating on its wings, windows growing yellow-dull, tyres sagging, bird shit ossifying on the fabric sunroof. As I always say, symbols are everywhere.

## a decent bit of buggery

So, I want you to imagine a summer's afternoon at school in Devon in 1946. Lessons are over and I am sitting in the cricket pavilion with some bootleg shandy, plimsolled feet resting on the old iron lawn-roller smothered in fragrant chopped grass. There is a light breeze and the sound of distant laughter. To be sure, enjoyment is somewhere on someone's agenda. Somehow, the atmosphere suggests the prospect of vague, but deliciously intense, romantic encounters, as thrilling as they will be uncomplicated.

But I was usually glum: I felt older than the other boys, more thoughtful, less playful, more intense. I did not laugh much and never at myself. Perhaps a father in jail does that to you.

The only friend I made at Fraylings was Rollo Pinkie, a pretty, but cerebral, olive-skinned boy with a flop of dark hair and fine fingers. Rollo was from the Scottish Borders, where his father had been the agent of an ancient, rebarbative and gnarled duke. He was sophisticated in mind and manner, but not at all the metropolitan type. He was a listener more than a talker, although witty and acerbic when he allowed himself to speak. I did not think it was a crush, but I was certain he felt a strong attachment. We provided each other with cover from the *mondain* realities of the Fraylings days.

Standing against the pavilion's chipped Ideal Standard urinal, dealing with the effects of the shandy, the smell of Izal disinfectant competing with latrines and cut grass for our attention, I said with fine affectation and a bluntness I hoped would be felt as admirable:

'You know, God made me handsome and clever, but He also made me cross and uncertain.'

Thoughtful words for a teenager, although that term had not yet been coined. I wondered, not without pleasure, if Rollo thought me deranged with self-obsession. With a calculated smirk on my face, I gave an expressive flick and buttoned up the flies of my cricket whites, zip fasteners being something only rich American relatives knew in 1946. And wanting to test Rollo, I added, beaming: 'You know there's a tradition in Fraylings that there's absolutely nothing wrong with a decent bit of buggery, don't you? If you shag one of the maids, you'll be expelled. But you'll only get a ticking-off if it's one of the boys.'

Indeed. So we all found.

Fifty years after this conversation with Rollo, a journalist wrote that both good and bad fairies had been present at my birth in Reigate in 1932. The good fairies, it was reported, had seen to it that I was notably attractive, if not in a demonstrative way. I had charm, they said, in abundance, even if, they hinted, it had an over-worked on-off switch. 'Please' and 'thank you' were not expressions I used readily. To do so would have been to acknowledge the moral significance of another person.

They told me I was handsome to women, but with a certain smooth and suggestive effeminacy evidenced in soft, clear skin that made me also a curiosity to men, an ambiguity in alignment I never quite bothered to dispel at any point in the years ahead. And the good fairies had also made me perceptive, original, industrious and energetic. There was, additionally, the keenest sense of personal style, a well-cut suit of character fit to dress – on rare occasions to disguise – the muscular ego beneath.

I was not bookish, but was an adroit lifter, and the second-hand wisdom I often repeated became, over time and with successive improvements in my own voice, incorporated into my own personality.

For example, I often cited William Morris whose principles my mother had taught me:

'Not on one strand are all of life's jewels strung.'

I very grandly mentioned this to Rollo as we ambled away from the cricket pavilion.

He arched his eyebrows and said, 'What on earth do you mean?'

'It's simple. There are always several ways of getting things done. You really don't have to do the obvious thing. In fact, I think it's sometimes better if you don't.'

## the good and bad fairies

I really do suspect good and bad fairies were present at my birth. They later each insisted on their part of the bargain. Handsome, clever me was restless and dissatisfied. I had acquired, or developed, an entire psychology, a personal dynamic, founded in notions of sharp-elbowed advancement, callous betrayal and calculated revenge under a camouflage of charm and elegant manners. No matter how fortunate and well-founded I appeared to others, I maintained an enduring internal sense of myself as a sufferer, an injured party who had been cheated out of what was deservedly his.

As a result, some found me shifty, if in a rather elegant way. I trusted no one and loved only myself, and that I possibly over-did. Favours and benefits were ever computed and calculated. My generosity was on a timed drip. Human debt became my currency. I learnt to add percentages of interest to every personal transaction. Emotional obligations were collected, even nurtured, as a banker nurtures debt. I detested authority and refused to salute the flag on Empire Day, suggesting instead that the Union Jack should be at half-mast.

And, of course, people loved me helplessly. To extract even a grudging nod of approval from Eustace Dunne was to have won one of life's battles, to have been given a nod and a wink and a nudge in the ribs by the Pope himself. Yet I lacked empathy for others to a degree that, in more modern times, would very likely have attracted professional clinical attention. Rollo said I had a real psychological problem: I was a total cunt. And because of this, I was fascinating.

The English master, an amiable, scruffy rascal called Yobbo Clarke, had taught us that P. G. Wodehouse believed a good autobiography required an eccentric father, a miserable childhood and an extraordinary time spent at school. The bad fairies had lavished this trinity on me in abundance.

## cordite and damp wallpaper

I only ever confided in floppy-haired Rollo. With him I shared my history.

Prep school had been in Chelsea when the bombs began to fall. In fact, I had been with my mother buying school uniform in Peter Jones during the very first air raid, when deadly Heinkels visited Sloane Square.

It is not difficult to sense how shocking it might have been to have this primary rite of passage, one curated by your own mother, interrupted by murderous high explosives. While newsreels make the Blitz look almost comforting, a demonstration of indomitable sing-along tribal London spirit, my experience was a brutally different reality.

'The panic was contagious, you know,' I said to Rollo. 'Forget all that heroic newsreel. People actually weren't at all calm. There was running, screaming and panic. But I was too confused and fascinated to be really scared. In fact, I was more afraid of the shelters than the bombs.'

Why? Because snobbery and cruelty occupied compartments of similar sizes in my mind.

'Sleep was impossible,' I continued. 'The thumps and tremors were continuous, the buildings above rocked and swayed and we sat with our feet in foetid slurry. I taught myself not to wince because that would be under-bred.'

I told Rollo about once leaving the Anderson shelter after an all-clear. There was a grey dust everywhere which was so fine it made you sneeze helplessly. Satanic curling coils of black smoke emerged from the drains. Wrecked buildings looked like sightless death's hands. In broken windows, curtains fluttered.

Everywhere the smell of cordite and damp wallpaper. The contents of shops were strewn over the pavement. I suspect all of this contributed to my later reverence for merchandise, my uncontained anger at people who disrespected stuff, who wasted things, who made messes. Once, I bent down to pick up from the pavement a fine, mottled, plane tree leaf only to discover that it was, in fact, a severed hand made more terrible still because a wedding band remained on one finger.

I confessed to Rollo that the Luftwaffe had hardened me, but I still felt terrible pangs when I was delivered to Fraylings for the first time. Seeing my father's brand-new Bentley disappearing back to London made me homesick. I mean literally vomiting. Bombs had not made me emotional, but when I later unpacked my trunk and found a letter from my mother with a dried flower inside, I rushed to the lavatories and cried myself hoarse. It was a day of fluid evacuations.

'It was because the car was brand new that it was so terribly sad,' I said to Rollo. 'The car had its whole life in front of it. There were journeys to be made, things to be discovered. And I could have no part of them.'

And nor, now that he was in prison, was my father going to have a part of them either.

## the invincibly disgusting mutton stew

I was an advanced example of the school's preferred type: a talented misfit who was vain and good-looking. I had no academic interests whatsoever, not much in sports, although cricket whites flattered me, a universal conceit. I was, however, drawn to lepidoptery, which offered imaginary vectors of escape to destinations more exotic than Devon. And I excelled at art and craft, which took me away from maths, chemistry and Latin. I soon took control of the school's book-press in the basement and printed Johnny Fennell's dreadful poems, illustrating them with linocuts I designed myself. This got a notice in the local newspaper, my very first brush with fame. I still have the cutting.

One night in the dorm, as other beds rhythmically creaked, I whispered to Rollo who was lying awake staring at the ceiling, 'I can't sleep. Let's go up to the roof for a smoke and leave this mob of masturbating hooligans alone. I want to talk to you.'

This was intended both as a command and a touching request, expressing both authority and need. Like 'teenager', 'psychopath' was not yet a word in common currency.

'I hate this place,' I hissed, as we crept through a dormer window on the mansard roof to find a perch in the gutter with a view of Appledore's distant lights.

We smoked, and I wanted to enlarge my views on food as they formed in my mind. A dish, even an atrocious school dinner, I told Rollo who was nodding, was never mere fuel: it was a proposition about style and status. It could be read as an insult or a gift. At this stage in Fraylings' history, it was mostly insulting, although I dare say they are now on to avocado toast.

'Did you try that mutton stew?' I said. 'I thought it invincibly disgusting. Both half-cooked and over-done with that absolutely vile coagulating fat. And those stiff sardines in that filthy green, nacreous oil. The pies! Dear God, those are very suspicious. What on earth do they put in them? And what about those unidentified frying objects? I think they might have been testicles.'

We shared a dislike for most teachers, especially Yardley Letwin, the games master, who was inclined to put his hand down boys' shorts whenever circumstances allowed, which was quite often given that he supervised the cold showers after games.

Additionally and disgustingly, Letwin liked to recommend bathing 'after every evacuation', an instruction generally ignored, on practical grounds if no other: the water in Fraylings was never even temperate. Many years later, Letwin became Secretary of the Paedophile Information Exchange, bringing Fraylings unwanted notoriety.

## downstairs with bohemians

But the art room offered a reprieve, a remedy for homesickness, a site of worship, a place where special and comforting rites were observed. The paint smelt of pleasure, of independence. It was the sovereign territory of Swinfen Harries, perhaps the only man I ever truly admired. In fact, so profound was my admiration that many of the anecdotes establishing Swinfen's own colourful reputation were eventually, like his quotations, absorbed into my personal lore: plagiarism and inspiration being not very far apart.

For example, the nomad-artist Swinfen arrived for the first day of teaching at school with his every worldly possession carried on a magnificent and lustrous black Brough Superior motorbike. Eventually, significant entrances on a motorbike would become a part of my own well-polished repertoire of journalist-friendly anecdotes. They were not true, but respect for truth is a puerile temptation.

And the journeyman Swinfen had worked for Eric Gill, helping the rascal-genius zoophiliac with his Prospero and Ariel frieze at the BBC's Broadcasting House. Gill, it was often told by Swinfen, conducted the employment interview on the scaffolding, covered with Portland stone dust, with a chisel in one hand, a mallet in the other, wearing his quasi-medieval tunic which made his disdain for conventional underwear into an uninvited provocation for those on the ground or climbing the ladder towards him.

I never, of course, met Gill, but felt this vicarious contact via Swinfen validated my own credentials as a true source of the Arts and Crafts spirit. Often, in conversation, the unwary might have got the impression that we had, indeed, been intimates. I often used to say, knowingly: 'The artist is not a different type of person; every person is a different type of artist.'

This was an old saw of Gill's. But people now think it is mine.

As if to prove a point about the infinite variety of human potential, the bohemian Swinfen was also a Boy Scout. Magnificently, he had known both Auguste Rodin in Paris and Baden-Powell in Hampshire. I found this peculiar amalgamation of campfire DIY and cosmopolitan culture compelling to an almost erotic degree.

Ancillary to Swinfen's art room was Swinfen's cellar, an even more appealing resort with the character of a *club privé*, accessible (by a spiral staircase) only to an elect few who had been favoured with personal invitations. It smelt of heat, dust, ink and beer. Here was the book-press that I had learnt to use. And the kiln Swinfen had himself built. Here he drank beer at his rumoured all-night firings. In the cellar was the desk with his specialist collection of *de luxe* and rare inks: Ama-iro Iroshizuku from Japan, Jacques Herbin 1798 from Paris, as well as Kaweco and KWZ from Germany. Here too was a small collection of Japanese poetry books, together with some exquisite, small ceramic pieces by Urano Shigekichi.

Swinfen often said, 'I learnt precision from Japanese poetry.'

Later, I used to say exactly the same.

In his cellar, Swinfen passed on worldly advice with the warm beer as he worked. A bachelor before that term acquired its low associations, he once told me, 'I will never get married. I am both happy and miserable enough as it is. I don't want or need to add anything to either side of the account.'

Another day he said: 'The strangest thing once happened to me. I was visiting the Dormer tomb, it's in the church in Wing, Buckinghamshire. Do you know the one I mean? It has an impressively early classical entablature held up on Corinthian columns, not at all bad for the Home Counties in 1552! Anyway, while snooping around the rest of the church, I found a monument with my own name on it. Swinfen Harries. It's not a common name, you'll agree. I was amazed. And then I heard a voice saying, "We've been waiting for you." It was just like M. R. James. What do you think about the mysterious disquisition of ghosts?'

This he did while teaching me, an enthusiastic pupil, how to perform efficient gas-tungsten arc welding, a technique he practised with his shirt off. Above the Vulcanic roar of the torch, he would sometimes ask: 'What do you think is the proper use of riches? I think a man can count himself rich by the stuff he can do without.'

He taught me ceramics, which he curiously pronounced with a hard 'c'. Under his tutelage, I learned to throw and fire clay, but not before decorating it with abstract patterns inspired by the Swedish books about the Svenskt Tenn design group and the Gustavsberg ceramics factory I found on his shelves. By the time I was sixteen, I could design and make a credible replica of Stockholm modernity. A tea set of mine with a repeat painted motif of stylized lingonberries was on display in the school entrance hall for nearly a year.

With Swinfen, the esoteric and the mundane, the mystical and the muck, were part of an indivisible whole. In one welding lesson, he unforgettably asked: 'What would you say is the exact difference between a pipe and a tube?'

## too much torque

Welding, I found, was empowering. It lent an attractive Prome-
thean force to its adepts and would, in future, helpfully allow my
impressive claims to possess a fragile affinity with the working
man and his art. And it was welding that undid me.

Swinfen had introduced me to his precious, bound volumes of the
pre-war *Architectural Review*, whose good-natured modernist propa-
ganda and arresting photography in dramatic chiaroscuro cheered
him greatly. Sometimes pages were printed on textured, coloured
stock, pink being a favourite, yellow an alternative. It had some of
the characteristics of a revivalist tract, and a similar range of enthusiastic voices belonging to writers who appeared also to be hallucinat-
ing, but with much better typography.

I was particularly drawn to a photo-spread on the 1933 Stuttgart
*Stühle aus Stahl* exhibition of modernist metal furniture. It featured
pictures of smoking lesbian novelists with geometric hair, wearing
Bauhaus fashions and draping themselves over tubular steel chairs
designed by Erich Mendelsohn. In one of the pictures, I admired a
single stem of a rose in an unlabelled wine magnum upon a glass-
topped tubular steel table. I made a visual note.

An image more distant from Empire Day at Fraylings could not
easily be imagined: it was both coolly sophisticated and weirdly erotic,
suggestive of a world of possibilities and confidences not yet available
to Devon scholars. So I decided to make myself a copy of the table.

I used Swinfen's tube-bending machine and his stock of Rey-
nolds chrome molybdenum tube. Or was it pipe? There was trial and
error. I sourced the glass from a merchant in Totnes who cut it to my
pattern, finishing the edges to an impressive smoothness. I bought
clamps. I shamelessly copied the Mendelsohn original from *The Architectural Review*. And, applying too much torque to the last clamp,
the glass violently shattered, severing a tendon in my right wrist.

But the injury had a larger effect than mere indisposition: at sixteen, I was never able to draw properly again. To compensate, perforce, my eyesight became exceptionally, even ruthlessly, well-focused. Fifty years later, a Japanese architect called Kengo Kuma experienced exactly the same problem after a strangely similar accident. Kuma taught himself to draw with his left hand. But I taught myself to steal.

Swinfen visited me daily in the school infirmary.

'Poor chap,' Swinfen said. 'I knew you'd be better off with the Gothic Revival than with the bloody *Neue Sachlichkeit*. So much for clean lines.'

He tamped his pipe and added, 'Pugin's glass would never break, d'you know.'


## women in uniform

Rollo visited often, but they were dull days recuperating in the infirmary and, as its only patient, I could freely prowl its ward and offices since only my hand, not my legs, was compromised.

One afternoon, surprising her in the tea room, I asked the nurse, always known to the boys as Jinx, 'Is it really true what they say about women in uniform?'

As a result of events arising from this inquiry, I was commanded to Godfrey Boate for my sacking. While Jinx had not complained at the time of this flagrant flouting of school rules, indeed, had been an enthusiastic participant once she had put her bedpan down, the following week she had found it necessary to register some retrospective distress with school officials. As I entered the headmaster's study, Boate laid aside his copy of *The Forest Trees of Tasmania* and sighed very deeply indeed.

'Mr Dunne, I am very sorry about this. And I do not mean your indisposition, most unpleasant and unfortunate as your injuries are.

But I simply cannot allow this sort of behaviour. As I have often said, a little mutual masturbation can be ignored, provided it is discreet. I can even turn a blind eye to occasional buggery, although again I would counsel discretion and moderation in this activity. But interfering with the paid staff. With the paid *medical* staff. With the paid *medical* staff while they are on duty. This is simply not acceptable. It is bad for morale. I am afraid I must ask you to leave Fraylings, although we will give you the most helpful references.'

In this way, the British public school maintained its reputation of being able to spot talent and then carelessly expel it.

'A dispute about manners. You know: girls, that sort of thing,' I would always say when asked in future to account for my premature departure from Fraylings. Nurse Jinx, however, had not been a girl, but a married woman of thirty-four. And it had been raining.

# 2

# 1948 – Spaghetti, gin and fucking the missus

*'Culture is the one thing that we cannot deliberately aim at. It is the product of a variety of more-or-less harmonious activities, each pursued for its own sake.'*

T. S. Eliot, *Notes Towards the Definition of Culture*, 1948

*The original Land Rover: a symbol that Britain could make it.*

'JESUS. THAT UTTER BASTARD BOATE sacked me for shagging Jinx. Christ! God bloody knows, everyone has shagged Jinx, haven't they? She's got more miles on her than the school bus. And been serviced more often.'

It was two days – and a long, slow, reflective train journey – after the Boate hearing. I was prodding at a spot on my nose and talking to the hall mirror in my mother's flat in that part of London where smart Hampstead becomes suburban Finchley.

Some might even dispute whether it was London at all because it was nearer Barnet than the Heath, but the address suited my mother's ambitions and these ambitions eventually became my own. You are, after all, what – or where – you want to be. Presentation is important. Social mountains are there to be climbed.

And I had climbed to the third floor of a late Victorian mansion block, all pompous red brick and stone dressings with impressively polished brass door furniture and a lobby below that smelt of bees-wax, perfume and afternoon affairs. The flat was flooded with Finchley Road light and furnished with plywood *chaises longues* by an alcoholic Finnish architect of the second rank. This was the same furniture you found in Jack Pritchard's Isokon building, at the other end of Frognal, a bold, white, geometrical construct, a messenger from 'The Continent', a rare example in bosky London of what American and European architects were already calling 'The International Style'. It brought modernist flair as well as some adventurous, exotic spirits to the area.

Mother's rooms were also filled with Ambrose Heal's fashionably austere 'prison' furniture, a nice irony considering her husband was

26

in Pentonville. Of brown Victorian furniture my mother had much to say, all of it hostile. Bleached oak, pale laminated plywood and birch were more to her taste. Thus, the walls were painted beige, a bold choice for the day, but good in pseudo-Hampstead light.

Perhaps it was a little like a Scandinavian tuberculosis sanatorium: 'clean lines', you see, has an actual and a metaphorical meaning. A few drawings by Ruskin Spear, a student contemporary of Mother's, were the sole concessions to decoration, while a pair of Anglepoise lights and a pseudo-Bauhaus rug designed by a chain-smoking vegetarian novelist indicated the optimistic presence that the modernist exotic spirits down the road would recognize.

Then there were the orange Penguins and blue Pelicans, the very first generation of English paperbacks, although they were, in fact, imitations of German originals, but that could not be said at the time. The Penguins were ambitious modern literature by Thornton Wilder and George Orwell, the Pelicans earnest and instructive studies in the history of coal mining, collecting Bohemian glass and anarchist agriculture. They were housed in a little plywood assemblage – again, Finnish designed – a thing known as a 'Donkey'.

I was, as I tormented my spot, wearing a well-considered outfit of slept-in jeans, a novelty at the time, brothel creeper shoes and a red Harrington zip jacket with tartan lining and the collar turned up, anticipating James Dean and Elvis by several years. Or so I later realized. I was already comfortably ahead of the game.

## take it from here

George Orwell's *1984* was just out. I had already read Mother's copy – another orange Penguin – but I was at least as interested in the new television set which last night had shown a flickering grey and grey 405 line performance by Terry Thomas in the BBC's first ever comedy series. Bleak and humourless as it was, comedy was in the air. On the radio, my favourite show was Frank Muir's and Denis Norden's *Take It From Here*, a masterpiece of gentle sophistication. It was a first class education in the art of the pun . . . and I learnt all its lessons. Infamy? Infamy? They've all got it in for me.

The television news that same night may have featured the opening of London's first launderette on Queensway and later the maiden flight of the amazing new passenger jet called the Comet, which flew at five hundred miles per hour. This mixture of doomed apocalyptic vision, pop culture and democratized technology I can now see predicted the future. I mean *my* future.

Anyway, the stubborn spot was very nearly gone when the door slammed and Mother marched in.

'Dear God, Eustace, you look such a fucking sight. When you've finished straddling the world like a denim-clad Narcissus, will you please tell me what you intend to do with yourself? Or were you thinking of keeping your no-good bloody father company in prison?'

She looked me in the eye while lighting an untipped Sweet Afton cigarette, inhaling deeply, a process that simply seemed to make her more steady and threatening still.

'Actually, Ma, I was thinking of becoming a designer. I'd thought about *un été doux et reposant*,' I said, salvaging a phrase from a school French lesson. 'I'd considered going over to *le côté obscur*, but I think idleness and the dark side have – frankly – limited appeal. I want to be busy. And rich.'

That morning, on the train back to Frognal, somewhere between Dorchester and Reading, I had decided that the Lethaby Academy of Art on Kingsway was my means to this end. I was a delinquent, but I felt delinquency had some glamour and wanted to realize all its cash value.

'I'm going to art college,' I told her.

'Are you, indeed?' she replied, her head nodding in slow, contemptuous beats. 'And how exactly do you intend to pay? Do say when you have a clue. That is, if you ever have a clue.' She turned on her axis and headed out again for the ancient lift with its open-work metal shaft and squeaking cables. I like to think she was letting me go.

..........................................................................................................................

[R] ROLLO PINKIE: *Eustace was always vague about what became of his parents. In discussing them at all, he managed to combine an overt mawkish sentimentality with an occult, callous disregard. While he promoted his convict father to 'something in the City' and a county level real tennis champion, the truth was that when his parents, escaping their creditors, decamped to Bali to run a bar in Denpasar, he broke off all contact. At the time, the only Europeans in Bali were Dutch flotsam left behind after independence. Nor, many years later, did he attend their joint funeral, organized according to Buddhist rites, on Kuta Beach.*

## fat, pale, miserable models

The Lethaby Academy was, generally, a dispiriting place. There was a lift, but it never worked. Sweating brick walls were painted in cream and green gloss, indistinguishable from a hospital or an asylum, although somewhat less deliberately fine than Mother's Hampstead sanatorium.

It was populated to a surprising degree by talentless, demobbed soldiers enjoying their freedom by mooching listlessly in the yellow light of the studios, making roll-ups and eyeing the girls. Necessarily, they were older men than I. One of them explained to me with admirable candour that, ordinarily, in 1948 the best he could hope for in civilian life was a regime of tinned spaghetti, gin and fucking the missus. But art college offered several years on the coast of Bohemia, as well as, longer term, vistas – illusions, possibly – of escape from the humdrum.

Forgetting the demobbed, lethargic soldiers with their noxious Woodbines, the other students were idle and supercilious, as survivors sometimes are. I was soon a matter of social suspicion. Why?

Because, I suppose, I had a toxic confidence that people found more enervating than stimulating. I also took care of what I was wearing.

Meanwhile, the student body as a whole sat around in an unheated Junior Common Room whose only concession to decoration or cultural curiosity was the fading remains of Air Raid Precautions posters. Typhoo tea was drunk out of filthy enamel mugs, the stains recording the passing of time like the rings in a section of an oak tree.

It was just after the Land Rover launched at the Amsterdam Motor Show. As if to demonstrate the entire country's confused search for a post-war identity, no one could quite decide if the Land Rover was a car or a piece of agricultural equipment. Still, it was reported in all the newspapers as a symbol of national recovery.

Some of the Lethaby Academy's staff, I soon learnt, had been occupied by designing parts of the revivalist 'Britain Can Make It' exhibition at the Victoria and Albert Museum, an event intended to raise national consciousness by suggesting that the increased production and consumption of material goods would bring bliss from Plymouth to Perth, enthusing Leicester and Burnley in between. Yet there were few signs of revival or vitality on Kingsway itself.

But there were, at least, girls, mostly in army surplus duffel coats which they did not remove indoors. They did not smile much. Most of them were what my contemporary, Terence Conran, mixing smug wit with genuine horror, described as 'virgins from Surbiton'. We knew this to be true because, whenever possible, we tested their integrity. Many were found wanting. I enjoyed Terence's remark because it nicely combined cruel topographical snobbery with a lofty profession of romantic sophistication.

But, generally, sexual curiosity at the Lethaby was fulfilled at its first and most modest level by the life class. Fat, pale, miserable models sat, as buses grumbled by outside, goose-pimpled and nude under the tired grey light that lazily penetrated a wired glass rooflight. The first life model I saw, fat and pink, looked as if she wanted to cry.

The room stank of *bouquet de corsage* and varnish while the naked models were, if female, diseased barmaids; if male, punch-drunk boxers or bit-part actors. The milieu was not stimulating, artistically or sexually, although sometimes, by way of compensation, we were joined by the celebrated portraitist Rodrigo Moynihan, usually dressed in a tweed jacket and corduroy bags, who raised the tone. He was, I assumed, always heading somewhere better. Certainly, there were better destinations.

Top-lit white flesh is not a delight and I preferred to spend my time at the nearby Sir John Soane Museum on Lincoln's Inn Fields, which was deliciously crepuscular, absolutely deserted and inexhaustibly interesting. And the only nudes were classical statues.

Here, while avoiding the liberal arts lectures in college, I educated myself in the matters of hazard and surprise in Soane's spellbinding cabinet of curiosities, his Regency memory palace. In this network of chance encounters, wandering between Egyptian sarcophagi and Hogarth paintings, I learnt from experience how to create spaces, turn corners, use colour and play with light. These are the tricks of the interior designer's trade. It was Sir John Soane, a humble builder who became the Regency's greatest architect, who taught me how to be a designer.

Designers are people who have a vision of how things should be. They are essentially idealists, always wanting to alter, and, one hopes, 'improve' things. Everywhere I go, I interrogate my surroundings. I read streets and houses. I ask them questions. I have a habit that people tell me is an annoying one, of rearranging their desks, unasked. There's really nothing that can't be improved by design. It's not so much a specific style as an attitude. Sometimes people think it arrogant.

........................................................................................................

[®] *Rollo Pinkie: Eustace never really understood that he was really selling his personal taste, although he persuaded himself and almost everyone else that in rearranging someone's desk or designing a sofa, he was reaching for some sort of universal, timeless excellence. He never appreciated the ludicrous paradox that while designers believe they can always change anything for the better, they stubbornly insist that their own work is an eternal classic which should last for all time.*

I liked the way that Soane had risen from a local artisan to be an international tastemaker. Assimilation of another sort played its part too. While I tended to avoid my fellow students, I saw advantage in cultivating some of the more pleasing members of staff. Insinuating myself into conversations in the local pub, the atrociously smelly Seven Stars, whose olfactory range spanned vomit to urine via tobacco and stale beer, I gathered that in the Senior Common Room, people were reading Eliot's *Notes Towards the Definition of Culture* and Leavis's *The Great Tradition,* as well as, more lightly, Graham Greene's *The Heart of the Matter* and Evelyn Waugh's *The Loved One.* All of them then new and being reviewed. So I went as soon as I possibly could to Foyles on Charing Cross Road to shoplift them.

## modernizing the lazy rump of imperium

One of the most pleasing, which is not to say easy-going, members of staff and a great influence on me was a Hungarian-Jewish typography tutor, Ilona Jacobsen. She had arrived in London at the same time as Hampstead's Isokon Building on Frognal and with similar credentials and ambitions: she was a woman intent on modernizing the lazy rump of imperium.

Ilona used a cigarette holder to emphasize her lascivious mouth and kohl to emphasize her penetrating, yellow eyes. She was a connoisseur of fonts and of darker things too. Like Swinfen Harries at school, Ilona knew about ink and took it most seriously: she had an account at J. Herbin in Paris and regularly imported exotic bottles from Schlagmuller of Mannheim and Isozaki of Kyoto. I thought this a good omen.

It was a pleasure to watch Ilona suck up these fine inks into one of the many vintage pens on a crowded art deco platter kept on her desk. Ilona sucked up other things too. Injections of paraldehyde, prescribed as a cure for seizures in infants, were regularly used as a remedy for the *delirium tremens* she suffered. She always claimed, with her familiar glass of Fernet-Branca to hand, that her DTs were not caused by drink, but by the trauma of Hungarian fascists marauding around in the Thirteenth District of Budapest where her family lived so uneasily in the days before her forced departure.

Ilona once told me in a heavily accented and melancholy voice, 'Luxury stains everyone it touches,' pulling at the hem of her black Chanel dress as she spoke. Then, with a flick of the wrist, dusting the ash off.

Her opinions combined the oneiric romanticism of William Morris and the severe analytics of Marx with the sumptuous tastes of a privileged *grande horizontale* who had once been rich. She had no small talk. Her conversation was always political.

'By the end of the nineteenth century,' she would lecture me, 'the machine had made skilled craftsmen into mere labourers. Their sole interest in their work became their pay, and beauty, instead of being a universal right, became a social luxury. Huh?'

When she talked like this, in a delicious guttural accent, I was never sure whether she was teasing, but her story fascinated me. The daughter of a fashionable milliner, Ilona's Marxist dialectics were enforced by an austere aesthetic, acquired from a term at the Dessau Bauhaus in 1928. To this she added the keenest possible business sense.

It was this German art school connection that led her, after the Bauhaus, to the Berlin office of the architect Erich Mendelsohn whose chairs I had admired at school. Mendelsohn was just then working on the famous Universum Film Aktiengesellschaft, always known as UFA, studios, spiritual home of the German film industry. It's nice to think that some of the dark Expressionist horrors of

German cinema were made in a beautifully refined modern building, as sleek as a white ocean liner. I always enjoyed these paradoxes.

On leaving Germany, when it became no longer possible for people called Mendelsohn to stay, the architect travelled to London where his reputation, established in the Berlin magazines, assured a ready acceptance by the local architectural community. A first job was soon acquired: the design of a new Peter Jones department store in Sloane Square, soon to be a gloriously incongruous intrusion of hard-edged German *Modernismus* into elegantly sedate Chelsea. This was where my mother bought my school uniform.

When Ilona herself inevitably arrived in London, she immediately contacted Mendelsohn. He promptly invited her to design the first displays in the David Jones vitrines along King's Road, which she did with Bauhaus bravado, successfully adapting Oskar Schlemmer's puppets and Herbert Bayer's graphics to the sale of Jersey knits and practical shoes. This caused a sensation in the *Evening News* and marked the beginning of a relationship with the David Jones Partnership. This lasted until 1956 when Ilona committed suicide while watching Soviet tanks debauching Budapest. On television.

## the vanity of a self-mounted butterfly

Towards the end of the spring term she told me, over a cup of very thin and bitter coffee, possibly made of acorns, and in the High Holborn Kardomah, that I had the 'vanity of a self-mounted butterfly'.

'Whatever do you mean? I actually rather like butterflies.'

'I mean, stupid boy, that you keep on looking at your reflection in the mirror. You think you're too swell for words. You do know the story of Narcissus, don't you?'

'Don't you start on that Narcissus thing, Miss Jacobsen, I've had enough of that from my bloody mother.'

'But, stupid boy, I am not your mother. I am your tutor. Although, perhaps, now that I think about it, I will become your lover too. Normally, I prefer women. But it tends nowadays to be more a question of beauty and availability than of gender. I think you are beautiful and suspect you are available.'

'Oh, for God's sake! Your problem, Ilona, is that you suffer from goyeurism. You are one of those Jews who detests us, but wants to be like us.'

She smiled and blew smoke in my face. For my part, I had always found Jewish girls attractive. And Jewish women too. Ilona, I suppose, must have been fifteen years older than me.

Our affair began in the euphoria surrounding the foundation of Israel on 14 May 1948. We had been listening to David Ben Gurion proclaiming the brave new state on the radio in her studio. She stood up, I presume moved by Ben Gurion's patriotic rhetoric. I remained sitting, my bottle of Bass to hand.

Then she did a dramatic up-do of her hair, securing it with a long amber pin, and then knelt in front of me. I saw the fine line of almost invisible dark fur on her upper lip and found it infinitely touching. The experience was like being one of her Parker 51 fountain pens. When it was over, Ilona said, 'Elegance is elimination', quoting Balenciaga, and leapt upright as I did up the buttons of my jeans.

## a minor artist with a major style, or was it the other way around?

Then there was John Minton, although everybody called him Johnny, the tormented artist who looked like a headmaster's son. Minton taught drawing and the pictures he drew had a delicate and amusing charm, but there was a struggle between melancholy and *joie de vivre* for possession of his lovely soul. Someone said he was a minor artist with a major style. He was keenly aware that while, as illustration, his work approached the status of art, as art it was, the critics said, no better than illustration.

Like Baudelaire, Johnny elevated dandyism to the condition of a religion. Not to be well-dressed was to insult other people. His was the mystery of the gifted artist. Or that was how the *Daily Mirror* would describe his death nearly a decade later in 1957. But he knew his limitations. And I found him fascinating. It was something to do with vulnerability and talent, a poor combination if you are intent on survival.

'I am not a painter,' he told me. 'I am a decorator and a naturalist.' This was in the year he had returned from a visit to Corsica with the writer Alan Ross, another depressive. His illustrations for Ross's book *Time Was Away* made a romance of the Mediterranean, a world, as he pictured it, of lobster pots, *matelots* in striped jumpers and tables laid for a lunch of baguettes, fresh fish and carafes of rough wine in the company of ladles and pots. These haunting images later fed directly into the illustrations of Elizabeth David's cookery books, which changed the British way of thinking about food. I learnt from Johnny that dinner should be decorative and romantic, not a nutritional chore.

'It's marvellous being taken seriously for behaving so badly,' he liked to say, adding, 'I've come to understand that my fraudulence is the truest thing about me.' One day, when Johnny and I had decided that that morning's seminar was a total waste of time and therefore went for a drink instead, he showed me his rough designs for a wallpaper, commissioned by Sanderson, called 'Arcadia'. It was terribly poignant that this very sad man on Kingsway doodled in Arcady with its dreams of perfect delight. He gave me one of his sketches.

Johnny often took me to Nobody's, a club on the site of an old kosher butcher on Charlotte Street. It was the sort of place you'd find taxi-dancers – paid dance partners. On my first visit, one of them was loudly complaining that he had broken his ankle trying to demonstrate the *tarantella*. The fabulous proprietress, a glittergob Portuguese Jewess from Birmingham, called every customer, irrespective of age or gender, 'Miss'. If she took a dislike to you, she would bellow, 'Out, cunt.' When the moment came, members wobbling on their leopard skin stools in front of the bamboo bar were told, 'Time, gentlemen, please. Back to your lovely cottages.'

'What's that terrible smell?' I asked Johnny on our first visit to Nobody's, noticing a whiff of disinfectant unequal to the job of disguising the whiff of drains.

He laughed and said, with a look eloquent of his own defeat and loss, 'Failure.'

At Nobody's they drew the curtains on sunny afternoons and at night served Albanian schnapps in hot water bottles. Cocaine was delivered after eleven by a Daimler limousine. Cheap chandeliers had been painted crimson.

One night, Johnny in his cups, I asked, 'Ought we to be drunk every night?'

'Oh, yes, I think so,' he replied.

Indeed, he opened his appointment diary in front of me, wanting to make a date for a debauch the next week. I noticed that the week before, over the seven days making up a double-page spread, the word 'DRUNK' had been carelessly scrawled in purple ink.

He was a shy connoisseur of embarrassment, but full of wit and metaphor and provocation, the beau ideal of an art college tutor.

'When a piece of music is too long, you cannot shorten it. Try applying that principle to a drawing,' he liked to say. I think this, with admirable asperity, was lifted from Schoenberg. Poor Johnny's life was too short: he died at forty. Dead drunk.

## not quite first class

My art college education was in the hands of this ill-matched, but beguiling, pair. Ilona taught me about life, Johnny taught me about art, although when I think about it now, I feel life and art are really the same thing. I ignored most of the other tutors and developed my own curriculum, the system being so lax that such a thing was entirely possible.

At a time when draughtsmanship counted for a great deal, my drawings were good, but never great. The school injuries were an impairment. I knew that I was not quite first class, even if I was unusually industrious and unscrupulously ambitious. To supplement what I lacked, I began acquiring, 'filching' you could say, the drawings of other students to add to my own portfolio. I told myself this was research. Later I learnt that French psychologists once declared that collecting was a psychosis and perhaps it was.

In the beginning, I acquired drawings by consent. I flattered the authors, saying, 'Gosh, this is awfully good. Do you mind if I take a copy for reference?'

People rarely begrudged me when I asked to keep an example. In this way I was able, with everyone's consent, to build up a library of current design thinking in the college, including printmaking, furniture design, ceramics and glass.

Then I began to steal drawings, but no one seemed to notice or care. Students are notably unpossessive and always likely to leave bags or folders unguarded while they are in the bar with a half pint of brown ale. After six at night, the studios were empty and plan chests as vulnerable to pillage as North Yorkshire in 793 was vulnerable to Viking invasion. So, hell, why not? My ego was such that I readily assumed the drawings of others into what you might call my oeuvre. I did not really characterize it as stealing: it was more like research. And in any case, I was just showing how enterprising I could be. Was this inspiration or plagiarism? The answer to that depended on whether or not you liked me. A few people did.

In this way, when Ilona Jacobsen, reviving an old contact from the Mendelsohn days, took me to a meeting at David Jones on Oxford Street, my student portfolio was an impressive one. Indeed, it was entirely true to say that my portfolio represented – in the most comprehensive manner – all the talent available at the Lethaby Academy of Art and Design.

David Jones's furniture buyer, a slick, mustachioed man called Trevor Osborne in a brown suit and suede shoes with yellow socks, took us both to the cafe on the department store's roof. Over a smoked salmon sandwich and a glass of warm Riesling, he admired this enormous and wide-ranging portfolio, while I admired the view of the busy London Olympics site far off in the smoky distance at Wembley.

One of those vistas of opportunity, more distant even than Wembley, seemed suddenly to open up. Osborne was, rightly, impressed by the bulk and eclectic swagger of my portfolio. There were fabrics, chairs, light fittings, book jackets, silk-screen prints, woodcuts, moody photographs with the grain showing. He was specially taken by a tea service I had designed and then made in the college's kilns, a successor to my early Fraylings effort. The bold geometry of its pattern had been inspired really quite closely by something I had seen by Josef Frank, the Swedish designer. I did not mention this, although I saw no reason to be ashamed of having excellent sources.

Osborne quickly offered me one thousand pounds a year to leave college before graduation and work in his design department. Later, I heard it reported that I was paid this money not to compete with the other students. This was my first sense of success, achieved, jealous people who didn't like me said, by immoral behaviour and exploitation. They may not have been entirely wrong, but I have always wanted to accentuate the positives.

## ape's bum fodder

With my David Jones stipend, while no longer technically a student of a college I disliked, I nonetheless retained access rights to the

39

Lethaby where the guest lectures were the outstanding feature of otherwise humdrum college life. A particular highlight was when Philip Larkin turned up and gave a talk called 'Ape's Bum Fodder'. Johnny had warned me that the lugubrious Larkin was liked and respected by everyone who knew him . . . slightly. Larkin said to us of a rival poet, 'You know, he couldn't write fuck on a shutter.' We laughed appreciatively.

More to my taste was the American photographer Curtis Moffat, who had opened his Fitzrovia studio in 1925. It quickly became less of a studio and more of a salon. Here, Moffat brought London its first exposure to the surrealist photography he had learnt in Paris with Man Ray: women with cellos as backs, blurred nipples, artistic pornography, that sort of thing. And the very dapper Moffat, an inspiration to Cecil Beaton, was hugely distinguished both artistically and socially. I thought him exemplary in taste and ambition. We were introduced over a glass of British sherry in the Common Room while Ilona was smoking in the background, observing everything.

Moffat was from a very different world from Ilona's dispossessed Hungarian-Jewish community. He had adroitly married the daughter of an English theatrical knight, persuaded philanthropist Jock Whitney to sponsor his progressive gallery and was an early member of André Simon's Wine and Food Society. Moffat's London flat was designed by Frederick Etchells, translator of Le Corbusier. He was an early collector of tribal art and counted Diana Cooper, Augustus John and all the very annoying Sitwells as his friends. This high-concept eclecticism soon became an enduring stimulus to me.

## not worshipping the ashes

At drinks after Moffat's talk, where he had discussed 'Violin symbolism in Surrealist painting', there were two hundred bottles of Pol Roger champagne for two hundred guests. And more bottles were soon required. Vans came in fleets from Berry Brothers in St James's, delivering the extras.

'Mr Moffat,' I said, suppressing a small champagne burp, 'Your talk was brilliant, just brilliant, but do you think photography is killing traditional art?'

Moffat quickly replied, 'Yes, but only if you think tradition is more about worshipping the ashes than tending the flame. But look, young man. There's someone you should meet.'

Moffat now introduced me to one of his guests, the publisher of a California architecture magazine. This was John Entenza, visiting London to discuss an imminent collaboration with *The Architectural Review*, the local journal *du jour* in matters modernistic.

Entenza's dark West Coast tan contrasted with the grey-faced Londoners. He wore a pastel-coloured cotton suit, highly polished oxblood loafers and marmalade *oeil-de-boeuf* spectacles. On Kingsway in the wet, he looked like a superior being. I think perhaps he actually was a superior species. His magazine, *California Arts and Living*, was enthralling and mandatory reading for the ambitious students. Entenza had commissioned promising young architects and designers, Charles Eames and Pierre Koenig among them, to create their own dream homes in Los Angeles as demonstrations of modernist potential. These were the so-called 'Case Study Houses'. You read this magazine, or, at least, you looked at its pictures, and entered a dream.

One Case Study house, all horizontals and bold glazing, might be hanging over the ocean, another daringly cantilevered out over the Hollywood Hills. Each was equipped with a dream kitchen in pastel and chrome, and populated by beautiful people, dream homemakers in pastel and gold, as well as perfect children. And the magazine paid for them. The deal being that each house became the copyright of Entenza, who in this way became an inspired herald of guilt-free sunny modernism. Never before or since has there been a more explicit campaign about the pleasure of design. However, the extent

41

to which they were cynical real estate speculations was never made entirely clear.

'John,' Moffat said, 'I want you to meet Eustace Dunne, one of the most enterprising students to come out of the Lethaby Academy. He lacks English conservatism to a degree that I think you'll find . . . *refreshing*.'

We talked small for a while until, several more glasses into the evening, Entenza said to me, 'Young man, you need to see what we're doing in California. Let me show you Los Angeles.'

It was raining outside and I could hear the unhappy 168 bus gurgling on the street, briefly paused while ferrying passengers from one dank purgatory to a more distant and danker other. Ilona was across the room, still smoking and looking ever more darkly at me. She made a hand gesture that suggested either masturbation or disdain or, perhaps, both. In bright contrast to her *Mitteleuropa* melancholy, a primitive, but nonetheless powerfully intoxicating, vision of Californian sunshine and money began taking shape in my imagination.

So I said, 'Yes, Mr Entenza, I'd like that very much.'

He beamed and looked away. I now noticed that his flies were half unbuttoned and that there was a curious dun stain on his left lapel.

But an idea began to form about what it really might be like to be a designer. Not a mere student in a duffel coat, nor a simple artisan thinking of chairs and pots, or sketching interiors, but an altogether more stylish, influential (and very much richer) individual. I wanted to become that person. There was a vacancy for me to fill. I didn't have a Mephistopheles to help me, so I became my own Satanic inspiration.

# 1949 – The Gland Canyon

*'Fools give you reasons, wise men never try.'*

Richard Rodgers, 'Some Enchanted Evening'
from *South Pacific*, 1949

*Life on board a converted seaplane.*

I SPENT MY STIPEND FROM David Jones on tickets from London to Los Angeles, flying with the haughty British Overseas Airways Corporation, one of the only national institutions left proud and intact after 1945. In those days tickets cost four hundred dollars each way and you bought them from the air terminal at Victoria Station, a survival from when distant Croydon had been London's airport.

At the station there waited a special streamlined Leyland bus, in sky blue and cream duo-tone paint with BOAC's 'Speedbird' badging. Ambitious windows swooping from hip to roof and letting in the sky were somehow redolent of air travel. This striking vehicle drove fitfully from Victoria up the Bath Road to the airport, a dissonance between its sleek appearance and rude mechanicals. Inside, it was a thing of wonder, with upholstery in lush, tan-coloured West of England cloth and the seat frames in sleek exposed chrome. My seat, however, had a perfectly symmetrical cigarette burn on the cushion, exposing the horse-hair stuffing, perhaps a gentle reminder of the frailty of my adventure. Of course, the whole bus smelt of past smokers and present diesel.

And on the seatback in front there was a loose net, its elastic long since spent, holding magazines. As a cosmopolitan gesture, mine held a slightly dog-eared and mildly stained copy of the American *Saturday Evening Post* with a schmaltzy Norman Rockwell cover illustrating American domestic felicity: a perfect family with good hair, good teeth and red cheeks gathered around a primitive RCA Victor television. In the grimy London of 1949, the image seemed other-worldly.

I opened the magazine as we approached Osterley and admired the double-page-spread air travel advertisements, all of which used the identical design conceit of a giant aircraft circling a miniature globe, trailing streamers. Names of destinations were listed like sinful temptations. Los Angeles to Rio, Washington to Caracas, the sunny streamers said, mocking the Middlesex rain which had begun at Heston.

Although the Great West Aerodrome had been promoted to a more modern-sounding 'Heathrow', it was really not much more than a collection of poorly maintained, ex-military huts. Of concessions to cultural or aesthetic curiosity, there were few. These huts were warmed by paraffin heaters. A sense of fatigued army shambles was pervasive. As a rare grace note, transatlantic passengers waiting to board were offered trays of cucumber or egg sandwiches and glasses of *amontillado*. Fortified, they were then driven by jeep across the drizzly runway.

By contrast, the plane represented an altogether different world, an optimistic messenger from Norman Rockwell's better elsewhere across the ocean. Almost obscene in its grandeur, it was a shiny, new Boeing 377 Stratocruiser just bought by BOAC after the government reluctantly agreed the release of precious post-war dollars, expansion of civil aviation being held to be in the national interest.

The Boeing was technically astonishing: a comfortably pressurized double-decker that could fly above the worst of the weather and reach New York non-stop without refuelling at Shannon or Gander.

Delays were unusual in 1949, there being so little traffic, and the Stratocruiser soon groaned and shuddered into the sky in an ecstasy of slow motion. There were maybe forty passengers on board, only half-full. Or only half-empty. I couldn't decide if my mood was pessimistic or optimistic. It was my first flight, but curiosity was easily besting apprehension when, twenty minutes into the sixteen hour first leg to New York, the captain warned of some 'lively' weather just west of Ireland, but assured us in emollient Home Counties tones that the crew would be looking after our comforts.

## pas de flair

Early in the food and drinks service, I noticed an intrusive smell of *eau de cologne* from two rows in front, beating even the stink of aviation spirit and exhaust intruding into the ventilation system from the howling engines outside, their exhausts already glowing red in the dusk. No one familiar with the smooth jet age could imagine the continuous vibration and invasive roar from piston-engined aircraft. Unless asleep, diversions were required.

So I got up and asked the wearer what it was. Where could I buy it? He struck a look located somewhere between indignation and fascination and told me, 'It is Chanel No. 5. I also put it in the Cousteau wetsuits I use for diving: it disguises the stink of rubber.' His English was contemptuously fluent, but his accent theatrically French, as thick as the *à la française* onion soup BOAC was serving him.

'I am,' he said, 'Raymond Loewy.' He bothered a difficult onion skin from his teeth with the help of a gold toothpick suspended around his neck from a fine chain. 'I have been in your Birmingham discussing new cars with Leonard Lord, now so amusingly since his ennoblement called Lord Lord. He plans to revive your British Motor Corporation. And with my help he may well do so. I am the consultant designer. My principle is "The Most Advanced Yet Acceptable". I call it the MAYA theory and will soon apply it to the Austin A40 a dull little car. *Pas de flair.*'

Loewy was wearing an immaculate white suit that, airborne now for nearly an hour, looked as if it had only just been sponged and pressed. Around his neck, along with the gold toothpick, a flamboyant pink foulard. He wore an off-white, nearly cream, Charvet silk shirt. Decorating his chest, a pink pocket square. On his mottled wrist, a very fine Breguet watch with crocodile strap, on his upper lip, a slim black moustache, pomaded and scented like his hair. He wore three gold rings on his left hand.

During our short conversation, Loewy quite literally had his tongue in his cheek, signifying, or so he thought, a louche superiority. At least, as far as the messy eating of onion soup in turbulence allowed. When we hit the advertised patch of very rough air the plane banged and shuddered, Loewy's soup slopped around its bowl and he said a theatrical 'Ooh la la' without stopping eating. I returned to my seat, but resumed my conversation with this impressively sleek and special creature as soon as turbulence subsided.

'What have you designed?' I innocently asked.

He dabbed his lips with the napkin and gestured for me to sit on the arm of his chair.

'I created the consultant design profession when I opened my New York studio in 1927. Since then, I have, quite literally, you understand, transformed some of the most important corporations. I have designed everything from a lipstick to a steamship, with cars and trains in between. Do you clean your teeth with Pepsodent? Yes? Well, you have used one of my products. Do you smoke Lucky Strike cigarettes? My response is the same.'

His onion soup now gave way to a *paillard* of Bresse chicken, which immediately commanded his attention. With it, Loewy ordered XO brandy. Dismissing me fussily with his knife hand to return to my seat so he could continue work on the luxury fowl, Monsieur Loewy gave me his card as an adieu. It simply read 'Loewy', but underneath was the legend '*la laideur se vend mal*'. Ugliness doesn't sell.

'Look up me next time you are in mid-town or Palm Springs,' he concluded, not bothering to look up himself.

## ripe plums

Back in my seat, I adjusted the gooseneck light and asked the steward for champagne. He brought a cruelly sweet *demi-sec*. It was horrible. I had another. A little lightning was silently visible in the distance as I ordered and soon ate trout *amandine* followed by duck *à l'orange*. With these, I drank four glasses of claret. And two glasses of brandy with the *crêpes suzettes*.

Noise and vibration from the four Pratt & Whitney R-4360 Wasp Major radial engines made sleep difficult, but the wine had made me pleasantly somnolent. And as they dimmed the cabin lights for the long over-water stretch and a steward brought blankets and pillows, I reclined the seat and let my imagination wander. I knew from the Pelican Freud I had found in my mother's flat that the rocking motions of train travel might have an erogenous effect. I thought that if Freud had known about Pratt & Whitney, he might have been more convinced still of his theory about mechanical oscillations leading to thoughts of romance.

I looked at my neighbour, a handsome woman of about thirty with tumbling, rust-coloured Jane Russell hair and dressed in an extremely flattering Dior suit the suggestive colour of a ripe plum. She had been silent throughout the meal service, drank nothing, but smoked a cheroot rather theatrically with her coffee. Now she was apparently asleep, her body bent in a nearly foetal S-shape, her handsome callipygian bottom towards me under the blankets.

In the cabin darkness, relieved only by dull ultra-violet nightlights and the orange glow of the distant exhausts outside, no one was moving, someone snored and my thoughts wandered more rapidly. After three minutes of confidence-building, I put my hand on her hip. She did not stir. I waited a moment then moved my hand further down her leg. Still no response. Becoming reckless, my hand went under her skirt, reaching the top of her stockings. She shuddered a little, then relaxed. But suddenly, she sat up very straight, slapped my hand painfully hard, a diamond ring making contact with bone, leapt from her seat and marched along the aisle towards the galley.

For several harrowing minutes, my terrified assumption was that she was alerting the crew to an attempted assault by a drunken maniac. I was certain to be arrested on arrival at Idlewild. And then I saw her returning in the near dark, apparently unflustered, but equally ignoring me completely. She resumed her original position. And after some tormented speculation, I resumed my original fantasy and its attendant actions. The cabin was still silent, the engines droned on. I put my hand back on her hip. Once again, she did not stir. Again, I waited a moment, then moved my hand further down her skirt and soon underneath it. My hand travelled further north, navigating its way to the forbidden territory of the delta of Venus. There was neither resistance nor protest.

On the contrary, I soon found that she was enthusiastically expecting me: far from leaving her seat to alert the crew to an assault, she had left her seat to remove her underwear in the cramped toilet. The inevitable followed. Soon she sighed with evident satisfaction, and that was my introduction to transatlantic travel.

She left the plane at Idlewild still without having said a word to me. I wondered if she had seduced me. Or had I seduced her? I never had the chance to ask, and I think I began to understand that ambiguity might be one of the rules of the game.

Meanwhile, I waited for the connection to Los Angeles. The lounge chairs were gorgeous, pleated Naugahyde, streamlined in profile to suggest the prospect of flight. Soon, I was boarding an American Airlines Douglas DC-6, where, peculiarly, first-class accommodation was in the rear. This flight, I slept.

## mystique and menace

People talk about seeing New York for the first time, but I will never forget my first experience of Los Angeles. The year I landed, the old Mines Field had just become Los Angeles International, the place we now call LAX. That name's claim to cosmopolitanism was revealing of giddy ambition, since in 1949 Los Angeles was really only a dusty, sprawling, undistinguished provincial city that had been relocated to the desert.

There was first generation neon signage on the skyline, flickering uncertainly, but nonetheless alerting me to the lurid triumphs and temptations of American civilization: Coca-Cola, Camel, Westinghouse, Kelloggs, Pan Am, Hebrew National Hot Dog, Budweiser and Red Cross Shoes. Every human appetite was branded. At the Hertz desk, I was offered and accepted a '49 Ford Custom Club Coupe which the Hertz clerk pronounced 'coop'. This was the first all-new American car after the end of the war. With its 3.7 litre six-cylinder engine, the powerful Ford was a keen contrast to the wheezing Morris 8 I had used to pass my test in London. It made me feel ennobled, even enthroned, as I slipped on to the freeway. From behind the wheel, I could see all the resources of America were united in pursuit of a glossy productivity. In 1949, Los Angeles traffic moved; congestion and pollution were not yet facts of Angeleno daily life.

The Collier-Burns Act of 1947 had taxed gasoline to fund the building of the new freeways which were just then beginning to characterize Los Angeles' landscape. 'Once you build a piece of freeway, you determine future actions. Once those lines are laid in concrete, subsequent construction is going to have to connect them,' people were known to say. It was beautiful watching pastel-coloured baroque insects, pistachio Packards and pink Plymouths, migrating in swarms against a blue Pacific. 'Rent it here, leave it there,' the

Hertz ads said. Wasn't this the ultimate statement of America's glorious ease and wastefulness?

My only previous introduction to Los Angeles had been Raymond Chandler's Philip Marlowe thrillers. Chandler's city was a place of mystique and menace, still a frontier town with crime bosses, dodgy politicians, corrupt policemen and glamorous movie people. Briefed by Chandler, I was expecting palm trees swaying like South Sea dancers. And they did.

In a single vista you could see snow-capped mountains and tropical orange groves, while poinsettia brushed against cracked and scorched stucco. It all made the vistas of Kingsway seem even smaller and meaner. There was still a working oil well on La Cienega Boulevard. The city was sun-bleached. But the sun did not always shine. Sometimes in the distance you could see clear, hard rain in the foothills.

I wanted to understand the city's contradictions and its bewildering artifice. And I decided it was purgatory or paradise, simply depending on whether you had money. But everyone had a ringside seat at a real-life circus.

The architecture was like no other, evidently sourced in imaginations untroubled by Palladio or any prim European notion of decorum. This was a city where Grauman's cinema looked like a pharaonic temple and a restaurant called The Brown Derby looked like a hat. I wondered if all restaurants should be so explicit. There was the Richfield Building on South Flower Street, NBC Radio City, the Coca-Cola Building on South Central Avenue, Echo Park, even H. Gaylord Wilshire's very own Boulevard. The Hollywood Bowl sat in a natural canyon of chaparral, sage and Indian paintbrush. Architecture I had only before seen in magazines or in the cinema was everywhere about me.

On a scruffy site where Southern Pacific railcars rumbled past, Simon Rodia's heroic Watts Towers, a bizarre construction of crazed ambition, were just being completed: naive, outsider art on a Californian scale so therefore not really naive at all. Rodia's fabricated towers were a marvel of intuitive engineering designed by a self-taught Italian immigrant who had variously been a labourer, night watchman, telephone repairman, cement finisher and tile setter, only to become the ultimate outsider artist. 'I had it in my mind to do something big, and I did,' he said. Rodia was an artist at welding and an inspiration to me, like Soane.

Surely anything was possible in California? My guidebook told me that Wilshire – the man with the boulevard – had made his impressive fortune from the I-ON-A-CO cure-all electric belt with its only slightly disguised sexual purposes. So surely an English designer was not be excluded from the prospect of riches. The guidebook also told me that John Parkinson, a humble lad from Scorton, Lancashire, was the designer of Los Angeles' imperious City Hall. I felt this was a good augury for an ambitious Englishman abroad.

## the Great American Designer

Entenza had suggested staying at the Biltmore Hotel. Waiting for me at reception in its Moorish-style lobby, with incongruous Austrian crystal chandeliers, was an envelope containing an invitation to a party hosted the next day by none other than Charles Eames. In an accompanying handwritten note on Beverly Hills Hotel stationery, Entenza told me this was not to be turned down. He added he would meet me there.

In the same way that Jackson Pollock would later become the Great American Painter, Eames had already become the Great American Designer, fulfilling a national appetite for a home-grown hero against a wave of European imports. He was born in St Louis, worked in a steel mill and wore butch wash 'n' wear plaid shirts. Later, with growing cosmopolitanism, more sophisticated bow ties and a hopsack suit replaced artisan workwear: Eames was nothing if not alert to self-image. I studied him closely.

Eames had passed through architecture school, won a competition about 'organic' design in New York's Museum of Modern Art in 1940 and six years later was the first designer to have a one-man show at the Museum of Modern Art on West 53rd Street. MoMA was design's Vatican, Eames had been blessed by the Pope and the 'designer' phenomenon was born.

In those days, 'organic' meant sensible, rational and humane, although it was an expression that would inevitably become distorted. For example, Eames had learnt the technique of bending plywood to make splints for the US Navy during the Second World War. This he soon adapted to furniture design. And he too was one of the freemasonry of welders. Eames used his knowledge of welding to make elegant frames for the glass-fibre seating tubs he pioneered.

He was a synthesizer of genius, restlessly inquisitive and curious about how things worked. If you understood the behaviour of plywood or glass-reinforced plastic, if you understood the skeleton, he argued, you could design a perfect chair. And I am certain he was correct. He had a child's innocence and love of exploration. His two short films *The Powers of Ten* were breathtaking works of realized imagination. A graphic treatment of the relative size of things in the universe, the camera zooms in to and out of the Earth's surface, mystically suggesting our individual insignificance. And the graphic excitement of it all! But Eames was a professional more than a visionary: he was mindful about soundbites and very, very telegenic.

.......................................................................................................................

[®] *Rollo Pinkie: There is another view. You can find people who think the shamanistic Charles Eames a preachy bore whose work was only ever of interest to a privileged clique. And nor has it worn well. So far from being eternal classics, Eames' furniture is simply very dated Mid-Century Modern, as obviously fifties as a Chevy with tail fins or a Fender Stratocaster. The man's essential vanity and boastfulness were treacherously disguised by an easy-going, bluff mid-Western personality which took in everybody. Eustace, dizzy in admiration for his stature and success, never noticed.*

## well-known to the magazines

I left the Chandler-era Biltmore with its *azuleros* and coruscating *Mitteleuropa* crystal, telling the cab driver, a Chandler-era Mexican of unhelpful aspect with broken teeth in a grey Chevy Fleetline, '203 North Chautauqua Boulevard in Pacific Palisades, please.' This was the Eames House, Entenza's eighth Case Study. It was built on a site once belonging to Will Rogers, the vaudeville performer who was a native Cherokee. I loved these bizarre Los Angeles connections.

The idea of the Eames House was to use high-performance military materials at non-military prices: in this way, the entire house was composed of off-the-shelf components from a steel fabricator, but post-war shortages in fact meant that Case Study No. 8 was disproportionately expensive rather than impressively cheap. 'I thought I'd have pups when they told me the cost,' Eames told Entenza's magazine. The Eames House was 'functional' in name only.

And Charles Eames' secretary, a woman who suffered for her cause, was always claiming that its many windows made it impossible to clean. In reality, none of Entenza's Case Study Houses worked well. Another famous example by Pierre Koenig in the Hollywood Hills was badly made, always leaked and was impossible to ventilate, but like Eames', the Koenig house photographed beautifully, making a glossy case for 'design' in magazines all over the world. Back in London, we had been fretting about whether Britain could make it. The Eames House showed that America already had.

Although not quite finished at the time of my visit, 203 North

Chautauqua Boulevard had already become a home, a shrine and a collective. Here Eames, not at all resistant to publicity, was memorably photographed welding and sawing for *Life* magazine by Herbert Matter: the litany and iconography of the designer as can-do creator were essential to an emerging mythology. And I wanted to be a part of it.

The Eames façade was composed like a Mondrian painting; there was a gold leaf panel above the front door surrounded by eucalyptus trees. Inside: Noguchi floor lamps, *netsuke*, Chinese lacquered pillows, Native American woven baskets full of dried grass, Shaker cabinets, Amish dolls, old tools, letter-press Wild West 'wanted' posters, Basque *pelotas*, a ploughshare, African *djembe* drums, French educational posters and hundreds of Japanese *kokeshi* dolls.

Eames' busy publicist, Eileen Himmelfarb, made sure the house was well known to the magazines. Often it was used for fashion shoots, helping cement the image of the Eameses' high-concept domesticity in the popular imagination.

Entenza was waiting at the gate and immediately introduced me to the host. Eames, a large handsome man, was looking amiably professorial in a corduroy jacket and cravat, although neither was strictly necessary given the temperature. There was a meaningfully arranged display of pipe, spectacles and pens in the breast pocket. His wife Ray looked like a smiley American Gothic matron in her trademark wide skirts, a scary fantasy little-girl look. She whispered to me that Charlie Chaplin was there. He had, she explained, often shared Japanese tea ceremonies with them, while gazing at the Pacific. Then she mentioned Anaïs Nin, a name that meant nothing to me. 1949 was the birth of television. So Dominick Dunne, a pioneer producer, was there too, Ray confided, not displeased by her impressive contacts.

'But the most important person here, Eustace, is my good friend Billy,' Charles interrupted.

I found myself shaking hands with an intelligent-looking, deeply tanned, pugnacious man in sunglasses, wearing a yellow sweater over the shoulder and an aqua Madras shirt.

'This is the director Billy Wilder,' Charles explained. 'We met when my friend Alvin Lustig, he's a graphic designer, was broke and working in Billy's garage. Billy's just finished the final edit of *Some Like It Hot*. I gotta tell you, I learnt more about architecture and design from watching Billy make movies than I ever learnt at school.'

Wilder, despite his radiant and sunburnt Hollywood aspect, retained something of the grandeur of old Europe. Taking my elbow, he steered me towards the wet bar.

'I never forget that I come from Sucha … and I never forget that Sucha is a very small Polish town in the Duchy of Oświęcim,' he said, simultaneously directing the barman's attention to a bottle of imported Russian vodka. 'We nowadays call it Auschwitz. But I have learnt a lotta other things too. You gotta trust your own instinct. Your mistakes might as well be your own as someone else's. Straight up with a twist of lemon, please. And one for my young friend.'

'But what's the connection between cinema and design that Charles was talking about?' I asked as we clinked glasses.

'Ha! Isn't it all about telling stories? I bought Bauhaus chairs when I was in Berlin! They told a story. I knew those guys, the nut jobs with the welding torches and boiler suits and frameless glasses. It's all about presentation and performance. If you're going to tell people the truth, be funny, or they will kill you. Oh yes. And fuck deadlines and budgets as well. My aunt Minnie was very punctual and never over-spent, but who would want to pay to see my aunt Minnie in a movie? Never forget that. Oh, and one other thing. A director must be a policeman, a midwife, a psychoanalyst, a sycophant and a bastard. I guess that's the same for designers too.'

From over the room, as Wilder's attention drifted elsewhere, 'Are you queer?' a colourful woman on a Noguchi stool shouted at me. And when I demurred, she said, 'Well, then. Come right over here,' and patted the other Noguchi.

Her hair in a tight bob, a chunky jade necklace above an impressive crevasse of cleavage, she looked down at her chest and then up at me and asked, 'Honey, do you know they call this the Gland Canyon?'

'I can see why,' I mumbled.

She continued, 'I guess you're new to Los Angeles. Never forget that Cecil B. DeMille made a film called *Gigolo* more than twenty years ago. Sex is everywhere in this town, but we never see things as they are, we see them as *we* are. And we travel, some of us for ever, to seek other states, other lives, other souls.'

Not sure whether I was being warned or teased, whether the woman was drunk or deranged, I felt the conversation slipping away from me.

'To be honest, I'm not used to martinis,' I confessed.

'Well,' she said, drawing the single syllable out to extraordinary length, 'a martini makes an ordinary glass shine like a diamond at a coronation, makes an iron bed seem like the feather bed of a sultan, a hotel room like the terminus and climax of all voyages, the pinnacle of contentment, the place of repose in an altitude hungered for by all restless ones. And I'll tell you something else, honey,' and now she winked at me, 'good things happen to people who hustle.'

I felt a sparrow-like hand on my shoulder and a slight directional pressure. It was my hostess intervening.

'You have just met,' Ray Eames patiently explained, 'Angela Anaïs Juana Antolina Rosa Edelmira Nin y Culmell. Better known, perhaps, as Anaïs Nin. She does not need opium because she has a gift for reverie.' With that, Ray rolled her eyes, leading me to the door and the waiting Mexican with broken teeth.

## fellatio and aerospace

The next night, also at the Eameses' invitation, there was another party on a converted seaplane, anchored at Marina del Rey. Billy Wilder was there again. As Eames had told me at his own party: everything is connected . . . especially in Los Angeles. I reintroduced myself to Billy, mentioning a slight hangover.

He said, 'Forget the hangover. Instead, dream. You have to have a dream so you can get up in the morning.'

The Southern Californian Aircraft Corporation had acquired a batch of war-surplus PBY-5A 'Catalina' seaplanes, or what we British more quaintly called flying-boats. What, I wondered, was the difference? Perhaps one seemed practical, the other visionary. Anyway, the Southern California Aircraft Corporation made its business from converting these military craft into rich men's playthings, this conversion translating mere flying-boats to luxuriously equipped aerial yachts. King Farouk of Egypt was one of the first customers, although it was never delivered as abdication came before completion.

Now rebranded the Landseaire, these Catalinas had eight beds, two of them in the midships gun position under dramatic blisters of Lucite. There was sound insulation and carpet. The massive wingspan was adapted for partying and sunbathing and where bombs or drop tanks once hung dependent on the wings, cute little dinghies were slung on electric hoists. There was an electric flush loo. A Landseaire would cruise at 175mph and cost $265,000.

The galley had a three-ring electric range and a freezer configured to store bottles of gin and vermouth. The martinis arising were, on this occasion, mixed by a hostess in a red and white polka dot bikini. It was in this galley that, unbidden, the server said to me, as

I was being curious about the ingenious spatial ergonomics of the flying kitchen, opening and shutting aluminium doors fastened with marvellously technical-looking latches, 'Gee, you're so cute.' She pulled the curtain shut and we were invisible for a few moments. Kneeling, she giggled.

Los Angeles, I thought with my eyes shut, is most certainly not a city of the angels. Soon, after she had spat into the miniature aluminium sink, the mixing of cocktails was cheerfully resumed. This mixture of technical profession and lascivious indulgence is what I find ineradicable about California. Moreover, concepts of fellatio and aerospace are fused for ever in my imagination.

## rearranging the elements

Two days after the Catalina party, I returned to Pacific Palisades to say goodbye to Charles Eames. He beamed as he opened the metal door and led me towards the studio, a big hand on my shoulder. And then the phone rang. It was a Henry Dreyfuss Western Electric model 500 which, becoming famous first in movies and now on television, made the old marmoreally cold GPO handsets in grim Bakelite with woven brown flex that we had at home look primitive. It was another reminder of American prowess and style. As he took the call, from across the room Eames struck a pose of amused concern at whatever he was hearing. With one hand over the mouthpiece, he made an amiable open palm gesture to me with the other.

'Excuse me. Do you mind? I gotta take this call. But make yourself at home, look around. Carmelita will make you some coffee.'

'That'd be lovely,' I said. 'No rush. I'm very happy here.'

I wandered into the studio. The morning light was reflecting yellow from the glazed Pacific and those damned palms were swaying, just as advertised. I opened his plan chest and riffled through the drawings. I found some sketches of designs for chairs using glass-fibre tubs above a welded wire frame. I stole them because I could. And because no one was looking.

'OK, Eustace. I'm done and Carmelita's here,' I heard from the distance and went to rejoin him.

'I'd like to tell you that was a call from the President asking me to design the next World's Fair, but it was actually a call from SoCal Power and Light about an outage next Tuesday.'

I had brought him a gift of Evelyn Waugh's *The Loved One*, a hilarious account of the absurdities of the Californian funeral industry, and told him, 'It makes death funny.'

'Wow. That's too swell for words. But you know, I have never said that pleasure is useless.'

And then I asked if I could make some notes of our conversation. He picked up one of his *kokeshi* dolls and a little dried seagrass, smiled a well-practised asymmetrical smile and said, 'Sure.'

'Let's start with something very simple. What exactly is this elusive subject, "design"?'

Eames looked thoughtful and said, 'Design is a plan for arranging elements in such a way as best to accomplish a particular purpose.' Then he settled on to yet another Noguchi stool. Reaching for a little piece of *netsuke*, a scowling dragon, and passing it to me, he said, 'Look at this. Details are not trivial or subservient. They actually make the design.'

I asked him about talent or ambition. Or was genius something different?

'Genius? Nah! We just work harder. And we have never designed for a fashion or a market,' he explained with genial seriousness. He showed me a cutting from a New York magazine saying that he and Ray moved freely in a world of unlimited opportunity with intelligence and taste. I thought, Yes, of course he did. And soon I will too.

Never has it occurred to me that anyone is a better exemplar of 'The Designer' than Charles Eames. He had imagination, charm, humour and a keen practical sense. He had an eclectic eye and, fascinated by play, was an inspired educator.

He went on to tell me, 'I visited a good toy store yesterday. It was sick-making. There was just too goddamn much going on. I think children have better taste than toy store owners realize.'

And I understood that Charles Eames was distrustful of showy affluence, although very happy to be rich, comfortable and famous. It was a nice compromise, one I intended to imitate.

California was a thrilling insight into America as a land of surprise and opportunity. I was both exhilarated and saddened that I would never have the wit, style and ingenuity Charles Eames possessed and I so desperately wanted to emulate. But I had a plan.

I didn't want to be like Charles Eames, I wanted to *be* Charles Eames. I had touched his cloak of greatness and now I wanted to wear one of my own.

I remembered Simon Rodia's words: 'I had it in my mind to do something big, and I did.'

# 1951 – South Bank Soviet

*'I'm the most terrific liar you ever saw in your life.'*

J. D. Salinger, *The Catcher in the Rye*, 1951

*Skylon at the Festival of Britain.*

Returning from Los Angeles of martinis and sunshine to a London of Bovril, semolina and cabbage, from pink Plymouths and Cadillacs to black Austin A40s, I needed a job and needed somewhere to live and work. I had a little money in my pocket and a small fortune of stolen Charles Eames' drawings in my portfolio. I had bought the portfolio from the brightly lit, six-storey stationery store on La Cienega Boulevard, where I saw my first *electric* typewriter soon after I had seen my first oil well.

A friend of my mother's had absurdly told me to make myself known in the Pall Mall clubs, but I thought the student noticeboard at the Lethaby Academy was a more realistic starting point for me. Mostly there were postcards selling easels and used football boots, or desultory invitations to outings on the Norfolk Broads and advertisements for terrible singalong folk nights at the Queen's Head. I saw the word 'skiffle'. The Communist Party of Great Britain even had a presence, offering Russian lessons on Tuesday and Thursday evenings in Red Lion Square. Harp instruction was available too, yet there were, I think, few takers, no matter how alluring and biddable Blodwyn Twdwr Evans and her stringed instrument might prove to be.

## first names here, old boy

But there was one notice that stood out because it was elegantly set in hot metal type. And it was in significantly modern *sans serif*. Gill, I think.

This was more my style:

*Tallboy St Clair Architects seeks to employ a Design Assistant. This is a busy practice with an established record in commercial interiors. We are recruiting extra staff to meet the anticipated needs of the 1951 Festival of Britain. Please telephone BAYSwater 3970 for an appointment.*

I went straight to the red phone box on Kingsway, the one Scott designed after inspiration from Soane's own mausoleum in St Pancras. Death and the Telephone, I thought to myself. If only Schubert had known.

Naturally, Scott's noble design stank of urine and tobacco while the floor was a grimy lagoon with floating islands of cigarette ends, bus tickets and all too evidently used condoms. This was hazard and surprise of a sort that would have displeased Soane. A bus grumbled by as I ruffled for my change. Press Button A, Press Button B, the pennies dropped. And the telephone was promptly answered.

'Tallboy St Clair Architects. How may I help you?'

'I'm calling about the design assistant job,' I said.

'Very good. Your name is?' the telephone replied.

'Eustace Dunne,' I told the telephone.

'Excellent. We are holding interviews next Wednesday afternoon. Please come to 24 Westbourne Grove at three.'

Six days later in Westbourne Grove, with a portfolio of my own drawings to supplement the other dishonestly acquired treasures, I was introduced to three people in an interview room. The first was St Clair himself, an affable man in the contemporary architect's uniform of green corduroy jacket, dark shirt and knitted woollen tie. He immediately put me at my ease with his amiable body language and said, 'Mr Dunne, I want to introduce you to Sir Gerald Barry and Hugh Casson. Gerald is the Director General of the Festival of Britain and Hugh is his architecture and design director. First names here, old boy.'

Barry, I had read in prep for this interview, was a middlebrow Fleet Street editor. Cambridge educated, therefore left-leaning, but populist too and not obviously too pleased with himself. A vicar's son from suburban Surrey, he had a kindly, collegiate manner, but gave an impression of being a man who liked to get things done, one not very much inclined to be deterred by obstacles or diverted by dissent.

He went straight into his pitch. 'We have only just stopped eating Lord Woolton's bloody awful pies. We are still eating filthy government Cheddar. The old cheese-makers have been ruined by the Milk Marketing Board. Coffee is made of acorns. There are power cuts every day and dock strikes every week. The next election is going to be fought over rationing. About time we could all enjoy a bacon sandwich, as well as the Third Programme! I think people have had enough. Actually, I know people have had enough. They are exhausted and need a tonic. I want the Festival of Britain to be ... a tonic to the nation!'

Casson, as quick as a bird and still clutching his brolly, looked up and nodded briskly, eyes darting. 'Mine is just the role of the oil can in making the machinery clunk around a bit more efficiently,' he explained, although I sensed he was rather more than functional lubrication.

Barry continued, 'Hugh here joined us early in 1948 ...'

'And it has been nearly three years of almost total elation!' Casson cheerfully interrupted.

'Hugh,' Barry continued, 'is absolutely determined to hire young talent. That's why you are here.'

And Hugh, I later discovered, was a genuine patron and enthusiast. The type who was a clever dropout from games at school, Casson was a principled man, clever and well-read, but an enlightened pragmatist too. Ten years before he had published *New Sights of*

*London*, a guide to modern architecture accessible to citizens using the Underground and Green Line buses alone. In those days, London Transport – even the BBC – still seemed a noble experiment.

## nook-shotten London

'London is a city of secret places. Nook-shotten, as the poet said,' Casson went on. 'I want to introduce people to them through the Festival's design. And we can create some not so secret places of our own! I want to see bright colours against the smog and soot. I want new buildings! Fresh ideas! Visions!' He waved a hand in the direction of the future. 'I don't want servility to the past or plagiarism. The people deserve better than copies of what's already been achieved.'

I winced only slightly, mindful of my Californian felony.

'I want pleasure in the here and now, and excitement about the future. Leisured gaiety, I call it. A helicopter will connect the South Bank to Heathrow. We will show washing machines, vacuum machines and refrigerators. There will be a telekinema so you can see yourself on a television set! There will be a "Dome of Discovery" which will be the festival's brain. Just imagine entering a clever man's cranium! We will send radio signals to the moon and we will receive them back.' He was now getting very animated. 'At night, people will be jitterbugging under searchlights.' With that, he made a brief dance move and resumed clutching his umbrella.

'We certainly will jitterbug,' Barry confirmed. 'Now, show us your drawings ...'

They all nodded sagely, expressing admiration for the range and eclecticism of my work. And they were specially impressed by my designs for chairs with a seat tub of self-coloured, glass-reinforced plastic, suspended in an armature of welded steel rods.

'This is very sophisticated and mature work,' St Clair said, with settled gravity. 'I'll confer with the others when you have left, but perhaps you'd consider joining us next week? Marion in reception will give you more details.'

'I'd like that very much,' I replied.

........................................................................................................................

® *Rollo Pinkie: I don't doubt that Eustace's notable force of personality and amazing portfolio of stolen drawings helped secure this appointment, but I happen to know that as soon as he had read the notice on the art college's message board, he took it down and stuffed it into the back pocket of his olive-coloured corduroy trousers. This was to remove the vacancy from sight and thus remove the possibility of competition.*

## life in The Old Dairy

One of the many problems with the Lethaby Academy was that it had no neighbourhood. Art schools generally send ripples into their community, like a stone skimmed across a pond. The ripples comprise friendly pubs, student houses and cheap cafes, but the Lethaby Academy was isolated by busy traffic and large commercial buildings. Kingsway was no one's idea of Bohemia. Certainly not mine.

So I decided to explore Camberwell, where another famous art college had its origins in the South London Working Men's College. I liked this origin in honest trade, this focus on the practical arts: the first students were taught embroidery and stencil-cutting. Architecture was taught too, but it was construed as a refinement of the building trade, not a branch of show business. In Camberwell, architects very sensibly learnt about bricklaying.

Best of all, I knew that in this rugged environment, the pioneer abstract painter Victor Pasmore was Head of Fine Art and the gutsy figurative painter Frank Auerbach was a tutor. This was the peculiar pleasure of an art college: the incongruity of high-minded battles over figuration or non-representation, arguments about the 'pregnancy of the picture-plane', an expression as widely used in seminars as it was baffling in meaning. And there was the curious thrill of being taught in a neighbourhood which still had a workhouse and feral children on the street, fighting beneath washing drying on lines in the open air.

Until I discovered The Old Dairy in Artichoke Mews, I traipsed ruefully around Camberwell's sordid bedsits. They were identical in their sadness. A miserable smoking landlady, under-nourished, but overweight from a diet of filthy government Cheddar and Lord Woolton's bloody pie, would attend a reluctantly open door with no enthusiasm and a headscarf. Vague but certainly unpleasant smells, probably animal in origin, were always present.

The better equipped bedsits might have a single bar electric fire. You had to feed shilling pieces into the electric meter to coax it into a simulacrum of life. There would be a faded candlewick bedspread, a single pendant light with a conical parchment shade, usually stained by some agent, cracked, cold, cheerless linoleum on the floor. The windows would be grimy, while damp interfered with the floral wallpaper's adhesive bond to the wall. Mould, you soon discovered, has a distinctive aroma.

'Christ!' I said to myself every time. 'There must be a better way of organizing life than this.' I began to wonder exactly how it might be better. And I wondered too what Charles Eames, in sunny California, would think of this South London horror show.

After my fifth or sixth viewing, I was sitting morose with a Guinness in the Hermit's Cave, the art college pub, ready to give up on Camberwell. But, deciding to walk back to the Festival of Britain site, about two miles away on the South Bank, I came across Artichoke Mews at one end of a bombsite on the Walworth Road.

An iron gate, hanging from only one hinge, half-heartedly protected a small cobbled yard, rather as a naked Surbiton Virgin might hide her modesty with the back of her hand. There was a sickly smell in the air from a nearby biscuit factory, which had unfortunately, in my view, escaped the Blitz. And at the back of the yard was The Old Dairy.

Obviously abandoned since before the war, The Old Dairy was a double-height space. Top-lit, so ideal as a studio, although the broken glass would need replacing. Nineteenth-century iron trusses, rusting but handsome, supported the roof and there were remains of rugged white industrial tiles on the walls. Elsewhere, bare brick. I think some people might have been deterred, but all I saw was terrific promise here. After all, wasn't design all about transformation?

I ran to the library on Church Street where the local history assistant helped me find the landlord. A deal was soon done, since in those days a taste had not developed for semi-derelict industrial premises and there was no prospective interest. Within days I was exposing more brick with a hammer and chisel, using plenty of optimism and white paint, sanding filthy wood surfaces to modern brightness and fitting dazzling studio lights I found in a wholesale theatrical suppliers near the Old Vic in Waterloo. I hung undyed calico from three inch diameter wooden rods fitted above the windows and now The Old Dairy was my first studio and first home. But I did not want to make much distinction between work and play.

Michelangelo believed that his job as a sculptor was to release the angel trapped inside the block of marble. I felt the same about buildings. They are living things. And they evolve: you don't finish a building, you start it. And hacking the stained plaster of The Old Dairy's walls and getting back to the brick was a sort of revelation. You can repurpose anything. And, like Sir John Soane, you can create visual surprises. Because textures are so pleasurable in themselves, you don't need any superficial 'decoration'. Sandblasted

London Stock brick and grey powder-coated Crittall windows are quite enough.

........................................................................................................

Camberwell, Schroeder's biscuit factory apart, was in 1950 horribly scarred by bomb damage, but the local council was doing its own demolition as well. Seven hundred new homes had been built on a space created on nearby Denmark Hill when Henry Bessemer's and John Ruskin's houses were knocked down. I dare say the local authority took some sort of pleasure in this revenge against the propertied classes, a calculated insult to the memory of art and industry, since Bessemer meant steel and Ruskin was the champion of Turner. But the insult to me was worse because these 'council houses' were so badly designed. Shouldn't a council house be the very best of its type, not the very worst?

There were still trams, London's last, and if there were any cars they were those humble Austins or the new Rover 75s as perpendicular as the Gothic churches. The most prominent shop on the high street was an undertaker, still using Victorian signs. The most prominent local business was Everitt & Co, a hatter who, sensing the opportunities of the moment, had diversified into manufacturing crash helmets with a cork shell, a racy peak, ear flaps and a leatherette outer. A huge forty-eight sheet poster advertised the Everitt Clubmaster for 82/6d. 'Keep ahead in Safety and Style' it read, a sentiment illustrated by a couple on an Italian Vespa, a neat machine that was a herald from a very different world.

Then there was Wally's Fish Bar, always popular because fish and chips were not rationed. Nor, alas, was the foul grease they were fried in. Still, like the students, I went there often. One wet Monday lunchtime, two of us were in there. He was obviously an art college type: carefully considered scruffy hair, a baggy, paint-spattered, roll neck sweater, working men's boots and a thoughtful look.

He said to no one in particular, but obviously intended for me since the queue comprised only the two of us: 'In England, it's thought to be morally suspect to worry about what you eat.'

'Are you worried about Wally's? Perhaps you're morally suspect?'

'No, not at all,' he said. 'I come here every day. The rock salmon is specially good. I am Howard. I'm a painter. I feel isolated as an artist, but not as a person. Would you like to have a pint?'

I would, and we did. Howard explained the continuous conversation he had with his canvases, as he battled daily with his pregnant picture-plane.

'When I finish a painting, it usually looks as surprising to me as to anyone else!' he said, amused by the absurdity and warming to his self-deprecating frankness.

'So that's what's different between art and design,' I offered. 'We designers tend to know exactly what we want to achieve. I think design is intelligence made visible, not a mystery painfully revealed.'

That was my first meeting with Howard Hodgkin, who soon became a very good friend. After his debut show at the Institute of Contemporary Arts in 1962 (with the Pop artist Allen Jones) he became generally recognized as Britain's greatest painter in the second half of the twentieth century. His early pictures became very collectible. I have lots, but I paid very little for them. A chance encounter in a fish bar would make me rich, an absurdity to relish.

## the terrace and the wrecking-ball

The Festival of Britain site was, if anything, even more depressing than Camberwell. Again, there was severe bomb damage, but it was even worse on the South Bank because of its proximity to Parliament, although the active rumour was that Hitler had actually advised the Luftwaffe to avoid damaging Westminster and Buckingham Palace since he planned eventually to move in. In that event, never much of a monarchist, I thought there would at least be room for the royal family to move back to Germany.

As in Camberwell, the local authorities continued the work of the Luftwaffe, clearing what few useful buildings remained on the site. The landmark Lion Brewery was demolished and its famous Coade stone lion sculpture was despatched to Waterloo. Ealing Studios made a sentimental film about a South Bank family defending its sad terraced house from the wrecker's ball. Clement Attlee intervened and preserved the slum as a curiosity for display in the Festival.

Despite Mr St Clair's insistence on first names, I could not bear to call him Tallboy. So it was Mr St Clair who said to me in his Bayswater studio, 'I want you to work on the house and garden pavilion, and on the transport pavilion. In the one, you will be working on a mock-up of the interior of the new *Arctic Albatross* flying-boat. It's being built at Cowes by Saunders-Roe and is intended to be our rival to Boeing's Stratoliner, a clumsy plane if you ask me. Typically American. Brute force and ignorance. And in the house and garden pavilion, I'd like you to develop those very fine designs of fibreglass and metal chairs you showed me at interview. And there may be some work in the restaurants too, but we can come to that later. Oh, remind me to tell you about British Felt.'

'I'm not really qualified for any of this,' I said, more apologetically than I intended.

'Utter bollocks!' Mr St Clair said. 'You don't need qualifications. You need enthusiasm and a good eye. And you have both.'

This was the spirit of almost reckless commitment possessed by festival workers. One of St Clair's other young designers had sketched some chairs in the style of Ernest Race's 'Antelope', whose amusing wire frame seemed like a diagram of our collective optimism. I was the only one in the studio who knew how to weld, so the St Clair chair came into being in my hands. I felt it made a good addition to my portfolio. Whether it was 'mine' was a matter of angels dancing on heads of pins: without me, it would never have happened. Genius always needs the power of execution.

My pastiches of Eames' designs for chairs were amongst the first examples of mid-century modern the British public had seen. I had welded the metal frames myself and had them lacquered in black by a paint shop in Willesden. The brightly coloured fibreglass tubs I had made by a boat-builder in Leigh-on-Sea, a man of sound principles used to laying plastic and resin for trawler hulls. I assembled the frames and tubs myself and, without asking Tallboy St Clair, attached a little sticker to the hidden side of the tub's lip saying 'Design: Eustace Dunne'. The sticker also carried a facsimile of my signature.

For the *Arctic Albatross* flying-boat interiors, I drew on some of my Boeing passenger experience as well as the King Features Syndicate space hero Flash Gordon, a rival to Buck Rogers, my boyhood cartoon hero. A theatrical model-maker produced a full-size section of fuselage and in it we installed two pairs of seats. These were, strictly speaking, non-functioning models, but gave a convincing impression of pleasures – possibly – to come, with their extravagantly moulded head and foot rests and chrome trim contrasting with lush, bottle green leather. If *Arctic Albatross* had ever flown, they would have been too heavy, but function is not everything.

It was Sir Windridge McCluggage of the British International Felt Company who became my inspiring patron, a Lorenzo de

Medici on the South Bank. For him, I designed a stand inspired by Norman Bel Geddes' futuristic book *Horizons*, a compilation of pre-war *de luxe* fantasies by a Hollywood scoundrel with the gift of the gab. I still had the Lethaby Academy's copy of the book at home. The whole stand took the *Arctic Albatross* design language to the next step: it had swoops, curves, chrome trim, lavish use of the new plastic, and recessed downlights. Insulation, underlay, upholstery and stuffing, the basis of the British International Felt Company's business, were treated with the stylish reverence due to exotic treasures. With a gin and tonic in hand and his moustache twitching, Sir Windridge told me, 'Young man, never before has a stand looked so bloody sexy.'

## no visible means of support

But my favourite project on the whole Festival of Britain site was not my own. Rather, it was the improbable and absurd Skylon, whose name was chosen by a Mrs Fidler, wife of the chief architect of Crawley New Town. Outside London, the new towns of Crawley, Harlow and Stevenage were the representatives of the Festival spirit: modern architecture, careful planning and attractive design would enhance well-being for a population ungenerously described as 'London overspill'.

Evidently impressed by the Trylon that had appeared at the 1939 New York World's Fair, Mrs Fidler liked to explain that 'Skylon' usefully combined all the senses of sky, nylon and pylon. In truth, Skylon was something of a Potemkin village and in that, I must confess, an effective symbol of the whole festival, since it was something of an artful deception. So far from being poised to launch itself into space, Skylon was a temporary assemblage of wire and the effects of a theatre designer. Not exactly a deception, but quite close.

Other than to astonish the viewer, especially those on the north bank of the Thames who enjoyed a distant view, it served no strictly functional purpose. People joked that, like the country itself, Skylon had no visible means of support.

What, in fact, Skylon's rocket profile, a hundred yards tall, achieved was a delightful illusion of floating and a stirring suggestion of progress … even if this was progress to an ill-defined destination with a departure time not yet agreed. Nor, being a construction of wire, essentially a theatrical prop rather than a functioning device, could it carry any passengers. I suppose we should all have realized that it was a symbol in more ways than one.

Near the Skylon installation, where every day I followed the progress of its construction, I introduced myself to an interesting figure who spent his days swearing and welding buckets on to a bizarre, chain-and-belt-driven contraption apparently of his own invention. The contraption's buckets scooped water out of a pool, before being raised on an unreliable mechanism (which often stalled with a crash of metal) to a height from which the water was discharged to dramatic effect, only for the cycle to begin again. Was it sculpture? Festival people never bothered with such pedantry.

## sweat and red wine

Ursine, beetle-browed and smelling of sweat (both stale and fresh) as well as red wine, the welder was Eduardo Paolozzi who, I soon learnt, had made his reputation two years before with an exhibition at the Mayor Gallery where his slightly dotty collages of Americana anticipated what we now call 'Pop art'. He was an impressive man. During the war, Paolozzi escaped the Pioneer Corps (who stationed him on a football pitch in Slough for a whole year) by faking madness, although some felt little faking was required.

I told him rather recklessly, 'Do you know, that's not really the way to do gas tungsten arc welding.'

'And you can go fuck yourself,' Paolozzi replied, without emotion, in a strong Scottish accent. I liked him immediately. He had expressive lips and an astonishing amount of body hair, a lot of it erupting from curious moles and other small imperfections. And then, unsuccessfully welded, the red-hot bucket fell off the carrier and on to his foot.

Paolozzi stood up, shrugged and said, 'So show me, smart arse.' And I did.

Paolozzi became a great friend. He asked me what I thought of the interfering Herbert Morrison, the festival's sponsor in government who was always trying to check Barry's and Casson's easygoing instincts.

'He's his own worst enemy,' I said.

'Not while I'm around he's not,' Paolozzi quickly added.

He was as eclectic as his art. Born in Scotland to a family from Frosinone whose art was ice cream, his father, a Mussolini enthusiast, had sent the young Eduardo to a fascist youth camp. This, with an incongruous Scottish accent, he greatly enjoyed and the experience began his life-long fascination with aircraft, uniforms and badges.

He was fond of explaining how he met Brâncuşi, Braque and Giacometti in Paris. But his own vision was unique, conferring as it did a peculiar value on machinery, even the malfunctioning sort with buckets and chains.

Paolozzi was a marvellous scavenger: 'I have an African or Indian approach to what I find. I like to make use of everything. I can't bear to throw things away. A nice wine bottle, a nice box. Sometimes I feel like a wizard in Toytown, transforming a bunch of carrots into pomegranates.'

He became a regular visitor to The Old Dairy, bringing blue glass apothecary bottles, Scotch whisky, hessian sacks of coffee, model cars and planes, nicely patinated handtools, military badges, print ephemera, glass carafes, American pulp magazines, vintage cameras and Cornishware mugs with him on every visit. I still have them.

Journalists often report admiringly on my brilliantly eclectic eye. I don't correct them.

Later in the year, I went to a pub in Roupell Street to listen to the festival's closing ceremony on the radio. The Brigade of Guards band played while, the announcer explained, the Union Jack was lowered. The Archbishop of Canterbury held a thanksgiving service in the Royal Festival Hall. It had all been, his Grace declared, a 'real family party'.

People are nostalgic about the Festival of Britain, but distance often lends beauty to the view. Not everything on the South Bank had been a success. The Live Architecture pavilion promised visitors they would be able to hear how building materials transmitted the sounds of 'suburban orgies' next door. It missed its attendance targets by more than ninety per cent. And not every visitor was an enthusiastic one. Some found the sight of pipe-smoking men in gabardine macs wistfully seeking enlightenment in the Dome of Discovery a doleful and melancholy one.

But for me, the Festival of Britain was a personal triumph. It was when I really began collecting press cuttings. The *London Evening News* wrote, 'Eustace Dunne is a rising talent in commercial art. His sparkling Travel Pavilion serves notice on the days of brown paint, varnish and porridge wallpaper.' The *Express*, excited by the fibreglass chairs, named me as 'Britain's first modern designer'. And Sir Windridge McCluggage became something of a feature on the broadsheet business pages. 'Design,' he told the *Daily Telegraph*, 'has turned felt from a commodity to a luxury.'

*Picture Post* photographed me in The Old Dairy to illustrate a short profile: 'College prodigy Eustace Dunne contributes to British furniture what the Ferranti computer and Canberra jet contribute to science and trade. Asked what design means to him, Mr Dunne replied, "It makes you happy." We say he's one to watch.'

## a cameo of incompetence

The Tories won the general election of October 1951. There was a general feeling among them that the Festival of Britain had had a disagreeably Soviet character, what with all its references to 'people' and 'land'. Churchill himself encouraged the mean-spirited removal of the Skylon, thinking it a symbol of socialist ambition, believing perhaps that all ambition was communistic. As if to say ambition was a bad thing. Skylon was sold to and dismantled by an East End scrap metal dealer who turned what he could into commemorative cutlery and unceremoniously dumped the surplus into the River Lea.

A terrible, ungrateful man called David Eccles who ran the Ministry of Works told the nation that he was 'unwilling to become the caretaker of empty and deteriorating structures'. And it was true that without any visitors, an empty Festival of Britain site looked ludicrous. And the Dome of Discovery was becoming a rather melancholy sight, since it no longer welcomed discoverers.

In this way, apart from the magnificent Royal Festival Hall, a building I have always loved, the Festival of Britain disappeared from the face of the earth. But not from people's memory. The site remained contemptuously derelict and neglected for ten years which was, I think, not at all what the Archbishop of Canterbury had meant when he said the festival 'has set the standard by which we will face the future'.

Euphoria might have been premature. Macmillan bitterly called the Festival of Britain 'a little gem of mismanagement, a cameo of incompetence, a perfect little miniature of muddle'. But lots of us had found it the perfect opportunity to make connections and even get, no matter how fragile, a sense of a distant, but tangible, future where everyday life might one day, perhaps, be better designed. A place where everyone would have a better chair or even, when rationing ended, a better salad bowl.

At least, it gave me an idea of what I wanted: to make designing a better Britain my business.

# 1956 – The theft of *truite au bleu*

*'I saw the best minds of my generation destroyed by madness.'*

Allen Ginsberg, *Howl*, 1956

*Elizabeth David in her kitchen.*

THERE WAS NO SIGN ON the cracked and peeling door, although a passing dog had recently made its mark. And I felt this anonymity might be significant because the most important doors are never labelled, are they?

I'm talking metaphors here. The door was not locked, nor was the immediate vista it revealed enticing. One of two bare globes burned orange in the lobby, a fire extinguisher rolled on its side while a narrow staircase invited a descent on a stained and slippery carpet into goodness-only-knows-what of a mild hubbub below. The hand-rail was tacky to the touch and mouse traps, probably rat traps, were set at every tread. It was three o'clock in the afternoon, but below in the fetid murk, both cold and damp, I soon found that times of day were of not much concern in this underworld.

'And who the fuck are *you*?' the man leaning at the bar asked, without either malice or aggression. And equally without much charm or curiosity. It seemed to be entirely a formal enquiry, no more than a routine 'good afternoon', perhaps just a little coloured by the suggestion that a sacred tribal space was being invaded by me, a blinking and uncertain, but evidently not wholly unwelcome, visitor to his subterranean club.

This man at the bar? He had horny, paint-spattered hands; long, dirty nicotine-yellow nails curled over the fingertips; bulging, bright, but bloodshot, eyes. Around his permanently pursed lips there was a fine dessicated line of whiteness, evidence, I later learned, that he really did, as gossips claimed, clean his teeth with Vim, a well-known and mildly toxic kitchen abrasive of the day. This, the better to achieve a winning dental whiteness, useful, it was felt, in seductions of which there were an indiscriminate many.

In pursuit of a romantic notion of beauty, his hair had received similar enhancement from another branded product. Cherry Blossom shoe polish (dark tan) was rubbed into his spiky crop. You knew this because a slight penumbra of brown wobbled between hairline and forehead where the Cherry Blossom had been applied with more vigour than tact. He stank of brandy and cigarettes as well as something indefinably organic and possibly dead. He had just a trace of a refined Dublin accent.

'I'm Francis,' he explained, in a way that suggested it needed to be clear that he was not Declan or Gerry.

This was Francis Bacon: fifty years after we met, Christie's sold one of his paintings at a record price for a living artist. Francis was my second introduction to Soho.

We were in the Gutter Club on Foubert's Place, a rival to David Tennant's Gargoyle on Dean Street or the Moonglow on Berwick. At the latter, you might find the elegant jazz musician Humphrey Lyttelton, with his Eton old boys' tie archly done up as a bow. Home Counties posho. Later, he became a famous BBC voice, but during this period he spent his time dancing on tables. 'That cat sho' swings his ass off,' a visiting American trombonist said appreciatively. Or a Jewish gypsy temporarily exiled from the Hot Club de France might be playing, 'It Must Be Jelly ('Cause Jam Don't Shake Like That)'. This was sophistication, here was style.

The clientele at the Gutter was different, largely comprising Cypriot and Maltese pimps who had made Soho their home, murderous thugs who had driven out the milder-mannered Italian gangsters who preceded them. By contrast, the mean-featured and ill-favoured Cypriots and Maltese drank neat gin out of Robinson's jam jars and drove obese pastel-coloured Cadillacs or Chevrolets along Soho's thin lanes. They parked where they pleased. In 1956 there were no yellow lines or parking meters.

Additionally, Gutter company included obscenely rouged old whores with rolls of fat and crude tattoos. One of them, dressed as a schoolgirl, liked to fake fellatio with a bottle of absinthe as a graphic illustration of her skills. There were, moreover, shifty cabbies, builders on the cusp of becoming Macmillan-era developers, half-naked negroes (as they were then called) smoking marijuana, and public school voyeurs, including me. A small contingent came from French Gabon. I once overheard a snatch of conversation:

'Hi, darl,' the girl said.

He replied, '*Ma chérie*, you are my roly-poly. I warm you up and eat you.'

There was no plumbing and, a relic of the eighteenth century, I soon discovered that a hole on the landings served all the building's floors as a latrine. I immediately liked the place and was drawn to Francis, as I was so often drawn to extreme circumstances and extreme individuals. I came later to understand that if you could catch him in between sobriety and drunkenness, he was very, very funny.

'Hello. My name's Eustace Dunne,' I said.

He blanked me, unblinking for maybe thirty seconds, then replied, 'Eu-stace,' deliberately getting the emphasis wrong, 'that's a queer's name, isn't it? Poof. Homo. Nonce. Bender. Bum bandit. Anyway, tell me, Eu-stace, do you think there are only seven deadly sins?' He sounded very disappointed: I am certain he was hoping to find this new visitor might introduce him to rather more. Perhaps, in a way, I did.

'I'm afraid sin is not my subject, but design is,' I offered, sounding more prissy than I intended. 'I'm here because I met the Gutter's owner, Thanasis. I made some furniture for his house in Chislehurst. I'm wondering about redesigning the Gutter's interior to make a truly modern club. London's first.'

He blanked me again and then said, 'Ah, yes. Design. Christ on a bike. That's the business of telling imbecile women the colour to paint their cornices, isn't it? Fucking ridiculous. I don't like the sound of it and I am sorry you are so very keen. I have found, dear boy, that what people feel to be enthusiasm is only a desperate attempt to conquer boredom. Tell me now, are you bored?'

And then he explained that, to conquer his own encircling boredom, he had just been on a road trip, or 'motoring holiday' as it was called at the time, to the Veneto. Companions included his friend, another painter called Lucian Freud, and Michael Wishart, also a painter, but of less distinctive talent. Freud had cheerfully told him en route, 'I am not made for happiness, but for something beyond despair.' An aestheticized, camp misery was apparently part of the group mentality. The art critic David Sylvester went with them too. He had to be carried in and out of the car, on account of his gout. Still, this did not prevent them from seeing Giotto in Padua, the Palladian villas on the Brenta canal, Pisanello in Verona and Tiepolo in Venice, in this way letting great art do what it can with boredom and despair.

'You remind me of Tony Jones,' Francis said. 'You'd like him, he's a pretty boy too. A photographer. He talks design bollocks as well, for sure he does. You should meet. The two of you could paint some cornices. Tell him I sent you.' On a wet beer mat, Francis wrote an address with the well-chewed stub of a 2B pencil.

## a handsome Welsh rascal

Tony was just then starting at *A La Mode* magazine, one of London's few sources of glamour. He was a charming, talented, handsome Welsh rascal with a sharp wit and a sharper eye who had been sleeping on a sofa in Francis' studio while his own premises on Pimlico Road, next to the Sunlight laundry, were being transformed. Here I went to see him. I rang the bell of an altogether smarter door and when it opened a beaming face said, 'Hello. Would you like a Guinness?'

It was ten in the morning.

Eventually, with Tony's guiding genius, 20 Pimlico Road would become a laboratory of late fifties style: with its guest bedroom and photographic studio on the ground floor and a living area above, accessed by a self-designed spiral staircase, human interest traffic here was very intense. Some great photographic portraits were taken. Some preposterous love-matches were played; several won, many lost. The theatrical comings and goings, unimpeded by social divisions or sexual conventions, only ended, or, at least, diminished, in 1960 when Tony married a rebounding Princess Margaret. Over Guinness, we discussed travel. And we decided, in imitation of Bacon and Freud, we would go on a motoring holiday, but our destination was to be France.

These were the days when a succeeding 'executive' might have a Humber Hawk, a Ford Consul or a Hillman Minx. Hawk, Consul, Minx? I often thought. Predatory bird, Roman official, feral felid. What do these names tell you about the status preoccupations of the customers? Why not Sparrow, Tax Collector, Dormouse?

Tony, however, owned, or had acquired by some irregular means, a superb, dark-blue, three-litre Lagonda with red leather upholstery. It cost three thousand pounds and its W. O. Bentley-designed engine would power it to an exceptionally dangerous and unstable 104 miles per hour. Seat belts were not yet a glint in the eye of even the most perfervid Swedish safety engineer. Tony insisted on calling the car's colour 'knicker blue' since the better class of schoolgirls in 1954, some of whom had passed through 20 Pimlico Road, were required by custom to be in (or more often out of) elasticated navy underwear, usually flecked, I recall, with lint.

In those days, speed was not limited. Nor was fast behaviour much inhibited, even where it was technically illegal. Neither was stigma or penalty attached to drink driving. En route to France, Tony drove along the South Circular Road with a Guinness at the wheel while I sat under a Welsh blanket. Waiting at Folkestone, we played US journalist Sylvia Wright's word game, a literary coup of 1954. Wright's 'mondegreen' was a humorous mishearing of something.

She had cited an old Scots ballad which began, 'They ha' slain the Earl of Moray and laid him on the green.' The laid-him-on-the-green had been heard as his wife, (Lady) Mondegreen. Hence, a 'mondegreen' was a ludicrous homophone. Tony enjoyed this sort of wordplay, which gave new meaning to nonsense.

'He went down on his niece,' Tony said, discussing the formal demands of marriage and laughing at seventy-five miles per hour through Bromley.

'I think one should get married in church,' Tony declared, briefly turning solemn. 'A registry office is no more inspiring an experience than paying the rates.'

He talked salaciously of mixed-race marriage, citing a rumour long familiar in palace circles that the curious African aspect of some Windsors was attributable to historic miscegenation in the Caribbean, something to do with the Lascelles family and their sugar plantations. This gave me a counter mondegreen: 'Your oasis' for 'You're a racist'.

. . . . . . . . . . . . . . . . . . . . . . . . . . . . . . . . . . . . . . . . . . . . . . . . . . . . . . . . . . . . . . . . . . . . . . . . . . . . . . . . . . . . . . . . . . . . . . .

® *Rollo Pinkie: I always thought that this tolerance of cognitive dissonance was simply evidence that both Tony and Eustace were hobbled by dyslexia.*

## elegance is elimination

Before we had left the ramp of the cross-Channel ferry, Tony had begun a soliloquy on style in the stinking and heaving saloon. 'Balenciaga, you know, said, "Elegance is elimination" . . .'

And I then remembered how it had been a favourite observation of Ilona's. Amazing how often Balenciaga featured in my life. As he spoke, he was looking around thoughtfully at adverts of Player's cigarettes, Vimto and health warnings about 'venereal disease' illustrated with a graphic of a sadly limp penis. On the bar, a doleful, illuminated, transparent plastic box contained yellow sausage rolls and grey ham sandwiches. It was scratched from within as if earlier captive life-forms had been trying to escape. There was a dull and stained tea urn. The boat shuddered, lurched and the diesels grumbled, rattling the catering crockery, still in those days made in Stoke-on-Trent. The whole place smelt of vomit and ozone.

'Elimination? You mean like evacuating your bowels?' I asked, feeling sick. It was blowing force eight.

'No, you idiot. I like Cocteau's idea that for most people, style is a complicated way of saying very simple things. But for us, it's a very simple way of saying complicated things. Anyway, I adore Cocteau because he was a *poète maudit*.'

He lit another cigarette.

At Boulogne, a crane lifted the Lagonda off the ferry. Roll-on-roll-off was, you see, still part of a more mobile and democratic future. 'Motoring' in France was still the pleasure of a privileged and adventurous few. We were one of only three cars on board and were soon on the deserted RN16 along the coast towards Montreuil. I had a Michelin Guide Rouge to hand and suggested, for purposes of absurdity alone, only stopping at towns and villages beginning with a B: Baboeuf, Belcourt, Beaucouz, Buissencourt . . .

And then I remembered to ask, 'Anyway, what does *maudit* mean?'

'*Eh bien, c'est moi, si tu veux.*' Tony smiled very broadly and toothily.

'If you insist on French, these plane trees are like an *enfilade*. And I think they are passing rather too fast. I want to survive until dinner, you know.'

'Oh fuck off!' he said, changing down and sweeping left into the Vallée de la Course, a scrabble of gravel and a mild squeal of tyres his background music.

'We are stopping in ten minutes. At a village called Inxent. Yes, I know it begins with an I, but it's still in the Boulonnais, so that counts.'

The Auberge d'Inxent was a low-built inn of few architectural affectations on the banks of the River Course. The village itself offered no concessions to cultural curiosity apart from two unusually grim war memorials, forbidding even by the high standards of northern France. Any small community losing twelve people all called Pettitot in the space of thirty years cannot entirely dispel residual melancholy.

However, the Auberge had acquired a modest reputation for its food and wine ever since André Simon, founder of the Wine and Food Society, had served notice to his members that it should be everyone's first stop on any road trip to France. Inside, framed and autographed menus were memoirs of exceptional dinners. One from 1932 included the bill and showed that *pain d'écrevisses* and a truly remarkable amount of Meursault had been enjoyed. This Auberge d'Inxent was where London's most famous modern food-writer made her temporary home.

How to describe the interior of the Auberge? Polished dark-brown wooden floors punctuated by threadbare turkey carpets, fussy lace cloths on rackety chiffoniers, annoyingly polished horse-brasses, an insistent smell of drains and gas mingling with an aroma of horses from the yard outside, a fire set in a scarlet-tiled *cheminée* even on this bright spring day. The proprietor had a wall-eye, a limp and wore a dirty cardigan. My bedroom had its faults as well: a faded green candlewick bedspread, laundry-thin darned linen sheets, a mean hard pillow, a chill damp causing the wallpaper to separate from the wall, a medley of structural stains and a nasty little black crucifix over the bed. It was cold and cheerless, so I went to the bar.

## Chardin with a Craven-A

Here I found, *à contre-jour*, as the painters say, or silhouetted as we might, a magnificent female creature sitting by a sunny window at a table untidily and precariously piled with books and papers. The sunshine made an aura around her turban. She was in profile and looking distracted. You might have taken her as a Chardin portrait had she not got a Craven-A filter cigarette on the go and a large glass of red wine, held not quite horizontally, in the other hand. From evidence of the empty bottle and the full ashtray, neither was her first of the afternoon.

I was embarrassed, but fascinated as well. A stately woman with an air of superiority that was almost tangible, she was very obviously as tipsy as a tart. Her nails, I could see, were finely manicured, but also very slightly grubby. Evidence of what? Carelessness? Not really because her elaborately tied turban argued against any charge of negligence. Manual labour? Scarcely. She looked instead like the severe headmistress of a very expensive girls' school. I wondered if she was drinking because of pleasure or compulsion.

Slowly, she turned to me and in a manner both steely and diffident, said, 'David.'

I took it to be a question and replied, 'Actually, no. Eustace.'

'Don't be ridiculous. *I* am Elizabeth David. Mrs David to you. I liberated the English palate and gave it a taste for garlic. There used to be a superstition that rubbing a clove of garlic around the bowl was sufficient for flavour. And I say, that depends whether you want to eat the salad or the bowl.' She laughed rather drily, then recovered herself.

'Oh my God, I am sorry,' I said. 'Of course I know your books. I bought the first edition of *Mediterranean Food*, the one with the lovely Johnny Minton cover, when it came out in 1950. It's so much more than recipes. It provides a sort of philosophy of life, a guide to taste in every sense. That cover alone shows us how to live. Makes me crave sardines and baguettes and flasks of cool wine. But what are you doing here and can I buy you a drink?'

She looked at me severely for several seconds and, when appetite had overcame its short struggle with doubt, languorously offered her hand and the glass it held, saying, 'Gamay. Since you ask, I am here to think and to write. And to eat. The kitchen here is exceptional, you know. It's famous for its *truite au bleu*. The trout is a stupid fish, but this dish ennobles it. As soon as it is landed on the banks of the Course, the fisherman stuns it with a little mallet called a priest, designed for the very purpose. It is quickly gutted, cleaned and set in good wine vinegar. The vinegar turns the subcutaneous mucus blue ...'

An acidulous woman with an acidulated fish, I thought.

'... and then it is very gently poached in a nice *court bouillon* and served with pickled parsley, tiny new potatoes and a *hollandaise* sauce. Delicious. It proves that every day has the possibility of a miracle. You will see. We'll eat it at dinner tonight. Bring your young friend with the smart motor. Then again, maybe not. Perhaps he is your chauffeur?'

With that, she arose (that stately term is appropriate here since there was a regal aspect to her style), abandoned her table of books and papers and, swaying slightly, set off across the polished wood and turkey rugs.

........................................................................................................

® *Rollo Pinkie: Eustace was always inspired by grand people, but none more so than Mrs David. And none was grander. She had an authority that he aspired to, but never quite achieved. So he copied her. At first just a recipe, but later it was a more ambitious sort of theft-by-appropriation. He often spoke of her as an equal in the revolution of British taste, but that was not a status the most superior Mrs David would ever have acknowledged, still less accepted.*

Tony and I were at the table by eight. Anticipating fish, we ordered a bottle of decent Loire white and poured ourselves a good glass each.

'She's come here to drink her meals,' Tony whispered a little too audibly as the regal Mrs David, cigarette in hand and a little more steady now, crossed the room to join us. Her sense of *savoir-vivre* was impressive, but so too was the sense that she was sad and bored and ruined and disappointed, even as she was rich and famous.

'Gaston,' she said to the dirty cardigan, '*encore du vin. Un magnum, s'il vous plaît. Et dépêchez-vous.*' And then, sharing a secret, she turned to us. 'I think any wine served *en magnum* becomes a luxury, even this wretched *pipi du chat* you both seem to be enjoying so much. Now. We will begin, as I have instructed, with the *truite au bleu*. I believe that Jean Giono was correct when he said it is ridiculous to cook this most stupid, but most subtle, fish in butter and almonds. *Au bleu* is the only correct method. And we will follow with *tarte à l'andouille flamiche aux poireaux* and *lapin aux pruneaux*. Perhaps we will finish with a little *crêpe* and some *Boulette d'Avesnes*. I would prefer the rabbit cooked over olive wood *en plein air*, but there you are. We are in the cold and bleak north.'

All of this we memorably ate. We learnt what the French mean when they say someone has *le droit de donner les leçons*. Mrs David had that right. And she exercised it.

'Basil, you see, must always be torn, never cut, since the presence of metal complicates the essential oil. Only a fool would take a knife to basil.'

With dinner we drank, after the Muscadet, an additional magnum of the afternoon's Beaujolais and an old *marc de prune* as *digestif*, re-covered by Gaston from a dusty shelf behind the terminally ignored

Cynar and the Suze. Mrs David relaxed a little somewhere between the *tarte* and the *flamiche*. She had once been an actress and slumped theatrically. I think I noticed a little *bouquet de corsage*. Moreover, she had *bons mots* to spare about her trade.

'I always admired Kenneth Tynan,' she noted. 'He was very funny and called Othello "Citizen Coon". He had the courage of his restrictions. And you know what he taught me? A bad meal is always expensive. That, and the tragic fact that simplicity – in food and in life itself – is so very elusive. Meanwhile, when you two are travelling south, I want you to visit my favourite restaurant in all of France: the Hôtel du Midi in Lamastre. Here, you will eat *poulet en vessie*, or chicken-in-mourning. It is unquestionably France's greatest dish.'

And with that, Mrs David stubbed out on a plate her twelfth cigarette of the evening, gathered her skirts, arose and left us. I moved to pour Tony a little more *marc*, but he waved a hand very slightly, got up and followed Mrs David. He was, I inferred, confident that he had a way with lonely, grand women of the upper classes.

Crossing the deserted dining room, I took my own glass of *marc* to Mrs David's abandoned window seat where the ziggurat of books and papers remained from the afternoon. I settled myself down and leafed through her notes, made with turquoise ink in a fine, nervous hand. And when I found a page headed '*Inxent le quatorze avril '54 truite au bleu*', I took out my new Biro ballpoint pen and wrote the recipe down on the back of my chequebook. As early Biros did, the new oil-based ink left ugly blobs.

And then I found a recipe for *pâté de la campagne*. I copied that down too, thinking to myself one day I might own a restaurant. *Dauphinois*? There was scarcely enough room left on the chequebook's cover, so I sacrificed an actual cheque to plagiarism of this fine recipe for potatoes cooked in cream, butter and garlic.

At breakfast, Tony beamed, rolled his eyes and simply said, 'Posh women!'

No more explanation was necessary, or offered. We set off for Lamastre and, I imagined, Mrs David began another day at her window seat, dreaming as well as thinking and writing and eating and regretting. Later she would write that the most important thing is, whatever you do, to affect the quality of the day. A stupid fish, she taught millions, could help achieve this.

Accelerating out of Troyes, Tony said, 'Here we go! I always think of Flaubert writing "other skies, other seas". We must keep looking for them!'

The Michelin Guide *Rouge* took us down the RN7, past that marvellous sequence that reads like a wine list: Auxey-Duresses and Gevrey-Chambertin are villages as well as bottles. At every opportunity, Tony stopped the Lagonda on dusty white Burgundy pebbles and took photographs of chateaux and vineyards, his Leica M3 an easy, unconscious extension of his hand and eye. And I used these respites from the road to consult Michelin Rouge.

I asked him about how he took photographs.

'You can never know. The big thing,' he explained, 'is that if you don't feel incompetent, you are actually just a hack. Got to experiment.'

The Hôtel du Midi in Lamastre is in the heart of the Ardèche, quite wild country. It was opened by the Barattero family in 1928 and was among the very first establishments in France to be declared *vaut le voyage*, receiving its three Michelin stars in 1933. Presiding here was Madame Rose Barattero, an imposing peasant rooted in *ancienne cuisine* whose chicken-in-mourning was the astonishing dish that validated the voyage. A fat fowl is stuffed with its own liver, slivers of black truffle are slid under the skin, hence the funereal reference. Then it is tied in a pig's bladder and poached in a double boiler, the result being the most extraordinarily unctuous and subtly flavoured flesh. Although I never learnt to cook it, *poulet en vessie* became, for me, a symbol of the French *l'art de vivre*. And so too did the severe, white Pillivuyt porcelain we bought in the markets and loaded into the boot. Madame Cadec was already selling it to knowledgeable Londoners from her little shop in Soho's Greek Street, but I felt it was my own discovery. Later, it became part of my vision of a new Britain. Design is about turning visions into projects. I made it so.

## a naked Persian lesbian witch

Driving back to Paris, Tony was in a reflective mood. 'I do have some *nuits blanches*, you know.'

He was referring to those rare occasions when, in bed alone, sleep was elusive.

'And the worst moment is four in the morning. The time, they say, of the Crucifixion. Your body is tired, but your brain is alert. It's a sort of agony. Like Christ. And terrible things come to mind. You get unwanted visitors. I know we all invent ourselves, but I've come to believe that it's very important to keep on good terms with the person we used to be. Otherwise, your original can come and disturb you in the middle of the night.'

I dwelt on this. And sometimes I still do.

................................................................................................

® *Rollo Pinkie: Eustace Dunne was a model of self-invention. The Eustace who became a public figure was not even remotely the same person who was born in Reigate in 1932. To what extent he recognized this, I have never been clear.*

I wanted to stay in Paris for a sort of *apprentissage* in French life and language, while Tony needed to get back to London, but not before he had introduced me to the Bal Nègre, a nightclub on the rue Blomet.

'It's wonderful. They have fire-eating black men from Equatorial Guinea. Cocteau drew murals on the lavatory walls in exchange for opium. Juliette Gréco sings gloomy Existentialist songs written by Raymond Queneau and Jacques Prévert. And Mistinguett? Did I ever tell you that she injects paraffin wax into her legs to maintain the curves?'

Of course he had not.

Apparently unaffected by two bottles of Ayala champagne served by a naked Persian lesbian witch, a resident *serveuse* at Bal Nègre, Tony drove off into the night and towards the new seas and skies of Calais and Pimlico. Myself, I had arranged a room at a little hotel on rue Vaugirard for ten shillings a night, but fell asleep on a bench at the Pasteur métro, next door to a binman, and woke to find the station closed. I used a fire escape and, like Dante leaving his dark wood, I saw the stars again. And discovered my Paris.

In pre-digital 1954, the old telephone exchanges still existed. Just reciting them now seems like poetry: Botzaris, Nord, Suffren, Danton, Jasmin, Odéon and Daumesnil. Here was style. The Brasserie Royale still existed on Boulevard Saint-Germain until, in a telling sequence of decline, it became for *les soixante-huitards* Le Drug Store, then, for the twenty-first century *bon chic bon genre*, an Armani shop. But the Brasserie Royale offered a fine perspective on the *flâneurs* and *boulevardiers* of the Sixth: pipe-smoking *philosophes*, *intellos* in berets aping the binmen, *grandes dames*, *grandes horizontales*, priests and even, on a good day, American tourists pretending to be Ernest Hemingway.

And I walked the streets in the dark. This is real theatre: in that moment between the lights going on and the shutters being closed, the city reveals itself with these amazing real *tableaux vivants*. True, this was a city where Sartre and Camus were celebrities, but after time with Tony, I was infatuated with the Paris of the builders, the waiters, the truck drivers, the house painters, *garagistes*, sign writers, off-duty policemen, the market porters. In Les Halles there were still *porteurs à béret* with their shuffling trolleys. They wore *bleu de travail*.

## France's greatest poof

My hotel had its own grubbily charming little bistrot called Le Bec Fin, where a bottle-blonde in red acrylic with a wasp waist presided.

'*Tu veux me baiser?*' she asked nonchalantly on my first night. School had taught me this was the word to kiss, but in the 15ème it meant fuck. There were ashtrays, by no means always clean. People smoked as if it were compulsory. There were paper tablecloths and open bottles of unlabelled wine on every empty table. But there were few of these: Le Bec Fin was always crowded and noisy, a beetle-browed Algerian continuously refilling whenever refilling was necessary, which was often.

I went to Chanel on rue Cambon and bought buttons that I wired together with paperclips to make what I thought were stylish cufflinks, almost Surrealist *objets trouvés*. Or what Coco herself called *misérabilisme de luxe*. Tony had disappeared with a boot full of porcelain, so I was fortunate to discover Dehillerin, the kitchenware store in Les Halles. I bought a working-man's blue jacket and, despite the warning of Mrs David that garlic should only ever be squashed with the flat of a knife, I bought two dozen different types of garlic press to bring home as trophies of my new sophistication. There was a lever-action press and a screw-action press, a crusher and a grater. I even found a fabulous new so-called *presse-Marseille* made by Peugeot on the Mouli principle. Best of all, the *vendeuse* in Dehillerin persuaded me to buy a gorgeous antique Brune et Cie device, made by an *horlogerie* in Brignoles just before the Revolution. It works on the piston principle.

*Rollo Pinkie: Here is an exquisite example of Eustace's genius at engaging, self-serving fantasy. There are nothing like as many as twenty-four different types of garlic press. But this is typical of the man. He wanted to claim attachment to the artisan by showing an interest in a simple kitchen tool, but then wanted to express his sense of superiority by demonstrating how he knew more about simple kitchen tools than any artisan. At the same time, it shows Eustace ignoring the admonition of Elizabeth David, who detested garlic presses.*

Determined to stay several weeks, I made my *apprentissage* real by getting a job as a *plongeur* in a restaurant called La Mer near L'Odéon, where the students collided with the *beau monde*. Its front door was extremely shiny: lacquered and rubbed-down, lacquered and rubbed-down, lacquered and rubbed-down, until a mirror-like finish had been achieved. Of course, dishwashing was for an English public schoolboy an example of what the French call nostalgia for the mud. But it was my university. I learnt kitchen French and saw knife fights. I learnt the base mechanics of the romantic restaurant trade, how so much glamour is supported by so much heat, sweat, violence and exploitation.

At lunch one day, I saw Francis Bacon arrive with his friend Lucian Freud, who I knew kept a room, more glamorous than mine, in the Hôtel d'Isly on rue Jacob. I wiped my hands on my striped apron and, barging past the waiters scuttling through the swing doors, made my way to the blue velour banquette. Bacon and Freud had joined a refined looking gentleman who wore a red *Légion d'honneur boutonnière* in his lapel and an air of exquisite pain on his face.

Francis leapt up and said, 'Eu-stace! It's still a poof's name, isn't it? So I want you to meet Hugues de Geoffroi, one of France's greatest designers, and one of France's greatest poofs.'

Hugues smiled thinly, looked at the painters, then returned his gaze to me.

'The trouble with your countrymen, Eustace, is that they have such very bad manners and such very execrable taste. My clients, you see, include the Windsors. Or did. I felt I had to part from them when I discovered that the Duchess had ordered military drums from Harrod's to turn into coffee tables.'

And I swear he said, '*Bouf!*'

Francis responded, swivelling round, 'Just look at this fucking place. Do you have to be ugly to get a reservation here? Do they give a discount to the ill-favoured?'

I returned to my dishes, but after service at La Mer, I walked back to rue Vaugirard, reflecting what a very curious smell Paris had. Later I was at my table in Le Bec Fin with a *blanquette de veau* and my second carafe of red. Do-you-want-to-kiss-me looked on, contemptuous and provocative at the same time, hand on hip, head lowered. I thought to myself how very much I detest *de luxe* and how much I loved this more ordinary world. And I agreed with Mrs David that human happiness could be better achieved with superior distribution of well-designed salad bowls than by the availability of free false teeth on the health service.

In the inside pocket of my *bleu de travail*, I found my chequebook. And on the back, the recipe for *truite au bleu*. I had not learnt much French, but felt I knew what I was doing.

# 1957 – The Gardens of Ninfa

*'Hey buddy, don't you be no square*
*If you can't find a partner, use a wooden chair.'*

Jerry Leiber and Mike Stoller, 'Jailhouse Rock', 1957

*No blocks of stone in a shabby chic interior in Chelsea.*

About the time Ilona overdosed in protest over Hungary, methedrine I am sorry to say, I decided to move the studio from Camberwell to north of the river. A pleasantly steady flow of work had given me ever more personal confidence as well as a small measure of financial stability.

For example, I had worked on ribbons for a cushion maker, anxious to acquire a little metropolitan glamour, who produced over a million yards to my design. I think this was a record. Not exciting work, but a million of anything is rather a lot and 'million' is a word journalists readily pick up. 'Eustace Dunne Proud' the headline in *The Draper's Record* said. I was photographed with bolts of cloth. I kept the cutting.

Spode had commissioned modern china from me. I had seen an article by my old school chum Rollo Pinkie in *The Architectural Review* about Sweden's Gustavsberg porcelain factory, an early source of my inspiration. Rollo had cleverly interviewed Stig Lindberg and Wilhelm Kåge, artisan-designers who ran studios within the factory. This, it reminded me, was a model arrangement and one I found inspiring. Or so I told the people at Spode.

Now you could go into Thomas Goode on South Audley Street, London's poshest shop, and see modern-shaped, Swedish-style cups and saucers decorated with stylized flower motifs with 'Designed by Eustace Dunne' printed underneath in a facsimile of my handwriting. This signature, by the way, was a work in progress: I have always thought handwriting extremely important. Only a fool would neglect it. I practise every day.

And in The Old Dairy, I was making more and more of my own furniture, adding basketware seats – we sourced the cane in Madagascar – to my established repertoire of Californian fibreglass. Most of this was to order – delivered to clients rather precariously on my wobbling scooter – but I made quite a lot speculatively and did my best to sell into the department stores, not often successfully.

In the fifties, a department store buyer was not a well-travelled cosmopolitan individual with a finger on the pulse of popular taste, but a thin man with a dreadful pallor, a tobacco aroma and a brown suit operating unenthusiastically under bad lighting. Frankly, I thought I could do better. And decided that perhaps I would.

'Why,' I always asked people, 'does shopping have to be such a dreary ordeal?'

Contract work kept coming in from the David Jones store and Tallboy St Clair. David Jones asked me to design their own-brand ceramics and glassware. And I still had a valuable portfolio of Lethaby Academy student drawings to help with that task. Meanwhile, Tallboy St Clair asked me to design stands for Austin at the annual London Motor Show. Here I used clear plastic and luminous felt, furnishing the stands with chairs of my own design, vaguely Scandinavian in spirit.

And this was the stage for my reintroduction to that fabulous *boulevardier*, Raymond Loewy, who turned up at the Earl's Court opening incongruously bronzed, perfumed and white-suited in a wet and cold London autumn.

As part of its troubled post-war reinvention, the tired and under-resourced 'Austin of England' hired a slew of international designers to inject some vital style into its battered and moribund carcass. Inevitably, the very visible, very expensive and very available Loewy was one of them. He had eagerly responded to the brief, produced renderings of ludicrously trashy originality and been promptly well paid.

But sitting in Manhattan or Palm Springs, he had become curious to see what progress was being made in Birmingham on implementing his design proposals, for surely the Austin customer wanted to drive around the West Midlands in a garish vision conceived in the Californian desert by a man who wore women's perfume.

'And you are the young man on the plane,' he said to me through a miasma of Chanel No. 5, while stroking the wing of an old-fashioned-looking Austin Somerset with evident and fastidious distaste.

'I really do not know why your people so doggedly refuse to implement my design,' Loewy said with princely disdain to the crowd on the stand at this opening night.

And then the chairman of Austin intervened.

'My dear Mr Loewy, I am so very sorry if I have misled you, but we never intended to *implement* your designs. It was just necessary for us to find out what you are thinking.'

I had seen the drawings and knew that what Raymond Loewy was thinking about Austin of England was that its future should consist of whitewall tyres, huge gunsight bonnet mascots in glass, an ovoid chromed grille like an alien's anus, metallic paint, opera windows in fake hardtops and more chrome on the weedy tailpipe. This? In Birmingham? I learnt from this exchange that designers really should never be too far in front of their clients, let alone their customers.

---

® *Rollo Pinkie: Raymond Loewy was a huckster and a pimp, but a magnificent one. He raised schmooze to the level of genius. He accepted work in the depressed UK car industry because no one in Detroit, of all places, could tolerate his pushy vulgarity. He was too crass for middle America and off-the-scale in middle England. Eustace was at one level a snob about Loewy. But I am certain he was helplessly in awe of the man's brazen confidence and impeccable personal presentation. 'Correspondent's shoes' he would always mutter when Loewy's name was mentioned. It was meant to sound disdainful, but I happen to know it was admiring.*

Meanwhile, my friend Paolozzi had recently been making news with an exhibition called 'This Is Tomorrow' at the Whitechapel Art Gallery. With the architects Alison and Peter Smithson, Eduardo had presented a strange structure of three walls roofed by corrugated plastic that stood on sand. On this artificial 'beach' were scattered old bicycle parts, a bugle, a ramshackle deckchair and a broken clock. Fantasy or reportage? Who could say? The critics said it was a 'watershed in British art' and I suppose it was.

But I didn't want to remove myself to the grimy East End of the Whitechapel Art Gallery. No matter how many watersheds the area could boast, it was still Jack the Ripper territory. I wanted to go where my clients were, where the money was, in the more prosperous south-west. So I began riding my *farro basso* Vespa to the north, parking it near Buckingham Palace (you could park anywhere in 1956), to walk the streets of Belgravia, Chelsea, Kensington and Fulham, looking for sites. *Farro basso* means 'low light': the very first, and therefore most original, Vespas had the headlight mounted on the front mudguard. Which I happen to know is *parafango* in Italian. Such a lovely word.

I had been reintroduced to this part of the city by Bernard Ashley, who, after leaving the City, had established himself in an attic flat in Pimlico's Clarendon Street, back in 1954. Bernard's parents had been friends of my mother. When my father was released from Pentonville, it was the older Ashleys who threw a party for him in a private room at The Dorchester.

In Pimlico, with his new wife Laura, Bernard began dyeing and printing fabrics, and turning them into eye-catching oven gloves, napkins and tablecloths which soon found a ready market in Peter Jones' clientele: Chelsea ladies seeking post-war colour. And he was beginning to do a little work for me, printing fabrics to my design. Bernard, besides being a shrewd businessman, was a trained engineer. It impressed me that the noisy, dirty printing machinery he kept at the top of his Cubitt house in hushed and genteel Pimlico was all of his own design and making. To me, this studio-workshop, reminding me of Gustavsberg, confirmed that this was the part of London I wanted to be in.

Bernard liked telling me, with a rattling background hubbub while trying to keep the six rollers of his cylinder printing machine in register, that I should read Seneca.

'Bloody good chap,' he shouted over the din, waving inky hands. 'I wouldn't be doing this if it wasn't for Seneca. "It's not because things are difficult that we do not dare attempt them. It's because we do not dare attempt them that they seem difficult." That's what he said.'

I thought such a view was very wise, even if I also realized it would actually license almost any sort of reckless adventure. But reckless adventures seemed a good thing.

'Damn and blast!' Bernard exclaimed, as the rollers juddered to a messy halt over a snagged bolt of cloth.

## the coffee-coloured habits of the monks

My spitting and burping and rasping and smoking two-stroke Vespa was evidence that some small sense of vital Italian style was penetrating sluggish Britain, but cappuccino was still a novelty in 1956.

I had, however, already found a favourite Italian coffee bar. The menu explained that cappuccino 'is named after the coffee-coloured habits of the monks', which amused me a lot, thinking of their obscene practices. I blew a little brown nest into the coffee's white froth, and considered – with only moderate enthusiasm – my cream cheese and gherkin sandwich. I looked around.

There was now an emergent genre of coffee bars where the decoration was theatrical. I had heard it called camposity. This one was called The Gardens of Ninfa, after that celebrated garden near Rome.

It was in that strange London territory where Belgravia becomes Victoria and camposity dominated whether invited or not.

In Soho, coffee bars had been rather different. You'd find a cheap rental premises, perhaps an old clip joint, let's call it Chez Max, rip out the filthy linoleum, rip out any fittings, put in a tough wooden floor and a jukebox. The result would be no more glamorous than an all-night urinal. Of course, Camberwell had no coffee bars of any sort: Wally's was our Ninfa.

But in the prosperous south-west it was not the same. Sure, the Kray twins were establishing a nightclub and money-laundering casino called Esmeralda's Barn on Knightsbridge, where they cleverly recruited (an already superlatively debauched) Lord Effingham to do front-of-house and give it some tone, but this was not the London of the spielers, cops, chorus girls, soubrettes, narks, exhibitionists, musicians, gangsters and whores, at least not whores of the conventional rub-and-tug sort.

This was genteel London, a London of Ashley oven gloves and Elizabeth David recipes, and to its established communities of diplomats and old money were now being added new tribes: advertising people, television people, smart dressmakers. (The miniskirt was only a few years away). And, of course, interior designers. This was John Fowler's, Sibyl Colefax's and David Hicks' territory. These were people who had marked a space I wanted to occupy.

A few years after me at the Lethaby Academy, David Nightingale Hicks – and, yes, that really was his name – was making a reputation for himself with the interior he designed for his mother in South Eaton Place. When it was featured in *House & Garden* in 1954, it caused a sensation. And journalists found his idea of 'tablescapes' engrossing. So obvious to me, Hicks held reporters hypnotically rapt when he explained that you could view a dinner setting as 'design', or that interesting Surrealist-style *objets trouvés* – my blue apothecary bottles, for example – could be conversation pieces on the new 'coffee tables'.

I decided he needed some competition. Hicks, whom I never liked, partly because he wore salmon-pink cotton polo necks with a pale grey suit that was emphatically tailored and waisted, once said to me at a little *vernissage* on Yeoman's Row, 'As I was telling the Duchess of Westminster, the best rooms, you know, say something about the people who live in them. Everything speaks to you.'

He was looking over my shoulder while he talked, scrutinizing the rest of the crowd for better prospects.

And I replied, 'Wouldn't it be absolutely astonishing if they did not?' I added 'You pompous fucking idiot', only just *sotto voce*.

But in full conformity with the spirit of the age, a spirit which I insist I sensed first, as the *Metro* eventually confirmed, Hicks was industriously, some might say too industriously, expanding the role of what a designer might be. For example, he made some breakfast cereal packets for a client of the J. Walter Thompson ad agency. I mean, they were awful. Execrable. He had a lot of taste, all of it bad. But I was impressed by his ambition and his achievements, which seemed effortless.

And it was said that after his wife, demented by his niggardly martinet pomposity, started slinging retributive bottles of Coca-Cola at the man, he began to add glossy brown lacquer walls to his interior design repertoire. Originally as domestic camouflage of the Coke stains, eventually as a taste choice for his very stupid, wealthy clients.

Soon he would win as clients the genius of the blow-dried bob, Vidal Sassoon, Helena Rubinstein, the yenta of the powder puff industry, and King's Road's infamous Chelsea Drugstore which made deliveries using girls in electric-blue catsuits riding scooters. Nightingale, I conceded, had a genius for clients who would generate publicity.

In the Gardens of Ninfa, the seats were carved out of stone, a fake *pozzo* strewn with artificial ivy was a centrepiece and gloomy Piranesi prisons were printed on to the plastic laminate tabletops.

Pleasant, I suppose, to think about ruins and incarceration over coffee. I think there might even have been a mummified Roman corpse.

You could not get egg and chips in Ninfa, but London's first *panini* were served here, even if they were filled with unauthentic cream cheese and gherkin or luridly pink Hungarian salami and industrial margarine made in Stockport. Avocado (still in those days called 'pear') was five bob, cover charge exclusive. The waiters wore impossibly tight trousers.

Borders always fascinated me and none was more curious than this one between Belgravia and Victoria. On the one side, that solemn hush which in London indicates respectability. On the other, the bus and the air terminal. In the one, glamorous folk on the way to paradise as I had been once, with vinyl Pan Am or BOAC vanity bags, tropical suits and sunglasses. On the other, shuffling travellers in cheap tweed, plastic macs and sad, parlour curtain dresses. Is it a truth that the rich are quiet and the poor noisy?

Anyway, Belgravia beyond Ninfa. This was a strange planet of cream stucco, flower boxes, awnings, lush garden squares, home deliveries. I had parked my sky-blue Vespa in a cobbled mews smelling slightly of horse shit, possibly originating in the Queen's stables. A purple Pontiac convertible had diplomatic plates, and a figure in a mauve Thai silk summer suit was watering an olive growing reluctantly in a tub. It was wonderfully exotic.

I returned to Camberwell, contemplating my discoveries, savouring my thoughts and not, digestively speaking, being allowed to forget the gherkin. Back in The Old Dairy, I went to the bathroom, splashed Bay Rum and cantharides on my swept-back hair, poured a lager and lime and put a Modern Jazz Quartet stereo record on low. I had just bought an RCA Model 7HF45 Orthophonic hi-fi, bypassing the original speakers with more impressive Wharfedales, which had more profound bass. The quartet sang, 'I feel that I could be a hit / If life would only quit upstaging me a bit.'

Fuck Nightingale, I thought. And I decided, metaphorically at least, that I would.

## a genius at curtains

I wrote a letter to John Fowler at his King's Road premises, using my streamlined, acetate Parker 51, inspired by Ilona. She had told me that her countryman, László Moholy-Nagy, another Bauhaus teacher, had used this fountain pen as an exemplum of modernity. This pen I had had to buy at W. H. Smith, but my writing paper I designed myself: 'the old dairy, artichoke mews, london se5. CAMberwell 7456' it said. The paper was a laid stock in light grey and the type was Baskerville, all in lower case, except for the telephone exchange. I liked this old font because it proffered an essential Englishness, but using it in lower case suggested a very European sort of modernity. I knew this because I had seen an extremely interesting feature on architects' stationery in Gio Ponti's Milanese magazine, *Domus*.

John Fowler never called himself a designer, but he was the most influential decorator of the day: a 'genius at curtains' the American magazines called him, not meaning to make it sound like a slight. He was old Chelsea and, I knew, lived in a shabby, flimsy house off King's Road, a more adventurous area then than it later became. At the time, the poet John Betjeman lived in Radnor Walk and cheerfully described it as a 'slum'. If you look at old photographs of Tite Street, where Oscar Wilde once lived, taken in the mid-fifties, you can see bedraggled children playing run-outs and rounders. There will only be one parked car – by no means always a grand one – and it always seems to be slightly foggy.

This was a Chelsea that still had a music hall. Max Miller, Max Wall and Anne Shelton played at the Chelsea Palace at the bottom of Sydney Street. But it was all on the cusp: very soon the Palace was taken over by the new ITV commercial television station for 'Spot the Tune'. Soon after that, it was happily demolished.

Fowler's friend, the architectural writer and acidulous old queen James Lees-Milne, lived in another shabby-flimsy house nearby on Bazalgette's Embankment. It was Lees-Milne who created the National Trust's country house scheme, prising splendour from dispossessed dukes, and Fowler who did the renovative decorations of repossessed mansions and castles. These were buddies you could rightly call 'bosom'.

Of course, I knew Fowler by reputation, but we also had David Jones in common. As an apprentice, he had learnt how to imitate Chinese wallpaper and how to do *faux bois* graining and fake marbling. It interested me greatly that this antiquarian was, in fact, dealing with dissimulation and artifice, if not actual forgeries. Fowler's biggest client for fake Chinese wallpaper and painted furniture was Peter Jones in Sloane Square, source of my school uniform.

And I loved it when I learnt that Fowler had dyed army blankets and used them as the drapery for which he had such a genius. So close was he to paint that he created his own private language of colour: mouse's back, dead salmon, *caca du dauphin* and *vomitesse de la reine* were my favourites. Indeed, so regal was Fowler that some wits claimed he was a reincarnation of Marie Antoinette. Certainly, I learnt that his habit was to enter rooms sideways, as if wearing an invisible, ghostly pannier dress.

I wrote:

*Dear Mr Fowler,*

*My name is Eustace Dunne and I do hope you don't mind my writing like this.*

*I became aware of and began to admire your work while I was myself engaged by David Jones as a designer.*

*It is true that we work in rather different styles. I am not at all a classicist or a specialist in heritage buildings. On the contrary, I have been influenced by Californian modernism and by the work of the new Italians shown at the Milan Triennale.*

*But I sense something shared in our design. We each take great pleasure in appearances and we are each moved by the practical and psychological aspects of 'comfort'. I feel, for example, that it would be quite impossible to be truly comfortable in a room one felt to be ugly.*

*I am planning to move my workshop and studio from Camberwell to Chelsea. And I would be so grateful, if at all possible, for the opportunity to introduce myself to you since your presence so defines the area.*

*Yours very truly,*
*Eustace Dunne*

A reply very soon came, inviting me to tea. Fowler's writing paper was a cream stock so heavy it was almost board. He used black ink and his hand was florid. The address was engraved, not merely printed. But when I arrived at Shawfield Street, there was no suggestion of tea. He went to the kitchen, fetched a three pint jug, poured in an entire bottle of Tanqueray, a tray of ice, a whole sliced lemon and a very small amount of Martini Bianco. The room was all neatly faded splendour: vaguely classical, spare rather than cluttered, with *objets de vertu* artfully placed, and with light and colour that made it feel modern. Someone eventually called this shabby chic.

Two pink stem glasses were briskly presented and Fowler sat back in an overstuffed chair of threadbare, maize-coloured damask, crossed his hands on his lap and, looking over the top of his depressed clerical spectacles, prettily asked, 'You're not a flit, are you? Only flits wear suede shoes.'

'What's a flit?' I asked, looking guiltily at my suede Chelsea boots.

'Dear boy,' he said. 'A flit is a cross-dresser.'

I coughed and spilt my gin.

'Never mind. We can't always be counting the cost. Sometimes awful things have their own beauty!' Fowler looked at the spreading stain on the Turkey rug and smiled thinly. 'Anyway, these Turkey rugs cost nothing. This one came from Bermondsey Market. In any event, we don't own anything. It's all on loan. All of it.'

'But I wonder,' I mused in the fading light, seeing the Chinese Chippendale escritoire across the room, 'if, in design terms, you are actually living in the past.'

'No, no, no. Not at all. The past is simply something that's over! I mean to say that it's important one knows about the *cavetto*, the wedge and the box. One means the traditional profiles of a picture frame. But one likes also to make the best of all contemporary opportunities whatever they may be. Everything is contemporary. That Chinese wallpaper over there. Do you think it's real or fake? And whatever the answer, do you think it really matters? Have some more martini.'

'What would your advice be to someone at my stage in his career, looking for premises?' I asked.

'That's very simple. First, go to look at the artists' studios in Sydney Close. Simply perfection. Old Willie Cadwallader – such a crook! – will grant you a short lease if there's one empty –' (and, for emphasis) 'if I ask him. Second, when you've done that, make it your business to get to know Walter Biles. He'll adore you and you will find him very useful indeed. Third, buy a crystal Lalique vaporizer, fill it with white vermouth and carry it with you everywhere to transform mere gin to dry martini.'

'And who is Walter Biles?' I asked while thinking to myself, *Not another stately homo.*

'Well,' Fowler went on. 'A very interesting individual. Trinity man.

I mean Trinity, Cambridge, of course. But he comes from, if you will, a successful family of butchers.' This last word was pronounced as if it were ridiculous. 'He was briefly and not terribly successfully a Jesuit missionary in India, but essentially he is a literary queer. And an absolutely first-rate pornographer. One of the very best. I think he finds more promising material in Chelsea than he ever did in Jaipur. More buggers, you know.'

I suspect my misgivings now revealed their construction on my face. Fowler continued. 'He's an English Gore Vidal. Do you know who I mean by Gore Vidal? You must, surely, have read Gore's book *The City and the Pillar*? I am told that the pillar bit is phallic symbolism.'

I winced.

Fowler continued, 'Walter was prosecuted at the Old Bailey when his second novel fell foul of the Obscene Publications Act a couple of years ago. And foul it was. There must be a bigger word than obscene. It really was very filthy indeed, but Walter was very disappointed when Christopher did not support him, at least not publicly. Do you know who I mean by Christopher Isherwood? Christopher described poor old Walter as a tragic, self-pitying drunk with a philosophy of failure. But the thing is, I happen to know, Walter has now abandoned writing dirty books. He wants to spend the family money on making a new restaurant. Dear Walter, always involved with tripe. You should go to see him. He might have work for you.'

## victory sponge

Walter Biles and his restaurant were moving into territory as fresh as his literary circle was fetid. He was an interesting man. Biles had a military stature, a refined voice, a fastidious dress sense and the red face always associated with butchers. His knowledge of food was both technical and idiosyncratic, piquant and peculiar. I believe Norman Douglas's writing on aphrodisiacs was one of his sources: larks' tongues and bull's testicles stewed in Falernian wine are examples of the dishes he would talk about with relish. He also spoke confidently of the charcoal-grilled sheep's balls he had eaten in Marrakech's Djemaa el-Fna. He was fond of the culinary underbelly of fries, *criadillas* and the euphemistically named 'white kidneys'.

...............................................................................................

® *Rollo Pinkie: I find it fascinating, and possibly revealing, how Eustace was so often drawn ineluctably towards the most challenging foodstuffs as well as to the most grotesque old queers.*

Biles, I think, was a sort of visionary. Just after the Festival of Britain closed, the very first edition of *The Good Food Guide* was published. The editor Raymond Postgate – interesting man, a Fabian hedonist popularizer of wine – could not find many causes for optimism in a food landscape he described as 'a plain of desolation'. What was for dinner? A dire cornucopia of tinned Empire fruit, synthetic cream and tough beef from Argentina. You might eat lentil roast or open a tin of pork casserole with apple. For pudding, Victory Sponge. This was a concoction of grated potato, sugar and breadcrumbs boiled in a basin smeared with cheap jam. And it was disgusting.

Against this, there were small flickers of gastro-enlightenment. In Bath, George Perry-Smith was cooking salmon *en croûte* with ginger and currants at his restaurant, called the Hole in the Wall. In the women's magazines, devilled eggs tentatively introduced the more daring British to paprika, and in 1953 Constance Spry, taking a break from flower arranging, created 'Coronation Chicken', with its respectful whiff of the Raj and the imperium. I think we can agree that this dish was a pioneer of all the apparently exotic dishes that the British eventually made their own: a sort of reverse colonialism which ended with Neapolitan pizza becoming a national dish.

Anyway, Coronation Chicken with its confident mixture of chutney, curry, raisins and nuts was very delicious, if not quite *cordon bleu*. It was a signpost to a multicultural future.

Biles had found an old ladder store on Brompton Road, long and thin, but with nice terracotta external mouldings mixed with red brick. He had an idea the interior should be painted yellow and filled with glossy rattan furniture and trinkets – Moghul prints, *zenana* windows from Gujarat in terracotta – acquired from his extensive tour of buggery in India. I felt differently, as I explained over drinks in the Coleherne on our first meeting. This was the Earl's Court pub, which was the point of contact between the new folk music and skiffle movements, and London's more flamboyantly costumed homosexuals.

Bathed in light from the strange stained glass windows, I slid my glass as best I could around the sticky tabletop and said, 'I honestly don't think yellow is quite right for interiors. Yellow makes people angry. You want something more soothing in a restaurant, more Swedish. Even if it has a French name.'

I had never been to Stockholm, but had known Swedish design since I began copying it at school. I liked Josef Frank's full palette of muted colours and his gentle patterns.

'On the other hand, may I compliment you on that blazer?' I ventured.

'No, you certainly may not. It's a boating jacket!' he barked good-naturedly. 'I want to call it "Pied de Mouton". Because I am fond of mushrooms.'

'Let fungus be my inspiration,' I replied, I thought rather stylishly.

## stripping for design

I stripped out the ladder store, which overlooked the magnificently gloomy Brompton Cemetery. There were generous oak floors and I hired Lethaby Academy students and a belt-sander to improve them. If the stains did not budge, we used a dilution of hydrochloric acid which left a nice white fuzz on the surface. We tore the remaining plaster from the brick and I bought more theatrical lights, but installed the reflectors on wires overhead. Then I made an extra batch of my Californian chairs. Most memorably of all, I had all the very tall, old windows covered with wooden louvres, made for me by a cabinetmaker in Stockwell. I painted them off-white. And the walls were mushroom.

Biles was thrilled by the result and within six months, Pied de Mouton had become one of London's most popular French restaurants, certainly the very best in Chelsea. In those days, *sole Véronique* was a provocative talking point. He cooked there himself in a lovely, coarse, dark blue apron. '*Bleu de travail*,' he told me. Everybody said Pied de Mouton was about the food – Biles' *noisettes d'agneau* and Steak Diane were notorious – but I knew Pied de Mouton's success was at least as much to do with the calm interior design as the exciting menu. Besides, Biles never acknowledged me in all his conversations with gossip columnists, diarists, food writers, hacks, hostesses, playboys, motley queers and the Pinewood studio starlets who now comprised his society. So I decided to make my own restaurant.

A restaurant, I was coming to realize, is a laboratory of taste in every sense. It is an advertisement too. People learn about design and manners from dining out. They are not paying for Biles' deep-fried gonads, but for an introduction to style. Tell me where you eat and I will tell you what you want to be.

......................................................................................................

[®] *Rollo Pinkie: One of many hilarious paradoxes about Eustace was that he wanted to appear a democrat, but was, in fact, a raging snob. Once in a restaurant he looked around at the customers and said, 'Tell me, do you think they give a discount to ugly people?'*

Sydney Close was too expensive and 'old' Willie Cadwallader, Chelsea's aristocratic landlord, was very much disinclined to do deals, so I found a sad tobacconist on New King's Road with a five-year lease left to run. It was an unpromising building between a chilly Welsh chapel and a grubby filling station. Once again, I stripped the interior, taking it back to bare brick. My Stockwell cabinetmaker made huge louvres to cover the shop windows. A stylistic routine was being established. And students from the Lethaby and from Camberwell were again recruited to help. This time, they built a suspended ceiling which neatly camouflaged the hideously stained Victorian plasterwork. And in this we cut holes, installing downlighters which I had copied from a recent edition of the magazine *Stile Industria*, always a reliable source of inspiration.

And dangling around the edges of the room, in the gap between the suspended ceiling and the wall, there were old colanders painted copper to serve as lampshades, their curious glow defining the tables set around the perimeter. I say 'perimeter' because I had this idea that the central space should be filled with a huge, communal refectory table. I did not yet own such a thing, but determined to have one made. Biles had given me an old French butcher's block and that was my starting point: the Stockwell cabinetmakers scaled it up to impressive refectory size. There was tongue and groove, tiled tabletops, dark brown quarry tiles on the floor and grey slate countertops.

I lent the students my two volume *Larousse Illustré* encyclopaedia, telling them to choose pictures related to food: *épis de blé, vache, cochon, poisson, coq, vin, sel, fromage, pain, boucher, boulanger*. We enlarged the Larousse engravings and printed them on giant panels of Formica laminate, which we attached to the walls. These walls were painted 'Dead salmon', as I decided 'Queen's sick' was not best suited to a dining experience. And we also had an engraving of a magnificent, over-sized *soupière*. Why? Because I had decided to call the restaurant 'L'Oignon Rouge', a name which nicely balanced a Francophile exoticism with a sense of down-to-earth practicality.

## export drive

Then my idea was to drive to Italy to buy a used espresso machine to rival the one the Moka Bar had recently installed in Frith Street. The route was similar to my recent French trip, but now – I felt significantly – I was on my own. And I had found, advertised in a trade paper, a nearly new Castiglioni-designed machine, as chromed and lascivious as a Raymond Loewy vision, in a wholesale coffee dealer in Novara.

I had already bought a 1951 Riley RMC to supplement the Vespa. It was not quite Tony's Lagonda, but near enough. Most of these Rileys were built for export, and mine was an example that was a distressed sale by a bankrupt antique dealer in Lillie Road, expensively thwarted in his ambitions for transatlantic business. So, the car was left-hand-drive and painted a very West Coast sky blue with cream leather upholstery and white-wall tyres.

With one hundred horsepower, it was really quite fast, although nothing like as fast as the American Ford V-8 whose style it aped. There was a column change: three on the tree, as they would have said in California. I remember, the side screens were celluloid with holes cut out for hand signals. After Lyon, the route diverged and I signalled my intention of turning towards Chambéry by sticking my hand through the flapping canvas. But soon the sun was shining and I lowered the hood.

I stopped for lunch at the Hôtel du Comte de Challes, a rather grand place and very deserted at this time of year. Walking its plush corridors looking for the dining room, I heard the strains of a single violin. Investigating, I discovered the ballroom: here, dancing entirely alone and without expression in muted Alpine sunshine, was Grace

Kelly, accompanied only by that solo violinist. It was an image I have never been able to forget.

Soon I was in Modane, on the French side of the Mont Cenis pass, where I stayed at the Hôtel du Commerce, a place where some of the ancient character of the Grand Tourists (and the cruel hardships they suffered) remained. At the end of dinner in an empty dining room – *filets de perche* and *blanquette de veau* with a grey wine from the Jura and some Beaufort cheese – I was admiring the fruit and sniffing the cleft of an apricot, something I have always found extremely sensuous. Assembling schoolboy French, I said to the waitress as she cleared the table, '*Cet abricot rappelle un peu le fond d'une femme.*'

She did not look up, but said, brushing the crumbs of the stiff napery, '*Aurez-vous besoin de service le matin, monsieur?*'

'*Peut-être même plutôt. Chambre dix-sept,*' I said, catching her eye.

'*Peut-être,*' she replied and bustled off to the kitchen.

Waking up with the waitress the next day, the sun was coming up over Mont Cenis long before *le service du matin* had begun. In the lonely car park, the cockpit of the Riley was inundated with snow. I had forgotten to put the hood up.

Novara was only a short drive. At Filipetti & Figli, I found the espresso machine and also found it would not fit into the Riley. But I did find the three different rices they grow in the wet paddyfields that blur the distinction between earth and sky: *vialone nano*, *carnaroli* and *arborio*. The espresso machine was sent by lorry to London, but I drove back the rice. The first person, I am told, to have brought these varieties home.

Consequently, at L'Oignon Rouge we made London's first risotto, not strictly French, but I think pedantry is the last refuge of the scoundrel. The rest of the menu? Of course, I already had Mrs David's recipe for *truite au bleu*, but now a few years on I also had her first published books as well. And in them I was beginning to find a connecting principle between cooking and designing. If you want to make ratatouille, would you not also want to have the kitchen to make it in? And don't designers and cooks do something essentially similar? You need to have good ingredients or good materials. You need a sound recipe or a good plan. The result of your work should be beautiful, useful, nutritious and delicious. Isn't it all the same thing?

I was determined to make all my own stock, as a moral principle as much as an economy. You need ample stock if you are to *create* (and I think that is absolutely the correct term) a proper risotto, with authenticity. The ingredients for stock should never be expensive and you can use bones, offcuts of meat the butcher does not want and any leftovers of old vegetables you can find, but never cabbage which makes it sour. Nor fried bacon, which makes it fatty. Simmer it, don't boil it. Boiling it will make it cloudy. Add some herbs, naturally. A *bouquet garni* is easy to make. Near the end, if you add a calf's foot, it becomes jellied.

With a good stock, I could make real soups! Tomato, mushroom, onion, beetroot, cold cucumber and *vichyssoise.*

And without ever realizing it, Mrs David helped me with the menu. *Truite au bleu*, obviously. But there was also going to be *pâté de campagne*, fish pie, fish cakes, poached salmon, *quenelles* of pike, chicken paprika (and more devilled eggs), kidneys with mustard, *carbonnade de boeuf*, soused herrings, macaroni cheese and a simple *paella*. For wine? Mouton Cadet, Macon, Liebfraumilch, Tio Pepe dry sherry and a mouth-purpling Antinori Chianti in a gay wicker *fiasco* for ten shillings.

And then I began to gather all the equipment I would need in L'Oignon Rouge, besides the espresso machine. First I bought white, French porcelain, now imported by Madame Cadec in Soho's Greek Street: plain, simple, honest, gutsy stuff. But pretty too. Then: Duralex glasses, a paella pan, knives and cleavers, a demilune, graters, squeezers, zesters, mashers, crushers, mincers, sieves, terrines, platters, cellars and mills. I loved the sound of all these words! Whisks, forks, spoons, skimmers, colanders, spatulas, tongs, bowls, boards, casseroles, moulds, carafes, jugs, glasses, scales, racks, jars, smokers, skillets, trivets and steamers. Possibly even an asparagus kettle. And what I began to realize is that this was the inventory not just of a restaurant kitchen, but of a shop. A shop that did not yet exist ...

The opening night was a party. Howard Hodgkin came, and so too did Eduardo Paolozzi. We made a huge cauldron of simplified *bouillabaisse* and served the very first authentic *rouille* in London, using *pimenton* from La Vera in Extremadura. Baguettes were stacked in teetering pyramids while Normandy butter was in glass jars. All the guests received a card with the *bouillabaisse* recipe on one side and an engraving of a classic French *marmite* on the other. Additionally, we gave each a wooden spoon tied to a tin of Ortiz sardines by tough jute string.

Maybe there were five good restaurants in London at the time? Because of this, the response to the pure theatre of L'Oignon Rouge was astonishing and at least as much of it was about the interior as the food.

........................................................................................................................

® *Rollo Pinkie: This is typical of Eustace's lavish self-mythologizing. He actually had no idea whether this was the first authentic* rouille *served in London. But then none of us did. I suspect there were predecessors at the Café Royal on Piccadilly and at Chez Victor in Soho. But it was this sort of bold, even outrageous, statement that helped make his reputation. Dutifully reported by the papers, an imaginative fib soon became established fact.*

## a star designer in the soup

The *Daily Rapid* sent its new art critic, a florid, bloviating, pustulated, broken-veined, bow-tied old fag with the X. Pobjoy byline, who accepted any invitation where drinks might be expected, especially if that expectation might be champagne. He was alerted when a stringer reported that students from the Royal College of Art were brawling with tramps on the street outside, interrupting the serene day of posh Chelsea with what looked very much like an avant-garde Parisian manifestation. Promising stuff! With him, Pobjoy brought a handsome, confident-looking woman he introduced as Beverley Grim – the owner, he said, of a Fulham gallery.

Both students and tramps had been excited by reports of giveaway food, each misinterpreting the spare aesthetic of London's first bistro as a charitable soup kitchen run by Social Services. Sensing an opportunity, I distributed enamel mugs of *gratin à l'oignon* and chunks of crusty baguette, at the same time offering students future discounts and exhibition space on the walls. Beverley Grim, I noticed, took notes.

When Pobjoy turned his free lunch into copy for his awful 'Eye Say' column, it caused a sensation. The entire cast of the new John Osborne play scheduled for Sloane Square's Royal Court Theatre abandoned rehearsals and turned up hungry and thirsty the following day. These gossipy characters spread the word like clap. In this way, a useful myth was established: I was not only a designer and a philanthropist, but a patron of the arts.

'Britain's star designer in the soup!' the *Express* wrote. Breathlessly, she described those lampshades I had made using the colanders from charity stores, sprayed copper. The 'In London Tonight' column of the *Daily Portrait* said, 'Eustace Dunne has triumphantly imported French style to London's first bistro.' I was photographed holding a huge *pain rustique*, baked for us by Solomon's of Bethnal Green. The French illustrations from *Larousse* looked on sternly. 'Eustace Dunne is a talent to watch!' *Everybody's* magazine said in a centre-spread. They had interviewed me while I was washing up in the kitchen. I kept the cutting.

If sometimes in future I gave the impression that I invented soup, baguettes and pâté that is because that is exactly the impression the coverage gave. Certainly, before L'Oignon Rouge they were not well known. Really quite suddenly, I had become the owner of French food. As well as a second-hand, Italian espresso machine. At that time, no one really understood coffee, but that would happen later.

# 1961 – Cars were important to us

'*It goes boom boody-boom boody-boom
boody-boom/Boody-boom boody-boom
boody-boom boom-boom-boom.*'

Peter Sellers and Sophia Loren,
'Goodness Gracious Me', 1960

*Jaguar E-Type, King's Road chariot.*

CARS WERE IMPORTANT TO US.

I should explain. There were now three of 'us'. Contract work for the studio continued to come in: the publicity around L'Oignon Rouge had created ever more new interest in the design business. 'Eustace Dunne never stops moving. He always arrives with a squeal of brakes!' Cheri Stunt told *Woman* magazine with some approval when she was photographed in L'Oignon Rouge with a carrot salad and a glass of Loire rosé for an article about her new miniskirt, then dismaying grumbly matrons and delighting youth of both sexes.

My friendship with Cheri had been confirmed when we worked on the second version of her successful King's Road shop, Soukh. I built a freestanding staircase as a central feature: it was photographed for *The Architectural Review*. And I showed her how to arrange bolts of cloth.

'No, no, no, no! You've got to *stack* them up!' I explained to her with my jacket off, sleeves rolled up, in red braces, with my third espresso of the morning to hand. Then I showed her with theatrical squats and harumphs how to stack with meaning. She rolled her eyes and flicked ash into my *demi-tasse* saucer.

Other big jobs included creating all the textiles for the interior of P&O's new ocean liner, the *Pretoria*, a task I acquired because the ageing Tallboy St Clair found its scale too daunting. I found it just daunting enough. These designs I sketched on the backs of several used envelopes, rescued from a workshop bin. I *did* always tell people to use both sides of any piece of paper.

Economy was always on my mind. Our furniture workshop was,

even so, still supported by worryingly long lines of credit from suppliers of foam and steel for the furniture. In the meantime, the old Camberwell premises were expensive to maintain and some of the workshop people were grumbling about all the attention I was giving to L'Oignon Rouge.

But I remembered Ashley's Seneca quotation, and felt daring enough to recruit some help. First, there was John Davidson, sharply dressed with a taste for chisel-toed monk's shoes, black polo necks, Senior Service and vodka. John, I think, had a Beatles haircut before The Beatles. His real ambition was to be a car salesman and it was these skills he brought to us. An open nature, a line of plausible patter and no reluctance whatsoever to lie in pursuit of a sale were his professional equipment. To us he was priceless since his own *milieu* was the suburban, philistine middle-manager who was usually the point-of-contact at our clients. I couldn't bear to deal with these people, but John positively enjoyed taking them to the pub.

......................................................................................................................................

® *Rollo Pinkie: This is a perfect example of how Eustace ruthlessly consumed people of value. Davidson was one of the few people in the business who could actually read a P&L.*

Second, there was Quentin Huskisson, a tough but twinkly eyed and personable artisan, whom I grew to trust.

Quentin had been introduced to me by one of the waitresses at L'Oignon Rouge. This was Susan Wellbeloved, a Cheltenham Ladies' College blonde experimenting with tan thigh boots, a tight sweater and *nostalgie de la boue*, assisted in the last by her relationship with a rat-like French waiter with an earring who smelt of *saucisson* and acted with the *hauteur* of a depressed Napoleon.

She was living in digs in Richmond and one day said to me, 'You know, Eustace, you should really meet my landlord. He's interested in furniture. Just like you. And just like you, he's really, seriously, fucking difficult. I mean. Seriously. Fucking. Difficult.'

And that was my introduction to Quentin. He had been brought up, to the extent that he was brought up at all, in a Leicester council house. To learn the trade of shop-fitting, he went, with characteristic cussedness, not to an apprenticeship, but to Australia. In Melbourne, his rise was rapid: this was through a combination of great application, hard-charging ambition and a local misreading of his distinctively East Midlands accent as 'posh'. In Melbourne, Quentin was taken for a duke, not a talented delinquent from the provinces.

By the time he left Australia, Quentin was a partner in Myatt Fields & Chatwin, one of the country's biggest architectural firms. Not a firm to win great prizes with great work, but a firm to win big money with big contracts: they designed the state of Victoria's first shopping precinct in the City of Moonee Valley, and Quentin had been the supervising partner.

And back in Richmond, Quentin was sharing a house on the hill with the ebullient Liverpudlian architect James Stirling, whose engineering building at Leicester University – all angles, shining brick and glass – was a sensation of the day. At least in the influential magazines of advanced taste, if not with heat-frazzled staff and students. James, who later became my good friend and worked on several restaurants for us, never did understand the principles of thermal gain. Nor did his clients budget for air conditioning.

Susan Wellbeloved had given me a phone number and I called.

'May I please speak to Quentin Huskisson?'

'And who wants to?' a gruff East Midlands voice, perhaps with a little Australian admixed, replied.

'My name is Eustace Dunne. I am a designer and I have been told, on extremely good authority, that you are also interested in furniture.'

'Well, m'dear, I am certainly sitting in a chair. And I am very well upholstered. Overstuffed, even. If that's what you mean.' I was certain I could hear a muted squeal of female laughter in the background. It was the middle of the afternoon.

Quentin and I met in a pub in Putney one lunchtime the following week. It couldn't be called an interview. Quentin drank several pints of Guinness and I explained to a bewildered bar girl how to make the Negroni I had ordered.

Throughout our conversation, Quentin smoked Havana cigars end to end, preparing one after the other with a twist of a horny thumbnail, dispatching the tip to the floor.

'That's how rabbis do circumcision,' he smirked, inhaling deeply and worryingly on contraband Montecristos, acquired as part of a large stash in lieu of fees never paid by a Maltese Soho club owner for a bar Quentin had designed. It was either that, Quentin explained to the wretched Mr Caruana, or an unscheduled meeting with a ruthless and hungry Australian wrestler of his acquaintance, recently arrived in London and looking for work. Alternatively, an unwelcome introduction to the Inland Revenue.

## my man of business

In this way, Quentin was able to smoke very many fine cigars. I liked him immediately. He was a person with no affectations, or, at least, the affectation of having no affectations. And he knew how to get things done. Not the type to ask questions. Quentin became my man of business.

And we needed cars. I sold the Riley and bought one of the new Jaguar E-Types, recently launched at the Parc des Eaux-Vives in Geneva in front of a world press that was almost unbelieving that a thing of such shamelessly provocative beauty could exist. No one could decide whether it was phallic and masculine or lascivious and feminine. I think it was probably both ... and this was an ambiguity to be exploited. Mine was a roadster in an icy metallic blue with navy leather upholstery. It had a brightwork luggage rack on the boot lid. I had it fitted with a 45rpm record player and a radio-telephone. There could be no better vehicle for transiting the King's Road.

And I let John Davidson buy the car of his B-feature dreams, a Ford Zodiac. This was Detroit kitsch adapted for the Home Counties, just about European in scale, but still indisputably vulgar in any polite context. There were chrome-plated ferrules beneath the boot and starburst Dagenham heraldry beneath clear vinyl on the steering-wheel boss. John chose sunburst yellow and ivory. This car he would use, more or less – usually less – effectively for taking samples of our furniture to show incurious department-store buyers in Leeds or Carlisle.

Quentin, however, made the most sensible choice. This was the 'Neue Klasse' BMW 1500, the first ever 'executive' car whose crisp lines and generous glass-house windows spoke of the Bauhaus if they spoke of anything at all. Quentin chose his in that grandma's corset shade of beige that they use on German taxis, after dallying briefly with one in a metallic finish he called Jewish Racing Gold. The perforated vinyl seats were dark tobacco brown. Both the perforations and the colour were ideal for a man whose upholstery was continuously exposed to an unruly smoking habit. Quentin's paunch was always covered in ash. Very soon, Quentin would write a remarkably unusual and very popular book about burns, stains, rips, tears and how to deal with them.

## Beverley's huge amber bangles

A week after the opening of L'Oignon Rouge, the *Daily Rapid*'s Beverley returned, unannounced, to see me. Finding my Vespa parked outside, she had acted on a whim. Inside L'Oignon Rouge, I was investigating behind the bar. One of the things I was learning about the restaurant trade was not that staff steal from you, at least not directly. Instead, what the dishonest ones like to do is bring in their own bottles of drink and serve it at bar prices, trousering the sale while not criminally depleting the stock. Clever.

So, while I was on my hands and knees, frowning at bottles of liquor and crossly marking levels with a chinagraph pencil, I heard: 'You down there! Lost something, have we? Got time for a drink?'

Dusting my knees and wiping my hands with a dishcloth I had designed myself (this one with an engraving of 'Un esclave' lifted once more from the very useful Larousse), I saw Beverley and was reminded what a handsome woman she was. Today she was in black Capri pants and a striped sailor top with huge amber bangles on each wrist and a cigarette on the go. Not obviously beautiful, whatever that means, but well put together with an attractive confidence and impressive *savoir-faire*. She nodded her head at a red and white Mini Cooper she had parked outside with all four wheels on the pavement.

I got into the passenger's seat, noticing the door was dented. The horn of a 22 bus blared as Beverley ignored Chelsea traffic to get in at the driver's side.

'Let's go to Battersea,' she said, adjusting her Capri pants, which were evidently causing a problem in her crotch.

I shrugged.

Minis always whined like food mixers. Something to do with the transverse gearbox, I think. The Beaufort Street corner was taken flat out in second gear and before we reached Albert Bridge, we were approaching sixty mph. I had also noticed on the parcel shelf three soft packs of Peter Stuyvesant filter-tipped cigarettes, a Zippo lighter, a copy of yesterday's *Le Figaro* and several German condoms labelled 'Ritax. Made in Germany. *Liebe Lust und Leidenschaft.*'

I didn't know whether to be astonished, intimidated or excited. Moments later, the Mini was being jerkily manoeuvred outside the Prince Albert pub. During the to-and-fro, she put her hand on my knee. This affected, if not her judgement as a woman, then at least her coordination as a driver using reverse; the Mini noisily shunted a

Commer milk float parked behind. Beverley turned the engine off. But her hand did not move and I felt myself reacting with that curious light tingling in the perineum.

'I'm not worried about broken glass, are you? Life's too short to peel potatoes. Kill or be killed. That's what I say. Let's go in.'

## the trouble I've seen

Inside, she bought the drinks and the crisps. A large gin and tonic for her, a large Scotch for me. The crisps were made by Smith's and sold in greaseproof bags for thruppence, with the salt in little twists of blue paper. Sometimes, if you were lucky, the Smith's production line glitched and you found two twists of blue paper in a single pack.

'This is all extremely amusing,' I said, chewing a crisp, 'but would you mind terribly explaining what's going on?' I tried to look indifferent.

'I was impressed by L'Oignon Rouge,' Beverley said. 'I like to see a man in an apron. Butcher's blue suits you. *Bleu de travail* the French call it, you know. And I think a wooden spoon accessorizes you well. You should carry them more often. Or perhaps a rolling pin. Anyway, I'm working on a multimedia art project about the new women's movement called *Bust My Balls*. And I thought I'd interview you since you seem to be a rather modern man. Unusually modern, in fact. And my first question is a test. Everything depends on this. Will you marry me?'

I tried to look unperturbed. I guessed Beverley was possibly five years older than me.

'That seems a little forward, if you don't mind my saying so. But perhaps you would tell me what you have in mind? Were you thinking of getting married this very afternoon, or shall we leave it until after dinner?'

'Look,' Beverley said. 'I'm not really very interested in explaining myself. But put it this way. I am new money. Worse, I am new South

African money. Even worse, new Jewish South African money. You will have met many resourceful and successful South Africans. But never, I think, a nice one. I am not nice. Anyway, my dad, Morrie, opened the first television rental shop in Durban in 1949. Made a fortune and came as fast as he could to St John's Wood to spend it. But he couldn't get through it all before the Balkan Sobranies and Macallan overtook his programme of redistribution of wealth. Did you know 'Eshkenazi' means 'German' in Yiddish? Anyway, I'm more interested in art than money. I had thought about journalism, but the only Fleet Street vacancies open to a woman are being a secretary who becomes a one-gin screamer at five o'clock or a char lady. I love art because it takes a woman out of cake-baking and flower-arranging and dress-making territory. Besides, art is about sex and power. So my point is: will you marry me? A simple yes or no will do.'

'That was quite a pitch. I suggest we continue this conversation at another time ... or place,' I said, with what I hoped was evident meaning.

And soon we were again parking, once more very noisily, this time scrubbing the Mini's neat little cream-painted ventilated steel wheels against the kerb. We were outside her magnificent mansion flat on a very leafy and dappled Prince of Wales Drive. Horribly, the smell in the lobby reminded me of my mother's place near Hampstead, but Beverley's interior on the second floor was altogether different. It was a mess of discarded clothes, abandoned shoes, jumbles of mismatched furniture, second-rate works of art leaning in piles against the *toile de Jouy* walls, unwashed mugs, glasses and dishes on the floor, stockings and underwear (best not to look), piles of books and newspapers, and full ashtrays.

I stepped over a fur coat. The television, I presumed one of her dad's, had been left on and the screen was crackling with foggy static. The flat stank of cigarettes and Hermès' Calèche perfume. I think there may have been cats in the kitchen so it stank of cats too, but that was only a suspicion because I began to sneeze. I certainly saw well-thumbed copies of Martha Gellhorn's *The Trouble I've Seen* and Mary McCarthy's *The Company She Keeps*.

Now Beverley said almost, but not quite, apologetically, sensing my distaste, 'You know, people talk about the movement as a sort of shrill and spurious masculinity. As if we are all man-hating bull dykes in boilersuits. But as Shirley Conran said, I would simply rather lie on a bed than make it.' And with that she rattled her bangles and kicked her shoes off.

And the bed was indeed unmade. And the sheets by no means fresh, river-washed, air-dried linen. Instead, pale pink easycare nylon, slightly rank.

'Here's more wisdom from Shirley Conran: you have to be efficient if you're going to be lazy,' Beverley said.

The following week we were married at Chelsea Town Hall.

Quentin was best man and drove us to Claridge's in his taxi-coloured executive BMW.

## streamlined one-pot dinners

A large Suffolk cottage, pretty in pink, was a part of Beverley's dowry, although I do not think she would have cared to hear it put like that. Still, it was touching that an inheritance from a chain of black and white television rental shops should include a building so distinctively colour-washed. We began to use it at weekends: two hours from L'Oignon Rouge to the thatch and inglenook, if you timed the traffic right. The E-Type and the Mini Cooper were the first in the village, confident statements about metropolitan fashion near the banks of the sluggish River Alde. Often, we raced there. The Jaguar was very much faster on the straight stretches of the dual carriageway, but Beverley's Mini Cooper always caught up on the winding country roads. She drove like an indestructible madwoman.

Decoration when I arrived included hideous reproduction art and detestable, fussy knick-knacks. Along with Constable's *The Hay Wain* and Yeames' sentimental *And When Did You Last See Your Father?*, there was Vosper's *Salem* of 1908, a painting which Lord Lever bought for his collection. At mid-century, these reproductions found their way into every house of a certain standing. If you bought seven pounds of Sunlight soap, they would give you a *Salem* calendar showing an old Welsh shrew in an unpronounceable Baptist chapel near Harlech. Worse than one of Conran's Surbiton Virgins.

I admired the commercial promotion, if not the art. Mawkish. I threw it out. The Constable and the Yeames too. Horse brasses, fire irons and bellows also went in the bin. And all the brown furniture. Plus the faded chintz. I binned anything with associations and set about furnishing the house with simple, honest and useful things. I kept, however, the Aga which was, thanks to a lackadaisical cleaning regime, turning a beautiful, mellow off-white, rather like a well-done *crème brûlée*.

The local builder, a Homerically disobliging individual with a cast in his eye and an appetite for dishonest practices, waxed and polished the stone floors and painted every wall white. I imported a handsome, black crackle-finished wood-burning stove from Norway (it came by road from Harwich) and colourful dhurries from Gujarat. These I sourced from Sobhita Bhatt, the Gujarati textiles heiress, who had been at the Lethaby with me.

I had my studio make Roman blinds in undyed calico. They muted the enormous Suffolk light beautifully. My Californian chairs – new ones in aqua, pink, orange and lime green – looked surprisingly handsome in so austere a rural house. I bought more studio lights and found a local cabinetmaker who could turn oak stumps into salad bowls. We had many more than we could use, but they looked most impressive in stacks. And we had ten of the gorgeous, flame-orange 'Coquelle' casseroles, which Raymond Loewy had designed for Le Creuset. Simple. And perfect for Beverley's preferred one-pot dinners.

Old copper pans we found in antique shops, while a local workshop was our source of baskets in all sizes as well as gorgeous Sussex trugs made of sweet chestnut. I designed wine storage using old stock brick, which the disobliging builder constructed in the kitchen: floor to ceiling. Galvanized buckets and watering cans were easy to find in the country and I think we had collected perhaps two hundred of them within the first six weeks. Bundles of dried willow were tied together with rough twine, making corner features that cast enchanting shadows.

The space left by *Salem* and *The Hay Wain* was superbly filled by framed bills of sale from local agricultural auctions in Beccles and Framlingham, robustly set in Victorian Grotesque type. Sixty-four of them were arranged, eight by eight, on one drawing-room wall. Old agricultural tools, a bandsaw, a spade, a hoe, a pig-scalder, a scythe, a broadfork, a cattle prod, a Pyecombe hook, a hay knife, a goad, a dibber and an adze on the other. I specially liked the goad.

And, naturally, we had another oversized refectory table made in limed oak. We sat around it on long benches upholstered only by old jute sacks thinly stuffed with kapok. And one evening there we were eating an *omelette aux fines herbes* with a fresh, crisp green salad and a rather grown-up Beaujolais from that maker with the flowery labels in Romanèche-Thorins. Frank Sinatra's *Come Swing With Me!* was playing jauntily on the hi-fi.

## legs, or the Marangoni effect

'Did you know it's called the Marangoni effect?' I said, while holding the generous glass of wine up to the light cast by twelve oversized church candles on the table. 'It's what you call "legs". Those dribbles down the inside of a glass that suggest the happy presence of alcohol in the wine. Would you like another? It's a Saint-Amour. Perhaps he was the patron saint of love.'

'Of course. But I've been thinking,' Beverley said. 'You know those amazing photographs Herbert Matter took of Charles Eames making furniture in California, and Jackson Pollock doing his action painting on Long Island, the ones you find in absolutely every magazine everywhere? Well. They helped secure an image of the American artist in the popular imagination: a man of action as well as a man of taste, even if Pollock was a coarse, sexist brute. Anyway, I think we should be seen doing the same here. Cooking, smoking, lunching.'

'So what are you going to do?' I asked.

'I'm going to call Mark Boxer at the new *Sunday Times* magazine. Get him to send a scribbler and a snapper. It's ideal for his pages.'

And Mark was duly called. An elegant and handsome man with the look of a wicked gypsy possessed of a Cambridge education, he carried the air of someone bent always on clever mischief.

'He's sending the new homes editor of the magazine!' Beverley exclaimed triumphantly.

And I went to meet her at Ipswich station. Naturally, I took the Jaguar and drove very fast back to the house, establishing in her mind what I hoped would appear to be a sort of stylish urgency defining our lives.

'Do you always drive in the middle of the road?' she asked, not evidently perturbed.

'Only when I'm in a hurry,' I replied. 'And I am always in a hurry.'

Beverley had pitched Mark Boxer an idea about lunch in the country, at the time an impossible vision for the majority of *Sunday Times* readers. Girls from L'Oignon Rouge had arrived earlier, by bus, to help with the arrangements. We had some interesting guests. Dickie Chopping, the best *trompe l'oeil* illustrator of the day, came with his partner, the decorator Denis Wirth-Miller. Chopping had taught at the RCA, but was now a Colchester native. Dickie had, like Biles, written a filthy novel, but his real preoccupation, buggery aside, was James Bond. He was working on the dustcover of Ian Fleming's *Thunderball*. Dickie explained with amused malice: 'I was thrilled that Ian Fleming called me "The Executioner"! He first asked for a flick-knife on the cover of *Thunderball* because it's the sort of thing teenagers use on people like us. But in the end, he let me use a gorgeous, old-fashioned dagger. Ideal for stabbing in the front. Or back, if you must. Fleming said *Thunderball* is immensely long, immensely dull and only my jacket can save it. And then I said, "We will see about *that*!"'

Another guest was Robert Carrier, the first modern food writer. He wore a bow tie and white shoes. Cedric Morris came too. Cedric was the gay baronet who had founded the East Anglian School of Painting and Drawing at nearby Benton End. I liked him: he was a painter of real style and authenticity, but not above designing extremely successful posters for Cresta Silks and British Petroleum. As well as teaching me how to prime and stretch canvases, Cedric had taught Lucian Freud to paint. Recently, he had done Dickie Chopping's portrait.

Lunch began with white Burgundy, naturally served *en magnum*, in the garden. I told people Terence Conran's dictum: wines served *en magnum* always seem a luxury, no matter if they are *pipi du chat*. Cat's piss, as Mrs David used to say. And lunch continued inside around the refectory table with red Burgundy. We ate a *quiche lorraine* made with bacon from Emmett's of Peasenhall, who won a royal warrant from Queen Victoria for pig husbandry. Then we ate *truite au bleu*, followed by a magnificent Cheddar.

The conversation was lively, indiscreet and genial. Cedric was a great plantsman too.

He explained to the baffled *Sunday Times* editor: 'You know, very little of what I know was actually learnt in either the Académie Delécluse or the Artists' Rifles. I learnt a lot more as a dishwasher, a *plongeur*, in New York. And I was a bellboy for a while too. Really, I have learnt by doing. I have cultivated more than ninety new varieties of iris, most of them named after Benton End. And, no, I certainly don't have any children, but I do breed birds and keep a macaw as a pet.'

We drank a *marc de Bourgogne* with the coffee. In this way was an image of domestic felicity, style, generosity, *bonhomie* and glittering connections made in an impressionable journalist's mind. I drove her back to Ipswich station, first at impressive speed, until I stopped on a whim at a lay-by near Grundisburgh.

I pointed out a thicket of elms and said, 'Did you know the sight of beautiful trees gave John Constable what he called an "ecstasy of delight"?'

She met my eye as the Jaguar made ticking noises, the hot engine contracting. She smiled slightly, said nothing and we missed her train.

The cover story, when it eventually appeared in the *Sunday Times Magazine*, said 'Design Man's Country'. It was rhapsodic.

## an enterprise zone

The next day I was standing in the wet grass of the orchard, posing in a butcher's apron for the photographer. He was using three Pentax S1s, the new single lens reflex cameras that were revolutionizing newspaper and magazine reportage. Their handy size made them very portable and well adapted to informal compositions and improvisational views.

And I was holding a sweet chestnut trug that was over-filled with apples in one arm. I had a ruddy country complexion on my face. This was, after all, a *colour* magazine. Then I heard the phone ring inside the cottage. I marched through the wet grass, drenching my custard-coloured corduroy trousers. The phone was, naturally, a GPO device, but I had insisted on the latest model, vaguely Californian in design, red with a coiled flex. Modern.

The voice said, 'Mr Dunne? This is Vincent Philbeam from the Department of Trade. Have I caught you at a bad moment?'

'No, of course not,' I lied smoothly.

Philbeam continued, picking up pace a little. 'I work with the

London County Council Expanded Towns Scheme. We are interested in persuading exciting, modern businesses to move out of London. Northamptonshire, Gloucestershire and Wiltshire are our favoured regions for expansion. Better air, better housing, more commercial opportunities, better communications. Actually, more golf too, but I imagine that is not your chief interest. Essentially, if you were prepared to move your manufacturing activities and your staff out of London to one of our EZs ...'

'And an EZ is precisely what?' I asked, wrestling my arm free from the top-heavy trug and spilling several Granny Smiths on the polished stone floor.

'Oh, I'm sorry. Enterprise Zone. We get very used to initials and acronyms in the DoT, you know. Anyway, the government would essentially underwrite the costs of a new factory, if, that is, you were prepared to make a ten-year commitment. Perhaps you would care to come into Thornhill Street to discuss the matter? May I ask my special assistant, Griselda Pollock, to make the arrangements? We will happily send a ministry car for you.'

'That won't be necessary,' I said. And the next week, an ice-blue Jaguar E-Type with navy-blue leather upholstery was parked outside the Department of Trade's imposing HQ in Victoria. Although it was cold, the hood was left down because it suggested a sense of urgency. Besides, Philbeam's PR department had said the several photographers waiting under the building's *porte-cochère* would prefer it that way. Twelve months later, the name 'dunne' (with a lowercase 'd') was written in gigantic Baskerville on a twenty thousand square foot factory in the EZ of Salisbury.

Like the red phone, the factory was impressively modern: a low-rise building in corrugated metal that was painted cherry red. And Philbeam had also underwritten the cost of our lorries: six Ford Thames Trader fifteen ton panel vans were also painted cherry red with 'dunne' in enormous Baskerville on the sides. The publicity photographs always had them in the car park next to my blue Jaguar, John's yellow Ford and Quentin's beige BMW. We were learning about colour in those days.

Most of the workshop joined us in the move to Wiltshire, whose benefits of fresh air and peaceful communications were readily appreciated by a team that had been working for too long in Camberwell smog. And Philbeam's new machinery, mostly imported from Germany and Sweden, allowed us to increase production. We designed new ranges, adding office furniture to our popular domestic seating. There was ample demand from the new businesses of the new towns. This was among the very first flat-pack furniture produced in Britain, an idea inspired by the great Austrian chair designer Michael Thonet whom I have always admired.

But the months pass slowly in the country, and the idea of a ten-year commitment to a rural idyll, a healthy prison, was becoming onerous. I missed the lustre of London. It was impossible to find trained staff in Wiltshire. Bank credit was always difficult. Export credit impossible: the Italians, frankly, designed and made better product. The air may have been fresher, but life was duller in the country, trade insurance a nightmare and salesmen never quite as energetic or improvisational as I actually wanted them to be.

I was explaining my growing resentment to Quentin, less than a year into the misadventure. He had his feet on my desk, his tie loose, his hair floppy and a familiar cigar clenched between his teeth. Through the enormous windows of my office, shielded only by bamboo trees, I could see the cherry-red 'dunne' vans being languorously serviced by forklift trucks, moving like mating insects.

'Quentin, I've very nearly had enough of this,' I groaned.

He looked at me very steadily and was silent for maybe thirty seconds.

'Anything you want me to do about it?' he asked in a breezy, non-committal way.

At the weekends, there was Suffolk. But I was also growing to detest country social life, with its predictable rounds of stuffy dinners, drinks parties with nearly dead people and private views of dud artists in third-rate galleries. Then there were the appalling aristos who exercised their *droit de seigneur* not by sexual exploitation of the obvious sort, but by expecting positive responses to invitations to their numbing gatherings. And good behaviour at them.

One such was Lady Henderson who organized regular and earnest sculpture tours of the country churches, followed by niggardly drinks in her beautiful but frighteningly cold Jacobean house. It was one of those Sundays and I was discussing a Roubiliac bust of a syphilitic Henderson ancestor with a shockingly empurpled homosexual from the National Trust. Then, carrying a nasty little silver tray of dry sherry herself, Lady Henderson interrupted with, 'Mr Dunne, one more drink before you *rush*?' Cooking smells were now evident. Other guests were being vouchsafed a benefit to which I was not yet entitled by Wiltshire nobility.

Before I could rush, a uniformed policeman found me in the throng and took me aside. With no preamble, he explained the Salisbury factory had burnt down. No one had been hurt, but it was completely destroyed. Foul play was not suspected so there would be no inquiry. It was clearly an act of nature.

As I walked with the policeman to his Austin Westminster patrol car, I thought to myself, Eustace Dunne, your friend and confidant Quentin just burnt down your factory. Then I did a quick and timely and pleasant calculation. And I smiled.

The insurance proceeds would be enough for me to open a shop. Back in London.

The following week, Quentin presented me with a file of before and after photographs of the inferno. He was a keen amateur photographer and the pictures from his Leica Visoflex were pin sharp.

# 1964 – Bleu de Travail

*'A man who lives a part, not to others but alone,
is exposed to obvious psychological dangers.'*

John le Carré, *The Spy Who
Came In from the Cold*, 1963

*Chelsea . . . pendant le déluge.*

'Do you know the difference between a pipe and a tube?' I asked.

Quentin grunted while fingering his surviving bishop and concentrating on his next move. He tended to play silently, I filled the quiet spaces with what I thought were stimulating provocations.

We were playing chess, drinking brandy and smoking. It was Soho, late at night, and we were in the flat I was temporarily renting above Foale & Tuffin's Ganton Street shop. Three pounds a week.

I had met Sally Tuffin and Marion Foale through the Royal College of Art. The pair was now extremely busy revolutionizing women's fashion: 'What all the young chicks are buying', the newspapers said. *A La Mode* lionized them in its 'What's Hot in London' column, a regular account of how London began to swing. It seemed 'young chicks' were indeed buying acid-yellow trouser suits and jackets with op-art patterns: Sally and Marion, young chicks themselves, made trouser suits, hitherto reserved for district nurses, sexy.

So soon after the Lady Chatterley trial, the 'sexy' word was becoming familiar in conversation, even if the more extreme of Lawrence's obscenities were still taboo. Only a few years before, Colin McInnes had told me that the publishers of his teenage novel *Absolute Beginners* had insisted on asterisks in 'f★ck' and 'a★se'. Not for much longer they wouldn't. The era of blushing asterisks was nearly over.

We had earlier eaten at the new Trattoria Terrazza, which defined the Italian restaurant for this generation: *pollo cacciatore*, chicken with tomatoes, olives and mysterious Sardinian herbs. White tiles, spotlights and those Chiavari chairs. And we started with a *bruschetta* of chicken liver, which I felt had a little too much garlic. Despite the old jokes, Italian cooks tend to be quite cautious, or, at least, delicate, with flavours and spicing.

Over the 'broosketta', I had to tell Quentin to pronounce 'ch' as hard as a 'k', but I think he knew already and made these mistakes for effect, that effect being to make me shudder. Fond as I was, there was always some doubt in my mind about whether Quentin was mocking me. If he had an emotional life, it was under very tight control.

We drank two bottles of Barolo which Mario himself had recommended. He comped us one of them. Stolen, I imagine. And now we were back in the flat, it was after ten and the drunks were being noisily thrown out of the pubs. We could hear the muted, but insistent, bass line from a group performing at the Bag O'Nails. I think it may have been The Swinging Blue Jeans.

But we preferred chess to pop, at least on this occasion. Headless tailor's dummies in trouser suits surrounded us as we played, reminding me of a haunted archaeological museum. Apart from the neon intruding from the street, the light in the flat was muted.

I returned to the question of pipes and tubes.

'Well, it's really very simple. One is defined by internal dimensions, the other by external. So the Underground is a tube, but your willy is a pipe. Although not in your case, I think, a very impressive one. If you see what I mean.'

I think I can say that Quentin was more moved by practical matters than theoretical ones.

## sexy furniture

'But don't you agree,' I asked, admiring a mannequin wearing a tunic in shot silk the colour of a Gordon's Gin bottle, 'that if you

can make a trouser suit sexy, you can make furniture sexy too?'
This very briefly caught his interest, but still Quentin said nothing.

And I was always fond of telling him on every occasion: 'You haven't, you know, finished your day's work unless you know how to start tomorrow.' So I told him again, adding, 'I hope your desk is clear tonight, Quentin, m'dear.'

He moved a piece, sneered and growled, 'Check.'

'So tomorrow,' I said, 'I think you should start investigating sites. Sexy sites.'

He looked up. I thought he might be thinking of hitting me. Quentin had the aspect of a bruised, ruffian cherub with a violent streak and a grievance.

He moved another piece and said, 'Check. Mate.'

But the next morning, Chelsea *flâneurs* saw a beige BMW slowly cruising the streets, a tousle-haired, cigar-smoking man at the wheel, his head swivelling at building sites and empty shops. They would not begin to suspect a boot full of an arsonist's propellants, accelerators and fuses. As well as a Barbour jacket, a camel-coloured Kangol 504 woollen flat cap and an unlicensed shotgun.

Additionally, Quentin was carrying £1000 in cash as a lubricant in negotiations should they become sticky. His other technique was to introduce himself, uninvited, to tenants of attractive properties and say, 'Hello. I am from the Inland Revenue. We're making an emergency investigation. Do you happen to know where the landlord is and how I might find him?'

In this way, introductions were soon made and it was not long before we acquired a corner site at a junction where Knightsbridge, Chelsea and Fulham meet. The property was ground floor, with a basement, in a nondescript fifties building, near Draycott Avenue where theatrical agent Daphne Rye had just opened Daphne's, her fashionable restaurant. And our building had huge windows that would eventually allow us to create an open effect, so very different from the claustrophobic brown-ness of department store furniture floors.

And I knew exactly what I wanted it to be. Shopping as a sort of theatre. I had met Morris Lapidus, architect of Miami's astonishing Fontainebleau Hotel. This was a spectacularly vulgar design, which even included grottoes and mermaids. Liberace was the permanent glittering cabaret. Not at all my taste, but Lapidus's chutzpah was infectious. Most usefully, he had told me, 'If you create a stage and it is grand enough, everyone who enters will play their part.'

This is what I wanted: to direct customers in a play I had written and staged and directed myself. But besides theatre, I also wanted the shop to have the sense of a utilitarian warehouse, a cornucopia of useful things. Beautiful too. And it would be called Bleu de Travail.

I explained to a journalist that I had always loved traditional workwear. Apparently she did not notice the anomaly – let's not say hypocrisy – that I was actually wearing a bespoke Dougie Hayward suit in dove grey and a yellow Jermyn Street shirt gathered at the wrist with white gold and garnet cufflinks. But no tie.

'The classic French indigo-dyed workman's jacket is a masterpiece of vernacular design: it is durable, handsome and its capacious pockets make it as useful as a bucket. And, like all good designs, they improve with age. *Bleu de travail* looks even better when faded, worn and patched. My favourite brand is "Le Laboureur". The workman. The French understand *l'art de travailler* as well as *l'art de vivre*. And I think Bleu de Travail's customers will come to understand both too.'

I would explain to Quentin how I wanted the shop to look. 'Empty, white, bricks, ordinariness and light.' I wanted the merchandise to be the drama. And Quentin would make sure that was exactly how it happened. He never asked any questions.

'Measure twice so you only cut once,' he would tell all the tradesmen on site, wisdom acquired from carpenters, but like all good folk-wisdom, it had a universal sense. And workmen never questioned

147

Quentin because they knew that, despite the BMW and the Havana cigars and the Italian restaurants, he was, fundamentally, one of them.

Old plaster was removed, bricks laid bare, just like in Camberwell. Electrical conduit exposed. There was industrial metal shelving, spotlights, painted tongue and groove ceiling, while the staircase furniture was made of scaffolding poles and knuckles. The floors were polished, dark-brown quarry tiles.

And while this tumult of building work was going on, newly recruited staff had to be trained.

'You've got to stack them like Cheri Stunt's boutique!'

I was addressing a girl isolated in a floor covered with white porcelain ramekins and wooden breadboards.

'Stacking is a form of repetition which is good for emphasis, and is also highly decorative. But it also happens to be an extremely effective way of getting all the fucking stock on the floor and reducing our warehouse overhead.'

## it's called a Mouli

'Dear child, it is called a Mouli,' I explained to another girl handling a piece of kitchen equipment with a mystified look, 'and it is used for grating vegetables. Vegetables are those things that grow in the earth. They are not to be confused with crisps. Make that mistake and I will spank you with a spatula.'

Cheri put all the girls and boys in black jeans and polo necks, irrespective of gender. Vidal Sassoon cut their hair. Equally irrespective. Very soon, Bleu de Travail became like a club for both the staff and the customers: it was so amusing working there with its prosperous, bohemian ambience and visiting popsters that our people actually volunteered for Saturdays. I like to think you would always find something you wanted to steal, or bump into somebody you wanted to meet. The light from the huge windows, enhanced by the spotlights, made even shell-shocked provincials look like Rank Organisation starlets.

Everything we had used in the kitchen at L'Oignon Rouge was now for sale in Bleu, as it came to be known. Perhaps the shop even looked like *Larousse Illustré* come to life. There were Duralex glasses, paella pans, knives and cleavers from Wusthof and Sabatier, demilunes, graters, squeezers, zesters, mashers, crushers, mincers, sieves, terrines, platters, cellars and mills. Whisks, forks, spoons, skimmers, colanders, spatulas, tongs, bowls, pasta jars, boards, casseroles, moulds, carafes, jugs, glasses, scales, racks, jars, smokers, skillets, trivets and steamers. Possibly even an asparagus kettle.

And, additionally, we had scented candles, fat cushions, paper lanterns, Braun electrical appliances and fishermen's chairs from the Ligurian coast. These last had a red lacquer frame and a rush seat. A writer from *Design* magazine quizzed me if they were not, in fact, copies of Marino Morosini's Modello 115 chair, the one designed for a golf club near Como, but no, I said. It was Morosini himself who had copied the fishermen of Chiavari who sat dockside, their feet surrounded by nets, cleaning squid in exactly such chairs made by anonymous local artisans. I had seen them myself on a buying trip.

Then there was the party. To succeed, you do not need just a good idea, ambition and energy. You also need a very good accountant and very good public relations. And parties are always excellent public relations. A flower truck from Amsterdam was parked outside. And so too were two *camions* from Dehillerin in Les Halles, the source of our kitchenware. We borrowed a Citroën 2CV and a Citroën DS and parked them all in *enfilade*: so in this way a tin snail and a goddess were both in attendance at our opening. The waiters and waitresses were, naturally, in *bleu de travail* binmen's jackets. No one was certain if this was a shop, a warehouse, a theatre or a museum.

The Beatles came. And I knew that John Lennon's song 'Norwegian Wood' was about an unsatisfied lover's revenge-arson, in which the singer sets fire to a Scandinavian wood interior. These thoughts were on my mind as I approached him. I am not musical, but we could always discuss arson.

Offering a French ceramic Pernod ashtray from a teetering stack, when I saw him about to stub out a Gitane in an oiled oak salad bowl, he contemptuously said, 'Fucking posho twat!' before he even said hello. But then he always spoke like that. Mellowing a little, through squinty eyes, Lennon then offered, 'Your mate Paolozzi taught my pisshead mate Stuart Sutcliffe in Hamburg art school, you know.' Lennon refused the larrikin role his manager Brian Epstein had assigned him and I liked him for that.

Amusingly, Bridget Riley wore a Foale & Tuffin op-art trouser suit. So that was life imitating art imitating life. David Hockney came in very bright colours. The William Hickey diary in the *Rapid* spoke of 'celebrity being money in motion'. Tommy Nutter of Savile Row arrived wearing a boa of fuchsia-coloured ostrich feathers over his *pied-de-poule* Edwardian draped suit.

We had copied Nutter's Savile Row habit of attaching champagne bottles to the doorknobs with hot pink ribbon to advertise luxurious decadence within. There were top-drawer queers as well: Walter Biles brought an entire entourage. Cheri Stunt, obviously. I heard Dandy Kim Waterfield explaining his new Topless Miss World project to the photographer Terence Donovan. David Niven, Kingsley Amis, the Kray brothers, the Duke of Kent, Barbara Hulanicki and Lester Bookbinder were also there. Lester was the film-maker who said art direction is 'turning crap into mediocrity', which I think is what we very successfully did with our theatrical presentation of a red saveloy tin.

Since we had beautiful Braun record players on sale, the ones known as 'Snow White's Coffin', the designer Dieter Rams had flown in from Frankfurt. The several glasses of champagne he consumed at the party were clearly not his first drinks of the day. Rams was heard telling a confused reporter, '*Gutes Design muss wie der gute englische Butler sein.*' And then he backed into a good English butler in *bleu de travail* and spilled his tray of drinks.

Marino Morosini, seeing our flagrant copies of his wood-framed red lacquer and rush-seated Chiavari chair, was a little less pleased.

'*L'imitazione è una sincera forma di adulazione,*' he said, clapping his hands and not smiling at all. At the time, I had no idea how that reaction would return to haunt me.

Marion Foale was there in one of her own trouser suits. She was saying to a BBC reporter, 'I won a Blue Peter prize when it started on the telly. I told my parents I wanted to paint. And they said, "No you can't. You're a woman. You've got to get married and have babies. You can't go to college." So I said, "Blow it. I'm going."'

## a diet of coal and borscht

And then there were the suppliers. The people from Dehillerin, naturally. The trug and breadboard makers from the countryside. Italian coffee importers. The manufacturers of the foam we used in our upholstered furniture, the ticking makers. And best of all there was Varvara Woda from FSW, the Firma Szkliwa Warszawskiego: the Warsaw enamel company who supplied our blue and red tea and coffee pots.

Varvara was not at all what you might expect from a native diet of coal and borscht. She was one of the most beautiful women I have ever met, with skin like an apricot, a dimple in her chin and tumbling brown curls like a pre-Raphaelite angel. She smelt almost overwhelmingly of strong Communist soap, had huge eyes and an enchanting accent. Perfect teeth. This was a version of Socialist Realism that was extremely pleasing. She also wore immaculate white lace underwear, as I had discovered one afternoon when showing her our stock of dhurries and throws in the shop's attic.

........................................................................................................................

® *Rollo Pinkie: Eustace's modesty here is most uncharacteristic. He was a flagrant, resourceful, ruthless and selfish philanderer.*

Of course, I gave a speech.

'Retail is detail,' I declared. There was a ripple of note-taking. 'I am not so much a designer as an editor of merchandise.' I didn't say plagiarist and thief.

'There is a painting which I discovered in the Kunstmuseum in Basel by Joost van Gelder. It has always been an inspiration to me. "Still life" is too limited an expression. *Nature morte* even more so; I like my nature to be very lively indeed. But what you find in van Gelder is a sensuously peeled lemon, a handsome carafe, a dead rabbit or hare, a generous glass of wine, a loaf of bread, a carving knife and a lobster. Perhaps also an hourglass as a memento mori. But this is actually what *life* can be like. If you shop at Bleu de Travail you can live like a Dutch prince of the Golden Age. Making a home, making lunch, making dinner. These are forms of creativity available to everyone.'

Again, the press reaction was spectacular. 'Thanks to Eustace Dunne,' the *Daily Post* wrote, 'the asparagus kettle has been democratized.' Another headline: 'Smart Chicks and Binmen's Jackets: Dunne's Designs'. Someone picked up my line that 'The designer's job is not to see the world as it is, but to imagine it as it might be.'

The *Sunday Times* explained: 'Breadboards, pestles and mortars, wine racks are the routine impedimenta of happy wholesome marriage.' Ironic then that the last I heard from Beverley before the party was 'No, I am not coming to your bloody party. Do I want to be Mrs Dunne? No, I do fucking not. And I've got better things to do. First things first, second things never!' Then she slammed the door so hard the house shook.

A woman from *Le Figaro* (pleated skirt, V-neck cashmere, very evidently no bra, French bob) asked, '*Est-ce que le bon goût, votre magasin?*' Without hesitation I answered: '*Le bon goût fait ce que vous croyez. Peut-être que vous croyez en différentes choses pour moi.*'

## what's the point of a chicken?

Rollo Pinkie was in the audience and asked about our market. I told him: 'Students in the new universities who need to buy their own furniture now have somewhere to buy it.'

'What's the point of a chicken brick?' a difficult-looking woman demanded.

'What's the point of a chicken?' I retorted.

Quentin was there throughout. He did not speak to any journalists. In fact, I don't think he spoke to anyone. Out of the corner of my eye, I saw him and his cigar leave early through a side entrance.

I knew what was on his mind. He was scouting an original Friese-Greene cinema in Fulham, a tobacco warehouse in Bristol, an electrical substation on Tottenham Court Road, a defunct police station in Bromley, a shopping precinct in Cardiff, a Quaker meeting house in Plymouth and an 1870 Board School in Leeds. Then a Victorian chapel in Cheshire. Soon, the papers were saying, thanks to Eustace Dunne you could buy a newly democratized garlic press in Macclesfield. Making money out of having good taste would soon come to seem almost easy. Sometimes I feel guilty for never having thanked Quentin. At least, not while he was alive.

Like John Davidson, Quentin was what my other half would have called NQOTOPD, or Not Quite Our Type Of Person, Dear. But with him I felt a real camaraderie. I think this was because of his strong, not to say intractable, character. Perhaps because of his experience in Australia, Quentin completely lacked any inclination towards silly bullshit. He was completely straight. Sometimes uncomfortably so. And he had practical skills, which I confess were superior to mine. He could lay bricks blindfolded. Genius is of very little value without the power of execution and Quentin was my executive. So much so that we got to a point where it seemed he could almost read my mind. I never had to tell him what I wanted because he could anticipate it. And his tough, artisan style always worked well with the troops.

..................................................................................................

® *Rollo Pinkie: This is a rare confession of a failing on Eustace's part. I can add that the self-taught Quentin Huskisson was a much, much better cook than Eustace, who once tried to replicate Quentin's fresh calamari in raw tomato sauce and it was an abject calamity. Mention this to Quentin and he would simply grunt. And he was the only person I have ever met who smoked more than Eustace.*

The following day, I woke up with a pyrotechnical and hypoglycaemic hangover. I was sweating slightly, my mouth felt dry and tasted of incineration. My eyes were sensitive to light, a subtle creeping nausea inhabited the back of my throat and I was a little unsteady on the stairs, absolutely craving strong black coffee. And, crashing into a mannequin in an op-art summer frock, I started wondering what we should do next.

Then I remembered that I had asked John Lennon to come to stay with us at the weekend.

# 1965 – Tremors and oscillations

*'When I was younger, so much younger than today
I never needed anybody's help in any way.'*

John Lennon and Paul McCartney, 'Help', 1965

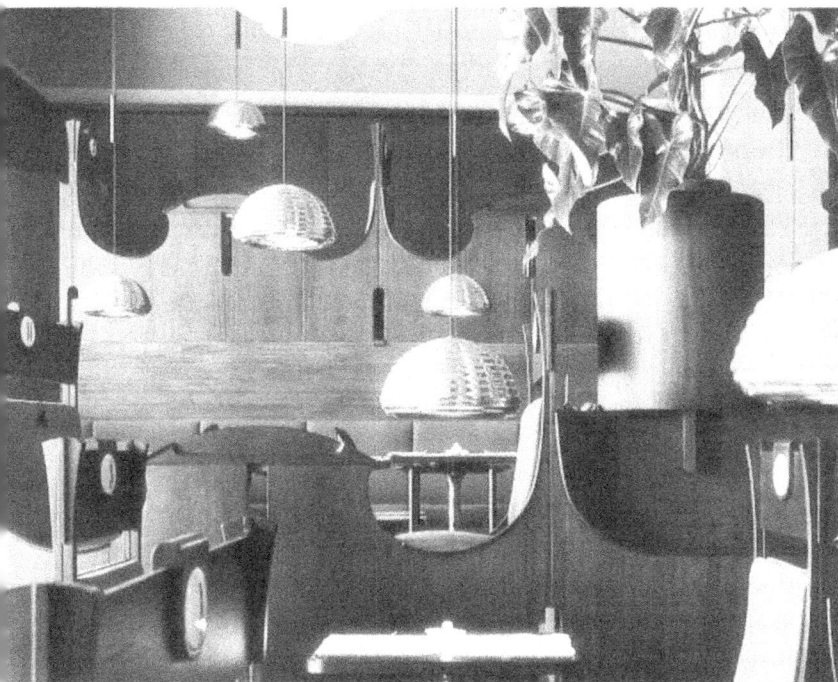

*Splügen Bräu, Milan.*

John Lennon never made that trip to the cottage. But instead I planned a trip to Milan. It turned out that the argumentative Beatle did not like being driven and that a helicopter offended in some obscure way the very approximate Buddhist principles he was cultivating. For my part, after the success of the Bleu de Travail opening in Chelsea, I wanted to begin a European adventure.

There was, I felt, certain business to be done with La Rinascente, the department store that – with its annual Golden Compass design awards, begun in 1954 – had made '*stile industria*' the expression of Italy itself. And I wanted to visit the Triennale, the irregular exhibition of art and design in the Parco Sempione.

Besides, I wanted to meet Gio Ponti, editor of *Domus*, and the designers Piero Fornasetti, Ercole Spada and Carlo Mollino, although the latter would require a side-trip to Turin. In any event, there was unfinished business with Marino Morosini, who had left the Bleu de Travail opening party muttering, '*L'uomo e un ladro! Copia tutto cio che vede!*', violently kicking one of my chairs across the room on his way out, something the gossip columnists happily missed since they had all left early to file their copy.

And then there was the Biffi restaurant in the Galleria, where everyone from Elizabeth David to Quentin agreed the white truffles from Alba were the very best. In order to impress, I had read and memorized the relevant passages in Mrs David's *Italian Food* before leaving London and was able to explain to anyone who looked even half curious that Milanese food tends to be white. *Risotto* is white. *Vitello* is white. The red tomato comes from the peasant south and is an unruly intruder here in the patrician north, a Lombard-Gothic city where people tend to formality. More German, perhaps, than Italian. In any case, who could not love a city where 'Gorgonzola', in fact a blue cheese, is a stop on Line 2 of the subway?

But I took a car, not the metro, to the hotel. In those days, you could hire an Alfa Romeo at the airport and I chose a lovely twin-cam Giulia Ti, painted a fine sky blue. It had cherry-coloured vinyl upholstery. Alfa was the car of Milan: its badge was the city's coat of arms. And I thought that 'Alfa Romeo' sounded more like an invitation to make love than the name of a vehicle manufacturer. If you had seen *Roman Holiday* and Gregory Peck's stylish handling of his Vespa, you'd understand the way Italians attack the streets.

It's only five kilometres from the airport to the Piazza del Duomo and that's not much more than five minutes if you are in the mood and the trams don't get in the way. After some amusing tyre squeal through the sombre streets, ignoring red lights in native fashion, I parked on via Manzoni and went straight into the Campari bar at the opposite end of the Galleria, facing the cathedral square.

This is an exquisite, tiny, very old bar with solemn, slow waiters in white bum-freezers serving perfect *aperitivos*, whatever the time of day. I liked it that Davide Campari himself had actually been born in the Galleria, adding extra authenticity to the experience. And, more darkly, that the architect of the Galleria, Giuseppe Mengoni, had died in a fall from the scaffolding during construction. As I sipped my third or fourth Campari, served with a spritz of soda and a twist of orange, I thought of these ghosts and of Mengoni's unfinished business. I made my plans and watched the richly plumaged *carabinieri* strut by. Quite literally, Milan's policemen have panache ... or feathers in their caps. And their uniforms, I am told, were designed by Valentino.

My plan was to use the wonderful new Splügen Bräu pub on Corso Europa as my headquarters. This was perhaps the most complete expression of design sensibility in all of Milan. Long before anyone had thought of the idea, it was a concept store. Much more than a pub or a shop, it was an engaging experience which demanded from visitors a sort of obeisance, but repaid them with lashings of acquired style.

Pub Splügen Bräu was the work of the Castiglioni brothers who had already distinguished themselves with a flair for magical improvisation that would not have shamed Marcel Duchamp at the very peak of his conceptual impertinence. For example: a chair using an agricultural tractor's seat. A floor lamp made from a lump of heavy, polished marble and off-the-shelf electrical conduit.

The brewery's name was cast in massive letters at right angles to the pavement. Inside, the Castiglionis spoke of 'scenography': they changed floor levels and used mirrors to create illusions of space. They were designers as film directors, using beer-drinking pub customers as actors on a stage.

## the man's a thief

It was in Splügen Bräu that I decided to meet Marino Morosini, a man who apparently still felt plagiarism was nearer to theft than to inspiration. As I was absently snapping some *grissini*, he strode in wearing a green loden coat (Schneider's of Salzburg, I imagine). That, and a double-knotted cashmere scarf in the bright red of the *vigili del fuoco* to match his fiery mood. He sat most deliberately and pointedly did not take his coat off.

'May I buy you a drink?' I asked, busily hiding my sketches at the same time. He said nothing, nodded just once and I waved at a waiter.

'*Due bicchiere de birrone di Chiavenna*,' I said and soon two handsome litre glasses were served us.

He took a draught, wiped his mouth with the back of his hand

and said, 'Mr Dunne, I think you are a thief. In fact, I know you are a thief. My Volcano di Stromboli chair won a gold medal at the Triennale and now without my permission we find copies of it in London.'

'If you'll allow me, Marino, you must not confuse inspiration with plagiarism. I am inspired by your designs and I simply want to bring a sense of your style to my customers in England.'

'But you pay me nothing!' he shouted and banged his glass on a Castiglioni table.

'Be reasonable, Marino. It's impossible to put a price on inspiration, you know.'

'You flatter me, but I would still like money. My reputation in London has been destroyed by your heartless copies.'

'That, Marino, is simply not true. We will *make* your reputation in London. But I will tell you what I will do. The chair will now be called the Morosini and I will give you a royalty of one pound on each chair we sell.'

'*Tentare non nuoce*,' he whispered, then stood and left.

And in this way, we acquired the masterpiece of Italy's leading designer without having to pay National Insurance contributions.

The next day I went to see Gio Ponti in the Torre Pirelli, Milan's sabre-thin first skyscraper, which he had designed. Its fridge-cool *modernismo* contrasted shockingly with the hot, mannered swagger of the Mussolini-era train station nearby.

I was there at Ponti's own invitation: he had invited me to discuss a future interview for *Domus*. His office was a design education in itself: the floor was the durable rubber Pirelli patent with round studs, intended for airports and subways, but soon becoming popular in fashionable houses. The room was lit by contrasting chandeliers: a series of Ponti's modernist designs made by Fontana Arte and more baroque designs in coloured glass for Venini.

After admiring the view, we sat on his signature Superleggera chairs, whose super-light design I thought, but did not say, was somewhat mannered and over-designed. An assistant served *espresso* in the tiny blue cups Ponti had recently designed for Alitalia. There were little *biscotti*. Ponti himself was in a nicely patinated Italian version of a *bleu de travail* work jacket, but wore a bow tie that changed the sense entirely. His wispy, white, all-over-the-place hair seemed to suggest an implicit cerebral energy.

'I advise you to look at my *Compasso d'Oro*,' he said in flawless, but heavily accented, English, referring to the Golden Compass design awards. 'You English, I feel, are too pragmatic. Enchantment is a useless thing ... but it is as indispensable as bread.' With great elegance, he offered me some more lightly sugared *biscotti*.

'Everything is going from the heavy to the light,' he continued. He quickly stood and, to demonstrate his point, lifted his chair with a single virtuoso hand. I asked if I could take a photograph and the resulting portrait became part of the great man's iconography.

He put the chair down then rearranged his wispy halo.

'Now, Mr Dunne. You are, I know, *fare onde* – how do you say? – "making waves" in London. I think we shall come to interview you. Perhaps in a gentlemen's club. I have heard such good reports of White's whose origins, I believe, lay with a certain Signor Blanco.' He made a cathedral of his hands.

'I think you'd prefer Whisky-a-Go-Go,' I suggested.

'Lucrezia will send a telex,' Ponti said. 'But before then, I have a proposal for tomorrow which I think you might find amusing. Perhaps you would like to meet Mies van der Rohe.'

## the Holy Redeeemer of domesticity

So the next day found me at noon in the Bar Basso on via Plinio, the place famous for creating the *negroni sbagliato* wherein prosecco replaced gin in the Campari and red vermouth cocktail. I felt I had to try one. In fact, I was able to try two because Ponti arrived forty minutes late, arm-in-arm with an elderly Mies, visiting Milan from Chicago for what would be the very last time. Brief pleasantries were exchanged between us and then Ponti explained: 'It is my pleasure to introduce the world's most famous architect, the last director of the Bauhaus, to London's most exciting shopkeeper, the first Holy Redeemer of domesticity. They say, Mr Dunne, you have brought the Bauhaus to the high street, so this introduction seems to me a good idea. Or, at least, appropriately symmetrical given your shared enthusiasm for clean lines.'

I did not know whether I was being flattered or patronized. I decided perhaps both.

'And we are going to drive to Pavia to visit the factory which makes my Superleggera chairs,' Ponti explained.

A navy-blue Lancia Flaminia presidenziale, a *sedanca de ville* limousine shared with the Pope, was waiting outside in the care of a grey-uniformed driver wearing sunglasses, even though it was an overcast day. Ponti and Mies sat in the back where the chairs had white linen antimacassars. I sat in the front with the uniformed staff, neatly indicating my status in this particular arrangement. Twenty minutes into the hour-long drive, I tapped on the glass division and suggested it might be a good idea for us to stop for lunch, which I offered to buy.

'No, no, no,' Ponti said, waving a hand dismissively. 'I have brought something. Look in the glovebox.'

I did, and found a packet of mints. I passed them to Ponti who shared them and, evidently, a private joke with Mies. We had no lunch and the journey continued in silence. Somebody later told me that Mies found Ponti 'bourgeois'.

Returning to the city after a factory tour, which Ponti and Mies had found consummately engaging, but I myself found dull, I asked to be dropped at the Piazza Diaz. On the fourteenth floor of a *grattacielo* was the Terrazza Martini. Here I went to consider my next explorations of Milan's design culture. The Terrazza Martini was a perfect venue for such a form of contemplation: *la dolce vita* aloft with an encompassing view of the entire city.

The next day I visited Piero Fornasetti, then living on a barge in the *Navigli*, Milan's canal zone, and not at the time the popular resort it was to become. At eleven in the morning, Fornasetti offered visitors a glass of port and a plate of Stilton cheese. He also offered lessons in optimum mastication of a cheese and wine mix, disgustingly illustrated with an open mouth. This was in deference to his English mother, although I feel he had misread English tradition.

Just as I had exploited illustrations from *Larousse* in L'Oignon Rouge, Fornasetti exploited nineteenth-century magazine illustrations in his designs, turning furniture into art with a mixture of pastiche, appropriation and collage. That same Lina Cavalieri could be found not only on furniture, but on a wheel of cheese, a clock, a commode, a platter and a leaf. '*Tema e Variazione*' he called it.

'Signor Fornasetti, you turn furniture into art,' I said, appropriating a line I had read in *Domus* and intending to flatter. 'You are well on the way to creating a complete universe to your own design.'

'Certainly,' he replied, waving a wooden toothpick as if it was a conductor's baton. 'Art takes us into imaginative worlds. Sometimes they are beautiful too. But I feel an essential part of beauty is that it cannot be explained. I am, you see, a stickler for details who loves uncertainty.'

Fornasetti offered me a Lina Cavalieri platter with little trapezoids of cold, griddled polenta, a slice of pickled porcini on top of each one. 'Salvation is in the imagination,' he said. 'If I were a government minister, I would set up a hundred schools of imagination in Italy.'

'Maybe one day you would help me start just a single one in England,' I suggested, leaving the matter hanging and my eyebrows arched.

I left the barge with an agreement that I would have exclusive Fornasetti distribution rights in England.

And then I drove the Alfa very quickly to Terrazzano di Rho, to meet Ercole Spada, the most exciting car designer at work in Milan. Out in the north-west, Spada's employer was the coachbuilding firm Zagato, one of the grand old *carrozzerie*, which, quite literally, had their origins in the days when inspired artisans and practical artists, metal-bashers and errant sculptors turned the old horse-drawn carriages into rolling sculpture. Phaeton, limousine, *berlinetta* and *spyder* all became types of car, but these names had their origin in the carriage trade.

## massimo edonismo

I found Spada in a huge, silent drawing office where very fine Venetian blinds diffused the light. He was a slim man with an enormous Roman nose, slicked hair and crocodile shoes, a cornflower blue shirt with a black silk knitted tie. No jacket. He smoked coarse black tobacco Nazionali cigarettes continuously. Along one wall, an enormous 1:1 outline – using sticky tape – of what would become a Lancia Flaminia Super Sport whose subtle radii Spada was defining using classic wooden French curves.

His own workstation was a six foot wide, parallel-action drawing board with layer upon layer of grid-patterned overlays. Overhead hung vast grey enamelled metal reflectors. It was one of the most beautiful places I had seen since school. And Spada, juggling a French curve, told me: '*Una macchina è emozione. Una bella macchina è massimo edonismo. Assoluta!*' I remembered these lines for the meeting I had scheduled the next month with Land Rover in Solihull.

## only here for the women

I met Enzo Apicella at the Furniture Fair. Apicella was making a name for himself in London with his cool, modern interiors for Pizza Express. These included the branch in Fulham Road where Eduardo Paolozzi had painted idiosyncratic murals in exchange for a lifetime's supply of margaritas. He spoke perfectly good English, but in Milan had gone native so asked me in his hoarse and mischievous Italian, '*Sei qui per le donne?*' (Are you here for the women?).

Feigning a sort of outrage, I priggishly replied, '*No. Sono qui per la salone del mobile.*'

Apicella, who liked puns and wordplay, promptly replied, '*Ah! La donna e mobile,*' which was to be heard, translated either as 'woman and furniture' or the famous 'woman-is-fickle' aria from *Rigoletto*. I rolled my eyes.

And I met Massimo Vignelli at the Triennale. Vignelli was working on the signs for the New York subway, cleaning the infernal guts of Manhattan by the application of a crisp Helvetica font. I introduced myself and he told me, in American English, 'If you can design one thing, you can design anything.' I was not at all sure this was true, but it was a line worth remembering.

Back at the Grand Hotel et de Milan, I went straight to the *jardin d'hiver* for a drink. Some of the ferns looked as though they dated from 1867, like the hotel itself. Here guests were promised '*tutto lo charme del passato, discrete e raffinate.*'

'Alfa Romeo,' I said to one of the etiolated ferns in front of the mirror-backed bar. I said it again, a little more loudly.

The woman on the adjacent stool turned. 'Excuse me?'

'The words sound so beautiful,' I explained winningly. 'Just like an invitation to make love. Can I buy you a drink?'

'Certainly. But it might annoy my husband,' she countered. 'I'll have a large Cutty Sark straight up. He won't be here for five minutes. And tell me, what do you do? I'm a professor of law at Bocconi University.'

'Damn, I'm a designer,' I said, adding, 'and I thought seduction was Italy's national dish.'

'Not on the menu today, sweetheart. And please don't give me that Verdi and Giordano shit.'

She twirled her glass with what I wanted to see as suggestiveness. Her husband arrived, stooped and assisted by an ebony cane. He must have been eighty.

Back in my room, I rang for room service, using the thick, crimson silk cord by the side of my bed. Outside were muffled sounds of traffic. A maid soon arrived and, together with the pot of coffee I had ordered, presented me with a package that had been waiting at reception.

Indicating she should wait, I opened the heavy brown paper envelope. Inside, an edition of Ludovico Vicentino Arrighi's *La Operina* of 1522. This was the book that had taught me my handwriting: that expressive italic style which Arrighi called 'chancery cursive' and had been adopted by most of the world's architects and designers in their various and doomed bids for self-identity.

With it, a note on a stiff card with 'MARINO MOROSINI' engraved in black grotesque. And in his spidery handwriting it said:

'You will see that this edition of Arrighi is in fact a worthless facsimile. Inspiration, you might say. Meet me at noon tomorrow at the grave of the sculptor Medardo Rosso in the Cimitero Monumentale. VM.'

The next day at eleven fifty-five, I parked the Alfa among the taxis and buses crowded at the Cimitero's main gate. The Rosso tomb was easy to find, since an autograph statue of an artist, sculpted as if drowning in veils, was an element of the design.

And here too was Morosini in his green loden coat and fireman's red scarf, sucking hard on a filthy Nazionali. I handed him an envelope containing five million lire. He handed me a pigskin attaché case containing drawings for chairs, desks and lights.

For a trifling sum, I had acquired the rights to a substantial part of what the world identified as 'Italian design'. I don't think Morosini was very pleased with this transaction, but, then, I don't think he was ever pleased with very much at all.

................................................................................................................................

® *Rollo Pinkie: This was a typical Eustace deal. Unscrupulous, brilliant and self-serving. He could now claim to be a patron of Italian design.*

I cancelled the plan to see Carlo Mollino in Turin. There was enough to do already.

## winging it

That afternoon I met Quentin at Milan's Linate airport, returning to London after some busy days. Or attempting to return. The hot, still, damp air did not suggest the possibility of movement.

Linate had history going back to Enrico Forlanini, one of Italy's aviation pioneers who had devised this idea of *Aeropittura*: aeronautical art in the Futurist manner, inspired by the string and cloth planes of the Wright brother's era. And conditions in the Vespucci lounge had not changed much since those distant days of farting engines, canvas, glue and string, when pilots dressed like the *Savoia Cavalleria*, in leather coats and flapping silk scarves, lurched through the sky no more than a hundred feet from the ground.

The style, if there was one, was Futurist, although Quentin said the upholstered chairs in pistachio and tangerine were by Marco Zanuso, now making his reputation in *Domus* and the other Milan architecture magazines. I roughly sketched them on a paper napkin. Anyway, few things date more quickly than visions of the future. On the whole, Rome's 'La Dolce Vita' style had not yet reached Milan's airport.

When we arrived after a spirited drive in a twin-choke-carburettor Fiat 1500 taxi, which ignored red lights with vivid contempt, the first thing we had heard over the crackling tannoy was, '*Tutti i voli sono cancellati*', but that was familiar at Linate where the discipline of air traffic controllers and ground-handling personnel was, at best, relaxed.

That was two hours ago and we had since been comforting ourselves with *caffè corretto*, that magical elixir favoured by travelling Italian businessmen everywhere from Bergamo to Reggio. Those handsome men, slumped in conversation at railway buffets or airport lounges, are not sipping mere *espresso*, although they are content to be thought to be doing so. Instead, their coffee has been 'corrected' with a generous splash of grappa or Vecchia Romagna brandy. Thus, in an entirely Italian way, exhilaration was potently tranquillized.

On the flight, there was a shudder of turbulence as we climbed over Monte Bianco. The cabin lights flickered and we were on our second whisky. I had had to explain to Quentin that it was common to say 'Scotch'. A trolley rattled and we were served gammon and pineapple with a carafe of Châteauneuf-du-Pape. A pink linen napkin was folded to resemble a swan.

Chewing, I said, 'Do you know, my father once asked me whether I wanted to be a captain or a sailor. I don't see much of myself in him, I have to say. I acquired some habits of mind from him, but he led a messy life. He seemed to enjoy chaos, whereas I rather like tidying up. I used to feel troubled by him, but now I don't think I care. To be honest, since I stopped thinking about him, I feel much better. He was once a huge presence for me, but now his moment in my life seems very remote.'

The plane thumped, the red wine spilled and I knew I was telling a terrible, destructive lie.

# 1968 – Invention of the scented candle

*'Two possibilities exist: either we are alone in the Universe or we are not. Both are equally terrifying.'*

Arthur C. Clarke, *2001: A Space Odyssey*, 1968

*Sad semi-detached houses.*

Quentin and I often used to have our meetings in The Connaught hotel, a fortress of burnished privilege with red brick, stone dressings, dark wood, brass (polished hourly by Filipinos) and stained glass gathered together in the heart of old Mayfair. It was where visiting old money came to spend itself. Of course it was incongruous for people like us, but I liked the way the doormen called me 'sir'.

At five o'clock on a weekday afternoon, the bar was more or less deserted. The atmosphere was clubby: wood panels, more polished brass, heavy drapes, bevelled glass and deep, somnolent red plush. A hideous, floral carpet was there to make the artistically sensitive or socially maladroit feel seasick. With every visit, I refreshed my sense of outrage.

Quentin often asked me why I saw no inconsistency between a professional advocacy of democratic clean lines and no fuss with a personal preference for old-fashioned luxury, servants, over-stuffing and velour. I explained that being concerned about hypocrisy was a puerile temptation.

A memory of many cigars lived on here in an ineradicable fug of expensive smokiness. The empty bar contained only a sense of absence, of tycoons past. I had a tumbler of whisky and it was not my first of the day. Quentin was on his fourth dry martini. There had been many afternoons like this.

A pyramid of half-smoked Havanas was in a heavy glass ashtray, a dog-eared and torn paper book of Georges V matches beside it, a Paris trophy.

## the disobliging Rollo

We were here to meet Rollo Pinkie. My school friend was establishing himself as the country's senior commentator on architecture and design. Superior, well-informed and ever so slightly bitchy. And Rollo was the author of a recent disobliging profile of me. It had been a sort of personal memoir, a where-are-they-now account of his young contemporaries from school.

> *Eustace Dunne was not intellectually inquisitive. In fact, he was intellectually lazy and complacent. Nevertheless – by a mysterious process I never fully understood – he always had privileged access to what was new. It was a sixth or seventh sense. There were always annoying boys at school like that, the ones who got the jokes, the shirts, the records – or the girls – first. With Eustace, people never quite knew whether to envy, admire or hate him for his easy success. Perhaps all three.*
>
> Rollo Pinkie, *The Architectural Review*, February 1968

Rollo walked in, affecting slight bemusement to demonstrate his amazing worldliness and refinement. Desert boots, black corduroy trousers and a black leather jacket did not win him access to the bar. The conservative Connaught dress code required a tie, but he was not wearing a garment with a collar. He was wearing an aubergine polo neck sweater, which hotel officials now accessorized with a stained Hermès tie, pressed upon him from the concierge's collection. He looked ridiculous.

Quentin and I half rose.

'Hello, Rollo. Our recent Italian trip was *exceptionally* rewarding,' I said, drawing out the 'exceptionally' while lowering my gaze and gesturing to a waiter at the same time. More drinks. 'We thought you might like to know something of our future plans.'

Rollo adjusted his stained tie. Knowing he would report to his readers in full, since costume revealed the soul of its wearer, I had dressed for the occasion. A double-breasted Prince of Wales check two-piece suit, a very bright white cotton shirt, a red silk tie with white spots and a matching pocket square, insouciantly ruffled. Dougie Hayward's shop was, after all, just down the road in Mount Street. The cufflinks were beautifully simple silver dumb-bells. I had left my fine hair in a bit of a mess to convey insouciance.

I liked to think this was a dandyish presence, but masculine nonetheless. On my wrist was a handsome Breguet Roman duo-dial watch on a fine black leather strap. I had decided this was not a Rolex or a Cartier occasion: something more equivocal (and more expensive) was called for.

Quentin was slumped and looking grumbly in his familiar battered chalk-stripe, under which he wore a round-neck woollen jumper with a shirt and tie beneath. Like Gianni Agnelli, he made a bit of a thing about the cuffs. But Quentin's were frayed and rolled over the sleeves of his suit, not artfully undone like the Italian's.

A grovelling waiter arrived.

'My friend here will have . . . Actually what will you have, Rollo? Chablis? Yes. A glass of the Christian Moreau Clos des Hospices? You know they make it with old pre-phylloxera vines and use paraffin heaters in the vineyards to protect against frost?'

Rollo said he did not, but found it very interesting nonetheless. When the waiter brought the tray, I snatched the glass and held it up to the fading light indicating, or so I intended, my deep appreciation of wine.

'My good friend Christian's house is one of the finest in all Burgundy: it is older even than the Hospices de Beaune. Wonderful little turrets and polychrome roof-tiles.' I made an illustrative hand gesture. 'I like the idea of God's Hospital. Good name for a restaurant, when you come to think about it. When I visited, Christian gave me a set of copper chafing dishes and four brace of ortolans. The man is *hallucinant!*'

'Delicious,' Rollo offered, sniffing and then sipping the Chablis. And struggling, I thought, a little for effect, added, 'I am sure you know James Thurber's line, "It's a naive domestic Burgundy without any breeding, but I think you'll be amused by its presumption." But there's nothing naive here at all, apart, that is, from me,' he added, unnecessarily.

Completely ignoring this effortful tilt at erudition, I prepared to make a speech. I coughed and swirled my glass.

What was in my mind was a way to enlarge my territory and to make more money from selling my taste. It was all about scale. We were no longer just designing packaging and chairs or selling pots: the Dunne name would soon annex graphics, furniture, products, interiors and retail. And everyone was going to be a client, Her Majesty included.

'Our workshops are doing well,' I began. 'The shop is doing extremely well. But I feel we could be doing more. People want to buy our designs, but there's a limit to what we can sell. Retail is very restricting. Of course, Bleu de Travail can grow. And it will. Quentin, bless, is already looking for sites in Cardiff, Bristol and Plymouth. But I want to sell ideas as well as furniture. I want to have an agency, a consultancy. I'm fed up with doing small graphics jobs for clients who don't know what they want. Just the other day, we did some packaging proposals for a perfumier who said she liked peacocks. She even showed us Polaroids of her awful flock of ghostly turquoise shitting things, or whatever the collective noun for peacocks might be. A plumage, I suppose.'

Rollo nodded.

'So we used peacocks as a decorative motif on her horrible boxes of foul scent, moisturizer, foundation and deodorant. And then she rejected the work. So I had to scream at her, "But you told me you *liked* bloody peacocks!"'

Rollo laughed, although he did not look as though he thought it very funny.

'We want to get to the stage where we move beyond servicing any client's poorly thought-out whim. We want to get to the stage where we realize possibilities beyond any client's imagination. We don't want to work for other people, realizing their dreams. We want to realize our own.'

In conversations like these, I always found the first person plural a helpful rhetorical device.

'There are advertising agencies. There are public relations consultancies. There are accountancy practices. There are legal firms. Why not a design agency, a design consultancy or a design practice? We could do more than sell Italian beanbag chairs to students or French casseroles to Chelsea housewives. We could sell "design" itself to Marks & Spencer and Land Rover. We could sell design to the fucking Queen!'

A second glass of Chablis arrived. Rollo Pinkie had just witnessed, and would soon report on, the conception, trouble-free gestation and entirely painless birth of The Dunne Design Group. And I had asked him to help. Keep your enemies close!

His article was published two days later.

*No one ever accused Eustace Dunne of modesty. But then no one else has troubled to drag the Britain of brown moquette and stale air into the twentieth century with quite so much style and vigour. Sometimes it seems like a single-minded obsession. And to hear it from Dunne, you can be persuaded that it is. But the Buddha himself would never have acquired so many followers without religious commitment. And that's what you sense in conversation with Eustace Dunne. That felt-tip pen he plays with in conversation is an instrument of liberation:*

*his designs will free us from drudgery. He wants to democratize
pleasure and he finds pleasure in the execution of everyday things.
Dunne is a man who has never drunk instant coffee and wants you
to join him. And you can, but only if you buy a French press from his
booming Bleu de Travail stores. And now, you don't have to be in
Chelsea to do so. Watch out Nottingham and Skelmersdale! A store
will be opening near you soon. With Eustace Dunne, zeal is the deal.
But now, Dunne is moving beyond sexy furniture and trendy shops.
He wants to apply the same revolutionary vision to British businesses
and British institutions.*

........................................................................................................

® *Rollo Pinkie: I remember this encounter and the resulting article very well and
how queasily uncomfortable I felt. Eustace was rich and had acquired that extra
dimension of easy confidence that being rich brings. Could I say no to his offer? Of
course I could. Might I have bargained harder? Probably not. I could not say that I
liked what my schoolfriend had become, but I respected his achievement, as well as
his inextinguishable confidence and his belief in 'progress'. It annoyed me that his
lazy intellect never allowed self-criticism, but redesigning the world seemed an interesting task.*

## a democracy of talent

There would have to be premises for the new design business. Soho
was no longer all sex shops and gunrunners, Maltese loan sharks and
Albanian hustlers, Chinese herbalists, drifters, Portuguese pimps,
desperate transvestites and laboured 'characters' drunk in loud suits.
It had now become Adland, with Wardour Street a strange Madison Avenue in miniature. Not perhaps so glamorous, certainly not
architecturally, but just as busy with its runners, Italian restaurants,
black cab accounts and air of sordid prosperity.

This was my plan. The advertising agencies made Soho a hybrid culture of posh boys slumming it and barrow boys gentrifying themselves: a real East End boys meet West End girls theatre. And all of them knee-deep in money. But The Dunne Design Group was to be different, idealistic even. I wanted a democracy of talent. The Dunne Design Group would be the first professional refuge for the many bright art students who were presently directionless and unemployed. There would be good coffee, flowers, art on the walls, real towels and proper soap in the loos. And every detail would speak quality. The studio and its people would be a permanent advertisement for a world made better by design, a unique vision which had been granted as one of the many natural, possibly even supernatural, privileges I enjoyed. Or so I told myself.

'It will be as the Bauhaus should have been,' I told Quentin. 'But the problem with Walter Gropius is that he was very dull.'

'How exactly can you claim to know that?' Quentin asked.

'Tell me three funny Walter Gropius stories,' I demanded.

## fighting bullshit

And this new studio would be in Soho's neighbour, Covent Garden, *terra incognita* to most of us. If we thought of anything, we thought of *Pygmalion*. The old fruit and vegetable market out, but no one had yet moved in. Studio space in crowded and expensive Soho could now only ever be acquired by Quentin's 'Jewish Lightning', creating property vacancies where none had hitherto existed.

But Covent Garden had cavernous abandoned warehouses with pretty loading bays, cobbled streets and low rents. Quentin may have been adept with his mystery propellants and murderous accelerants, but they were not necessary here. The fruit and vegetable market had succumbed to market forces.

The new building was in Alleyn's Rents, a narrow cut between

Garrick Street and Bow Street. It had once been frantic with seedy pubs and busy brothels serving the voracious market trade with beer and clap, but was now mostly lifeless and derelict. The day after our meeting at The Connaught, I drove Quentin there for a site visit in my new Lamborghini, a happy by-product of the recent visit to Italy. I liked how Ferruccio Lamborghini had so recently created an impertinent start-up, a calculated affront to the established and magnificent Ferrari. Rod Stewart kept one in a garage at his house near Totteridge: it was painted the same yellow as his bottle-blond hair.

And when the importer had explained that all Lamborghinis were named after fighting bulls, I liked them even more: a Miura being a specially large and truculent *toro bravo* from the province of Seville. Mine was in a bellicose tangerine.

Parking in Alleyn's Rents and causing an obstruction, I took a moment to stroke the central instrument binnacle, a violently projecting trapezoid covered in delicate black suede, with just the lightest suggestion of padding beneath.

'Absolutely gorgeous, don't you think?'

Quentin scowled.

The shopfitters were at work as we marched up the stairs. Quentin had designed an impressive reception desk in ash, with his signature bull's nose moulding. It was lit from above by recessed downlighters. In the vast studio upstairs, four rows of twenty reflectors, very similar to those in Splügen Bräu, defined the ceiling. New galvanized ventilation trunking was left exposed. The brick had been cleaned and the once rough wooden floor sanded and waxed.

My new desk was designed as a statement. And that statement was: 'This is design.' In a glass cubicle at the far end of the studio, it was given the status of a sacrificial altar. A piece of limed oak nearly the size of a ping-pong table was supported by legs of perforated metal which looked like the hidden spars in an aircraft's wings.

There were two task-lights and a piece of grey Welsh slate, a welcome gift from the adman David Abbott. It had engraved on it a line from the Canadian humorist Stephen Leacock, cut in Bodoni: 'Advertising is the science of arresting human intelligence long enough to get money from it.'

'Let that,' I said, tapping my Pentel marker on the slate, 'be an inspiration to all of us.' Adding *sotto voce*, but meaning to be heard: 'Especially our accountant.'

And I decided to hire Rollo Pinkie, partly to discourage his very well-informed, but persistently sour, commentary, but also because I wanted a writer and a communicator, an intellect, in our democracy of talent.

Rollo presented himself in my office late afternoon just two days after I had called him with the hint of a proposition. He was looking amused and confident, always more agreeable in person than in print. I offered and he accepted a generous glass of whisky.

'I really do think, Rollo, that you should come to work with us. I'll be extremely happy if you continue your own writing. And I will give you an office of your own. We can work on books together. Articles too. And our catalogues. There may even be other forms of writing we haven't thought of yet. I think, for example, one day we might start our own advertising agency.'

Rollo smiled and nodded. 'Thirty thousand?'

I frowned and said nothing.

Two weeks later, he moved into Alleyn's Rents. From these campaign headquarters, we attacked the whole country.

Rollo immediately ghosted a fifteen-hundred-word article under my name. This was eagerly accepted by the *Protector*, where 'I' described the lacklustre character of the high street that was crippling the economy and compromising the life of our cities. Once in print, this was an ideal calling-card, sent out to every managing director of every chain of stores in the country, with an engaging covering letter which I signed 'Eustace'.

In this way, our first meeting looking for new business was at Marks & Spencer in its Baker Street fastness, a building whose character was somewhere between Soviet and Presbyterian, but decisively neither. This was a middle-England untouched by sex, pop or style. It was the uniform of real virgins from Surbiton.

The lobby here was populated by hopeful souls seeking benediction, as if Dante had imagined a circle of Purgatory reserved for the retail trade. There were suppliers with crates of oranges on their laps, live chickens in cages, bolts of cloth and knitwear. Given the nod by a munificent Marks & Spencer buyer, the suppliers of oranges, chickens, cloth and knitwear would make a fortune.

## middle-aged England

In its way, a visit to Marks & Spencer had an equivalence to an audience with the Queen. But, equal and opposite to the chance of preferment, there was the hellish prospect of rejection, and the ruin it implied. This made the air brittle. The atmosphere was tense, but I was oblivious of the feelings of others. Striding up to reception, I thumped Morosini's pigskin attaché case on the counter, smiled broadly and said, 'Eustace Dunne for Sir Peter Pilsbury.'

The receptionist was about to say, 'Let me see if he's available' but got only as far as 'Let' before I said, 'Actually, we'll go straight up.' I had called Pilsbury yesterday to fix the meeting.

'Time spent in reconnaissance is never wasted,' I said to Quentin, who had heard it before. This line he knew I had lifted from my friend Jocelyn Stevens, proprietor of *Queen* magazine, a man with officer bearing who had spent time in the army.

Pilsbury did not have officer bearing. He was a tall, balding, puffy, red-faced, white-haired man with that very smooth, baby-like skin which celibate priests often acquire. His fingernails were just that little bit too long, his handshake fat and wet.

'Tell me, Mr Dunne, what it is we can do for you,' he said through pursed lips. 'We seem to have been doing quite well without you.' He smiled acidly.

'It's actually more a matter of what we can do for you,' I said brightly. 'Beginning, perhaps, by letting us design you out of this pit of mediocrity you've dug for yourself. Has anyone ever told you that the problem with mediocrity is that it recognizes no level higher than its own? How do you expect anyone to have an appetite for buying Marks & Spencer food if they have to traipse through an ocean of dreary knickers and bras before they find the *patisserie*? And, as for the knickers and bras, they should have a fuckability even without the tits and the arse in them. And to be absolutely honest with you, Peter, fuckability is a quality they most certainly do not have. Actually, it's a quality Marks & Spencer does not have.'

Pilsbury looked both grotesquely pained and intensely curious. 'And what is it you propose, Mr Dunne?'

'So glad you asked. I'll tell you exactly what,' I said. 'For a budget of £100,000, we will redesign the ground floor of your Oxford Street flagship store. We will modernize your trademark. "St Michael" sounds like a leprosy charity or a failing church. People don't want to spend money in a church. Or catch leprosy. Most disagreeable. And we will redesign your bestselling lingerie, making it sexy, not just serviceable. When I see a woman undress, I want to think about my mistress, not my grandmother.'

Then I flipped open the attaché case, produced a sheaf of architectural renderings, sketches of a new M&S logo, a non-disclosure agreement and a contract in triplicate. All had been prepared the night before.

'I'll need to discuss this with my board,' Pilsbury said in a tone of voice that conceded he really did need to do no such thing.

## a successful Riviera thief

The next day we visited Hawker Siddeley in Hatfield, with much the same combative style.

Hawker Siddeley was the successor to the legendary aircraft manufacturer de Havilland and occupied its original, magnificent art deco factory. But the de Havilland name had now disappeared, even if its handsome planes will never be forgotten. It all spoke of a fading grandeur. On the way to the meeting, we stopped at the famous Comet Hotel, once again more exuberant art deco. Its plan form was based on an aeroplane and a model of the record-breaking Comet stood outside on a pylon, with decorations sculpted by the war artist, Eric Kennington.

My costume for the day was designed for success: a white mac, black drainpipe trousers, a white French-cuffed shirt, sky-blue silk tie and white shoes. I looked like a Riviera thief, and a successful one at that.

We were given lunch in the boardroom. The dining table had a glass top and was lit from above by a magnificent art deco luminaire in chrome and frosted glass. Framed on the walls were certificates celebrating de Havilland's success in the Schneider Trophy and various round-the-world air races.

Just audible from outside was the noise of machine-tools at work on the shop floor, three axis lathes from Cincinnati and the country's very first computer numerically controlled mills, imported from the US. In an act of defiant, calculated insularity, we ate Scotch eggs, York ham and Caerphilly cheese. There were bread rolls that exploded into powder, German wine, dull wax-coated fruit and evil, thin black coffee from a plastic Thermos.

The managing director explained to us that Hawker Siddeley's new project was the HS125, Britain's first 'business jet'. Just as he was beginning to discuss Mach numbers, specific fuel consumption and stall characteristics, I interrupted and said: 'My dear fellow, this is all very well, but the businessmen who are actually going to pay for this aeroplane do not care about aeronautics. In fact, I'd go so far as to say that they do not give a flying fuck.' I paused for laughter, but there was none. 'Anyway, they are no more interested in Mach numbers than a writer is interested in the chemical composition of ink. They want a working environment. But they also want the cognizance of pleasure. Their reference points are not wind tunnels, but the great hotels and restaurants of the world. They want Cannes, Nassau, New York and Paris. Not, if you will excuse me for saying so, a shop floor or lab in suburban St Albans.'

I paused and eyed the table. 'When I buy *my* HS125, the interior will not look like a municipal bus. It will look like a *club privé*, a casino or the boardroom of an extremely exclusive Swiss bank. There will be soft beige leather, light Norwegian wood, mood lighting and luxurious carpet. In my HS125, you will not want your journey to end. Gentlemen, what do you think?'

The gentlemen mumbled amongst themselves and agreed that The Dunne Design Group should create a mock-up business jet interior in time for the imminent Le Bourget air show. Hands were shaken and a little bit of drabness retreated from British life.

We drove back to London down the A1, the Lamborghini howling like an angry bull tormented by picadors. We passed the spot where the horn player Dennis Brain crashed his Triumph TR2 one wet night. Quentin mentioned this, but my mind was elsewhere: a cigarillo would not fit in the cigarette lighter, an atrocious design fault, I said, so I asked Quentin to light my Phillies with a match.

I inhaled and confessed. 'You know Beverley was only ever a starter wife?' I changed noisily from fourth to fifth and the Lamborghini shimmied as I accelerated hard. 'After we married, I never really slept with her at all. Mark Boxer told me it's very bad manners to sleep with anyone fewer than three times. And I hate being bad mannered, except when it's deliberate. Did I tell you she's Jewish? I know what an anti-Semite is. An anti-Semite is someone who hates Jews more than is necessary.'

I changed gear.

'I'll tell you what.' I wagged my cigarillo and looked sideways at him as we overtook a Commer van at improvident speed. We were on the crest of the road. 'After an extremely promising start, Beverley lost interest in love-making and preferred looking at the ceiling. Instead of sweet nothings, all I ever got was, "Be quick, no kissing and don't sweat." So I'm getting divorced. I suggest you do too.'

Beverley was interviewed about our separation in *Novelty*, the high-concept journal of sixties and seventies style where nudity – meaning psychological exposure as well as posing with no clothes on – seemed an editorial compulsion and, therefore, attracted many voyeuristic readers too fastidious to buy pornography. The interview, intended to fan the early flames of the second wave of feminism, was illustrated with a picture of the two of us (actually fully clothed) in the E-Type on King's Road. It was a touching image, but Beverley's tone in the interview was notably unsentimental. She accused me of systemic misogyny, bigotry, knuckle-dragging sexism, gender imperialism, sexual colonialism, male supremacist fantasies, grasping selfishness, warped egomania, a dirty mind and a crude but all-embracing insensitivity. This was fair enough. She added that I was 'careful' with money and, for extra effect, that the size of my penis did not match the size of my ego. Despite *Novelty*'s encouragement of sexual frankness, she neither flattered nor condemned my bedroom performance. Of course, this silence was intended to be cruel. As she had confessed at the outset, Beverley was not nice.

Exasperated, I waved the cutting at Rollo in our weekly meeting when we surveyed recent press coverage. I said, 'I suppose I should never have told all those people that the only way to stop a Jewish woman fucking you is to marry her.'

Rollo winced and said, 'Please don't say that. I've asked her to marry me.'

## you are the Spitfire of agriculture!

Our next new business meeting was at Earl's Court for the Motor Show. On display were Vauxhall Crestas and Sunbeam Rapiers, Ford Corsairs and the new Austin 1800. But what I most admired was the Peugeot 404 Familiale, a seven-seater estate car that combined a nice utilitarianism with seductive French chic.

Quentin whispered that the body had, in fact, been designed by Pininfarina, an Italian, but I was never one to let dismal facts get in the way of strongly held opinion. The Peugeot, I insisted, was Frenchness incarnated: 'The perfect car for driving down the tree-lined N7 in that marvellous gap between lunch and the *cinq-à-sept*. Or if you cannot wait until five o'clock, I note that the rear deck is extremely capacious when the seats are folded flat. You could very easily do a *deux-à-quatre*.'

But my real target was elsewhere: the Land Rover stand where we had an appointment with the chief designer, a sober individual with pipe, tweed jacket and maroon cardigan. The Series II was a new product and its virtues were demonstrated with black and white photographs of cars crossing ploughed fields and hauling themselves up riverbanks with the help of winches.

'Have you,' I asked the man with the pipe, 'any idea how very dull your stand is? Do you really think your customers here are interested in pictures of mud in Norfolk? Your customers are global. They work in deserts and snowfields and Alps, not in the one-eyed fucking fens. Your stand here says nothing about your values or beliefs. It only says Land Rover is boring machinery. But you are so very much more! You are Britishness! The Queen drives a Land Rover! You are the Spitfire of agriculture! Your customers are not wall-eyed, incestuous Welsh hill farmers, but citizens of the world. And I think your motor show stand should say that.'

And next year it did: Land Rover gave us a five-year contract to design all their motor show stands. What good they did for Land Rover is perhaps hard to measure, but these served as useful advertisements for Dunne in Frankfurt, Paris, Geneva, New York and Tokyo, where we were careful to invite our own prospective clients as well as mere Land Rover customers.

A press conference was arranged in Alleyn's Rents to announce the new business wins of The Dunne Design Group and the continued growth of the Bleu de Travail shops. Eventually, this became an annual review, a calendar item in the diaries of admiring journalists. Rollo Pinkie was commissioned to write the very first press release:

### Dunne Design: from nylon knickers to titanium aerospace.

*In its first year Eustace Dunne's new design consultancy has won substantial business from Marks & Spencer, Hawker Siddeley and Land Rover. The style that made Bleu de Travail a shopping sensation is now at work for British commerce. Expect a revolution on the high street, in the air and on the farm.*

Forty journalists were gathered in the graphics studio at the top of the building at breakfast time. There were French press coffee-makers with aromatic grinds from the Algerian Coffee Store on Old Compton Street. There were croissants I had bought first thing from Harrod's, bagels were delivered on a bike from Brick Lane, with lox from Forman's. Cartons of filthy pasteurized supermarket orange juice had been surreptitiously decanted into Bleu de Travail enamel jugs to disguise its character and source.

Terri McGonagal of the *Protector* asked: 'Eustace, isn't this all just posh? Your French coffee? Your smoked salmon? Aren't you just a snob?'

'Not at all,' I replied. 'I'm not a snob. I just enjoy the best.'

'And who defines what's best?'

'I do! Simple, honest, beautiful things that work well. A lack of fuss. A concern for function. An appetite for quality. These can be available to everyone. Design is not exclusive, you know.

'Take what we have done with the scented candle. These were popular in Paris in the time of the *grandes horizontales*, you know. Monsieur Rigaud even made one called "Kiss Me Quick" because in those days, smart Parisians were Anglophiles and the use of English was *à la mode*. Of course, now it's *le monde à l'envers*. I am not saying we invented the scented candle, only that we realized its potential. In the bathrooms of Fifth Avenue co-ops you will always find a guttering Manuel Canovas Palais d'Été candle along with the Frette towels. Frette towels are extremely warm and thick. Careful attention to these small things can make big improvements to existence. And our civet and cypress blend offers decadent luxury at modest prices so that a council house in Stoke-on-Trent can (at least) *smell* like a smart Parisian bordello or a Manhattan apartment. And the thing about candles is this: electricity murders darkness. Candles illuminate it.'

I was very pleased with that, but then I carelessly dribbled Quentin's precious Algerian Gold coffee down the leg of my dove-grey Dougie Hayward suit, the French press I was using having an ill-fitting lid.

*In the past, I have written that Eustace Dunne 'opened a whole generation's cognizance of pleasure' with colourful, affordable furniture and accessories. Like Terence Conran's invention of the duvet which certainly took drudgery out of the bedroom, leaving more time for pleasurable activities, Eustace's scented candles made even the drabbest of interiors exotic, seductive and mysterious. But now I need to write that line again. In the same way he once revised the domestic landscape, Dunne will now refresh the business landscape too. Might Marks & Spencer work better if the chairman drank proper coffee made in a French press? Eustace Dunne thinks so. I have never met a man so visually perceptive. Without ever saying so, Dunne would notice a ladder in my tights before I did myself.*

Terri McGonagal, *Protector*

Someone asked if we will open in Amsterdam. I said, perhaps a tad too smartly, 'No. I only ever go where the vine is indigenous.'

...........................................................................................................

® *Rollo Pinkie: This was a bald lie. For years, Eustace carried on an affair with a young designer in Dublin and travelled there frequently. Late at night, he would often make mawkishly sentimental claims to Irish ancestry, even though there are no vineyards in Eire.*

We were asked to gather for a group photograph. I made sure to stand on the right, because when a group photograph is published, the person standing on the right will appear on the left, hence his name will be first in the caption. I do think attention to detail is important.

As the group dissolved, Quentin said to me, 'That went well,' as we ambled to my office for my whisky and his martini.

'It did, didn't it?' I said absent-mindedly. My attention was now taken by a piece of paper on my desk, next to the inspirational Welsh slate.

I read, smiled and passed it to Quentin. It was a telex from Charles Eames:

'Come to New York soonest. New Museum of Modern Art exhibition of my work and I want you to meet curator Philip Johnson. Ever. Charles.'

# 1970 – Remember, son, I'm a whore

*'I am what I am. To look for reasons is beside the point.'*

Joan Didion, *Play It As It Lays*, 1970

*Philip Johnson's House, New Canaan, Connecticut.*

I was writing this on the in-flight stationery Pan Am provides in first class, a nice, pale blue, very light-weight onion skin paper with an adorable thermographed image of the old Stratoliner, girdling the Earth like a roaring, kerosene-powered Ariel.

Bound for New York again.

I loved flying. Saint-Exupéry was required reading at school. Not *The Little Prince*, which is maudlin and sentimental, but his heroic aviation books. His reasons for flying returned to me whenever I climbed an airstair or ascended a jetway or sank into an embracing recliner: '*car cela libère mon esprit de la tyrannie des choses insignifiantes.*'

There's nothing quite as helpful in forgetting the tyranny of everyday things as adjusting the backrest and starting on a generous Manhattan, knowing there are many more to come in seven hours of relative tranquillity. Although I do appreciate that this was not precisely what Saint-Exupéry had in mind. Still, ours is not a heroic age. Or not just yet.

And I loved the new Boeing 747 immoderately. So inappropriate to call this majestic ship 'Jumbo': it may have been huge, but it was graceful, not cumbersome. The aircraft had the authority and presence of a sublime cathedral, not a clumsy elephant. Indeed, if you cared about the modern world, travelling on a 747 was a form of worship at a shrine dedicated to technical gods. I had even told the architect Norman Foster the 747 was better than architecture, and he agreed, really quite enthusiastically.

And I loved the 747 because of the can-do business attitude that built it. These were people, after all, who set to work in a shipyard on

Seattle's Duwamish River. Boeing's William M. Allen confessed, 'It was really too large a project for us,' yet the team managed to design the 747 in just twenty-eight months. Some people take longer to do a chair. It nearly bankrupted the company, but that was soon forgotten when they began calling it the Queen of the Skies and Her Majesty began to democratize travel. As Billy Wilder had told me, when you have a success, concepts of under-budget and over-budget seem suddenly less clearly defined. All bankers should be made to learn that.

I ate a salted cashew.

And every passenger loved the 747 interior. Milton Heinemann said that for the very first time, passengers would be in a quiet spacious room, not a noisy claustrophobic tube. This was, for goodness' sake, a two-storey aircraft with a spiral staircase linking the different levels! You could be on a ranch or in a hacienda. First class featured a sunken well, a sort of upholstered love pit, and a cocktail bar all of its own with discotheque lighting. I may be imagining this, but I think there might have been fountains and palms as well. Meanwhile, at the back of the plane, the designers had created the sedate, sensitively lit, modernistic environment that, I would argue, was, in terms of exposure to serial millions of tired bums and sore eyes, the most familiar and successful interior design ever.

And on this particular Pan Am 747, the cabin crew, whatever their sex, had been evidently selected for poise, charm and figure. Additionally, they knew how to mix real cocktails. These were the days when a bottle of maraschino cherries, Angostura bitters, preserved lemons, fresh limes, green olives and Peychaud's were on any decent airline's minimum equipment list.

In style and demeanour the cabin crew were more like skilled courtiers or expensive courtesans than downtrodden, indentured aerial servants. What did Wordsworth say about the French Revolution? Bliss was it in that dawn to be alive. But I thought, William, you can forget your Lake District. If only you could be with me now, seven miles above Nova Scotia.

The cabin lights were dimmed and I could see now in the far distance, nearly a hundred miles away on this beautifully clear night, what the in-flight magazine told me Truman Capote called a 'diamond iceberg floating in river water'. New York was always thrilling. And I thought twenty-five minutes was ample time for another ruminative Manhattan. I pressed the call-button.

An hour later I was in the seething terminal looking for the De-Witt Carriage & Limo driver, a man of sound principles and dark colour called Winston. I always used him on New York trips because he knew the back doubles through his native Queens, useful when the Van Wyck Expressway was jammed.

I also liked Winston because he had been expelled from Columbia for dealing cocaine. He was now learning his way around Rockefeller's proposed laws as well as he had learnt the backstreets of Queens. Winston, you see, provided his clients and friends with a first-rate drug delivery service.

Two hours later, his black Lincoln Town Car was nosing down FDR Drive delivering me to the River Club on 52nd Street and I was pleasantly high. This was old New York, with a *porte-cochère* of faded red canvas, liveried flunkies, Edith Wharton manners, a light, but inoffensive, layer of dust in a bathroom lit by bare bulbs, plumbing like a destroyer's, a tight view of Roosevelt Island and a broad vista of Brooklyn through slightly opaque glass. The beds were made of beautifully laundered, but very fatigued, sheets. There were Puritan comforters and a smell of history.

Inside the River Club, when the traffic was stopped at a red light, you could even hear the slapping of the filthy East River and the grumble of tug-boats. I'd like to think you could hear a curlew as well, but that was fantasy. Old New York was, if I am honest, the way I wanted new New York to be.

## breakfast on Lexington

'Say, fella!' Charles Eames growled as he leapt out of an enormous leather chair in the River Club's black-and-white marble reception at eight the next morning. He thrust one huge mid-West hand at me for a gentlemanly shake, reserving another huge mid-West hand for a brotherly grip on my shoulder.

'Let's get us some breakfast at my favourite diner. Do you know the Lexington Candy Shop Luncheonette?'

Of course I did not, but I pretended I did.

Americans, I always think, have a categorically different idea of scale from Europeans: the Lexington Candy Shop Luncheonette was a whole thirty blocks north of the River Club, involving a time and distance for breakfast which a Londoner might think more appropriate to a summer holiday.

But thirty minutes in the back of the creaking Ford Crown Victoria cab with its yellowed and scratched Plexiglas partition gave Eames plenty of time to explain the plan.

'My private view tonight is the first time the Museum of Modern Art have given so much space to a living designer. It's a great honour. I'd like very much for you to see all my work in this context. And, if you could be persuaded, I'd be very happy if you were to say a few words from the perspective of London. It's also a perfect opportunity for me to introduce you to Philip Johnson. He can be difficult. Doesn't suffer fools. In truth, doesn't suffer a damn thing. But he's New York's greatest architect and the curatorial brains of MoMA. And he knows everybody. You know his first exhibition there on "The International Style" still defines what we think of when we think of "modern architecture"? And that was long ago. He's a sort of cruel genius, but very funny. And, by the way, a Nazi faggot.' He said that last bit in a very matter-of-fact voice.

The cab pulled up at the Luncheonette on 83$^{rd}$ Street. Eames, in his Donegal tweed suit, theatrically bid me enter, holding the swing door open and bowing slightly. Inside, pure Edward Hopper, an instantaneous hit of nostalgia sourced, in my case, not in experience, but in Hollywood pulp. A long counter with tall stools upholstered in red vinyl, neon signs offering burgers and sandwiches, blintzes and pastrami, servers with grease-splattered jackets. Nothing had changed since it was last fitted out in 1948, including the fabulous Hamilton Beach mixer used for fixing malts. It was pearlescent green with chrome details, more like a car than a kitchen appliance.

As we settled down to enjoy eggs benedict, home fries with garlic pickles, ranch sauce, banana walnut pancakes and French toast drenched in maple syrup, plus, of course, absolutely foul coffee, the sound system began playing the song of the year: Simon and Garfunkel's 'Bridge Over Troubled Water' and Eames told me over his fourth cup of filth: 'I've got to record NBC's *Today* show at lunchtime.'

Back at the River Club, I turned on the Zenith television, found NBC and saw Eames in a bow tie explaining to an interviewer in a spangly dress: 'We are in Noo York to introduce a noo chair at a noo exhibit.' His wife, Ray, stood beside him in her American Gothic outfit. I spent the rest of the afternoon effortfully digesting Lexington's grease and sugar, and writing my speech for the private view.

## what it is to be a designer

And this is what I said.

> 'Charles Eames is not so well known in London as he is New York. But that will soon change. For me, he is what it is to be a Designer. And, ladies and gentlemen, we are entering the Age of The Designer. Of that I am certain. The famous Eames chair has never been bettered and nor will it be until someone discovers a new material or human anatomy is decisively

changed, each unlikely. And never has anyone been a better exemplar of "The Designer". Charles Eames has imagination, charm, humour and a keen practical sense. He has an eclectic eye and, fascinated by play, is an inspired educator. He once told me in Santa Monica, "I visited a good toy store yesterday . . . it was sick-making." You could say the same of almost any store! He is distrustful of affluence, but dedicated to comfort. I am not one to defer to others, but Charles Eames has the wit, style and ingenuity every other designer wants to emulate.'

The applause was polite and then the audience re-formed into its huddled groups of coiffured women and dark-suited men, more intent on each other than the art. Waiters with trays of canapés swirled like midges around a fire. If, I said to myself, you want to know what God thinks about money, just look at the people He gives it to. And then I was interrupted by a large hand on my shoulder.

'Eustace, I want you to meet Philip Johnson. Perhaps I should say *the* Philip Johnson.'

'I've heard an awful lot about you,' I said to a bald, skeletal, immaculately tailored man wearing outrageously emphatic spectacles, just like Le Corbusier's. (As soon as I sourced them at the Bonnet *lunetterie* in Paris, I got a pair of my own.)

'I don't care what anybody says about me as long as it isn't true!' Johnson smartly replied, smiling like a headhunter's desiccated trophy skull. 'Please, call me Philip.'

Taking a flute of Great Western New York State champagne from the tray of a passing midget, Johnson whispered to me, 'I like Eames. But I see him as a little bit like Edward Hopper, don't you? He's a great American figure, for sure. But perhaps a little bit corny as well. I don't much like that homespun Yankee wisdom, that virtuous showboating. I think you need a little acid in the system to be taken seriously by serious people.'

I nodded. Already, I had plenty of acid in my system from this tart domestic fizz.

'I find Eames impressive,' I said, perhaps a little too weakly.

He put his flute down, took his spectacles off, asked a waiter to stop and polished them on the server's white jacket.

Replacing the spectacles and regaining focus, Johnson continued, 'Do you know Hopper's *East Wind Over Weehawken* in Philadelphia? It's his greatest picture. I see Eames like that. Very American, but a little melancholy despite his success. And that wife! She scares me to death! Creepy-creepy. Meet me for lunch tomorrow at the Seagram Building. I eat at midday.'

## gay and happy

Philip Johnson was rich, gay, Harvard, metropolitan, squeaky clean, sleek, successful, brittle and unconstrained by principles of any sort. He had been described as a cultural corrupter, a maestro of manipulation. In Germany before the war, he had cheerfully noted that the Wehrmacht's 'green uniforms make the place look gay and happy'. His schmoozing the Nazis led to a cameo role in CBS reporter William L. Shirer's *Berlin Diary*, which became notorious when it was published in 1941. He later apologized for being a Nazi fanboy, but I suspect rather enjoyed the notoriety, if not the reason for it. The CIA maintained a file on him.

Philip had a genius for imitation, for observing trends and usurping their proprietors. His most famous buildings were all either collaborations with his mentor, Mies van der Rohe, the last director of the Bauhaus who had found sanctuary in Chicago, or imitations of them. And in appearance, he aped Le Corbusier, sourcing those statement spectacles from Maison Bonnet in Paris. And he always wore a bow tie.

Philip's 'Glass House' at New Canaan in Connecticut became one of the most photographed buildings in the world, thanks to the slavish attention of *Town & Country* magazine and *Architectural Digest*. They loved his acid quotability. Then there was the Seagram Building on Park Avenue, the ultimate corporate temple where the golden ratio was put into the service of bourbon sales for the Bronfman family. Somehow geometrically austere, yet lavish at the same time, Seagram's exposed L-beams in Corten steel soon became beautifully patinated and a perfect complement to the copper-tinted windows. If anybody questioned Modernism's grasp of beauty, the sight of Seagram would extinguish that doubt. It was as 'beautifully conceived as anything by Palladio or Hawksmoor', my friend the painter Michael Wishart told me.

I arrived at 11:57 and stepped into a lift which, twenty or so floors later, opened directly into Philip's office. Like every office in Seagram, it had a luminous ceiling and the total effect was discreetly vulgar: there were eight of the 'Barcelona' chairs Mies had designed for the Spanish king in 1929. The originals were black, but these were mud brown. The carpet was deep and lush. It was manically controlled opulence.

## easy to copy

Seeing me looking around, he said breezily, 'I like Mies because he is so easy to copy,' adding quite unnecessarily, 'Remember, son, I'm a whore.'

I knew he said that to everyone, being promiscuous even in his quotability. Settling down, I questioned the difference between inspiration and plagiarism. Philip had been asked this before and quickly replied: 'I get everything from someone. We all do. Nobody can be original.'

I wrote that down, but with Philip, you never quite knew exactly who was the whore and who the pimp and who the punter. He was magnificently contrarian.

'The first complete sentence out of my mouth,' he told me, staring at the East River, 'was probably that line about consistency being the hobgoblin of small minds. I see no conflict in admiring the Bauhaus and also in enjoying cannibal fetishes.'

We went down to the Four Seasons grill at Seagram's core. Again, it was a Mies shell fitted out by Philip in his mature 'Rich Man de Luxe' style. In a rushing culture where busy men had traditionally lunched on oysters standing up, sitting down in comfort to be waited upon conveyed a very special sort of status. Say '99 East 52nd' and every cab driver knew you were someone. Or, at least, that you knew someone who was someone.

'Which is the best table?' I asked Philip as we strolled into this fantastic gilded menagerie of bankers, senators, Great American Novelists, ambassadors, socialites, Supreme Court judges, heiresses, magnates, auction-approved artists, Nobel Laureates, tycoons, billionaires, film stars, Hollywood agents, three-martini admen and their various shoals of adoring and compliant pilot fish.

'Whichever one I am at,' he replied tartly, then confessed, 'but they do tend to keep the very best for David Rockefeller.'

We settled into a booth with leather just beginning to acquire the crackled finish you might find in a vintage Bentley. Its rough texture meant that even Philip's silk and cashmere suit did not squeak.

'All of this we owe to George Lang,' Philip said, waving an explanatory hand around the room, then polishing his glasses on a board-stiff napkin. 'Fascinating man. Began as a violinist in a Hungarian *shtetl*, came here, graduated to organizing wedding banquets in The Bowery and soon invented himself as a restaurant consultant. Perhaps the very first. This is his masterpiece. The *Evergreen Review* described it as "the most expensive restaurant ever built", I am very pleased to say. I might be a whore, but I am not cheap. All my own work. And George's, naturally.'

'Whatever happened to the Rothkos?' I asked, flicking open the menu.

'That's very interesting,' Philip replied. 'We commissioned Mark Rothko to paint huge Four Seasons canvases, but he was a terrible bellyacher, a pain in the ass, and said he would paint them with the express purpose to "ruin the appetite of every son-of-a-bitch who ever eats in this room". Mark hated the posturing, the money, the pretensions, the airs, the graces. That's to say, the very purpose of the place! He returned the advance and kept the paintings for himself. I dare say they are now ruining his own appetite. Anyway, in compensation, we have the Picasso curtain designed for Ballets Russes in 1919.' This he indicated with a nod of the head. 'I think we won the bargain.'

'I will have the little neck clams and the *paillard* of Vermont chicken with morels,' I murmured.

'One of the interesting things about the food here,' Philip said as he looked at the wine list, 'is that it was among the very first restaurants to understand and sell seasonality. As you'd possibly expect for a place called the Four Seasons. So, a native American gastronomic culture, if that's the correct word, based on industrial chicken biscuits, grits, Texas toast, burnt ends and gravy was given the shock therapy of discovering asparagus in spring and funghi in the fall. I think we'll have an Oregon Pinot Noir.'

He waved in the direction of the Picasso with a fork. 'Did you know that the cutlery here, as well as the champagne flutes, were designed by Ada Louise Huxtable, our greatest architectural critic? Only a pretentious fool would mouth the stupid word "*Gesamtkunstwerk*", but I think you know what I mean.' With the device of this patronage, Philip had corrupted New York's ablest architectural critic. I found this inspiring.

## rushing and the Rockefellers

Philip's favourite building was the Guest House he designed for Blanchette Ferry Hooker Rockefeller in Turtle Bay, the East Side's artistic quarter. It was built in 1950 for $64,000 on a twenty-five by one hundred foot in-fill plot. It was in Philip's most austere style, but its purpose was not really to accommodate guests: the Rockefellers had plenty of spare rooms in their very many other houses.

Instead, it existed to house a collection of Clyfford Still and Willem de Kooning paintings that were not at all to John D. Rockefeller III's taste. More importantly, the Guest House served as an informal laboratory for the Museum of Modern Art. New art – potential acquisitions – was shown here to the Rockefellers' glittering circle without the bother of curatorial bickering or the fuss of museum security. Donors to the potential Museum of Modern Art were flattered by invitations to cocktail parties and seduced by the glamour of it all.

And Philip invited me to a Rockefeller cocktail party as his guest.

I told him, 'The sole piece of useful advice my father gave me was: never refuse a glass of champagne because you can never be absolutely certain where the next one is coming from.'

He smiled wanly and led me to a butler called Charles, who was distributing more powerful drinks from a bar invisibly located behind flush cupboards in the entrance hall.

We were in a corner sipping martinis when he said to me over the roar of the rich, 'Dullness is the enemy,' and arched his eyebrows.

'Who do you think is the richest person in this room?' I wondered.

'Come, come,' he said. 'They do not even think in such terms. Once you have passed one hundred million, you enter a curious sort of egalitarian democracy. They could all buy each other twice over, but none of them actually wants to. They want to buy status.

Put it like this, Blanchette's father made his money from seeds.' He pronounced the word as if it was intrinsically hilarious.

I leant my head slightly to one side.

'Just think of how that vicious little wormdick Hilton Kramer described my work: "publicity, showmanship and the exercise of power". He was trying to be a bitch, but he was exactly right. Publicity, showmanship and the exercise of power! I cannot think of a better description of the art world.'

And he was also impressively cynical about the social purpose of design.

I said to him, 'My shops in England make people happier. If you cannot afford a good de Kooning, you can probably afford a good salad bowl.'

'You're going to change the world, Eustace? Well, go ahead and try. You'll give it up at a certain point and change yourself instead. But no hurry. Here is your chance to meet Mrs Museum of Modern Art. The woman who has everything, plus twenty-seven de Koonings. Blanchette, may I introduce Eustace Dunne from London? He is recently divorced and feeling very lonely,' Philip said mockingly.

She had a regal presence and an imperial composure learnt at Miss Chapin's School for Girls, a demeanour lately enhanced by Chanel. She had only one flaw. She was perfect. Otherwise, she was perfect.

'Young man, how many wives have you had?' Mrs Rockefeller enquired, blowing smoke.

I caught her eye and held it for three or four heartbeats. 'My own, or other people's?'

'My oh my. Will you have one more drink before you rush?'

She summoned Charles, and I searched my memory as to where I had heard that before.

Philip said, 'It should take you about four seconds to reach the street door. You've got two.' We hailed a cruising Checker yellow cab on Beekman Place and in the soft drizzle, the windows steamed quickly. I felt as if we were in a Saul Leiter Kodachrome.

Philip continued as if we had never been to the party. 'I always say that architecture is the art of how to waste space. And I am designing a very great deal of wasted space on Madison Avenue. This is the headquarters of AT&T. That's a very boring telephone company and I will make it look like a Chippendale cabinet in pink granite. Consistency is the glory of slaves! There will be two hundred thousand feet of retail space at the base of the atrium, and I think you should test your salad bowls here in Manhattan. I'm sure I can cut a deal with the developers to give Bleu de Travail rent-free space for a year.'

'That,' I said, failing to conceal my excitement, 'would be splendid.'

The Checker cab stopped at an address on Mott Street with a discreet sign above the bell push that said 'Adult Services'.

'Do you know what Truman Capote believed?' Philip asked.

I said I did not, so he told me.

'"More tears are shed over answered prayers than unanswered ones."'

## great theatre or tawdry fakery?

I took myself to La Fonda del Sol in The Time Life Building for a final lunch on this visit: nice to keep last night's Rockefeller memories alive in this most amazing Rockefeller monument. Lunching alone is one of life's chief pleasures: it's a form of research, not of waste. I always carry sketchbooks and there was lots to fill them with here.

La Fonda del Sol was, like the Four Seasons, conceived as a total work of art, although the atmosphere and style could not be more different. One was hushed old money, the other was a raucous *cantina* transplanted from Guadalajara to the Rockefeller Center. The designer was Alexander Girard.

The restaurant was an innocent, perhaps even patronizing, tribute to all things Latin American, possible in the days when the most sinister South American character was Speedy Gonzales. Girard designed every single element: salt shakers, book matches, even the ponchos which the waiters wore.

The menu cheerfully began '*Bienvenido! Esta usted en su casa*' and the walls were a tribute to Latino gastronomy and printed ephemera: ESCABECHE, MOLE and POBLANO made fabulously exuberant word-play patterns on the walls. Girard had commissioned his old friend Charles Eames to design bespoke chairs known as 'La Fonda'. The architectural space was complicated and meandering with niches containing colourful pre-Columbian sculptures of the gods Ixtab, Kukulcan and Yumil Kaxob. 'It is like an Aztec Soane Museum,' I scribbled in my notebook.

Eames had told me that Alexander Girard insisted a restaurant must be as much about feeling as about food. I tore the front off a book of matches decorated with an image of Huitzilopochtli, the sun god of the South Americas. I even liked the memorable phone number: 'PLAZA 7-8800'. My mind was full of mezcal, beer and ideas. Was La Fonda del Sol great theatre or tawdry fakery?

I decided it didn't matter. I had a plan and I was determined to implement it.

# 12

# 1978 – Don't count the shit, just count the inches.

*'Just one more year and then you'd be happy.'*

Gerry Rafferty, 'Baker Street', 1978

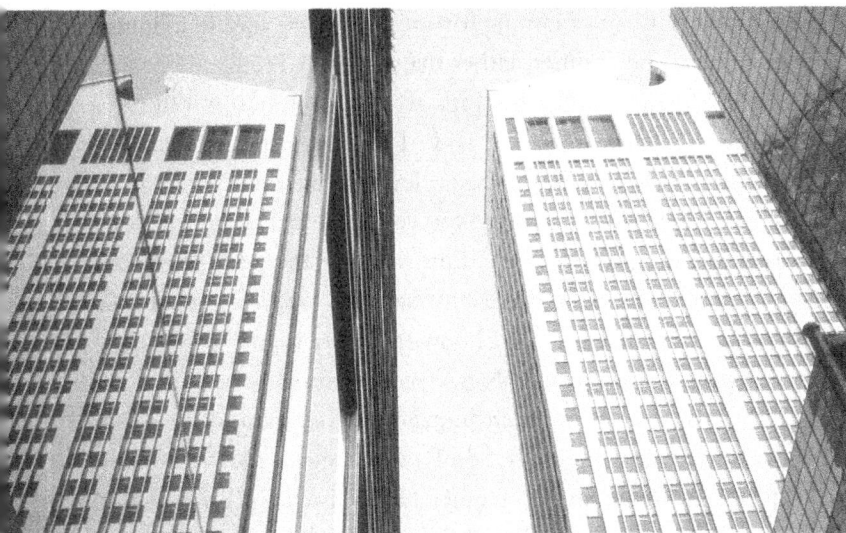

*The AT&T Building, New York.*

Lou Rosenberg was the developer of the AT&T Building.

Of his tastes and affections there could be no doubt since he was, in all matters not related to business, a stranger to confidentiality. I supposed he was here in London to enjoy, besides his own garrulous presentation of his vision for mid-town property, *le vice anglais* on its own *terroir* – once business was done.

Conversation with Rosenberg was, by the way, a little like a one-way ratchet: a form of rasping torture you might find in a dungeon. Something to be endured rather than enjoyed. He liked bacon and shellfish. Shiksas too. WASP girls were a compulsion, often more than one at a time, or so he said. 'Those regal uptown kids with white shoe dads, they bounce a fat Jew like me off the ceiling once they get into a rhythm. "Baby, you've got nostrils like Satan's feet," a Vassar girl with huge jugs told me once on the floor of my office. She screamed when she came and she came a goddamned lot. They think they're princesses, but I know they're tramps.'

Rosenberg was remarkably free with personal information, often of a sort you'd prefer was left imprisoned. I spent a lot of my time with him wincing internally. Lou Rosenberg was a Jew who did not keep kosher. He did not keep quiet. He did not keep his zipper done up. He could not resist picking his nose. I think you could say he was a transgressive controversialist.

You could also say he was a very big man indeed, similarly proportioned to the Alaskan brown grizzly bear, a likeness emphasized by the choice on this occasion of an extravagantly double-breasted mohair suit the colour and sheen of Branston Pickle. He had generous, perhaps over generous, lips. They reminded me of pink oysters. He was a striver from Greenpoint, a part of Brooklyn that had not yet succumbed to fashion. His big head appeared to be slightly pointed. His father had been an associate of the gangster Meyer Lansky, the mob's accountant, and known as Duddy the Jew. His teeth were remarkably white and his hair receding.

I asked Rollo to come with me to meet Duddy the Jew's son in London. I called him at the university where he was maintaining some academic credentials as a part-time lecturer.

'Look, Rollo. We're going to open in New York. First, the shop. Second, the design consultancy. I want you to do for me here what you did so extremely well in Covent Garden. We'll take Manhattan, the Bronx and Staten Island too.' That last bit I cheerily sang as a tribute to Lorenz Hart. Rollo sounded crestfallen, but acquiesced.

We had agreed on Duke's, the spiritual home of the dry martini. This is a hotel in a silent and nearly secret cul-de-sac in St James's. Its air is thick with gentlemanly privilege: Ian Fleming was a familiar here, proved by a framed letter in the bar from his apartment on Ebury Street. Indeed, it was Duke's martinis which were shaken not stirred, a technique that so impressed Fleming it became a James Bond motif. Rosenberg was, however, staying at the Dorchester, a short stroll away. This was, I think, because the concierge had reliable and cost-effective methods when negotiating a good deal with the hookers who pretended to be guests in the lobby. Basically, they agreed his price or they were out of the revolving door. In Duke's, by contrast, people were more interested in money than sex.

Rosenberg insisted on taking the Dorchester's courtesy car, a Rolls-Royce Silver Shadow in midnight blue. He wore a gold Rolex Daytona that was much too shiny.

'I think of myself more as a paragraph guy than a sentence guy,' Rosenberg said, fiddling with his watch bracelet as he sat back in a green velour tub chair not quite adequate to the task of supporting him. He spread his arms theatrically: 'I don't have charts. I hold everything in my head. They told me at school I was too sensitive. I have never gotten over that. I fight against it, I fucking really do.'

## the martini ceremony

A coruscating trolley with frozen bottles of gin, ice, lemons, a zester, tongs and enormous green olives rattled towards us over the carpet: Duke's martini ceremony was about to interrupt the monologue. Rosenberg chose Tanqueray, influenced, I suspected, by magazine advertisements rather than by any personal preference diligently acquired in comparative tastings. I chose a more recondite Plymouth gin and Rollo followed my example.

Luis Buñuel had said that for a perfect martini, the requirement was merely for a shaft of sunlight to pass through a bottle of vermouth before refracting into the glass of gin itself. The waiter – like a priest – produced a dropper which drizzled vermouth on to the gin, settling in globules on the surface. Lemon skin was rubbed around the rim of the ice-frosted cocktail glass, almost painfully cold to the touch. A green olive was drowned in gin.

We drank. With martinis, Lou explained, you are in the same territory as women's fucking tits. One is never enough, but three are possibly too many. We had four and by the time we had finished, Lou Rosenberg had persuaded us to occupy a hundred thousand feet of his new AT&T Building, rent-free for thirty-six months on a non-repairing lease.

'It's all about human traffic' was the way he summarized the deal – word by slowly enunciated word – as if he had just cracked the human genome code and was giving the acceptance speech for his Nobel Prize. Meanwhile, as he spoke, Rosenberg's eyes followed a waitress across the room.

'And, man, this will have traffic like you have never seen,' he said, still looking at the waitress.

'I don't mind lying, but I detest inaccuracy,' I said above the gin-soaked murmur of the crowd. 'You, Lou, and I are going to get on very well.'

We shook hands.

The next day, the *New York Times* business page ran a headline: 'Rosenberg Corporation's Coup: Po-Mo Madison Avenue Monument Pre-let To English Designer'.

Philip Johnson's AT&T Building on Madison Avenue was designed as a challenge to orthodoxy. Its open pediment six hundred feet above the ground was meant to suggest Thomas Chippendale, the Georgian cabinetmaker whose trade was bookcases six feet above the ground rather than skyscrapers. In functional terms, this open pediment achieved nothing. In semantic terms, it achieved an awful lot: the formal austerity of High Modernism was over, at least according to the Philip Johnson version. And then there was the seven-storey atrium, the first thing any human traffic discovered on entering from the street. And Bleu de Travail was on the ground floor: a new shop for Manhattan, the first of its kind. The game was on.

## the attention span of a gnat

Rollo Pinkie told me I had to meet Kelly Hoffmann, the matriarchal architecture critic of the *New York Times*, a paper still in those days known as 'the Grey Lady' on account of both its incorruptible seriousness and its solemn refusal of colour, actual and metaphorical. Kelly, a fast-talking, exhausting, bleed-your-contacts, break-the-news, bust-your-balls type of journalist with the attention span of a gnat, but the tenacity of a boa constrictor, was different.

She was egomaniacal and clever and shockingly bad at planning her time or meeting her deadlines. Weary friends would complain that, in order to meet Kelly for what would in any event be a stupidly rushed lunch, three or four phone calls were required that same morning since the venue was always changing, as was the appointed hour. Sometimes she had lunch at four, but this might be the second lunch of her day. With her deadlines, she was often found handing sheets of hastily subbed copy to the compositors, moments after they came out of her long-suffering portable typewriter.

Yet her influence was enormous. An endorsement from Kelly Hoffmann could make a business, create a fad, cause a sensation, start a career. Just last year, an article by Kelly on medical glassware had had all of the East Fifties sipping their margaritas and mojitos out of 250ml laboratory conical flasks while snorting their cocaine from petri dishes. At one party she attended, the waitpeople wore green surgical scrubs and masks. She titled her story 'Hospital Chic'.

The year before, Kelly had made tangerine the colour of summer. When she was interviewed for her own newspaper about vacation plans, she made the North Fork of Long Island newly acceptable. Somehow, she managed to mention that she would drive there in a Datsun 510, which suddenly acquired the status of a BMW. She had all the views that were fit to print.

'The woman's a nightmare,' Rollo had explained when we met in New York. 'A chromium-plated, Royal Bengal pain in the arse. A meddling yenta to end all meddling yentas. But in this city she's important. You don't count the shit, you just count the inches. She'll get the column inches. They will be noticed. And you'll get the customers.'

I agreed to meet Kelly Hoffmann at Studio 54, a club whose pitiless velvet-rope door policy gave regular thrills of shock and fear to the institutionally insecure, but ambitious, of New York. The damned looking into Paradise, as someone put it. Mere entry was a test of social approval.

Yet it was, as Andy Warhol had said, 'A dictatorship at the door, but a democracy on the dance floor.' They alienated everybody because they would not let everybody in. But neither was Bleu de Travail interested in everybody. These were our people and the thought occurred: could we make the opening party like a busy night at Studio 54?

An easy arrogance and English accent won trouble-free admission past the velvet rope, although the $100 passed to a surly buzz-cut bouncer was no handicap to progress. Kelly was fifty minutes late.

## fucking traffic

'I can't fucking stand this fucking traffic,' she said, striding across the floor towards me at the bar. This was as if the fucking traffic had been a very specific condition localized on Kelly Hoffmann alone, rather than a general blight on Manhattan as a whole. When she stopped moving, she stopped twirling her Hermès Kelly bag.

'Club soda and no weird stuff,' she beamed, settling an ample rear on a bar stool. Kelly wore a floor-length down coat and denim dungarees from Norma Kamali. Like Jean Cocteau, who in no other respect did she resemble at all, she wore two Cartier Trinity rings on her severely manicured right hand. Kelly Hoffmann was about five feet tall, but had a giantess's ego.

'Studio 54 I wrote about in the *Times* last year. It's in a tradition of great nightclubs that goes back to the Moulin Rouge, Copacabana and The Cotton Club. And, boy, do these guys know how to organize a scene. The opening night was a riot. Literally a riot. When you get in, you're a star. But look! There's Michael Jackson! I mean everyone's star.' Michael Jackson was leading some exotic animal on a gold chain towards a private room.

'Might I explain the Bleu de Travail proposition?' I asked with the patience a psychiatrist would reserve for a severely disturbed patient.

I then quietly explained my design principles, my Francophilia and my love affair with food. I mentioned scented candles. The equivalent in its way to the revolution in Britain's sex life that was caused, not by contraceptive pills nor newly won social liberties, but by Terence Conran's genius in importing continental quilts and claiming them as his own.

'Actually, you look as if you're wearing a Habitat duvet!' I laughed. 'But what I really mean to say is, I very much believe in that old German maxim: the best is always simple, but the simple is not always the best. I like the ambiguity. I have a puritan's eye, but the taste of a voluptuary. That's what Bleu de Travail will offer. Simple pleasures.'

'Look,' Kelly replied like gunfire. 'I just can't flash on that. Players here don't like ambiguity or complexity. They want to be told. Straight. They don't want to interpret. That's why we all speak English. And let me tell you right now: there's no appetite for European workwear in the United States. We have enough of a problem with Oshkosh, Dickies and Carhartt. Who wants to look like a garbage guy or a fucking dirt farmer? C'mon!'

She lit a Pall Mall and sucked deeply.

'So no hope for modern design here in the commercial centre of the world?' I said, mockingly.

'To be honest,' Kelly countered, 'Design Research in Boston just about exhausted any domestic taste for that stuff in the sixties. Conran flashed on that. But Marcel Breuer is so 1927. He's what we call "dead". And Williams Sonoma has got cookware covered. You want a black skillet? They got it, dude. Anyway, that's all too Marin County. This is New York, sweetheart. As for Danish Modern! My arse, my friend. I'm thinking Korean this year. Maybe Oceania next. Frankly, I think the Bauhaus sucks.'

'You seem very confident in your judgements.'

'Even more so since I gave up spontaneous rap sessions and

began studying the Fischer-Hoffman Process. This shrink Hoffman was my dad.' She extinguished the Pall Mall, looked briefly bored, but her face lit up as she asked, 'Want to go party at the Chelsea Hotel? Or would you prefer Plato's Retreat?'

In this way I was introduced to a career choice defined by my preference in decadence.

Plato's Retreat was a swingers' club located in the basement of a grimy residential hotel on East 23$^{rd}$ between Lexington and Third. Its proprietor, Larry Levenson, had acquired some modest, but lasting, fame when in an interview with the *Village Voice*, he claimed regularly to ejaculate fifteen times a day. This was a statistic which few who had ever heard it could resist repeating, either shocked, awed or envious. Yet Plato's Retreat maintained a certain sort of sophisticated dignity at odds with its sleazy offer. Levenson, when not otherwise occupied, expected a version of good manners and propriety from his clients.

...................................................................................................

® *Rollo Pinkie: For such a fastidious and sophisticated man, Eustace had a juvenile sense of humour and enjoyed crude, dirty jokes. He liked to explain when serving Stachys affinis, Japanese artichokes, how they made you fart helplessly. He told me how at Plato's Retreat he had met an off-duty Braniff hostess who knew Alexander Calder. But more than that he did not say. He could also be maddeningly discreet.*

The Chelsea Hotel was, by contrast, scripturally Bohemian, a product of the same counter-culture that birthed the *Village Voice* itself. That paper had begun when another English hopeful in New York placed a postcard in a Sheridan Square bookshop, rather like my laying out our stall on Madison Avenue. But the Chelsea Hotel had a deeper history: built as an apartment block in 1883 with utopian-socialist collective principles, its proprietor encouraged what he liked to call 'celebratory orgies'. A respectful tradition acknowledging this was soon established among the clients.

The survivors of the *Titanic* were lodged in the Chelsea Hotel: a metaphor if ever there was one! Dylan Thomas died here after drinking eighteen straight whiskies of unspecified size and Jackson Pollock threw up in the lobby, very much in the style of his paintings. *2001: A Space Odyssey* was written here, while Andy Warhol's *Chelsea Girls* took its name from the hotel. Mark Rothko was a resident in a perpetual depressive tumult of morbid colour. The playwright Arthur Miller, Marilyn Monroe's husband at the time, said, I think approvingly, that the Chelsea Hotel had 'no vacuum cleaners, no rules and no shame'.

And it was to the Chelsea Hotel that I decided to travel with Kelly Hoffmann. When I later explained to people that I had no idea what was on my mind, no one believed me.

In the cab, Kelly said, 'You know what Marlene Dietrich thought? I like men who are poets. But that doesn't mean they have to write poetry. Know what I mean? I too like men who are poets, even if I think poetry is a waste of time.'

The cab pulled up at 222 West 23rd, near Pier 54. This was a world as different from the Seagram Building as Sitting Bull was from Gore Vidal.

The Chelsea Hotel was full of art and artists, overflowing ashtrays, music and musicians in poses demonstrating the different degrees of stupefied inattention which doctors use when describing the Coma Scale.

## uh, gee, great

Kelly knew her way around and muscled towards the bar where a man dressed like a geography teacher, but wearing a hundred per cent nylon blond fright wig, was snorting cocaine off the zinc counter.

'Eustace,' she said winningly, 'I'd like you to meet Andy Warhol.'

The most famous living artist in the world, pre-eminently visible, but maddeningly and artfully opaque at the same time, looked up, giggled, brushed the snow off his nose and said, 'One good line leads to another. It helps me write.'

Kelly asked him, 'Will you come to the opening of Eustace's new shop when it opens in AT&T next fall?'

'Uh, gee, great,' Warhol said, returning to his tightly rolled $50 bill and his inhalations.

Kelly said to me, 'If he's sober tomorrow and, as a matter of fact, he sobers up quite fast when business is involved, I'll take you to his Factory. It's his playground, his toy theatre. It is dense with superstars in a delirium of inverse snobbery: status is achieved through competitive manifestations of performative debauchery. Human space debris. The more out of it you are, the more in it you become. Anyway, I like Andy's idea that art is anything you want it to be. Maybe he'll make you a superstar. Or perhaps,' she said reflectively, 'I will.'

At this moment, three shrieking girls in sequins and fishnet tights with their hair dyed magenta, each one carrying a flash-popping Polaroid camera, wobbled on their heels up the bar to shuffle a giggling Warhol out of the room.

Kelly changed her order from a club soda to a Four Roses.

'What,' I asked, 'are all the synonyms you can think of for "peculiar"?' Screams could now be heard from the lobby. A police siren wailed.

Kelly said, 'Unusual, odd, funny, strange, curious, bizarre, weird, queer, different, idiosyncratic. Next question.'

Next day's *New York Post* carried pictures of Kelly and me leaving the Chelsea Hotel, leaving readers to draw their own conclusions. Liz Smith, the vengeful and competitive gossip columnist, had muttered gleefully that her rival Kelly was a tramp. 'Sordid over-boogie' she called it, quoting Eve Babitz.

We arrived late morning at Warhol's Factory, shuddered upstairs on a wobbly and graffitied goods lift. And we found Warhol engrossed in his copy of the *Post*. By the Factory's tranquillized norms an early riser, Warhol himself looked as if he had not slept, although his clothes looked like they had been slept in by someone else.

'This is uh, gee, great,' Warhol said, nodding at the newspaper. His nose was very obviously running. 'My idea of a good picture is one that's in focus and of a famous person. Check that! You are beautiful people.'

## industrializing art

The Factory was so-called because Warhol wanted to industrialize art, to depersonalize it, rob it of mystique and to mass-produce it like soap or a carbonated beverage with herbal extracts. He let people confuse vanity for genius, he ridiculed history, mocked connoisseurship. Brands of fast-moving consumer goods were afforded the status of high culture.

Robert Hughes had accused Warhol of producing art that was 'flat and perfunctory'. Hughes was a truly great art critic, but he sometimes let his anger get the better of his judgement. Flat and perfunctory was the point.

Warhol explained to me that what became the Factory had begun in 1963 at what he called a 'haircutting party'. Here he made walls decorated with scrumpled Aluminum Corporation of America tin foil and this happy improvisation was inspiration to do his own apartment in the same way. As the Factory enlarged, broken mirrors were added to the tin foil repertoire.

And the Factory was a nomadic enterprise. From East 47th it moved to Union Square, then to Broadway then to East 33rd. On any day you might meet Salvador Dali, Allen Ginsberg, any number of Warhol's own tranquillized Factory-endorsed Superstars, diverse celebrities, groupies, hangers-on, drag queens or even

216

DeVeren Bookwalter, the star of Warhol's film *Blow Job*. Of course, there was a nasty edge to all of this, but I was, on the whole, extremely impressed.

'Say what you like about Andy,' Kelly later explained to me, 'but he understands the speed and values of the modern world. He sees no distinction between high culture and low culture. He senses that beauty can be manufactured. He values his films as highly as his paintings and he produces each using industrial methods. I've heard him called a self-important, self-mythologizing, vainglorious, money-obsessed pain in the ass, but perhaps one day people will also say that about you.'

'They already do,' I said to myself.

...............................................................................................................

® *Rollo Pinkie: Eustace rather over-played his relationship with Warhol. They were never more than passing acquaintances. I once interviewed Warhol for* Vanity Fair *and mentioned Eustace. Warhol said, 'Gee. Do I know this dude?'*

And the idea formed in my mind, almost as a fever dream, that the Factory could be imported to London and then, indeed, to any other city big enough to cope with the egos and the chaos they generated. It could be a laboratory for designers, a showcase for new work, a continuous experiment in beneficial public relations, a playground for staff, a tax break, a popular entertainment, a source of inspiration, an image-building project of stylish majesty, an everlasting media phenomenon, an incubator of ideas and a temple of taste.

The relationship with Bleu de Travail would be symbiotic: curiosity generated by the Factory would lead to desire and desire would lead to sales in my shops. In my version, the Factory would usurp art galleries. It would be a twentieth-century Soane Museum. Just as Sir John Soane's bizarre eclecticism had inspired me when at the

Lethaby Academy, the Factory would inspire a new generation. And I would be the beneficiary.

## a ziggurat of kilims

The opening of Bleu de Travail in the AT&T Building was on a perfect New York October day: the sky a flawless blue, the air crisp and clear, the skyline diamond-cut. And the party that evening was catered by La Fonda del Sol: a thousand guests ate tacos and drank Mexican *cerveza* while stepping carefully past towers of Breuer chairs, pyramids of Polish enamel, ziggurats of kilims, monuments of butcher's blocks and minarets of pepper mills.

Lou Rosenberg was photographed with Andy Warhol. An incongruous pair, but framing the event as effectively as the pious, kneeling donors in a Flemish Renaissance altarpiece. Each beamed for the cameras.

And Warhol was taking his own photographs too: he signed the Polaroids in black felt-tip and sold each to its subject for $100. They say he made $50,000 that night.

As he positioned me against a wall of French casseroles and switch brooms, I beckoned with a finger.

'Andy, come here. I have a proposition for you. Just as I have brought Bleu de Travail to New York, I want to bring the Factory to London. It will be a transfer of taste. What do you think?'

'Uh, gee, great,' Andy said, thoughtfully putting his Polaroid down.

I then cornered another guest, the architect Timothy Clever, whose Fondation Voltaire had just opened to great controversy in Montreal. People said, with an ever-so-knowing nod to the sage of Ferney, that I disapprove of what you design, but I defend to the death your right to design it. Even the hip settlers in the Mile Ex quartier had objected that it had a bullying presence, pushing real life out of the area. Patrons of the Dinette Triple Crown on Clark Street even staged a demonstration with Molson beer and poutine, a hot mess of chips with cheese and gravy. But others thought it a design of original genius, executed with uncompromising conviction and rare energy. I was simply aware that it had caused a sensation, blowing a very noisy framboise at the stiff Canadian establishment. And that was what I wanted.

Clever said in his fine, slightly hesitant voice, 'Last night I ate at The River Café in DUMBO, the new acronym for Down Under the Manhattan Brooklyn Overpass. Extraordinary place. It's built on an underwater pier in the East River. Sensational sunsets. And Larry Forgione's food surely makes it the best Italian restaurant not just in Brooklyn, but in the world. They have perfect little dishes of bright green olive oil on every table. They make *focaccia* on the premises. I'd like to see something similar in London. You'd be interested in that, wouldn't you, Eustace?'

'Timothy, I have an idea bigger even than The River Café, bigger even than the Voltaire . . .'

But at just that moment, Kelly Hoffmann interrupted with a bottle of Corona in her hand, reeling very slightly.

'Sweetheart, I need a quote from you for tomorrow's paper. And my deadline is only twenty minutes away. Can we go somewhere quiet? My Dictaphone is being killed in here.' She waved the microphone at the crowd to indicate the source of the problem.

We went to the private office.

'Your quote will only take a minute. What'll we do with the other nineteen?'

I blocked the door with a beanbag chair.

Next day the *New York Times*' home page led with a story: 'The French Revolution, English style. Eustace Dunne brings Bleu de Travail to Manhattan. The next revolution will be indoors.'

# 13

# 1980 – High-concept chips

*'Suicide is painless.'*

Johnny Mandel and Michael B. Altman,
the theme tune from M*A*S*H, 1970.

*Andy Warhol in New York.*

I WANTED TO TEST THE Factory idea in London with a new restaurant. To me, restaurants are always laboratories of taste. In every sense of the word. The food and the style should, ideally, fix an idea in the customer's mind.

There is a very particular environment where you would want to eat *foie gras* and a rather different one where you might, if such a thing can be imagined, want to eat a hamburger. Like a glass of good, and I do not mean 'expensive', wine, a restaurant should be a convergence of all the senses. But that's what 'taste' is.

And Quentin had a site in mind on an unpromising street near our Covent Garden studios. But to me 'unpromising' simply means a promise that's not yet been realized. Unpromising can always be broken, I like to say. If you are a designer, you perceive patterns others do not.

For me, it's all about seeing opportunities and making revelations. Everything I have ever done has been involved with finding a neglected property and realizing its value, whether that property was the intangible business of 'design' itself or, in this case, an extremely tangible half-ruined hat factory on New Row, next door to a dangerous-looking minicab office and a sad Pakistani newsagent with a dusty window display that included dry cell batteries, bags of crisps and condoms. Just down the street, the Israeli artist-inventor Dov Nomad had opened his studio-store. Here, he sold recycled cinema seats containing pressure pads that played Schoenberg quartets through hidden speakers when you sat upon their cushions.

Quentin took me to the site and, kicking an old bottle of Guinness across the street under an abandoned Bedford Dormobile with three flat tyres and yellow-crazed glass, he barked a laugh and said, 'We'd have to be as mad as shit-house rats to take this place.'

'But we are, Quentin, we are,' I said.

He pressed his nose up to the opaque window and said in a voice of high-camp approval, 'Ah! The foul-smelling mould of the ghetto! I'll speak to the agent.'

The agent was a man Quentin later described as wearing a Sinai tie and having perfect teeth, not intending to be kind. We bought the lease that same afternoon and Quentin promptly went to The French House with his sketchbook. Here I believe he stayed all evening and spent the time drawing, waiting for a pay-as-you-go soubrette who never came. It was an entire Havana wait, he grumpily explained later. But he had had time to think. Quentin's first sketches showed that our new venture would not be as ambitious as Andy's Factory on Broadway, but uh, gee, great as the artist might say, we would introduce depressed London to inflated New York style . . . in the company of French food and Italian furniture.

## popularizing the potato

Was 'Factory' too imitative a name? I wasn't sure. I began toying with *'usine'* or *'usine alimentaire'*, but thought most people would confuse these with a *pissoir* because *'usine'* sounds vaguely urological. And as I write this, it immediately occurs to me that the priggish English could benefit from more pissing in the street, at least in a more organized manner. I immediately made a note to self: I must design a modernist *pissoir*.

I often wonder why the English are so reticent about these things. In France they are different. Not only do bidets frankly acknowledge the reality of excreta and their side effects, but a flatulist like Joseph Pujol, *Le Pétomane* of Le Moulin Rouge, could make a celebrity career out of farting. In his stage act he could extinguish a candle at a distance of one metre as well as imitating musical instruments and animal noises. There really is something magnificently French about this.

Anyway, some things were immediately certain. The fascia board would say 'Factory', or maybe 'L'usine', in that stencil-like industrial font Le Corbusier liked to use on his drawings. We would have Eames chairs and Morosini chairs. The lamp fittings and luminaires would be inspired by Castiglioni, as would the drinking glasses. And I had just sketched some new cutlery inspired by Ada Louise Huxtable's designs for the Four Seasons.

And before I had left New York, I called Andy and asked if he would design the menu. He said 'Um, gee, great' and now I had in front of me a screen-print Andy had done of an abattoir, similar in spirit to his 'electric chair series', perhaps not quite as depressing, although the cattle in the stalls did not look best pleased. I would do the calligraphy myself. Arrighi's Chancery Script, I thought.

Besides *truite au bleu*, there would be *caneton aux olives*, as they do at Allard, and *poule au pot* like the one served in Lipp: it's a very Bleu de Travail idea that the people should, as Henri IV regally declared, have a 'chicken in their pot every Sunday'. I thought I might let them eat cake as well. Then we would have *boeuf à la mode*, *gratinée à l'oignon rouge*, *chou farci*, *coq au vin*, *bavette à l'échalote*, *jambon braisé au Madère* and perhaps even just a simple *croque monsieur*. What could be finer than a simple *croque monsieur* with scalding, melting cheese and a glass of shockingly cold white Burgundy? And, naturally, a very superior *steak frites*.

Certainly, the Factory would serve London's very best chips. This would not be a departure from my veneration of France and all things French. And, in any case, it was a Frenchman called Parmentier who first popularized the potato. I don't believe anybody who says he doesn't like chips. But a chip can, like anything else in this world, be well designed or badly designed. They have to be a certain shape. And a certain length. Not too fat, not too thin.

Too thin and they are *pommes d'alumettes* and that's not at all the same thing. And, of course, they have to be cooked twice. Then drained. And served with sea salt. Never vinegar. Anyway, what we call vinegar in this country is not vinegar at all. It is a non-brewed industrial condiment. A Frenchman would think 'malt vinegar' was a waste product. Everybody knows this. Precision is important.

## a recipe for bouillabaisse thirteen pages long

I don't like pedantry, but I do admire attention to detail. So I went to see Richard Olney, the most uncompromising of cooks and food writers, to check our menus and recipes. He was strict and demanding, but not at all pretentious. Really, quite the opposite. At least, his form of pretentiousness was to advocate a very pedantic simplicity. But who is to say how pretentious an ostentatious show of lack of pretension may be?

Wonderfully, Richard, of Puritan descent from Iowa, had a recipe for *bouillabaisse* that was thirteen pages long. Another, for chicken with forty cloves of garlic. His version of the local peasant dish *pieds et paquets*, sheep's feet and sheep's tripe, was poached for eight hours in a tomato-infused *mirepoix*. This was not a man in a hurry. He made Elizabeth David look like a frivolous flibbertigibbet.

He wrote a weekly newspaper column called '*Un Américain gourmand à Paris*'. On these pages, he fought against every convention: it was Richard who, devoted as he was to French food in the grand manner, taught the French about freshness, seasonality and the accurate pairing of wine with food. *Haute cuisine* ignores the seasons in preference for a lofty, rigid tradition.

Creamy and buttery sauces? Richard would prefer a disciplined reduction. Show a master of *haute cuisine* a fresh artichoke and a crude handful of sardines and he would not know what to do. It's a peculiar truth that the Americans and English know more about claret and Burgundy than the French do. And more about French food as well.

Besides, a visit to Richard Olney in his hard-scrabble house in Solliès-Toucas, a village of barely two hundred souls near Toulon, also gave me an excuse to visit the Restaurant Hiély in Avignon, one of Provence's oldest: an urbane and civilized place just steps away from the Palace of the Popes. It has been there, unchanged, since 1938. I sat down, got a Rhodia notebook from my music bag and started scribbling. *Bar sauvage de ligne* and a bottle of Miraval Blanc kept me and my thoughts company.

Three hours later, after a delightful drive in a Citroën DS that might have been chauffeured by Monsieur Bibendum himself, I found Richard busy in his herb garden. A professional, college-educated WASP peasant, he was wearing a well-worn plaid shirt, flapping open, not laundered recently, and dusty espadrilles. There was a pair of secateurs in the waistband of his skimpy Speedo swimming trunks. This was his domestic uniform. He rarely wore anything different. In his hand was a bunch of sorrel for the dish he was cooking for dinner, a composition of five different layers of vegetable omelettes, drenched in the herby sauce and then cooked again in a tin nestling in a *bain marie*. This '*gâteau de crespens*' became the Factory's first special. We called it 'Richard Olney's Provençal Feast'.

'You know,' Richard said, playfully snipping at me with his secateurs, 'Julia Child says I enjoy being difficult. But, as you are very aware, I can be perfectly charming if you treat me as the genius I so obviously am.' He posed theatrically, arms folded and head back.

As we settled down to an *apéro* of Bandol rosé under the vine-covered pergola in front of his kitchen, I asked about his discovery of French food.

'It was a dish of mashed potatoes in Paris. Made with no milk.

Just butter and cooking water. It was perfect. And for me it was a revelation. It taught me that "simple" is not the same as "ordinary". Then there was Lulu Peyraud of Domaine Tempier. She taught me everything.'

As we ate a starter of *consommé de crustacés en gelée* from gaily painted bowls decorated by an unsuccessful associate of Picasso, Richard explained wine as a philosophy. As he spoke of the mysteries of vinification, behind him I could see a Waring electric blender and, incongruously, some packs of Fluffo the Golden Shortening. Then he quoted an old proverb: 'Better than the scriptures can, wine reveals God's plan to man.'

## targeting iceberg lettuce

Then Richard explained his latest campaign. He had already scored with his readers a conclusive victory over garlic powder, stock cubes and dried herbs, but now he was targeting iceberg lettuce.

'You are a man who understands authenticity,' he said. 'So you must join my campaign for real salad. Did you know that the disgusting and tasteless iceberg – which exists only as functional transport for cheap mayonnaise and ketchup – was a sort of Frankenstein growth created by a hybridizer in the late nineteenth century? It is the polyester of lettuces. It has no taste, it has no season, it has no *terroir*, other than a laboratory in Pennsylvania. It's a lettuce that makes sense for growers and wholesalers, but not for cooks or gourmets. Do you know what the *New York Times* critic Mimi Sheraton said about it? "If you can't find iceberg for a recipe, substitute waxed paper."'

He poured more Échezeaux with priestly deference. In this way did rocket, romaine, lamb's lettuce and *mesclun* find their way on to the Factory's menus.

## another girl from the *Protector*

Fiona McCrum from the *Protector* came to interview me after the opening of the Factory. To lubricate the conversation, I offered her a glass of Beaujolais nouveau which was cautiously accepted, as if Satan himself had offered a bubbling and steaming bowl of venom.

Swirling the cheap, metallic Beaujolais with mock seriousness, I said, 'It's a naive domestic Burgundy without any breeding, but I think you'll be amused by its presumption.'

Fiona scribbled furiously. She was only twenty-six and had not realized I was spoofing Rollo's James Thurber character.

'You have been accused of having a mincing and finicking obsession with food,' Fiona said combatively.

'Well,' I said, accepting the challenge, 'I certainly care about what I put in my mouth. I imagine you do too.' I was probably smirking when I said that. 'Food and design are related, you know. As, of course, are food and sex. Creating a nice chair is essentially the same process as making Irish stew. You have to have a plan, or a recipe. You need good materials and must treat them with care, respect and skill. That applies to, say, a tomato, a leg of lamb and a piece of Macassar ebony. Get the stew and the chair right, and you will give pleasure to many.'

The next day, a photograph appeared in the *Protector* of me in a striped pinafore, holding a tomato and a leg of lamb. 'Designs On Your Taste' the headline said, and I was firmly quoted by Fiona as saying, 'I do think best when holding a tomato or a leg of lamb.' This was presented as evidence of lunacy at best, of privilege at worst.

And I was further rebuked for recounting a conversation with Elizabeth David. We had been discussing the importance of freshness in cooking and, entirely without irony, Mrs David had said and I reported, approvingly, to Fiona McCrum: 'One of my sisters turned up from Vienna with a hare which she claimed had been caught by hand outside the State Opera House.' To me a demonstration of high principle, this was presented by the *Protector* as detestable snobbery of a nearly criminal type.

For so long a hero of the paper because of the democratic instincts revealed in my shops, I was now being mocked for frivolity and decadence. I demanded the right of reply, and a letter was published on the women's pages the following week:

> *Better to think than not to think. And I think better holding a leg of lamb and a tomato than your reporter does holding a notebook and a ballpoint. She sneers at our selling good food while Ethiopians starve. But banning* caneton aux olives *in Covent Garden is not going to bring free-for-all farmers' markets to Addis Ababa. And what is decadent about caring? I feel we should all care rather more. In my experience, people who do not care about food will care about very little. You accuse me of 'piggery'. I blame you for 'priggery'.*

The letter was signed: 'Eustace Dunne, designer, Solliès-Toucas, Var, France.'

The next week, bookings at the Factory were nearly twice the budgeted estimate.

And now I wanted to return to the *pissoir* which, with its mixture of Frenchness and boldly explicit function, seemed a fine advertisement for all of our businesses. What could demonstrate a useful love of France better than translating the Parisian *pissoir* to the streets of London?

..........................................................................................

® *Rollo Pinkie: It's worth pointing out here that Eustace never really understood the French language, beyond a few well-rehearsed clever comments intended to make him seem sophisticated. And he always spoke with such quiet authority, no one ever questioned his competence. He was fond of saying* 'Mieux perdre un ami qu'un *bon mot' to excuse his occasional bitchiness (although he had never read a word of the French philosophers he supposedly quoted).*

I sent a young designer to Paris to photograph every *pissoir* in his favourite arrondissements, all, as it happened, in the Quartier Latin. He came back and composed some mood-boards with extremely interesting historical details. *Pissoirs* first appeared in the 1830s and were known as *vespasiennes*, a reference to the Emperor Vespasian who is, most unfortunately, forever identified with piss, and maybe wind as well, on account of his levying a tax on the urine collected from Roman public toilets for use by the leather-tanning industry. Ingenious.

But the Parisian *pissoirs* were more ingenious still. Not only were they useful conveniences and finely decorated street furniture, but they had an additional function of being a vehicle for advertising. I love this French sense of the utilitarian and the *chic* in combination, something so lacking at home. Marvellous, I think, to gaze upon an Art Nouveau advertisement for Suze, the gentian *apéro*, or Cynar the artichoke liquor, while expelling the remains of the same through the relief of micturition and a liquid rope of golden pee. Here was form and function of a high currency!

Our design for an English *pissoir* used the same advanced engineering plastics we had used on loo brushes for Woolworths, and I had a momentary spasm of anxiety that we might be developing an unwanted lavatorial specialism. And we proposed very bright colours. They were, appropriately I feel, organic in form and inspired, to a degree, by the sculptures of Brâncuşi. The *de luxe* version had a reservoir of five litres. I decided to call it the 'P-loo', a name which evokes both public and lavatory: the hope was, people would pronounce it 'pee loo'. Our P-loos would be mass-produced and portable. Our P-loos would bring style and character to the most mundane of activities, enhancing the nation's toilet habits the while.

Not since Thomas Crapper's original water closet had design so influenced hygiene and manners.

I presented our P-loo designs to the British Airports Authority and they were enthusiastically accepted. Publicity included photographs of myself and all the male staff apparently using a long line of colourful P-loos arranged along Long Acre. We were grinning and waving with our free hands while the other hands were occupied in the obvious and necessary way. Quentin had some trouble here with his cigar.

The public would see the very first examples – raspberry red, Gordon's Gin green and Positano yellow – in the new Terminal 3 at Heathrow. I offered a prototype to the Victoria and Albert Museum and it was immediately acquired for the permanent collection, taking its place next to sculptures by Giambologna, drawings by Leonardo and an English medieval altarpiece with forty-five scenes of the Apocalypse.

The *Daily Post* reported 'Museum Goes Potty' and soon after I was invited to join the V&A's advisory council.

## the industrial design of good food

Crisp Gascoyne wrote a sparkling review of the Factory in the *Metro,* the trashy but influential free-sheet. 'A retro-gastro revolution' she called it. I promptly sent her a fax asking if she would like to be co-author with me of *The Factory Cookbook* whose subtitle was 'The industrial design of good food'.

But what does it take to run a restaurant? The food is, while obviously significant, possibly the least important element. It takes luck, genius, experience and balls. It also takes a studious awareness of gross margins, unit cost analysis, food cost percentages, profit evaluation, portion calculus, sourcing ingenuity, an empathy for waitresses suffering period pains and shrewd investment stratagems. Preferably using OPM, or Other People's Money. We used other OPP as well. That's Other People's Pictures. The Warhol Foundation lent us some Andy originals for the opening. We had them copied, kept the originals and returned the fakes to Pittsburgh. I thought this a nice Warholian gesture.

# 14

# 1982 – Murder on the Canal Saint-Martin

*'If it is true that we can ever come to know another human being, even to a small degree, it is only to the extent that he is willing to make himself known.'*

Paul Auster, *The Invention of Solitude*, 1982

Canal Saint-Martin.

ONE OF THE MOST DELICIOUS sensations I know, a little like Philip Johnson vicariously enjoying storms from inside his Glass House in Connecticut, is lying in bed early on dark London mornings and hearing the breathy rattle of a taxi outside, competing with the hesitant, tentative pre-dawn birdsong . . . and delighting in the fact that it's not waiting to take *me* to the horrors of the airport. What's the acoustic equivalent of 'voyeurism'? I don't know, but this is it.

There are times of day I specially enjoy and others I dislike intensely. I have never enjoyed late afternoon, that moment when most of the working day has passed, but you are not yet properly released into the freedoms of the evening and night.

But early mornings, before much has begun to move, are moments of wonder and promise: the whole day is waiting to be designed, to be mapped and explored. And I was told that a compensatory pleasure of being single was to lie diagonally across a double bed, escaping pockets of warmth and exploring the cool sheets, something specially delicious in these privileged moments at the beginning of the day.

But today was different because I was not alone.

I had called last night and she had opened the door herself, not made up, but hot and pink from the bath, hair *en brosse* and smelling of Creed Green Irish Tweed soap. She wore a vicious yellow Indian brocade robe and, very obviously, nothing else apart from woven leather slippers.

She met my eye and said nothing, stepping back a pace. Still silent, she shrugged off the robe, which fell to her waist, then kicked off the slippers, reducing her height by about an inch.

As she led me me through a cluttered drawing room, I saw a Blüthner baby grand and a Buescher 400 saxophone, a jazz classic instrument from about 1941. One that Duke Ellington would have known. I said nothing, but she saw my brow furrow, so explained, 'The saxophone teaches me mouth skills while the piano teaches me hand skills. Do you know what I mean?'

In the bedroom was a bowl of fruit and vegetables. Again, my brow furrowed.

She said, laughing, 'I keep a cucumber near my bed, but not because I'm hungry.'

And this was the aroma in the bedroom as the taxi rattled outside: farmyard, spoilt fruit and spent sex.

Quentin's wife was truly one of the most extraordinary women I have ever met.

## drugging the Prime Minister

Crisp Gascoyne's reviews of the Factory had queues winding around the block at all times and in all weathers. 'Covent Garden Flowers Again' was my favourite headline. Cabs that had recently refused to go beyond Cambridge Circus now circled Seven Dials, hungrily looking for fares. The Factory had expanded the possibilities of London itself. There was lots of press to check every morning and there were soon many imitators.

After the success of the restaurant, we were emboldened to build a larger Factory on Andy Warhol's model: a hybrid of restaurant, theatre, workshop, studio, gallery, laboratory and public space. But this would require ambitious funding and the Prime Minister herself had offered to help.

We had met at a Department of Trade lunch. Carpet tiles, fluorescent lights, awful contract furniture in synthetic fabrics with square-section black-lacquered metal legs, and scrappy little pinboards with ugly messages scrawled in blue biro. I imagined a Fighter Command Nissen hut in 1941 might have been more glamorous and would certainly have smelt no worse. Filthy little burnt cocktail sausages on sticks, Ritz crackers, cubes of tinned pineapple and mousetrap cheese, ministers with halitosis, more Surbiton virgins, this time with ring-bound notebooks, plaid skirts and Alice bands.

As I struggled to swallow an under-cooked grey sausage, the Prime Minister, dressed in eye-searing cobalt blue, smelling of Marks & Spencer scent, took me aside and said in an engagingly hoarse whisper which commanded total attention, 'Mr Dunne, I wonder if I might have a word with you about procurement. I am finding it very difficult to get what I want.'

And now I was on my way to Downing Street from Quentin's wife's flat in Little Venice.

As we drove along Marylebone Road the cabbie said, 'Hey, guv, did you know the famous saxophone solo on Gerry Rafferty's "Baker Street" was lifted straight from "Half a Heart" by Steve Marcus?'

I did not, but resisted a put-down and simply said, 'Well, I do know that these days, in every field, it is increasingly difficult to be confident about matters of originality and authenticity.'

Eustace Dunne, what an arse you are, I thought to myself, not entirely displeased.

We turned right down Portland Place and on to Regent Street towards Whitehall. I lit a cigarillo. In the constipated traffic, the driver was now discussing the BeeGees (with gruesome musical illustrations) while I choked as best I could a long and deadly yawn. As I searched in my pocket for change, I found a little canister.

I have never much cared for drugs. If I need psychotropic enhancement, I am very happy with farmyard wine from central France. *En magnum.* I prefer agricultural products to pharmaceutical ones. People who take cocaine annoy me: the energy it provides is a spurious one. But when Merck stopped making methedrine in 1966 on account of it being too damned nice, I had laid down a little cache, rather as you might with a vintage amphetamine.

Methedrine was essentially the same as Pervitin, a stimulant used by the Luftwaffe and the Wehrmacht. It was known as Stuka-tablets, although I am surprised that people flying Junker Ju 88 dive-bombers were not already quite awake enough, given the noise, vibration and excitement. It was very good at keeping pilots and soldiers alert, although side effects included disabling headaches and foaming at the mouth. Given her weakness for military metaphors, I thought some Pervitin might be amusing for the Iron Lady, who had graciously agreed to host a fundraising reception for the new Factory.

Beyond its photogenically glossy black front door, Number 10 is one of the least romantic houses you could hope, or fear, to visit. The aesthetic is that of a shabby and under-funded old people's home. The lights are too bright and there is a vague, but insistent, smell of school dinners. The furniture is old style, but newly made. And much, much too glossy.

Of course, there are proper pictures from the Government Art Collection, but they have been chosen by someone who is either blind or has a barmaid's conception of country-house taste: third-rate eighteenth-century landscapes and portraits, weedy, sad, faded little watercolours by Cozens and Cotman. Given the choice, why not have some gutsy Turners from the Tate, or a pouting, post-orgasmic, Pre-Raphaelite harlot, a Biblically turbulent John Martin canvas showing the parting of the Red Sea or Armageddon, some cheerful Hockneys or a batch of sexy Allen Jones prints paying homage to killer heels and tight-laced basques?

Downing Street is like a rundown museum with an absentee curator. In some rooms, there are tilts towards a modernist conception of interior design, but these reminded me only of a municipal crematorium in the provinces. And we were in one such now. The Prime Minister, resting her cut-glass tumbler of neat Scotch on a pseudo-Chippendale chiffonier, strode towards a pale lectern made of plywood covered with a joke-oak plastic laminate; a battered, corset-coloured Anglepoise illuminated her notes with 25 watts of dullness.

She sang my praises with themes dictated by notes compiled in a scissors-and-paste exercise performed earlier that day by the press secretary and her cuttings book.

'Eustace Dunne,' she warbled, 'has proved that design is essential to both our economy and to our culture. He has made a public lavatory with the grandeur of a temple.' An audience selected by the Department of Trade and the Arts Council nodded appreciatively while I shuffled towards the chiffonier and dropped a single tablet of Pervitin into her Macallan.

There is something of an art, or, at least, a craft to spiking drinks. In Chicago's Lone Star Saloon, Mickey Finn used chloral hydrate to incapacitate his victims, the better to rob them. Of course, I did not want an incapacitated Prime Minister. I wanted a disinhibited Prime Minister. Macallan spiked with Pervitin would elevate her mood. I knew that William James, who happily coined the term 'pragmatism', had described alcohol as a useful 'votary of the yes-function in man'. In woman too, I was hoping.

'And the Factory,' I heard her say, 'will perform for late twentieth-century Britain exactly what the Great Exhibition performed for our impressive Victorian forebears. It will present our credentials as a creative powerhouse. They had the courage to build the Crystal Palace. I recommend that you all have the courage to support the courageous Mr Dunne. He may not be royal, but he is the true heir to our Prince Albert.'

She approached me as the applause was rippling, inviting me, by patting her hand on the upholstery, to sit on a bench covered in an alarmingly gaudy peppermint-green velour. The wallpaper in the room was acid-yellow Regency stripes.

'Prime Minister, what an astonishing endorsement,' I said. 'I am so very grateful. You could have had everyone eating the mushroom canapés out of your hand.' And I noticed that the Prime Minister had very fine hands indeed: elegant, long, sensitive-looking fingers, no polish, but finely buffed nails cut short in a most impressively business-like fashion. I found these hands both revealing and curiously erotic.

## may I call you Eustace?

'What I have learnt, Eustace. I may call you Eustace? Of course I may call you Eustace. I'm the Prime Minister and I may call you anything I want. What I have learnt, Eustace, is that if you set out to be liked, you must then always be prepared to compromise. I have never wanted to be liked. I have only wanted to be respected. And obeyed. Besides, I never, ever compromise. I am very patient, provided I get my own way in the end.'

Her eyes sparkled and I sensed she was becoming animated. And she was intent too on explaining her philosophy.

'Being powerful is like being a lady. If you have to tell people you are, you aren't!'

'It is the same with design,' I replied. 'Subtlety reaches a deeper part of the human psyche than ostentation. Which brings me to my point. If you ever feel in need of advice about interior design here in Downing Street, we would happily provide it. Pro bono, naturally.'

Before she could comment, William Whitelaw, the deeply troubled Home Secretary, hurried in a heavy man's fashion across the carpet, bent to her seated ear and, facing away from me, whispered something indecipherable in detail, but evidently portentous in character. He was dismissed with a brusque, pursed-lip nod and a wave of two hands. The ursine figure then disappeared into the crowd.

'I always say everyone needs a Willie' – coquettish now – 'but my dear Home Secretary does sometimes lack a sense of ... *timing*. As you were saying.'

She placed a fine hand on my knee. 'I do, I am sure you recall my saying, feel we need some help with our decor. Sometimes I think Downing Street looks positively Soviet. And that can never be a good thing. Come, I want to show you my private drawing room. It is my own little democracy. And I personally control its borders. I also raise its taxes. And I punish visitors who disobey me.'

And with that, the First Lord – or was it in fact a 'Lady' – of the Treasury led me by another fine hand upstairs in Downing Street.

## le style est l'homme

The next day, Quentin and I were due in Paris to show his first-draft Factory drawings to the architect of the Fondation Voltaire. We say 'first-draft', but the French grand manner calls it *'equis'*. Quentin had done his sketches, but now we needed them turned into what the French call a *'projet rendu'*. Another fine name for a restaurant, I thought as I repeated the words in my head.

We took a breathy, rattling taxi at dawn to Heathrow. The Terminal 2 lounge was thronged with a dyspeptic tribe of European businessmen. Each looked hungover, each clutched a folded mac and carried an 'executive' briefcase, some of them with combination locks which I find strangely annoying. Do 'executives' really worry that complete strangers are going to steal their P&L accounts and their copy of *Penthouse*? Maybe they do.

'Good morning, ladies and gentlemen. This is Graham Nicholson-Smith, your captain today for the short flight to Paris Charles de Gaulle. With me on the flightdeck is Emma-Louise Bassett.'

There was a disturbed rustle of pink newspapers.

'Our flight time today is forty minutes and we may have a few bumps on the climb out, but overall we are expecting a smooth flight, so sit back and enjoy the service. For those of you in the front cabin, I recommend the full English.'

Bump it indeed did, to the smell of hot black pudding. Below, the battlefields of Picardy were visible beneath scattered low cloud, offering some form of compensation. I hate Tridents because I cannot believe that a plane with three heavy engines in the rear can possibly be balanced and stable: only raw thrust was keeping us up there, a metaphor if ever there was one.

Although when I thought of the worse suffering of the trench heroes buried below, we seemed to avoid disaster and, thanks to the bump-generating tailwind, arrived in a miserable, rainy and blowy Paris five minutes early. Now I knew why macs seemed to be compulsory for *hommes d'affaires*, although I was only in my Dougie Hayward Prince of Wales check.

Charles de Gaulle is ugly as only French modern official architecture can be: it was evidently designed by the same lugubrious, sadistic amateurs of bush-hammered concrete who built the toll booths on the autoroute. You really would not believe this was the culture of Lalique, Ruhlmann and Mallet-Stevens, of Chanel and Dior. With only hand baggage, my pigskin holdall and Quentin's canvas military-style bag, we stopped very briefly to get a filthy French coffee before taking a truculent Parisian taxi stinking of Gitanes and garlic farts.

Why are the French so very bad at making coffee? No one has ever been able to explain that to me. But my thoughts were now on my destination: the Hôtel George V. Quentin's was the industrial houseboat on the Canal Saint-Martin he had recently acquired. *Le style*, as they believe here, *est l'homme*.

George V is one of the world's most magnificent hotels: hushed and opulent, extreme only in its subtlety. Quentin, on the other hand, had bought a classic *péniche*, a metal barge 126 feet long and 17 feet wide, a gauge designed for the Canal Saint-Martin. The artisanal character of this huge craft suited his personality. Once it had carried grain from a depot on the Canal de l'Ourcq to central Paris, but now it was retired and Quentin had berthed it near the Bassin de la Villette. The hull he had painted a very dark blue with a red stripe and, inside, Quentin had made it look like the Cheltenham Bleu de Travail: tongue and groove panels, spotlights, and the iron deck was now a floor covered in brown quarry tiles.

He called his *péniche* 'Peruggia', the name of the Italian mason who lived hereabouts and had become famous when in 1911 he stole the Mona Lisa from the Louvre. His rationale was that Napoleon had stolen it from Italy, so he had every right to steal it back for *la patria*. Quentin identified strongly with thieves. It was perhaps why we got on so well.

That night we were to meet Timothy Clever at Le Savy, an exquisite little bistrot on the quiet backwater of rue Bayard, close to the George V. Convenient for me, if not for Quentin. Savy was once the old Bar Elie, transformed in about 1925 into a miniature art deco masterpiece with a pewter counter, painted friezes, mirrored walls and a mosaic floor. Long and narrow, it was like the dining car of an express train, an effect enhanced by the SNCF travel posters advertising St-Raphaël and Biarritz. Contemptuous waiters breezed through in their floor-length white aprons, performing with impressive gravity tasks they obviously felt beneath them.

Le Savy was kept in business by the fashion people from nearby avenue Montaigne, what you might call *vendeuses de luxe*, and by the offices of Radio Luxembourg next door. While we waited for Timothy, we ordered a toasted baguette with bone marrow and an endive salad with Roquefort. We each had a flute of champagne.

Timothy arrived, deeply tanned, in a shocking-pink raw silk suit with a lime-green shirt and sky-blue brogues. This was how he liked to identify with the masses whose living circumstances he felt empowered to improve through the agency of architecture. I liked

Timothy because, without accepting such a thing himself, he was a titanic snob and egotist.

He often spoke witheringly about his hatred of the suburbs, arrogantly assuming that the only reason why everyone in Rickmansworth did not live in a glass cell supported by steel ties and visibly serviced by nursery-coloured conduit and trunking was because they had simply been denied the opportunity on account of being poor, homespun, uneducated and, therefore, not privileged to move in his own cosmopolitan, left-leaning perfect circles. It amused me greatly that Timothy himself chose to live in a superb Georgian house with no galvanized pipework.

As Quentin produced his sketches, the waiters offered us menus. These were wrapped in heavy and cracked clear plastic, bound at the edges with frayed ribbon. The restaurant's specialities were picked out in red boxes. Six different sorts of clams, as many varieties of oysters, a shoulder of lamb with *petits pois Lyonnaise* and herrings with potato salad. I sensed that Timothy was unhappy with the choices: he cultivated his Italian background and a version of his snobbery was to maintain that the crudest *cucina casalinga*, even that pasta made with burnt husks of wheat that were floor-sweepings, was superior to Escoffier.

Putting the menu down without ordering, he said, 'I am so sorry to be late.' He was always late, carelessness about timing being a privilege of genius. 'But I have just been to a champagne reception for Salman Rushdie. I do think you should get Salman involved in the Factory.' I saw Quentin, still reading the menu, wince.

## like a Gothic cathedral

Settling into his missionary position with his arms spread along the top of the *banquette*, his fingers curling around the rail, Timothy explained: 'I believe we can affect the quality of people's lives. I mean ordinary people's lives. The only way is forward!'

He stopped and told the hovering waiter he would have the *gnocchi Parisienne* (baked in butter and topped with ham and cheese), as near as he could get to Tuscany while on rue Bayard.

'If we are going to improve the quality of the environment, and I believe we must, everybody will be involved. It will be a high-tech collective. Architecture is about public space. And we can be kings of that realm. Or bishops. The Factory will be like a Gothic cathedral. But remember,' he wagged a finger, 'the great Gothic cathedrals were high-tech in their day.'

'Precisely,' I said. 'They had flying buttresses, we have cantilevered decks.'

'My architecture is legible, light and flexible. It can be read like a book. It's democratic and it is the future.'

Quentin said, 'What bollocks, Timothy. Your lips move and your fingers trace the lines when you read. You've no idea what reading a book actually involves! Still less writing one as, it seems to me, you want to do with this highfalutin manifesto.'

Timothy was now morose with his gnocchi, but he had made a point and so too had Quentin, who was becoming manifestly more troubled as I enthused about Timothy's vision for the Factory. Then Timothy made a dramatic intervention, asking the waiter if he had any balsamic vinegar. The waiter, looking astonished, had not.

Timothy pushed his plate of gnocchi away. 'Now, my friends. You must forgive me. I have an early flight to Rio where I am speaking at a conference about how legible architecture can save the environment.'

A black Mercedes was visible through Savy's net curtains and we watched as the chauffeur held the door for the shocking-pink socialist.

## wrestling with the angel

Minutes later, Quentin and I took a Renault 16 taxi to the Canal Saint-Martin for a stroll before a digestif in *Peruggia*.

'The Renault 16,' I said, 'inherits the great French car design tradition of the Citroën DS. Look at the clever modular seating and the hatchback loading door. Do you know, Quentin, I have a feeling that, one day, all cars will have a hatchback. I like this Renault because its form follows its function. I think that's what Timothy has in mind for the Factory.'

Quentin was staring out of the window and quite rightly ignoring me. He looked unsettled, strumming the glass with his knobbly fingers. And when he stopped doing that, he began scratching his arms and clearing his throat. Never the most communicative man, he was completely failing to engage with me. Even when I said, 'Let's go to the Bistrot Paul Bert tonight, I think it's time for some *escargots* and *choucroute*.'

........................................................................................................

[®] *Rollo Pinkie: This is such a typical Eustace Dunne account of things. A sensitive man, he was always insensitive to others, failing here to notice Quentin's evident distress. Or if he did notice, he imagined an invitation to dinner would solve the problem. He always did. Never mind plenty of optimism and white paint, Eustace always thought plenty of optimism and two bottles of Meursault were the most effective remedy for melancholy.*

The Canal Saint-Martin runs underground between the Faubourg du Temple and Bastille, and anybody who had seen Gustave Doré's dark illustrations of Dante's *Inferno* would be reminded of them by an infernal walk or boat ride here.

But on the surface its character is very different. The Impressionist Alfred Sisley painted its chestnut trees, creating an image of blameless, eternal spring. Lovers canoodle on the pretty cast-iron footbridges while working barges tackle the complicated locks below them.

You would never know it from the surface idyll, but the Canal Saint-Martin was used as a dump. Its periodic draining would reveal, to the regular delight of the popular press, an informal, submerged, urban museum: bicycles, prams, fridges, chairs, doors, the occasional rotting dog carcass, metal shelves, plastic buckets, bottles and, from time to time, dead bodies.

Quentin too, it soon turned out as we strolled and smoked, had submerged problems.

'Araminta's messing around. I'm totally pissed off. She's shagging the milkman, I suppose. Not a lot else to do in Wiltshire. For all I know she's shagging her bloody shire horses and the postman too. I think I'm going to stay on the houseboat here in Paris. She can keep the Little Venice flat and amuse her fancy men there, but I'll have to sell the farmhouse. That would mean I can no longer work with you, but there are some options. Would you like to buy the farm? Or lend me money, with the farm as security? About half a million would do it, I'd guess. And by the way, I think that Timothy friend of yours is a conceited, hypocritical arsehole. And I know what you do with arseholes. Certainly, you do not employ them.'

He beamed at me, somewhat falsely I felt, and pulled very heavily on his cigar, the blazing tip making his rumpled face look like an orange Mephistopheles.

I didn't know if he was joking, so said, 'Quentin, dear thing. None of us is making any money. In any event, you already live like a fucking millionaire. And don't be jealous about Araminta: you've treated her like a toe-rag for the past ten years. If you need money, you're going to have to find it for yourself. I'm already too far stretched. And you know everything I make actually goes back into the business.'

It is hard to discern whether someone suffused in an orange glow is looking ashen, but his tone suddenly changed. The gruff but usually affable Quentin suddenly became a whining supplicant with an edge of menace.

'But, Eustace, it would be terrible if people ever learnt about the fire in the country factory. I'd never forgive myself. And of course, I would never say anything. But I do know people are talking. Not everybody is your friend, Eustace. There are treacherous people out there and one of them called me last week. He wanted to know what you did with the insurance money. Actually, that's a very good question, but I will keep quiet about it. At least for the moment. I really don't want all my photographs to get into the wrong hands.'

'Don't be a total cunt, Quentin!' I said angrily. 'I have no idea what you're talking about. And anyway, you benefited from the insurance money as much as I did. You spent it on hookers, cars, booze and God alone knows what else. Probably this ridiculous barge. And now you are asking me to refinance your whole sordid project.'

He laughed and gave me what I thought was intended as a good-natured shove, but was, in fact, a little too vigorous to be ignored. I shoved him back. Suddenly, I thought of that Gauguin painting, *Jacob Wrestling with the Angel*. It was now very dark and we were alone and I had become horribly aware that this was becoming a real struggle, not negotiated horseplay between friends.

'Have *you* been fucking Araminta, Eustace? Have you?' Quentin, who was very drunk, made a horrible bovine bellow and rushed at me again. I, slightly less drunk, sidestepped and he fell into the canal, joining the bicycles, prams, fridges, chairs, doors, the occasional rotting dog carcass, metal shelves, plastic buckets, bottles and, from time to time, dead bodies.

I learnt later that Quentin could not swim.

And I did not care. I straightened my tie and walked towards Bastille. By the time I found the taxi rank, there was a distant sound of police sirens.

## fixing a blindspot

I might have had very good eyesight and feral coordination, but sports never interested me. Not even tennis, despite the persistent erotic undertow caused by the sight of a young woman's brown legs with straining muscles. Betjeman's Joan Hunter Dunn was, I thought, polite pornography. But also too suburban. And tennis would have required belonging to a club, something appealing only to people who actually value the company of others.

Equally, the idea of a 'hobby' was always repulsive since it implied that everyday life was so tedious that something pleasing must be maintained above and beyond it. But photography was different.

For years this had been a blindspot. I loved beautiful things, but had never owned a camera and had never taken photographs.

So the day after the fight with Quentin, I was walking along the rue Neuve des Petits Champs towards number 19 where the photographer Henri Cartier-Bresson had a studio in servants' quarters on the fourth floor. Tony, now married to the sister of the Queen, had introduced us by letter, but now I had decided – in a rare moment of critical self-examination – to remedy a personal failing and learn to take pictures.

Cartier-Bresson spoke perfect English, having studied at Cambridge. And he had the manners of privilege: his family was rich from the cotton trade. His first camera was given him by the American socialite Harry Crosby, whose motto was 'Living well is the best revenge', often found embroidered today on novelty cushions. I wish I had known Crosby.

Cartier-Bresson served Algerian coffee in Duralex glasses. His first words were: 'You know it was Dick Simon of Simon & Schuster who gave me the title of my book, *The Decisive Moment*? I had said to him, "Oops! The moment! Once you miss it, it is gone for ever." And he said gravely, "There you have it."' He clapped his hands.

Cartier-Bresson fetishized privacy and subterfuge: he painted his Leica matte black so it could be used unobtrusively. He offered it to me for inspection. I picked up the camera and considered it as you might a fifteenth-century illuminated psalter.

The photographer never wanted to be recognized: at an Oxford honorary degree ceremony he held papers in front of his face. This was an image that went around the world: 'no publicity' being the most certain way there is to achieve a very great degree of publicity.

'The greatest artist I know,' Cartier-Bresson continued, 'is Costantino Nivola, a man who is *hors de série*, unique, if you understand me, a man who cannot be classified. He understands the strange beauty of everyday things as well as the value of surprise. At which he is something of a master.' Nivola was a masterclass in social promotion through art and design. A Sardinian peasant with a flair for sculpture in a style we would today call 'mid-century Modern', he ended up in the Hamptons.

Mention of Nivola made me think briefly of Soane and then I soon wondered if I had just heard the first draft of an autobiography by Cartier-Bresson. But here was someone I could learn from, as much as I had learnt from Sir John Soane himself, Charles Eames, the Castiglionis or Marino Morosini. Cartier-Bresson was not going to do anything as banal as teach me how to use a Leica M3. Instead, he taught me a working method as relevant to design as to photography.

'You will find your first ten thousand photographs are your worst,' the Frenchman said. 'Your approach must be to have a velvet hand, but a hawk's eye. Never use flash. It is impolite and intrusive. It is like going to a concert with a gun in your pocket. And remember that in photography, the smallest and meanest object can be a great subject.'

'I know that to be true,' I said. 'You're talking to the man who turned an ordinary salad bowl into an object of almost religious significance. In my shops, a spatula is comparable to a fragment of the True Cross.'

Cartier-Bresson laughed and pointed to a decanter of whisky, arching his eyebrows. I nodded agreement.

As he poured a generous measure into Baccarat tumblers, Cartier-Bresson went on. 'My principle is edit, edit, edit! Reality offers us such wealth that we must cut some of it out on the spot. There are no alternatives other than to simplify! The question is: do we always cut what we should?'

I bit my lower lip and looked at the floor. I sensed my audience was over.

The next day, I picked up a copy of the Paris edition of the *International Herald Tribune* on my way to Charles de Gaulle.

'London designer dead in Paris at 55. Mystery of the Canal Saint-Martin' was a story on page three.

I cleared my throat and strummed the glass of the taxi's window. And I decided that Quentin had let me down.

....................................................................................................

[R] *Rollo Pinkie: Eustace defined all human relationships in terms of value and benefit, as well as loyalty and betrayal. It speaks of his pharaonic ego that Quentin's death is interpreted not as a personal tragedy, but as treachery. In a move that would bring a Roman tyrant into disrepute, after Quentin's death Eustace claimed the life insurance as his own, since premiums had been paid by his business.*

# 15

# 1985 – A designer who wants to be a billionaire

*'Live out your fantasy here with me.'*

Madonna, 'Into The Groove', 1985

*A superyacht.*

THE TAXI WAS TEN MINUTES late at the hotel.

No apology, just an unenthusiastic shrug.

'*Dommage, m'sieur, circulation vachement merde.*' The driver spat in the gutter and did not look sorry at all. But Sacré-Coeur was set against a blue sky and Paris was as it should be. Which is to say the Boulevard-Magenta and Porte de Clignancourt had tortuous, strangulated, anarchic traffic, and the fatigued beige Peugeot 404 driven by this passive-aggressive man in a biker jacker and a turban made only small progress.

He spat again, this time on to the floor, and cursed in a language that was not French.

How on earth, I asked myself, did Paris ever acquire a reputation for sophistication?

BA1756 took off at 11:40, later that morning. Conditions for the flight back to London were calm and we at the front of the plane enjoyed a smoked salmon and scrambled egg brunch while once bloody, now grey-green, battlefields sped by below.

But Quentin's 'accident', as I insisted on styling it, had made me maudlin and reflective, a mood as unusual as it was lachrymose. I looked for something to read.

'There is no thirst in the human soul quite so unquenchable as the thirst for youth,' I read, picking a little stray scrambled egg off my lapel. I was looking at a gushing article in a women's magazine found in the pocket of seat 1B. Grease stains suggested it had previously been enjoyed by another passenger also playing with a late breakfast.

Heathrow. Black cab. Cromwell Road. Home. Then the next day

it was a fast turnaround in the London office. Read the press cuttings, patronize the staff, return to Heathrow. Telling people I was seeing bankers in Geneva, in fact I checked into a clinic in Vevey, just an hour's drive down the lakeshore from Cointrin airport.

I took an S-Class Mercedes from Limos4Geneva, the car providing an interval to contemplate, from the back seat, German concepts of luxury, or 'luxus' as they called it in their maddening way. I was, for example, fascinated by the soft feel of the padded seat belt, intended not to injure delicate silk or cashmere. Or, I supposed, even naked skin, chilled to goosebumps by the efficient Swabian air conditioning. One day, I decided, we would open in Germany.

We rushed past Lausanne, Ouchy, Rivaz, Chexbres, Vernex and La Tour-de-Peilz. Beautiful names, all of them, I thought. In one tiny village with no traffic and no pedestrians, but several sets of traffic lights nonetheless, I spotted a huge showroom selling Bösendorfer pianos: culture caught like a fly in amber in this beautiful, but desolate and costive, country.

And I could not help nodding with solemn approval that the Route du Lac had wonderful vertiginous vineyards lining the road, perfectly trimmed vines of *chasselas* and *servagnin* running from the very near water to the very distant sky.

'*Les vignobles sont protégés par UNESCO*,' the uniformed driver told me with pride. We were doing nearly two hundred kilometres per hour. I reached without enthusiasm for a bottle of mineral water – Evian itself nearly visible across the misty lake – and thought of lunch. 'Fillets of *perche*,' I said out loud. 'Or perhaps *raclette* and *délice des Grisons*.' Then I returned my gaze to the lake.

The Vaudois littoral is lined with clinics to bust fat, lengthen life, dry out, retexture, transplant, groom, scrub, slim, buff, reprogramme, tan, beautify, detox, inject or do almost anything imaginable to enhance or preserve any body which still has a pulse and belongs to a rich, spoilt, ruined, vain customer. And in an internal battle between economy and vanity, my sense of economy had lost. After the accident, I had told myself it was time for a little redesign of my mortal self, although I wanted no one to know: the name I used to check in was Frank Steiner.

'Frank Steiner' was, I thought, a terrific joke because a local tradition of blood-sucking and body alteration had been established by Byron and Shelley at the Villa Diodati at Cologny, just a few clicks away. To compete with Mary Shelley's holiday writing project that became *Frankenstein*, Dr Polidori, Byron and Shelley's travelling physician, wrote *The Vampyre*. This was the first and best literary example of scientific intervention in human life: vital fluids being drained from one creature to regenerate another.

## sleep is a slice of death

In the clinic, traditional French hotel luxury competed, in matters of style and atmosphere, not altogether successfully, with the aesthetics of a Swiss nuclear medicine laboratory. It had been founded in the thirties by a disreputable Russian who was a pioneer of hypnopaedia, the science of learning while you sleep. Fyodor Turmansky deplored the fact that most people 'waste' 219,000 hours asleep during their lives. 'Sleep,' he insisted, 'is just a slice of death.'

Professor Turmansky also believed that grafts of monkey testicles inserted into male patients' scrotums would have a rejuvenating effect. Results were spectacular, demand was high, so a malodorous monkey farm was established on the Route du Lac to supply the clinic's needs.

When monkey glands became illegal, the clinic turned to lambs' foetuses. When lambs' foetuses became illegal, the clinic began to disguise the sources of its remedies and cures.

Like all patients, I had been sent a scary disclaimer, reporting that short-term side effects were occasionally stupefying, even disabling, so close medical supervision would be required for several days after injection. Longer-term side effects included hirsutism, possible rejection and infections that sometimes were terminal. These were to be considered and accepted before any procedure could take place.

There was a lobby bar with a handsome terrace, drenched in soft light from the lake. Its back-lit shelves carried bottles of *grande marque* champagnes, even if they were displayed in deterrent style as if they were plasma or disinfectant. But the bedroom mini-bars were stocked with water only and breakfast in your room was compulsory. Guests, or patients, perhaps 'clients', were expected to leave bio-medical samples outside bedroom doors along with the breakfast tray of rejected croissant and mint tea. Vevey, I thought, cannot easily be mistaken for Sodom.

The clinic's restaurant was vast, prim and humourless, as if A&E consultants had designed the first-class lounge in an airport, providing at the same time ample scope for medical emergencies. There were portraits of Churchill, Somerset Maugham, Pelé, Gary Player, Noel Edmonds, that idiot from Slade and Pope Pius XII, all evidently clients satisfied by successful reinvigoration.

Over a thin, puritanical and unappealing *escabeche* of mackerel, I sat down with the medical director who looked cheerful and declared: 'Obesity is nothing to do with enjoying food. It is an ugly compulsion.'

I nodded gravely.

'And with our injections we do not intend to make you live longer, but to age better. And that includes sex. If all goes well, you might find the experience intensified and the libido more alert. We recently had a sixty-five-year-old guest whose expense of sexual energy had been so prodigal after injections, he promptly returned for another course of glands and a penis transplant.'

Time was an issue, the medical director explained.

'In the west, time is like gold. You save it. You lose it. You waste it.

You don't have enough of it. And you always want more of it. I have studied a tribe in the Amazon called the Barasana who simply have no word for time and therefore no concept of it.'

'Why then do we procrastinate?' I demanded.

'Let me answer that in a moment,' the medical director replied.

Returning to my room, I found it strange and mawkish when so many guests, clients or patients were, one way or another, battling with the consequences of passing time, to have so many brightly lit promotional vitrines featuring classic Swiss watches. Hublot and Rolex looked like vanguards of the Grim Reaper. Especially so when diamond-studded.

And later, waiting in the treatment room, I picked up the clinic's house magazine. Wasn't *Inside* a terrible name for a publication of a clinic that was essentially a voluntary penal institution? Then soon the anaesthetic advanced its cause and I fell asleep.

When I awoke later, there was a dull ache in my scrotum. I recalled a critic of the therapy had warned the process was merely 'inserting dead meat in the wrong place'. And that was what it felt like: a small, but heavy, creature had died down there. I winced.

At the reception, a hatchet-faced harridan with hair scraped back and perfectly invisible make-up, almost certainly an extravagant masochist, I felt, took my order for a cab with a look that would freeze Satan's own barbecue.

## monkey glands are not enough

Twenty minutes later, I was in the candle-lit bar of the grand old Hôtel Les Trois Couronnes, the net curtains wafting around the French doors in the seductive zephyrs off Lac Léman. The suffocating atmosphere of discretion positively invited, even demanded, delinquency.

I picked up a facsimile copy of Harry MacElhone's classic 1927 book of cocktail recipes. Smiling to myself, I ordered a Monkey Gland: gin, orange juice, grenadine, syrup and absinthe. This I sipped with a pleasure that gripped that prehistoric node at the back of the neck. One Monkey Gland was certainly not going to be enough.

'Now I know what ballsache really means,' I muttered, while uncomfortably rearranging my weight on the bar stool. Still, soon the cocktail was having its analgesic effect. Entering an internal reverie about promised new vitality pursued by amiable thoughts of Mr MacElhone, I was interrupted by a heavy Russian accent and an even heavier Russian hand on my shoulder.

'My name is Dmitri Kozlov,' the accent said. 'Don't I recognize you from the clinic?'

He had escaped the regime as well.

Kozlov had a head like a Halloween pumpkin dressed with frameless spectacles and was wearing a vintage Adidas tracksuit in a difficult emergency services shade of blue. He looked more like a professor of accountancy than the exiled late Soviet-era fertilizer magnate of reality. He ordered a bottle of Krug for himself and a third Monkey Gland for me.

'I saw your Range Rover concept at the *Salon de l'Automobile* in Geneva. It is very funny to suggest a baby-bottom-pink suede interior for a piece of shitty agricultural equipment. Do you know what happens to pastel colours in farmyards? But I did like the idea of having a sunglasses case built into the steering-wheel boss. Your English sense of humour is really quite remarkable.'

'Actually, I never play it for laughs,' I said, a little priggishly. 'Design is a matter of applied intelligence, of practical solutions to everyday problems.'

'You really think so, Mr Baby-bottom-pink suede?' Kozlov pursed his generous lips. '"*On verra, on verra*," as our banking friends down the road say. We will see, we will see. But I am not interested in what you call practical solutions. Nor, I am very glad to say, do I have what you call everyday problems. Certainly, I have problems, but they are exceptional ones. Indeed, truly exceptional. I am a billionaire who wants to be a designer. And you are a designer who wants to be a billionaire. I think we will get along well.'

I found Kozlov repellent, but fascinating.

'How did you make your money?' I asked while providing myself with the silent answer: theft, vice, dissipation, extravagance, gambling, bribery, gun-running, corruption, pimping, fraud and influence-peddling. There is much to be learned here, I thought.

'Get up early. Work hard. Be lucky. And steal fertilizer factory!' Kozlov in fact replied, having no time for indefinite articles. 'We acquire great wealth because there is nothing to stop us. That, if you follow me, is what it means to be an oligarch. Now, Mr Baby-bottom-pink Suede. Perhaps you would like to design the interior of my new yacht,' Kozlov suggested, pouring more Krug and spilling some. He chucked back a handful of unsalted cashews.

He continued, 'I have a yacht already. But I am bored with it. Size matters and so too does shape. I invite you to enter a playground where excess is not merely tolerated, but actively encouraged. I have a boredom threshold that lowers itself automatically every twelve months. I refuse to be polite. I enjoy excess. We measure success in chandeliers. But I want you to teach me. I want you to improve my taste, but please, if you will, no baby-bottom-pink suede. Instead, I think, blue sky thought.'

I warned him, silently calculating the commission on billions of dollars, that, 'Billions of dollars do not equal taste. Every yacht I have seen has an interior that's a deprived child's vision of glamour: un-blushing, crass, spectacular vulgarity. All afloat on an ocean of fatuity. Yes. Of course, Dmitri, I can save you from yourself.'

*Princess Potassium Nitrate*, named for the source of his fortune, was built by Blohm & Voss in Bremen. She was seventy-four metres long, had a permanent crew of twenty-two and eight cabins for twelve guests, together with Kozlov's own stateroom, with panic room contiguous. The fertilizer magnate had specified a full-depth plunge pool, twin helipads and a tender that was itself bigger than the popular conception of a 'yacht'. There were twin MTU 20-cylinder Series 8000 diesels and *Princess Potassium Nitrate* had military spec navigation, automation and protection systems.

I was there at her launch into the Weser on a freezing day two years after the Kozlov meeting in Les Trois Couronnes. Somewhat contemptuously, she was flying a Red Ensign. My fees were $20 million, paid in Switzerland.

The twenty-two crew were dressed, at my suggestion, in Paul Smith. Cushions and curtains in a silk-cashmere fabric using a monochrome pattern derived from the historical flora archives at Kew. That touch had impressed Kozlov. Bespoke *objets d'art* (which I thought of as middlebrow junk) were commissioned to fill back-lit bays. The stern was like the apse of a cathedral with sacred chapels replaced by serving stations of champagne and caviar. Eames Soft Pad chairs were upholstered in a delicate, flawless gazelle hide, organically dyed the colour of *crème fraiche*. Decks were Moroccan ebony, Siamese teak and Tuscan *pietra serena*. Bathrooms were unique ovimorphic fantasies – inspired by Nivola – moulded in black Corian. It was as if all the expensive hard surfaces of the world were focused here on Dmitri Kozlov's ship.

It's a truth that the very rich like neutral colours, frosted glass, downlighters, fossils, suede, Alcantara, and objects or art so bland – a gourd, for example – that they yield nothing to contemplation. It was equally clear that the very rich did not much care for books. A pile of unread and unreadable, but coruscatingly glossy, Taschen art books constituted the library on Boksi's yacht. They were never disturbed.

'What we are doing here,' I told *The Architectural Digest*, 'is transcending the traditional limits of architecture.' The journalist scribbled obligingly. 'We are transcending costive, suburban conventions of taste.' The journalist scribbled now even more furiously.

But I knew what I was really doing was creating a safe place in the ocean where my client was unlikely to contemplate the fruits of his criminal greed, his rape of the planet's resources, or consider how wickedness had created the building of this ocean-going, rootless, nomadic, hedonistic principality.

## Satan's work

Kozlov's jet existed to feed, or assuage, these same anxieties. And it was my next commission. If you like, the creation of an aircraft interior is an inimitable design exercise. The space is constricted, the attention of the consumer extremely focused and the discipline a stimulus. Of course, I had spent a long time on commercial planes and we had done seating fabrics for British European Airways. But this was a bigger brief.

Once, when part of a government delegation to the industrial design fair in Kiev, I had travelled on a Russian plane in the Brezhnev era. You could not call it a 'private jet' since Communist orthodoxy allowed no such thing as privacy, but it was not a plane ever used, nor even seen, by fare-paying commercial passengers.

And it was an experience I would never forget. The aerospace engineer Oleg Antonov was a Kiev native and the Antonov An-24 was his personal transport for him and his guests around the Ukraine. The chubby, high-winged plane was painted a military matt green and was undistinguished from outside. Its belly was close to the ground and you entered by a very short airstair (to enable access to primitive airports). Yet the interior was, so I mused, like a Tsarist bordello: burgundy carpet, burgundy twill armchairs with antimacassars, lacquered brown wood, recessed lighting, bevelled glass, and a silver samovar surrounded by buckets with bottles of Georgian *shampanskoye.* It was, in its decadent lushness, the very opposite of the technical imperatives of aerospace which are based on lightness. And I wondered if in this way Russian revolutionaries in fact shielded themselves from the unsatisfactory modern world they had helped create.

By contrast, we gave the cavernous cabin of Kozlov's Boeing 737-400 nine enormous captain's chairs, upholstered in the lightest of grey leathers, decorated with gigantic blanket stitches, appearing like an enormous, enveloping baseball mitt. There were Lalique room dividers while a massive plasma screen continuously played soothing aquarium videos. Real windows had been replaced by LCD units showing imaginary views, so as to improve on nature. It was as if *glasnost* had invaded the aircraft interior: pale leather replacing dark red stuffs, plutocracy displacing democracy.

.......................................................................................................

® *Rollo Pinkie: It did not strike Eustace as risibly absurd, not to mention contradictory, that, in the same week Dmitri Kozlov's Boeing business jet made its delivery flight to Geneva from Lufthansa Technik in Hamburg, where it was fitted out, that, back in London, his Bleu de Travail had begun a well-publicized campaign about 'authenticity' in design and how to improve popular taste.*

Another oligarch, a Kazakh gas thief, had been a guest at one of novelist Toft Monks' penthouse lunches that were a London institution circa 1985. Monks was a cheerful rascal who reinvented himself as the writer of plonking, ham-fisted, wince-making, but very successful thrillers. He enjoyed his wealth and celebrity in an uninhibited style and his lunches were becoming a tradition among those well-connected in London media, politics, theatre and business.

And typical of Monks was the aggrandisment of 'penthouse' when his attractive riverside apartment overlooking Parliament was,

261

actually, two floors below the top. And the menu was invariable: a single, carefully policed, glass of champagne on arrival. A very masculine, meat-centric pie and a single glass of good red Burgundy, again carefully policed, followed. I do not think a woman was ever present. No one was ever over-served at one of Toft Monks' lunches, but then again, no one ever refused an invitation.

Someone had told a younger Monks that the secret of social success was to have an eclectic guestlist so, my first time, I had found myself struggling to make coherent conversation with a foul-mouthed Scottish stand-up comic on my left and the Archbishop of Canterbury on my right.

But on the latest occasion I was seated next to a Buckingham Palace official of ultramontane grace. We listened attentively as, over coffee, the Kazakh explained business opportunities in the Caucasus.

'Sometimes I think it's Satan's work,' I found myself saying to Buckingham Palace, explaining my own work for an oligarch. 'I mean, great temptations, but terrible risks as well—' and then I was cut off as I heard 'Tell us, Your Grace ...' and Monks grandly attempting to grab the room's attention as he nodded to the Archbishop, requesting a view on current affairs. So I turned back to my immediate companion.

'I wonder if progress from Oleg's Antonov with its flock to Dmitri's Boeing with its ruched leather and spot-lit fossils is evidence of larger changes in the Russian view of the world,' I suggested, as my neighbour looked thoughtfully into the distance through the vast windows above the Thames.

'That's very interesting,' the equerry said, returning to earth. 'We have been thinking about a refit of the Royal Train. To be absolutely honest, the dear old thing is beginning to look a teeny bit *tired*. Do you know, I think you can still see ghosts of LNER livery and the bogs are primeval. Worse than Sandringham and God knows they're pretty bad. HM would not wish to be thought an *oligarch*,' he said, 'but you might like to take a look. See what you think.'

'At last!' I said to myself. 'Designing for the fucking Queen!' I sank a last drop of Burgundy.

## coming far

Two weeks later, I took a black cab down The Mall, past the Victoria Monument and up to security at the main gate of Buckingham Palace. For the first time in my life, I was able to say, 'I have come to see the Queen.'

'If it's true, it ain't bragging' I said to myself with some satisfaction. I was wearing a navy-blue linen suit, a cornflower-blue shirt from Turnbull & Asser, black loafers and a black knitted silk tie. Additionally, there was an artfully rumpled white silk pocket square.

Of course, the guards by some mysterious process already knew the taxi's registration number and I was peremptorily nodded through to a car park hidden from the gawping tourists and reserved, if the tell-tale signwriting on the vans was evidence, for tradesmen alone. There appeared at the Queen's London home to be a special need for plumbers and central heating engineers, whose Transits outnumbered those of florists and fishmongers by a factor of three.

A uniformed valet, dressed like an extra from a Viennese opera, appeared as if from nowhere and bowed very slightly.

'Mr Dunne, this way please. Her Majesty will receive you in the Yellow Drawing Room.'

I was led to a creaking service lift, smelling vaguely of haddock, and two flights later, emerged through green baize doors into a corridor, more of a gallery, which seemed to be a quarter of a mile long. There were enormous battle scenes of Walcourt, Schellenberg, Elixheim, Oudenaarde and Malplaquet. There were Dutch flower pieces; one of tulips I noticed was labelled 'School of Dries van den Westenra, A Gift of Marcus Samuel'. He was the man who created Shell, a Prince of Pollution.

And then into the Yellow Drawing Room itself. With its dazzling light and upper-class clutter, I thought it looked like a demented chatelaine's take on David Hicks. I counted a Macedonian earth-mother sculpture, a wine-cooler in the shape of a Provençal *cigale*, several stuffed owls, a sword made of shark's teeth, a surprising number of ostrich eggs, a small Maori canoe, a totem pole, several oil paintings of horses in the style of Stubbs, and floor mats from Tonga.

Just as I was wondering if there might be little bowls of Fairy Dust, an unmistakable, slightly quavering voice behind me said: 'Have you come far?'

This was always, I later understood, the Queen's traditional question on meeting a strange subject.

I couldn't help myself. 'Do you mean geographically or socially, Your Majesty?'

A hovering man in army uniform, an equerry I imagined, looked exquisitely uncomfortable. But ignoring my suicidally mischievous wit, the Queen continued.

'One is told, Mr Dunne, that you are an expert on taste.' She spoke the word as though it was foul. 'So far as one is concerned, what I think about taste is that it does not help. Do you know what I mean?'

She had, I noticed, some chocolate digestive biscuits in a yellowing Tupperware box on a side table, next to a bottle of Gordon's gin and several splits of Britvic pineapple juice. For some reason, among these recent antiques I felt immediately guilty about having copied Ernest Race's 'Antelope' chair designs in 1951, welding up facsimiles and then taking credit. But the guilt soon passed and confidence returned.

'If I may, Ma'am, may I remind you what your very own couturier Hardy Amies said?'

'You may, Mr Dunne.'

'Well. He said that a man should look as though he has bought his clothes with intelligence, put them on with care and then forgotten all about them. That is the effect I would like to achieve on the Royal Train.'

'One's train is a matter very personal. Will you, for example, be choosing one's colours? I don't, Mr Dunne, want any of this newfangled functionalist nonsense. An English Queen's train is one's castle. Or palace.'

'Ma'am,' I explained unnecessarily, 'I had no part in the Bauhaus. Instead my culture is Pop. Some of my fortune comes from selling plastic stools and beanbags.'

'Oh dear. How very unfortunate. But we must all do what we can,' the Queen said, with the suggestion of exquisite pain.

'Ma'am, if I may. My salad bowls, scented candles, asparagus kettles and ramekins have changed the lives of millions of your subjects. You have no need for any refinements that I might humbly offer, but I can undertake to create a new Royal Train that will show British design at its best. It will be a superlative advertisement of national skill and a matter for national pride.'

'Of course it will,' the Queen said. 'The Duke of Edinburgh is most interested in "design". He has, one is told, recently given an award to an electric toaster and a tetrode valve. Maybe he will give an award to you too.' Her Majesty did not smile when she made that last remark. Instead, she looked somewhat crestfallen. A corgi scurried over highly polished parquet.

'That, Ma'am, would be splendid, but first let me show you what we can do. I am confident you will be pleased.'

'Very well, Mr Dunne. But none of those hard edges, if you will. One has enough of them in one's Land Rover. Colonel Vyvyan here will show you out. Perhaps, Colonel Vyvyan, you would make an appointment for Mr Dunne to show one his proposals for the Royal Train at Balmoral later in the year.'

Colonel Vyvyan obliged, since obligation was his calling. We walked to the waiting cab in military silence.

'What did you say, sir?' the cabbie asked as we drove up the Mall.

I had been talking to myself. 'I just said, "I am designing for the fucking Queen,"' I explained. And then I laughed. Although no conventional royalist and not at all a good supplicant, I declare I felt a thrill of exhilaration at this royal encounter. At the studio, I gave the cabbie five pounds and a matey tap on the shoulder, telling him to park on double yellow lines and wait.

## sea change

I now moved, with settled gravity, confidently up the stairs towards my desk and its regular daily pile of press cuttings, maintained and guarded by my secretary, an Amazonian Dutch lesbian in pop socks.

'You are not going to like this, Eustace,' I heard Anika say, adjusting her horn-rimmed spectacles to suggest a mood of intelligent sympathy.

The most prominent one was from the letters page of *Haul at Sea: the LuXXury Boat Report*, the extravagantly lush quarterly magazine published in Geneva. An aggrieved correspondent was not happy with the sixteen-page feature on *Potassium Nitrate* that had appeared in the last edition. The feature had been titled 'Sea Change'.

It had been gushing and not at all specific. In the security-obsessed world of superyachts, details are always fudged, specifics being for the little people. For similarly evasive reasons, costs are never disclosed since these might excite the curiosity of tax authorities or the vengeance of disappointed and less fortunate business associates.

But uncritical, even lavish, praise is a currency that can be spent very freely in this glossy medium. And the magazine had said:

*Eustace Dunne has set a new artistic standard for superyacht interiors. Just as Augustus found Rome brick and left it marble, London's top designer found a floating world of brass and teak, turning it into breathtakingly sophisticated beige. We call it a sea-borne sea-change that will alter superyachts for ever.*

The correspondent did not agree about all of these points. Gary Knobber, a reliably competent professional designer, had been subcontracted to us, charged with overseeing the Kozlov super-yacht commission. I had many other obligations: my role was an inspirational one, to achieve agreed ends by critique, guidance and commentary. A designer, in the theory I was evolving, was not necessarily the person who held the pencil. He was the source of the idea and the arbiter of taste. And now Knobber was claiming authorship.

His letter said:

*The interior designs you published are, in fact, my own work, not those of Eustace Dunne. Dunne Design was merely the umbrella company that won the contract. This was a contract that I managed. Moreover, creative decisions about colour, furnishings, fabrics, all other decor, fit-out and details were mine alone. If the concept of "authorship" means anything, I am the designer of the* Potassium Nitrate *interiors. In any future reference to this outstanding vessel, the credit must be: Designer, Gary Knobber.*

I was told by Anika I first went purple, then white, with fury. Immediately, I dictated a letter to *Haul at Sea*'s editor, an impression-able young woman I had met at the Café de Paris party during the Monaco Boat Show. It read:

*Design is always a collaborative process and I am extremely
disappointed that Gary Knobber, in whom I once invested so
much trust, now wishes to abuse the collegiate traditions of the
design business. At a time when some of us are doing our best to
establish design as a credible and effective business medium, it is
deplorable that Knobber exposes our profession in so callous,
squabbling and self-serving a manner. And I am personally
extremely disappointed that a once respected subcontractor should
so arrogantly claim a design credit for what was, in fact, only a
simple task of on-site contract management. I take partial
responsibility for this embarrassment to my client since I was the
one to promote Knobber to the position of influence which he has
now so deplorably fouled. But he forgets himself. Knobber is an
artisan, a manager and not an inspired creative personality. His
claim is outrageous. I am the designer of* Potassium Nitrate.

Then I called my solicitors, a partnership of unprincipled feral
chancers disguised by a sophisticated Chancery Lane address, and
asked them to draft a cease-and-desist letter to Knobber.

I sat back, lit a cigarillo and poured myself a drink. Swirling
the Macallan in its Georgian cut-glass tumbler, I wondered if dark
clouds might be appearing in my whisky. Knobber, I thought, was a
jumped-up little prick who owed his position, such as it was, not to
class, breeding or talent, but to my patronage. Never mind that this
patronage had served me very well. Knobber, the betraying bastard,
would never work again.

Who, I wondered, still worried that the clouds in my Scotch
which I suspected might be caused by a malfunctioning dishwasher, or a lazy kitchen assistant, would want to credit Gary Knobber
when they could credit Eustace Dunne? What did the French call it?
*Trahison des clercs?*

*Rollo Pinkie: The couriered letter to* Haul at Sea *was a rare error of judgement by Eustace. Perhaps the first marker of his own declining fortunes. The editor told me she looked at it with bemusement that quickly became delight. And then almost uncontainable excitement. Here was an international story about authorship and provenance. A messy spat in a yacht harbour, between a rich egotist and his pupil! It even had an almost Oedipal character, given Eustace's smooth patronage of the rough Knobber. She told me: 'I'll write it up for us first, but I am going to pitch it to* Vanity Fair.'

Haul at Sea *had faxed a copy of Eustace's letter to Gary Knobber who was in Hong Kong, celebrating the award of a contract to design a shipping group's new chain of luxury hotels. In the article eventually appearing in* Vanity Fair, *Knobber, by his own account, was at the China Club, lifting pork with black fungus to his mouth using jade chopsticks while a waiter poured ice-cold Puligny-Montrachet. The fax was brought to him on a superb black lacquered tray, the shape of a Komodo dragon.*

*The magazine described how Knobber read the fax and chortled.*

*'Eustace Dunne, what a conceited, fatigued, arrogant plonker you are.'*

*And the rogue designer lifted a fresh glass of delicious white Burgundy and remembered the recent death of an old associate, known also to the arrogant plonker, in an absurd accident about three years previously . . . a designer called Quentin, a man described by* Vanity Fair *as someone he used, but never praised. This made him solemn for a moment.*

*Then, suddenly brightening, Knobber had, in the magazine's account, told the Wan Chai bar girl who was his companion, 'Do you know, darling, I have only ever prayed once? It was a very short prayer. I asked God to make my enemies look ridiculous. And do you know what? He granted it! Eustace Dunne is beginning to look ridiculous!'*

# 16

# 1988 – Kiss my assets

*'Life would be tragic if it weren't funny.'*

Stephen Hawking, *A Brief History of Time*, 1988

*The Royal Train before Eustace.*

IT WAS THE MORNING AFTER BBC2 aired its documentary about the Royal Train.

I had watched it in the studio with Anika and, extremely pleased with the result, we had gone by taxi to Annabel's, the nightclub on Berkeley Square, which successfully maintained a delicate equilibrium between the wince-makingly louche and the breathtakingly posh.

Annabel's placed no higher a value on cultural consistency in its menu than it did in its clientele. If you wanted to meet a Saudi arms-dealer, grifters, a ruined Italian aristocrat, a *de luxe* pimp, money-washers, a stoned Old Etonian, an unscrupulous Harrovian pusher, a Ghanaian con man in a kente cloth smock, a French Murphy artist or even an over-dressed local millionaire in trade, it would be a good place to start looking.

It was a place I hated, but it seemed the right thing to do. We ate devilled whitebait then *goujons* of sole with asparagus mousse, then an over-cooked *crème brûlée* and raspberries to end. Three bottles of Leflaive's Puligny-Montrachet had been bookended by Macallan to begin and some, perhaps I found the following morning very possibly too much, Jacopo Poli grappa to conclude. Anika smoked State Express 555 cigarettes without enthusiasm throughout dinner. A pyramid of them piled up slowly on her side plate.

And then there was Anika herself. Like a mountain that demanded to be climbed, a bridge to be crossed or a metaphor to be coined, this impressively robust Sappho from Utrecht represented a challenge to my curiosity as much as to my libido.

She had been a loyal and efficient assistant for years, but remained a personal enigma. Anika did not disguise her sexuality, but nor did she invite investigation of it. She was confident enough to wear her pop socks to Annabel's even when the other women were in St-Laurent-of-Arabia or Pucci or Halston. She wore no make-up besides very bright red lipstick and her hair was drawn back so tight her skull was revealed like an Egyptian Middle Kingdom profile. She wore statement glasses.

And I was utterly fascinated by what might be going on inside her Dries van Noten dungarees. But every time, for the hell of it, I made a move, as I so often did, she withered me by absolute indifference and a puff of cigarette smoke. Two taxis were (always) called for the return journey.

## shower, shag, shave

It was seven thirty the next day. 'A millionaire in trade,' I said to myself, somewhat ruminatively. Despite the Royal Train, I was not feeling at all regal; in fact I was feeling rather crapulous and queasy.

'Shower, shag, shave,' I mumbled to my reflection in the bathroom mirror. Then, rallying: 'Given your age and habits,' I continued to myself, 'you are not in bad shape,' although the growing number of liver spots on the backs of my hands made me gloomy. I pushed both of them through my thinning hair.

That morning, because of Anika's nun-like focus, her frozen disposition and refusal of frivolity in any form, I was alone and, since peristalsis was a preoccupation and constipation a nagging fact of late middle age, shaving was today necessarily my first ritual. Certainly, a shag was to be a distant last.

My bathroom was wood panelled, painted an inky matt blue-black with coir matting. The dark paint, I always thought, showed off the sparkling white enamel and porcelain to good effect. I finished shaving and splashed myself with Dior Eau Sauvage. Then, in a floor-length hooded white terry robe and tan-coloured Moroccan *babouche* slippers, I moved slowly to the kitchen to select one of the fifteen enormous Brown Betty teapots on display in sequence upon an oak shelf supported by tensioned steel wire, all illuminated by very bright spotlights. In contrast to the bathroom, my kitchen was dramatically white.

..................................................................................................

® *Rollo Pinkie: Classic Eustace! He had an absolute conviction that to know some-one's bathroom (or kitchen) was to know their soul. He did not care about people. He cared only about the things people chose to use, the environments they occupied.*

To make tea, you must heat the teapot slightly with a direct gas flame then fill it with Fortnum & Mason English Breakfast, chucking each spoonful in with dashing and nonchalant ceremony. Someone who cannot be bothered to make tea properly is not someone ever to be trusted with anything, I would always tell anyone prepared to listen. A speckled earthenware mug, said to be made by a Ditchling apprentice of Eric Gill, was duly filled and I sat down to contemplate the day ahead. It was the day of my investiture.

Dull headache and sluggish or petulant guts apart, the signs were propitious. The BBC2 documentary about the Royal Train had been a glorious indulgence. And as the many late night calls had indicated, a popular success. Introduced by the ineffably smooth David Dimbleby, selected because he was Royal Household-trained, it was filmed in 35mm to provide a visual texture and colour palette that were still well beyond the scope of the new video technology.

After a wide, establishing shot showing the new, streamlined Royal Train arriving at Edinburgh's Waverley Station, the camera shifted to an onboard salon. The Queen appeared, evidently relaxed, in an interior looking a little like an expensive Copenhagen hotel.

As she looked around somewhat questingly, perhaps searching for a missing Tupperware box of biscuits or a fugitive corgi, Dimbleby's hushed and respectful voice-over intoned:

'Since the days of Prince Albert, the Royal Family has been a sponsor of the finest British art and design. And this tradition continues today with a Royal Train to rival the Royal Yacht. Pop goes Britannia!'

Apparently smothering an involuntary wince, Her Majesty then performed to camera.

'My husband and I believe that life is more than mere existence. We believe that symbols matter, that details are important and that one's country deserves the very best. The Royal Train is not a thing of whimsy. It is not mere rolling stock, it is a rolling showcase of our national virtues, of our nation's insistence on the very best in the world. And of our ability to manufacture the very best in the world. It has become one's intention to recognize the achievement and award its designer, Mr Eustace Dunne, with one of this nation's greatest honours.' She rearranged the hem of her skirt.

Anika and I whooped and clapped.

But I also blinked at this point in the programme because the Royal Train's communications equipment and lighting fixtures had come from Siemens in Germany, its upholstery from a small business in Como, Italy and its air conditioning from Japan; the armchair in which Her Majesty was relaxing was my own copy of Dieter Rams' original design of 1962. The locomotive itself was manufactured by Thomson S.A. of France while the marble in the bathrooms was from Carrara in Tuscany. British manufacture, my arse.

In the bathroom could also be found towels by Frette from Milan's via Manzoni while Toto of Kitakyushu was commissioned to make special lavatory basins: I had been impressed by the hot water-jet feature in Toto basins, whose soothing stream of warm, drying air had often been enjoyed on Japan's Shinkansen bullet train. And since a great national taboo was even to think about thinking of Her

Majesty the Queen using a lavatory, still less to consider the effect of a hot waterjet on the Royal infrastructure, my sense of mischief licensed me to indulge. Significantly, I felt, since they had been commissioned, there had been no Royal complaints about Totos on the train. My imagination wandered freely.

True, there was decorative wallpaper from King's Road's Osborne & Little, but it was printed in Switzerland. Smythson of Bond Street did the stationery, whose letterhead a junior in the studio had designed, using a nice modern cut of Caslon. At least, some of the modern art was sourced from students at the Royal College of Art. But, if anything, the Royal Train actually demonstrated the abject and humiliating failure of Her Majesty's subjects in manufacturing and the modern world, not their swaggering triumph. I coughed.

'But "design",' I said on camera towards the end of the programme, 'is a cumulative process. It is not one subject, but many. It is more perspiration than inspiration. It is popular and democratic, not elitist and exclusive.' The film showed me scrambling over scaffolding poles in the new Factory building, now taking shape and slowly rising above the ground. Workmen busied themselves out of focus in the background when I stopped scrambling to deliver a pleasant, thoughtful, modest and touching soliloquy.

This to-camera piece was filmed with me wearing a hard hat carrying a FACTORY logo, in a stencil font of Le Corbusier's, a nice confirmation of my unbreakable solidarity with the workforce. And the preceding shot had been from the air, very much in the lavish style Peter Montagnon essayed in Kenneth Clark's landmark *Civilization* series when looking at the chateaux of the Loire. This being a big budget documentary, the producer could not resist an expensive helicopter shot, the sort usually refused by the BBC's scrupulous management. Now, because of our success, 'design' was taking its place in the public imagination alongside 'art'. The Factory was my Chambord, my Loire chateau.

® *Rollo Pinkie: One of Eustace's many exasperating characteristics was to make inaccurate or inappropriate cultural references and to misquote sources. He was always saying 'less is more', but misattributing it to Le Corbusier rather than Mies van der Rohe. And I doubt he had ever been to Chambord.*

The helicopter shot concept was to catch me approaching over the horizon – naturally, driving myself democratically, not being chauffeured exclusively. Headlights on for drama! Then the gyro-stabilized camera fixed to an outrigger of the hovering Bell Jet Ranger that would follow my car up the path to the Factory. What with the wind and the sun and the damnable vagaries always present in any live-action filming, it took six takes and the best part of a day to get this fifteen second sequence to work. It added perhaps fifteen thousand pounds to the budget, but eventually looked splendid and my new gunmetal grey Mercedes-Benz S-Class, the one with the five litre V-8 engine, shone most impressively in the wintry sunshine.

® *Rollo Pinkie: Eustace, in fact, always drove a Porsche. Or, at least, was always photographed in one. He liked to say, 'The best is always simple, but the simple is not always the best' – a line from the German architect Heinrich Tessenow I had trained him to remember. Porsches appealed because of their elemental functionalism. But they were always hard work. When photographers were not present, Eustace preferred the back seat of an S-Class Mercedes or a plush Bentley. He understood nothing of the principles of internal combustion or vehicle dynamics, but drove recklessly fast on all occasions.*

And, in the company of my Brown Betty and my school-of-Gill mug, I now read the *Protector's* television review.

> *Was that really pop art you saw behind HRH? Was the Queen sitting on a modern plastic chair, not a feudal, gilt throne? Where have*

*all the aspidistras gone? Long time passing!* The Royal Train *was a masterpiece, BBC2 at its documentary best. Queen Victoria had coal-mines, cholera wards, winter gardens and child slavery. Queen Elizabeth is, in every sense, a breath of fresh air and bright light. Who knows? Modern design might yet save a medieval monarchy.*

I smiled. 'Designing for the fucking Queen!' I said to myself, then went for a pee.

## a bloodshot environment

People receiving honours are given elaborate briefings about pro-tocol. Arriving at the appointed time, you are led to a waiting area in the Ballroom, the most impressive space in Buckingham Palace. Here proud, nervous and expectant individuals reminded me of the hopeful suppliers to be found in the Marks & Spencer lobby, the ones carrying trays of sample tomatoes, knitwear and socks, their fortunes and careers to be made or ruined by exigent and demand-ing buyers. But this was different: social promotion was on offer.

What a ridiculous place, I thought, my latent republicanism quickly exposed by a Crimean War-era interior that was a turbulent ocean of red and gold. Red and gold carpet, red and gold curtains, red and gold attendants. Possibly attendants with red and gold balls, I wondered. A gold throne on a red dais and a monumental organ with gilt pipes surrounded by swags of red brocade completed the effect. It was a bloodshot environment.

And all of this pompous magnificence you access through the back fucking door! Here was additional symbolism: the popular face of Buckingham Palace in front of the Victoria Monument is the tradesmen's entrance. The impressive façade is on the other side of the building, addressing the garden, and is never seen by the public.

'You could call Royalty two-faced,' I said, to no one in particular.

I knew all of this. Never mind the gross imperial taste, so repugnant to a student of Charles Eames, I knew what a practical design calamity Buckingham Palace had been. I knew I could have done it better. It was commissioned by a temperamental and spendthrift client who had a muddled brief and originally promised the job to the magisterial, monumental, mystical and wholly original Soane, but in the end gave it to an inspired, but over-busy, hack called John Nash, a designer of platitudes built at scale. His concept was a replica Palais Royal and Tuileries, but before Nash's design had been even half-built it was thought so very bad, it was demolished.

A parliamentary select committee did not find Nash negligent, although nor did they trouble to re-employ him. His monumental arch for what was then still Buckingham House was moved to a corner of Hyde Park, where it became known as 'Marble Arch', and other architects were commissioned to cover up his bodged work. The Buckingham Palace where I was sitting today was not a noble design of the Regency, but Edwardian afflatus by the same architect as the Victoria and Albert Museum.

And then, interrupting my daydream, the over-warm atmosphere in the Ballroom chilled a little, following a rustle of silk. A military band played the national anthem and all rose, some of them reluctantly, some of them puffing and creaking. The Queen moved majestically, in company with her Gurkha bodyguards. After the anthem, a medley of patriotic hum-along tunes including the Dambusters March was played. I had taken two beta-blockers and an inch of Macallan to calm my nerves before getting in the car.

The Lord Chamberlain was sonorously calling people forward one by one. Not soon enough, I heard my own name. I walked forwards and then knelt, as instructed, on the Investiture Stool. The protocol had prepared me for the process of the accolade, the dubbing of Knights Bachelor on both shoulders. There are no warnings of what might be said.

The Queen said, 'Mr Dunne, you have come far.'

I felt a light tap from the sword used by George VI when he was in the Scots Guards.

'Your Majesty.'

'One is very pleased with one's train.'

'Thank you, Ma'am.'

'Arise, Sir Eustace.'

And then I returned to the crowd.

What a way to run a fucking ballroom, I now thought to myself. After the investiture I was ready for champagne and conversation. Instead, I was offered a cup of tea and some thoughts on the weather from a school-dinner-lady who had won an MBE for services to the Grassington Colliery Charity Appeal. And I was alone, a condition I never much enjoyed other than at lunch.

'The Queen never even said goodbye,' I complained to the dinner-lady, as much in perplexity as self-pity. Meanwhile, an un-motivated agency photographer took banal pictures, which would later appear in the gossip columns, the *Metro* captioning me as a 'Knight by Design'.

## shepherdess market

A red and gold attendant directed me to my parked car where Reg, my driver, was waiting with the engine insolently ticking over. Caught unexpectedly, Reg fussed to hide his forbidden cigarette. I ignored his fumbling and gave him an address in Shepherd Market, while lighting my Phillies Mexicali Slim with great concentration, a creased brow and closed eyes. The gun-metal Mercedes nosed silently out of the Palace Yard on to Constitution Hill and then on to Park Lane. It would have taken the newly knighted me less than fifteen minutes to stroll across Green Park, but the old me never walked if I could drive. Besides, I felt absurd in top hat and tails.

Shepherd Market is, in fact and metaphor, the heart of Mayfair, although sheep have not been seen there since 1735 when the old fairground was developed into handsome townhouses. The Mercedes stopped at an address with a mirror-finish lacquered black door. I left my top hat on the back seat, but retained my cigarillo as I effortfully removed myself from a low car parked at a high kerb. I also retained the insignia of the Knight Bachelor hanging around my neck. A highly polished brass plate said 'Elysium S.A. By Appointment Only'. I inhaled on the cigarillo and pressed the bell.

The door quickly opened and, without a word, I was led upstairs to a room with pink velour furniture, candy-striped Regency wallpaper, an atrocious electric chandelier and two girls dressed as shepherdesses, including authentic *bergère* hats.

Without letting go of my cigarillo, I allowed the shepherdesses to undress me, as they had done many times before. They were fastidious in their refusal to make this in any way erotic. Rather, it was a practical matter to be addressed at the beginning of the afternoon's proceedings. Still refusing to abandon the cigarillo, I was now invited by gestures alone to lie prone on a bed. This I did and a shepherdess took the smouldering cigarillo away. The other shepherdess now produced a spool of pink ribbon (which I knew to be vintage French double-faced *grosgrain* satin and silk, acquired to my own specification from a tradesman in Lyon) and tied my wrists – really quite tightly – to the brass bedstead.

The two shepherdesses now stripped themselves, wriggling out of their antique blue and white bustles, retaining their jaunty hats but nothing else other than the anachronistic pink spike heels each was wearing. Facing downwards, I had to struggle to see, but struggle, a Buddhist had told me, was what defined life itself. One pair of the spike heels now walked on my back. That done, the other shepherdess thrashed me with a wet newspaper, her breasts swaying agreeably as she gathered momentum. I wanted it to be the *New York Times*, but felt it was more likely the *Daily Mirror*.

## Sylvester from the bank

When I emerged, Reg was once again lounging against the car in that challengingly indolent way professional drivers have. Maybe if I put him in a uniform, he'd have better deportment, I thought to myself. Quickly, we drove to the Covent Garden studio where Anika was looking blithely concerned.

'Sylvester from the bank called. Will you call him back? Shall I get him for you?'

Sylvester from the bank was Sylvester Truelove, a man of ill-favoured aspect, but lacking the distinction of authentic ugliness. He was a cynical and oleaginous chancer, blithely unconcerned about the damage caused by his calculations, who had had his trading licence withdrawn by the Serious Fraud Office for malpractice. Sylvester had told them, 'It was not insider trading. It was very well-informed speculation!' When he wanted to say we are not going to make any money, he would say instead, 'The market has priced-in a more muted margin outlook.'

He was the product of a bad public school, a philistine and a boor. He had an extensive (and often trumpeted) acquaintance with the more accessible members of the peerage. Impressively knowledgeable about how many base points over Libor a syndicated loan to Liberia needed to be, he had made my financial destiny his unique personal occupation. The first time we met he tried to impress with an account of a country-house visit which began by walking from a parade of pleached limes into a dripstone cave, style of William Kent, where Lord Bigwig had once entertained his own dairy maids. In the house itself, he smugly explained, there were hunters, noise dirt and business on the ground floor, but 'expense, state and parade above'.

A fucking odious little creep was my first impression on meeting, but soon Sylvester had proved himself useful since he was constrained neither by ethics nor by good manners. Now the bank kept him on as a sort of indefinable consultant, a valuable asset to them since he knew where a very great many financial corpses were interred, and these graves he attended with great solicitation. He also had a very good sense of which financial bodies were soon to be incinerated, often because he held the matches himself. And Sylvester Truelove had attached himself to me as a barnacle does to a rotting hull.

Sylvester said, 'Eustace, hear me now. You are starting to worry me. I don't know whether it is despite or because of your dubious reputation as a cosmic creative genius, but I do have to say that you are hopelessly careless about management.'

I replied, 'If you are so fucking clever, Sylvester, why aren't you as rich as me? And do tell me, when you have stopped greasing your bloody awful quiff, and adjusting your disgraceful Windsor knot, why you have tassels on your shoes.'

Sylvester continued, unrepentant. 'Be serious for a minute, Eustace, you idiot. There is a big difference, I need to explain, between cash and profit, between turnover and revenue. Bleu de Travail's accounts are hopelessly muddled. I am all too aware how very busy you have been, away from the business. We all are. Some of us cannot avoid television and tabloids. But no one has yet found a way to put value on PR. I would argue that publicity is a mask that eats the face. And tell me, as your personal adviser, exactly how much did you get paid for work on your famous Royal Train?'

A mite too proudly, I replied, 'We got paid nothing. We cannot charge the Queen. We are not mere tradesmen. Fishmongers may charge the Queen, but designers do not. Our work on the Royal Train has been a huge intangible asset for our business and for the design profession as a whole.'

Sylvester groaned and said, 'Eustace, you really are a great pompous fucking ass. I know the reality of your business, not the Walt Disney version of it.'

'Do you now? Do by all means tell me!'

'OK,' Sylvester began, 'you ask, you get. Suppliers are not be-ing paid. And fashion is turning in another direction. Someone in the Chelmsford Bleu de Travail tells me you insisted, on grounds of "taste", that a certain floral Afghan dhurry be removed from sale. But it was their bestselling line. For God's sake, Eustace. This is not The Magic fucking Roundabout. It's business.'

'Go on.' I sighed.

'Just try to stop me,' said Sylvester. 'The whole business is under-invested and under-capitalized, although I doubt you know the differ-ence. The properties are all leasehold with little intrinsic value. Traffic is declining. You spend nothing on advertising and expect your own excessive PR to necessarily benefit the business through association. I am here to tell you that it does no such thing. Do you really believe that people think if they buy an artisan smock worn by a Provençal peder-ast, they will become like you? Bollocks. Utter, sweet Jesus, bollocks.'

'You are talking through your arse, Sylvester. You really are the one who knows the price of everything and the value of nothing, aren't you?' I stiffened a little. 'There really is more to all this than money. Honestly there is.' I made a money gesture with thumb and index finger.

'We'll see about that, Eustace,' Sylvester said. 'If we don't inter-vene, we may enjoy finding you explaining your interesting fiscal theory to the official receiver. But listen. I have lots of ideas. Some good, some bad. You have to decide. But I am certain this is a good one. To make an impression of a healthy company, we must use whatever liquidity we have to fund operations. When suppliers get nervous, and some of them are sobbing into their hankies, it spreads like a nasty rash. The credit rating companies are looking over our shoulders. Very soon, all the other lenders will notice the problem and banks less civilized than ours will say you are in breach of your covenants. And, believe me, then it will be all over, my friend. You'll have to take your gong to the pawn shop.'

'So what is it you suggest, Mr Clever Dick?'

'We will have to issue a note. I am not saying it's a profits warning. It can be drafted to read confidently. But we must be certain to appear absolutely honest, aware and straightforward.'

'That'll be a first for you, Sylvester.'

Overnight a fax was sent from the bank to Covent Garden. I picked it up on the new (and rather erratic) fax machine Reg had installed in the back of the Mercedes.

It began:

*Due to exceptionally difficult and unpredictable trading circumstances, a hot summer, a cold winter, a mild spring and hesitant consumer demand, the directors of Bleu de Travail have adjusted their forecast for the fourth quarter. The directors believe that in a highly competitive market this represents a solid result. They also emphasize that the fundamentals of the business are sound and they anticipate a return to double-digit growth over the next five years. The directors also express their confidence in the Chairman and Managing Director, Sir Eustace Dunne, who received a knighthood in the Birthday Honours List.*

A grumbling column appeared in the next day's *Telegraph* City pages. At the weekend, the *Financial Times'* influential Lex was more measured, but therefore more damning. It expressed doubts that my design genius could necessarily translate into business genius. 'Creativity is one thing, but "creative accounting" is rather different,' Lex decided. The retail analyst Bertie Fein of Gilchrist & Rosenblatt issued a worrying note, saying Bleu de Travail was 'below consensus' and published 'a poor trading statement that significantly lagged behind the sector'.

For the first time in my life, I was being criticized in public. Bleu de Travail was my life and now people – people who were know-nothings and philistines – were saying they did not want to buy my stock, not even to hold it. They wanted to sell it. I called Sylvester at his conquistador-kitsch ranch in Hampshire, where he kept his classic cars, his Laotian mistress, his Filipino servants and his Argentinian polo ponies.

'Don't they understand, I have made a fortune through the sheer application of hard work?' I moaned.

'And I think you're in danger of soon losing one,' Sylvester said.

'Kiss my assets, then please fuck off. And when you have fucked off, perhaps you would like to meet me for dinner at the Café Royal tomorrow night. I think there are some things we need to get sorted. Not least your own position in this mess which, I maintain, is all of your own creation.'

Two days later, Anika handed me a letter couriered from Paris. The sender was Elysium S.A.

*Dear Client,*

*As the new owners of 23 Shepherd Market, we photograph all visitors to our premises as a routine security measure. Polaroid copies of your recent arrival and departures are included here for your reference.*

*Archive quality 35mm photographs have also been taken to ensure the absolute security of your business with us.*

*You may be interested in maintaining the integrity of your status by subscribing to our new Members' Security Package, available to selected clients for £5000 pcm.*

*Additionally, for your personal pleasure, we have recorded all the transactions that took place while you were recently doing business with us. These are available in all formats, including VHS or Betamax video and still colour prints.*

*Naturally, we respect your privacy and subscribers to our Members' Security Package may acquire the original tapes and negatives at an additional charge.*

*Your Area Manager will be pleased to discuss these arrangements with you.*

*We look forward to your next visit.*

*Yours very truly.*

*Sylvie Fleury*
*For Elysium S.A.*

Feeling very sick, I looked at a surprisingly sharp Polaroid of myself wearing the insignia of Knight Bachelor and ringing the bell of a notorious Shepherd Market brothel. I could imagine the headlines in the *News of the World*: 'Design's Darkest Knight', 'A Knight To Be Forgotten'. I cringed. Then I picked up the phone to my lawyers to ask how much an injunction would cost. Presumably, I hoped, considerably less than £5000 pcm.

The taste of celebration and champagne was turning to bitter ash.

# 17

# 1990 – Simplify, then exaggerate

*'Ma il mistero è chiuso in me
Il nome mio nessun saprà.'
('But my mystery is closed in me
No one will know my name.')*

Giacomo Puccini, 'Nessun dorma' from *Turandot*,
1926, popularized by Luciano Pavarotti in 1990.

*The Pompidou Centre under construction: inspiration for my
factory.*

'To be a success,' Terence Conran had told me, especially when talking to financial journalists, 'you need excellent accountants and excellent PR.'

When I last said it on the *Today* programme at 6:45 a.m. one wintry morning, addressing a politely nodding BBC presenter, I forgot to add that you also need a sadistic ego, feral greed, a knack for shameless self-mythologizing, a brutal lack of empathy and a quite fantastic disregard for the welfare or happiness of others. But business is war and in war the first victim is truth.

'If you're ever going to say anything, make sure it's fucking memorable,' I also used to say, aware that people usually remembered robust fucking language, particularly on the radio.

My accountants had surpassingly achieved the excellence demanded of them and, with great creativity, helped me to ascend to national, even international, stature. If I failed to distinguish between turnover, revenue and profit, the accountants, happy with fees correspondingly engorged by their misleading figures, did not trouble to correct me. They left me undisturbed on a plane higher and more lovely than their grubby, matter-of-fact-and-fiction spreadsheets.

Instead, I had become the artistically and socially acceptable façade of capitalism. Ambitious, but sensitive. An expansive hedonist, to be sure, but one who wanted to share his pleasures. I was a well-spoken visionary, not an unsettling disrupter: a Joan of Arc of the property-owning middle classes and all who coveted white porcelain ramekins and a butcher's block. I was a rich man who cared. I was also a rich man who found it amusing that the dire trade of accounting was the one area of human activity where 'creativity' was frowned upon.

In a certain milieu, my fame transcended categories. In Paris's La Coupole, the huge Montparnasse brasserie I enjoyed because of its fabulous democracy of painted hookers, families, deal-makers, voyeurs, young lovers and seriously smoking *intellos* wearing scarves and scowls, there was a giant framed photograph of me with a scented candle. Neighbouring portraits showed other Left Bank cafe familiars: Picasso, Sartre, Camus, Barthes, Derrida and Lacan.

But this longed-for prominence, this lustrous presence, this permanent place in the gossip columns, my knighthood, the *maîtres d'* who recognized me in London, Paris and New York, the valet parkers who appeared from nowhere, the drinks on the house, the white goods manufacturers who annually offered to refit my kitchen, the private views, the privileged access to airline lounges, the comp'd holidays in Lyford Cay, the sommeliers who held back something 'Sir Eustace would enjoy', the automatic upgrades, the 7-series Beemer on indefinite loan (a car I never even used) and many millions of pounds were now under threat.

## jealous bastards

Not so much threat of extinction, as threat of contamination by jealous bastards. 'Eustace Dunne' was a well-respected brand, but brands can lose value as well as acquire it. Enemies were now like jackal buzzards circling around the rotting corpse of a wildebeest on the Great Karoo. Dishes were soon, I feared, to be enjoyed cold. Do not, the Arabs say, spit in a well when you pass it since you will pass it again on the way back. I was well aware that I had done quite a lot of spitting on the outward leg.

There was the ridiculous, megalomaniac little shit Gary Knobber, still undermining my reputation as an autonomous creative genius with his absurd claims. And now that smarmy, preening prick Sylvester Truelove was feeling tragic and I-told-you-so about money. Myopic wanker analysts were sending out warning notes. And Elysium S.A. was, with impressive French subtlety, suggesting blackmail on account of an entirely private taste for being systematically tortured by girls from Bromley dressed up as Versailles shepherdesses.

Worst was progress with the Factory, the ambitious – perhaps over-ambitious – enterprise that was to celebrate and define a lifetime's achievements: the collation of art and industry, of commerce and culture, of money and meaning. It was threatening to enter a death spiral.

The Factory contained two research institutes, a dance school, a model farm, saw mill, fabrication studio, perfume laboratory, experimental bakery, acoustic studio, book bindery, crafts workshops, a kiln, a forge, a CAD suite, weaving studio, library, two lecture theatres, a state-of-the-art audio-visual suite, professional kitchen, design archive, restaurant, two bars and more exhibition space than had ever existed in the country before.

Plus, twelve bedrooms for visiting conceptors, a useful word I had learnt and acquired during a recent trip to Japan visiting someone in Nissan's Ogikubo advanced design studio. These conceptors – architects, designers, composers, chefs, producers – would, the covert idea was, provide me and my businesses with a steady stream of interesting ideas in exchange for lavish hospitality.

Progress with the Timothy Clever building was not a problem. The architect's impressive design, with his signature funnels in primary colours, tensioned steel wires, heroic glass, bold profile, structural cross-bracing and splendid lack of concern with public utility or convenience, was already being spoken of as a Stirling Prize winner, even if it was being spoken of less generously by its neighbours who found it an unsubtle and bullying presence in the landscape.

Clever himself was even whispered as being in line for the almost sacred Pritzker Prize, awarded for a lifetime's achievement in architecture, or so he whispered himself to friends at champagne breakfasts for leftish causes, not excluding Salman Rushdie. The Factory, like any well-managed design project, a rare thing in itself, was on time and on budget. And like any well-managed design project, it was attracting publicity. There were important sponsors: keen to rub up against me and acquire some of my glossy allure were British Leyland, Kodak, ICI and GEC, all signed up as donors, each as anxious to be identified with the thrilling culture of design as the Factory was needy of their financial support. Indeed, David Bache, the justly celebrated designer of the original Range Rover (which had been shown in the Louvre), had, over a canteen lunch in Solihull, suggested that the Factory would be the ideal venue for the global launch of his new compact City-Rover urban four-wheel-drive.

## a bit of acid

No, the problem was one of personalities. Obviously, I had not had the time to direct the project personally. To do this, I needed a cadet version of myself. I wanted to look into a pool, like Narcissus, and turn the beautiful reflection into another person. I wanted someone who respected my values, but had a mind of his own. An envoy who, while on a leash, could nonetheless roam wide, teaching the faith. I wanted someone who would stand up to me. But not too much.

And I needed someone, besides Rollo Pinkie who was daily becoming more aloof and self-important and had an energy system of his own, who would also help write all the very many books and articles that went out under my own name, someone who would draft the lectures and speeches I gave. Someone, in fact, who gave me a voice perhaps superior even to my own. And if Rollo felt an unsettling twinge of competition that would be no bad thing. He was becoming insufferable.

I wanted someone I did not have to explain things to, someone who had some fucking initiative. And I found this person working in the Victoria and Albert Museum, a young man called Sven Roth, an academic expert on contemporary furniture who, tiring a little of the tedium of museum life with its costive bureaucracy, obsession with rank over ability and petty jealousies, had begun writing very polished popular journalism about design. And one recent piece of Roth's had been a profile of me in *Harpers & Queen*. It was appreciative and interested to the point of being very nearly flattering, but the ink contained enough acid to make it credible comment rather than brainless puff.

Like a good dish, Roth's article had perfect balance and left an agreeable after-taste. I promptly arranged lunch at Meridiana, Enzo Apicella's Chelsea landmark *trattoria* with its dramatic interior vaguely inspired by Constantino Nivola's Sardinian sculptures, or perhaps vaguely inspired by Emmental cheese, which also has similar dramatic apertures and perforations in its structure.

Apicella was a frizzy-haired, deeply tanned, mustachioed, eccentric and voluble Neapolitan rascal who had brought an end to plastic grapes and views of Vesuvius in the Italian restaurants he owned in Fulham, Soho and Earl's Court. With his white linen double-breasted suit and a *pizzaiolo* striped T-shirt, I was reluctant to admit that I admired Apicella greatly.

Not least because Apicella had very few deferential genes. Leading us to the yellow naperied table, he asked me, 'Eh, Eustace, you fat rich bastard. Why you no join my PCI?' – this referring to the Italian Communist Party.

'Because, my dear Enzo, I am not a stupid Trotskyite redistributionist from Naples. I am not even Italian. I have more than half a cup of brains, you know. And I'd like a negroni and one for my young friend. Now please fuck off.'

'Eustace, *sei un vero rompocoglioni*,' Enzo said, clutching his balls and grimacing, hopping away towards the kitchen like a *commedia dell'arte* character.

Moments later, he returned with two chunky glasses of dark red liquor clinking with ice and a platter of finely sliced *felino* and *finocchiona*.

'We in the Italian Communist Party believe in the best salami for everyone,' Enzo explained haughtily, while deferentially offering the platter with a flourish like an arabesque. Then he said sweetly, 'I suppose you know *finocchiona* is slang for "cunt". Be careful not to choke.' He did a theatrical twirl and left.

Next came the wine. As a cruel test, I asked Roth about its provenance.

'It's a Montepulciano d'Abruzzo,' the young man confidently said after sniffing and sipping a little more. 'I can't be certain, but I think it might be one of Zaccagnini's'.

I was impressed. I was even more impressed that I did not have to explain the menu to Roth.

And Roth knew exactly which model Breuer chair we were sitting on: the original was made by Michael Thonet, manufacturer of my favourite bentwood cafe chair. But what we were sitting on was made in Malaysia. Not at all the same thing, but they were the same fakes that Bleu de Travail so very profitably sold.

Roth also laughed at my jokes and was funny in his own right. He had read widely (calling our Chelsea a 'nook-shotten Cythera'), travelled a lot, knew interesting people and had an always open anthology of witty, apposite, memorable quotes. I was to adopt many of these as my own.

So I offered him the job of running the Factory over our second macchiato and my third cigarillo of the day. Roth accepted immediately. And over the next few months, he made a good, even very good, impression with everyone. And, to my enlarging annoyance, everyone included the press. Many of the newspapers and magazines that had once doted on me, now doted on my more eloquent and younger surrogate who was styled 'general manager' of the Factory, while I was positioned as a distant and irrelevant investor.

Roth's quotes made life for editors easy. He was even featured in *National Geographic* on-site at the Factory in wellingtons and a hard hat, complicitly presenting himself as a successor to my fiefdom.

Naturally, accountants, no matter how creative, were no help with this predicament, but I believed a new campaign of public relations might ease the torment I felt at my image being adjusted and my reputation compromised.

## a revolting human being

I called Bill Shein, a revolting human being who smoked eighty Marlboro Red a day and had yellow slicked-back hair. He wore cheap shoes and a bad suit with dandruff on the collar. I despised the cheap shoes, but Shein was the best public relations man in the country, the author of many award-winning talking points. He was the master distractor.

He had made his career working for Harold Wilson, spending as much effort keeping (ample) bad news in as letting (scarce) good news out. He worked like a *mafioso*, with a mixture of favours, threats, obligations and credits. His clients included unsavoury dictators, common criminals, disgraced footballers, bankrupt entrepreneurs, dishonest prime ministers, embarrassed royals, uncomfortably closeted actors and experts in genocide. And now his clients included me.

Shein's disgusting offices were in Curzon Street, in a building not far from Shepherd Market, that looked like a first draft of a casino in the Persian Gulf designed by a short-sighted Jugoslav not quite connected to the relevant contemporary concepts of luxury. It was not architecture that suggested tact and discretion, or even good manners. It was architecture that suggested money and sin, although not of the enjoyable sort. It was architecture to accommodate the unsavoury spirits who paid Shein's vast fees.

'I am told you do reputation management,' I said, seeing only a faint image of Shein's feet on the desk through a swirling fog of filthy, blue cigarette smoke. On the desk was a brown plastic blotter with a nasty ball-point pen in a little gold cup set in something like a gimbal. There was also a picture in a decorated silver frame of Shein with Harold Wilson, each holding a bottle of Newcastle Brown Ale and wearing football scarves. Both were showing off bad teeth, now fixed in Shein's case with an elaborate set of too shiny dental weapons recently implanted by a celebrity orthodontist in Santa Monica. 'And I am aware you have done wonders for Rachman and the Krays. Do I get you exclusively for these preposterous fees you charge?'

'No, you don't. You worried about associating with the crims?' He laughed explosively. 'Two's a conflict of interest, three's a speciality. You're helping me out here, old son.'

Shein shoved a prepared contract over the table. I signed it with his Montblanc, not bothering with even a cursory reading.

'You're in deep poop, Eustace, my love,' Shein said, grinning. 'But I have a chromium-plated shit shovel to help with the extraction.'

'I presume you don't mind if I smoke,' I said, concentrating on lighting my cigarillo without waiting for the answer.

Shein explained, 'We gotta simplify, then exaggerate. We gotta get a message out there. You are the *genoux d'abeille* of the design world. I know this is true because I just made it up! No. Honestly. Not really. Maurice Saatchi told me. And our Maurice, he's never wrong.'

As Shein doubled up with a horrible fit of bronchial coughing and spitting that turned his already blotchy face purple, I asked what exactly we should do.

'First. We will get you on the box more,' Shein said, using a handkerchief to dry his wet face. 'You know there's two offers you should never refuse? Free sex and going on the telly. You know that Blo Norton? "The Thinking Man's Crumpet" I call her. You are going straight on to her programme, old son. She'll give you free telly. Them chairs in the green room at Television Centre have seen a thing or two, I can tell you.'

'Actually, I think television is an extremely meritorious medium,' I said.

........................................................................................................

® *Rollo Pinkie: Eustace always muddled 'meritorious' with 'meretricious'. When I first heard him make the mistake, I was too embarrassed to mention it. Then I began to enjoy hearing him make an ass of himself.*

'Can one be honest on the box?' I professed ethical concern. 'I can remember hearing Richard Nixon say, "I never cry . . . except on television." It's all about dissimulation, but I stand for honesty and robustness. We must be sure that comes across.' I was slightly aware I was becoming ridiculous.

'It's a deal, then,' said Shein, ignoring my queasy misgivings. He struggled to escape from his vulgarly padded black vinyl swivel chair and as he led me back to the door said, 'Oh. And I think we should do *A La Mode* as well. They've never had a top gent on an *A La Mode* cover. But they will soon. I'll speak to Flea. She's a bit posh. A bit up herself. Actually, a lot up herself. But if anyone can help extricate her pretty bobbed head from her fiendishly tight little arsehole, it will be you, Eustace.' Shein patted me on the shoulder and I flinched involuntarily while waving at a cab, thinking I had just contracted Lucifer.

## heavy entertainment

Two nights later, I was on *Late Night Line-Up*, Blo Norton's small, brainy, cultured colony in the vast imperium of the lower-middle-brow

British Broadcasting Corporation. She was not 'Light Entertainment'. Blo Norton was Heavy Entertainment.

'We are not *Celebrity Squares*,' she privately explained to the curious. 'We are Celebrity Trendies.'

Sitting on a black leather and chrome chair in an austere outfit, relieved by an amusingly short skirt whose occasionally fascinating revelations the cameras worked not quite hard enough to avoid, Norton spoke in clipped, blue-stocking tones. Many viewers who did not share her interest in Jürgen Habermas, Messiaen or Alain Robbe-Grillet nonetheless found her a tele-spectacle of engaging, even compelling, erotic nuance.

She began, adjusting an exiguous skirt, her introduction to me.

'There was a time when "design" was something you found in museums or art colleges. There was a time when dinner was "tea" and we ate Spam and chips with a mug of Brooke Bond watching *The Black and White Minstrel Show*. But that time is not now. Having swung in the sixties, Eustace Dunne has come not exactly to rest, but has come to occupy a very well-designed position in national life. If we watch the telly while sitting on Bauhaus chairs, if we are eating *coq au vin* and not pork pies, it is because of Eustace Dunne. To us on *Late Night Line-Up*, this is what it is to be modern.'

Norton asked what was my greatest moment in business. And I explained it was telling the woebegone managing director of Marks & Spencer it was an error of taste to ask customers to walk past gondolas of ugly bras and erotically repellent knickers on their way to buying smoked salmon *roulade* or a television dinner of frozen fish pie. And all of life, I averred, was a question of taste. I spoke, with a quiet passion learnt from David Attenborough's treatment of orangutans on the same television channel, about how taste could be inhibiting yet stimulating. It was one of the creation myths, my stump speech, and I never tired of repeating it.

Second, I treated the audience to my story about the invention of the scented candle, an inspiring act of autonomous creative genius for which I let them believe I was uniquely and personally responsible, although this was presented with modesty enough to look convincing, or so I felt. My deprecating manner in fact suggested high achievement. Just as Michelangelo had been thought to be a mere conduit for divine revelations, I was a channel through which larger forces made themselves known.

'Design can change the nation's sex life and its bedroom habits. For example, why waste time with chatter when you can light a scented candle and make your point with delicious perfume and magical flame? A decent, honest scented candle can have a transformative effect. Do you know that for years our best-selling scented candle was actually called "Hanky Panky"? I have never met a woman who can resist civet.' I said this with a grin calculated to be winning and Norton gasped right on on cue. And then she clapped her hands in laughing approval.

'Eustace Dunne,' she said, 'whatever next?'

'Some Hanky Panky?' I suggested cheerfully.

The audience roared.

I gave a well-rehearsed shrug. A dutifully watching nation, approaching bedtime, wondered very seriously about the presenter's own bedroom habits and whether she would soon have some civet of her own.

## shoes stuffed with rose petals

Flea Crichton was the editor of British *A La Mode* who had changed the title from being the parish magazine of the fashion-conscious Home Counties matron into an internationally respected barometer of high style and expensive accessories and very costly advertising. Under her editorship, there were no longer personal ads for nannies and small display ads for comfortable shoes, but every issue was an encyclopaedia of international luxury and expensively acquired style. Handbags had here acquired the reverential status of religious art.

Her readers were smart and well-connected, neither *vendeuses* nor housewives on private roads in Surrey. Instead, they were urban, smart and ambitious. Crichton was famously exigent, fond of saying, 'You don't come second, you are merely first of the losers.' But there are quite a lot of people who say exactly the same.

Those of her staff who were not sacked in routine and regular cullings adored her, the ones who had been let go, a rather larger number, traded on precious stories of her foibles. They said she scrubbed her desk every night with Perrier water and Chanel No. 5, that she stuffed her shoes with rose petals and had a Filipina whose sole occupation was to launder her La Perla underwear in dew gathered from Green Park and interleave her piles of silk knickers with sheets of handmade Italian tissue paper produced by nuns in Ticino.

They said she was not too proud to stock her own wardrobe with frocks abandoned from the magazine's fashion shoots. They said her ice queen demeanour had a temperature control which money, position and power could readily access. She could be hot – very hot indeed, they said – when career vectors demanded. They said she kissed up and kicked down. They said she was a helpless starfucker, pitiably addicted to celebrity as a junkie is to Mexican Horse.

So she was happy to meet me, although very determined not to show it. The venue was Cecconi's, an Italian near Savile Row not yet touched by the emerging *nuova cucina* which Apicella was testing at Meridiana. In fact, not touched by any influence at all since about 1935 when most of the ancient waiters were hired. And Flea had got to the restaurant first, claiming psychological advantage as well as her place at the corner table which Pierluigi had assured her was 'the best' – a preoccupation of her class – although several other regulars seated elsewhere had been given identical assurances about their own position in the Cecconi's universe.

Her printed lambskin and gold metal Chanel 2.55 handbag was arranged as a part of the Hicksian tablescape along with her Cartier lighter, Marlboro Reds, an initialled Smythson onion skin notebook bound in red morocco and a silver Tibaldi fountain pen from that fabulous little shop on the via Borgospesso in Milan, this last something sent for review in *A La Mode* which Flea had asked her secretary not to return.

Bread had been offered while she was waiting and bread had been refused with a dismissive flick of a hand wearing many Swarovski diamonds, sent to her on approval, but never returned. And Swarovski's PR had been too terrified to pursue the matter. From behind her Chanel sunglasses, she was staring implacably and coldly across the busy room as if in a meditative trance. She ignored the polite nods and the 'Hi, Flea' greetings from passers-by.

Shein's pitch to Flea had been that for *A La Mode* to maintain the momentum she had so stylishly established, she had to break every taboo, challenge every prejudice, circumvent every custom. Including the one saying only women should be on the cover. Women may be the readers, he argued, but women enjoy men. Especially stylish men. Why not cause a sensation – an international sensation – and put Eustace Dunne, London's most stylish man, on the cover? This had been Bill Shein's argument. That, and the fact that it would attract new advertisers. Flea, through her assistant, had not said yes, but nor had she said no. She had simply agreed to this lunch.

'Good morning, Pierluigi,' I said as, with a very self-conscious, geologically slow Churchillian gait, waving my cigarillo to acquaintances, I moved most deliberately towards Flea's corner table. Two waiters hurried to adjust the Morosini chair behind my now descending bottom. I was wearing a new, densely black corduroy suit by David Chambers, a violently bright white shirt by Charvet and Edward Green black Oxfords. No tie. Flea acknowledged nothing. She just stared.

'Not been here for years,' I said, attempting melting trivia while looking around. 'Not since Marino Morosini, the designer of this very chair, was trying to sue me. Poor Marino. So misguided. I found then, as I will find today, that a perfect escalope Milanese with a little spinach is a perfect remedy for anguish. Not, that is, that I am feeling anguished today,' I corrected myself, but she continued to stare.

'Tell me what you're thinking,' I gently demanded, but she remained unmoved and incurious. So I consulted the menu, choosing the veal and asking for an Americano as an *aperitivo*. The silence remained.

When my escalope arrived, I ordered a half bottle of Barolo.

'King of wine and wine of kings,' I offered to Flea by way of worldly commentary. She still stared and said nothing. And, without her having spoken, a waiter brought her a single sliced tomato. She waved away the offer of oil and salt. And she ignored the tomato as resolutely as she ignored me, as I was busy attending to squeezing half a lemon over breaded meat.

Before I had finished, an *A La Mode* assistant in a little black dress arrived at the table and leant in to whisper into basilisk Flea's ear. The editor got up to leave still without having spoken, offering only the most peremptory of nods as a courtesy, and walked to her car.

'What the fuck?' I said to myself and ordered another half bottle of Barolo for company.

That afternoon, a little black dress sent a fax to Anika in pop socks with details of the cover shoot. I was still not sure whether I had won or lost the encounter.

## keeping it in your trousers

Terry O'Neill, an *A La Mode* favourite, was the photographer assigned to the job. Terry was very definitely a Terry and not a Terence.

'I think your pictures are extremely good, Terry. I have done ever since you shot Twiggy on a Moulton folding bicycle. How are your pictures made? Do you recognize Cartier-Bresson's moment critique or care about Sontag's theory of cameras imprisoning reality?'

'Nah. A lot of bullshit is talked about photography, Eustace, my love. It's instinct. You've either got it or not. I got it. And I got Nikons or Leicas. We're gonna do it like Faye Dunaway post-coital poolside at the Beverly Hills Hotel after the 1977 Oscars. Know what I mean?'

Dunaway later became his wife.

'I hope you're not expecting me to have sex with you,' I said, only half astonished. 'Although I might consider it if you can get me an Academy Award.'

'Nah. I keep it in my trousers nowadays,' O'Neill replied, entirely seriously, fiddling with the focusing ring of his Nikon. 'Frank Sinatra told me, "Just don't get in the way." And that's my technique, innit? Eustace, my love, I want you to be yourself.'

'In that case, I'll light a cigarillo.'

Two months later, a portrait of me blowing smoke into the camera was on the cover of the September edition of *A La Mode*, the issue fattest with advertising. And that advertising now included cars, razors, aftershave and Edward Green shoes. The editor's paymasters were well pleased. The headline said, 'Eustace Dunne Still Has Designs On You'. Bill Shein was thrilled, myself, somewhat less so, although Anika did arrange for a thousand copies of the magazine to be delivered to Covent Garden.

She also sent a gift-wrapped tomato to Flea.

## Desert Island Discs

Warming to the very well-paid task of reinforcing my reputation, Bill Shein now wanted me to appear on 'Desert Island Discs', the BBC's perennial radio programme where guests are required not merely to choose favourite records, but to offer a touching and intimate apologia for their entire existence to the unctuously avuncular vintage presenter, Roy Plomley.

As the top radio spot for plugging new books or old personalities, the process of acceptance for Desert Island Discs was one requiring great expertise in horse-trading, often of an unscrupulous kind, but in this black art Shein was as adroit as a Tipperary tinker: in exchange for the favour of having his client as a castaway, he was able to call in some showbiz debts and promise several coke-ruined popsters and farcically drunken and adulterous novelists for future programmes.

Since I had no taste for music, caring only for accessible jazz and classics for dummies, but generally preferring silence, Shein, many of whose clients were music industry calamities, created a playlist for me. This was a matter of careful calculation in terms of semantics, although that was not the term Shein himself used. Still, every chosen recording had to reveal a teasing facet of my personality.

There would be Glenn Miller's Army Air Force Band's 'Chattanooga Choo Choo' to demonstrate pop before Pop. And Lena Horne's 'Stormy Weather' to declare a taste for soulfulness. Victoria de los Angeles would sing one of Canteloube's *Chants d'Auvergne* as a profession of my love of rural France: a sort of acoustic *rillettes*. Then there would be The Beatles' 'If I Fell' as an example of two minutes forty-five seconds of perfectly designed music, beautiful and haunting, but catchy too. 'I knew John really quite well,' I was able to claim.

'If I Fell' was followed by Holst's 'I Vow To Thee, My Country' to show touching humility while 'Guantanamera' was chosen as evidence of fascinating exoticism and an interest in the folkloric antics of colourful third world peasants. In the conversation about it, I told Plomley about discovering Miramar and Vedado, Havana's art deco districts. And, while in virtual Cuba, Shein had tutored me, no linguist, how to pronounce Esteban Rodríguez-Castells and Rafael Fernández Ruenes, architects of the astonishing Bacardi Building on

Avenida de Bélgica. Shein insisted I mention the address because it gave a sense of authenticity.

Beethoven's Ninth was selected because it showed a taste for artistic majesty and was the 'Battle Hymn' of the European Union, a project of which I approved. My Desert Island Discs concluded with Erik Satie's 'Gymnopedie': clean, clever, bright, modern, witty and Parisian. A musical autobiography, I thought of my playlist, but did not dare say it.

Between the Beatles and Holst, Roy Plomley asked, 'Some may think of you as a great materialist, a man who cares more about a coffee pot than God. Does that mean you have no spiritual side?'

'Not at all,' I rejoined. 'I learnt precision from Japanese poetry. And that's nearly a religion, you know. I am not a church-goer, but I do have a keen sense of something more than we can comprehend. I think we humans, when faced with the awful vastness of the universe and the mysteries of existence, are like cats and dogs going into a great library. They can see the books and hear the conversation, but have no idea what is actually going on.'

I was very pleased with that.

And when Plomley asked about my luxury, I very quickly replied, 'A well-stocked cellar, a Baccarat crystal glass and . . .' a pause here for comedic effect, 'a very well-designed corkscrew. One both beautiful and useful.'

'And your Desert Island book?' Plomley enquired.

I had never actually read a poem, but Shein had counselled me on the need to appear sensitive and perceptive so I confidently said: 'Shakespeare's sonnets. You know, Roy, "so are you to my thoughts as food to life."' And I laughed. '"And lilies that fester smell far worse than weeds." This we know to be true. The way Shakespeare accessed mystical truths with such apparent simplicity, I find very moving. I love this sensuality, this contact with the senses, these metaphors of food, flowers and sex. And I love it too that Shakespeare could see into the souls of both princes and paupers. He was high-minded, but popular too. And he was indiscriminately liberal in his, how can I put it, personal . . . affairs,' I added with an acoustic smirk.

'Sir Eustace Dunne,' Plomley concluded, 'thank you for being such a very well-designed castaway.'

Then Eric Coates' 'By The Sleepy Lagoon' began to play.

Back in the brightly lit green room, Shein shrieked, 'You were *brilliant*, Eustace!' making a gesture with his fat little hands. Some flakes of puff pastry from a recent vol-au-vent were attached to his chin.

'If you ever again do that inverted commas thing with your stubby little fingers in the air, Shein, I promise I will punch you in the mouth.'

# 18

# 1992 – Skönhet für alle!

*'Control your own destiny, or someone else will!'*

Jack Welch, *Winning*, 2005

*A model for all of us.*

THE NIGHT BEFORE THE FACTORY was to open, I visited the architect Timothy Clever in his set at Albany, the storied ghetto of neoclassical privilege off Piccadilly. Most sets belonged to dispossessed aristocrats, the better sort of Tory MP (a diminishing category), distinguished elderly historians (an enlarging category) and the occasional gay actor who had been raised to the peerage with aspirations raised to match.

Wasn't it odd, I often thought, that an architect who made his reputation by a polemical enthusiasm for technology – in an oeuvre that owed more to Johnson Controls, Mitsubishi and titanium than to Vitruvius – should choose to live in the grandeur of a 1771 house designed by Sir William Chambers for the Earl of Melbourne, with a little bit of rococo *coquillage* here and the odd *fleur-de-lys* there.

Clever, careless of any inconvenience or disturbance that might be caused to his more discreet and right-leaning neighbours, had had three of his patiently acquired sets in the Albany knocked into one. It was a spatial arrangement that contemptuously denied all the constructional logic implied by Chambers' handsome eighteenth-century façade. The process of acquisition had taken five years, followed by two of construction. But he had his house in Lucca, his apartment in Cap-d'Ail near Monaco and his duplex in Brooklyn's Park Heights, so he felt no urgency about the site on Piccadilly.

Throughout, neighbours complained about the nagging and continuous building noise, of Polish builders banging up Chambers' cantilevered stone staircase in steel-toed boots, playing Capital Radio on their grimy, paint-splattered ghetto blasters and leaving empty cans of Żywiec strong lager and crushed Fajrant cigarette packs in the lobby. Once completed, they complained that the children from his fifth left-leaning marriage were up at five in the morning to learn Mandarin from a resident tutor. A noisy call-and-response was part of this learning process: before dawn, chants of '*wo xiang yao yi xie lucha*' reverberated around the hard, shiny surfaces.

Meanwhile, Mrs Clever marched to and fro in noisy Gucci boots while reading a new translation of *The Pillow Book*. Other residents laughed at staff who were required to be dressed in surgical scrubs and sheepskin slippers to protect the highly polished Szechuan ebony floor.

One of these crisply laundered scrubs, a Filipina wearing a name tag saying 'Concepcion', offered me a glass of champagne. Cristal this time, a wine which left a curious taste of ash on the tongue. Also offered was a white ceramic spoon whose bowl contained sliced lotus and abalone stewed with black fungus, decorated with a single coriander leaf. That, and the little spray of spit a vengeful Concepcion had aimed at this fussy canapé. And her aim had been true.

Timothy Clever said, 'I think the Factory will exceed even the Voltaire. It's probably my very best building.' If there was humility in this confession, it was not obvious.

## the Clever Voltaire

The Factory opening was a sensation. Six hundred design and media people were there, all perfectly coiffed and mostly in expensive black, from London, New York, Paris, Milan, Madrid and Tokyo.

There was no separate press launch and private view because this was a world wholly determined by the media. It was a perfect, hermetic echo-chamber of an event: reporters, reporting on the reported. I guiltily confessed that I worried when this community was described as 'the design world' because when 'world' is used as a suffix, it does not indicate vast scope and global ambition, rather an introspective clique.

But here was the design world, putting mediocrity to the sword. The crowd included the best writers from the *New York Times*, the *Protector*, *Corriere della Sera*, *El Pais*, *Le Monde*, *Asahi Shimbun* and *Süddeutsche Zeitung*. After a welcome speech, I asked Dieter Rams, dressed like a Frankfurt professor, to say a few words in his distinctively broken English. Then I spotted the Japanese fashion designer Issey Miyake, dressed as a Buddhist monk, in the audience and asked him to join us on stage. Cameras flashed.

## an adolescent playpen

The following week, the *International Herald Tribune* profiled Sven Roth, giving him the entire back page with a fine, moody portrait by Terry O'Neill. Sven was in silhouette and holding an unlit cigarillo. Finding the story in my morning pile of cuttings, I felt affronted: as if my body had been snatched and my soul invaded. The writer, apparently collared by Roth at the opening, wrote about him being Britain's next 'design guru', eulogized him for energy and vision as well as his keen sense of personal style and youthful vigour. He was even quizzed about political economy to which he gave very eloquent answers, drawing closely on his extensive knowledge of the more readable passages of John Ruskin.

But worst, I found myself in Gary Knobber's position with the superyachts. *I* was the genius of the Factory, the benevolent visionary who had made it possible and the socially responsible philanthropist who had largely paid for it. But to read the *Trib*'s account, I was no more than a semi-detached backer, a source of funds rivalled at least by British Leyland and Kodak. That ungrateful little shit Roth gave me acknowledgement that was enthusiastic in general, but deliberately vague on details of creative contribution.

But most disturbing had been Roth's confident presentation of a future for the Factory in which Sir Eustace Dunne's only involvement was to sit back … and to sit on his hands. To me, this robbed my future, burgled my destiny and suggested the unthinkable prospect of having nothing to do. As well as the even more unthinkable prospect of mortality which is, so obviously, the immediate consequence of inactivity. What was that about sleep being a slice of death?

So I asked Sven to a breakfast meeting at The Connaught, the Mayfair hotel where, over kedgeree and mango salad, admen, cabinet ministers, editors, fixers, plotters, hustlers and mere millionaires confirmed their sovereign importance to each other, while waiters worried little beaten copper chafing dishes making scrambled eggs, served with truffles for the occasional apex-predator plutocrats.

Many of the regulars did two sittings at breakfast. And often guests who were beneficiaries of two breakfast-at-The-Connaught invitations, something which always carried the sense of seriousness since the need to have breakfast implied both intimacy and urgency, simply cycled themselves from one banquette to the other in an absurd dance of High Importance.

With the *Financial Times* propped against the table's centrepiece, I had already started on some L. Robson & Sons Craster kippers and buck's fizz when Sven arrived, looking annoyingly pert, well-groomed and at ease in this menagerie of power-broking titans.

'Very good, Sven,' I said, picking an obdurate kipper bone from my teeth. 'In fact, extremely well done, my dear Sven. But are you now going to stop being a junior fucking celebrity, a cadet Kenneth Clark, a mini-me? Are you going to stop going on television every day? Might you be able to take time off from your so very, very busy journalistic circus and be a proper general manager of the Factory? Might you, Sven? I am only asking because some of us are getting a little fatigued by your publicity-mad antics, your refusal to be serious, your neglect of budgets. It's a Factory we have built, not an adolescent playpen.'

Sven, despite his boyishly vigorous aspect, was very tired and recklessly hungover. He looked pained and told me, 'If that's what you think, Eustace, I am very disappointed. What you call a circus was carefully planned promotional activity, which helped raise our profile, gain credibility and win sponsors. We needed those sponsors. Your endowment might have been generous, but it was never going to be enough to meet the recurrent running costs. And, to be absolutely honest, I really think you should go and fuck yourself. Possibly within the next quarter of an hour.'

He then picked up his glass of freshly squeezed juice, poured it over my head and walked out. A little stutter of amused applause went around the dining room while Hyacinthe, the epicene head waiter, rushed to my help with a very stiff starched linen napkin.

Two days later, newspapers reported 'The Factory Loses Its Manager' or 'Sir Eustace Dunne's Factory Folly' or 'The Factory Runs Out Of Steam'. Sven Roth had disappeared, and I had no idea who to hire in his place.

This I was pondering when Sylvester Truelove called.

'Eustace, we really need to talk. Can you meet me at Biggin Hill, tomorrow at noon?'

Biggin Hill may be one of London's busiest airports for general aviation, but the rich must access their private planes through the dreariest, traffic-clogged suburban arteries of south London, past pound stores, Indian restaurants, doner kebab stalls, tyre and exhaust fitters, Tescos, Roman Catholic primary schools, mosques built of breeze blocks, minicab offices, bus depots, all-night Turkish greengrocers, chippies and council houses. To avoid the risk of sadness, I took a helicopter from Battersea. Six minutes in the air. A Bell JetRanger with ruched beige leather seats. Well worth it.

Sylvester was waiting in the Biggin Hill 'VIP' lounge, a terrible place inspired perhaps by a dentist's waiting room in Croydon. The banker was already playing with a Styrofoam cup of mephitic brown water, acquired from what was optimistically labelled a 'coffee' machine. I dreamt of espresso days and refused Sylvester's offer to join him in a plastic cup of boiler scrapings.

A distressed and dusty *Ficus elastica* 'Robusta' was in a terracotta-coloured plastic pot in the corner and dog-eared copies of *Autocar* and the *South London Press* were jumbled on a nasty chrome-legged and glass-topped table smeared with the fingerprints of travelling millionaires.

'I thought we should go to Paris for our long-postponed conversation,' Sylvester said. 'Make it easier for you.'

A uniformed girl with a clipboard led us to a waiting Beech King Air for the short flight to Le Bourget. Sylvester added, while gazing aimlessly at cross-Channel traffic below, 'I think we should have our talk in L'Ami Louis. A table is booked for eight.'

## smells like shit

L'Ami Louis is on the otherwise undistinguished little rue du Vert-bois, and was an institution of the 3rd arrondissement. It had been founded in 1924 by a cantankerous peasant called Antoine Magnin; dark, wooden and tiny with just twelve covers with an always roaring *feu du bois* whatever the temperature. Its food was elemental: *foie gras* in enormous slabs, *gigots d'agneau*, Bresse chickens, Poilâne bread and always red Burgundy . . . a *vin qui sent la merde*.

'Smells like shit,' I helpfully explained as I swirled an excellent Beaune in a balloon glass. 'You'll adore it, Sylvester. You'll feel at home in a shitty farmyard.'

® *Rollo Pinkie: The funny thing is, Eustace never really understood wine. It was always bought for him by a reliable merchant. He had learnt early on that swirling the wine in the glass and appearing to sniff thoughtfully gave a convincing impression of being a true oenophile. Were you, for example, to quiz him about the grapes used in Pessac-Léognan, he would have been hopelessly flummoxed. But no one ever asked and the mystique of authority remained intact.*

Sylvester was not frivolous. 'You are going bust, Eustace, and you have two options.' Changing to the first person plural, he added, 'We put Bleu de Travail into administration, or we sell it. Selling it is the better option. So I want you to know I have been talking to Armin Arschloch. In fact, Eustace, I have been talking to him for some time.'

Armin Arschloch was the founder of LUXI GmbH, the world's biggest furniture company. It specialized not in charm or beauty or location, but in cheapness, convenience and vast, out-of-town warehouses. Cost and volume were Arschloch's interests, not taste or pleasure. He was a frugal man who used teabags twice and whose idea of dinner out was to eat a curried bratwurst in the LUXI GmbH canteen. He had a simple desk in a shared office.

I pushed away a gloriously smeared plate that had recently supported nearly five hundred grams of landais *foie gras* but now carried only toasted Poilâne crumbs. 'What *are* you talking about, Sylvester? I really do not understand.'

'Then let me explain.' Truelove tightened his Windsor knot despite the intense heat caused by the flames and the farmyard-flavoured Pinot Noir we were drinking. I recalled that wine mervchant John Armit had always insisted that good Burgundy should smell like shit. Right now, I could sense shit in the air.

'You are' – reverting to the second person – 'in a business with very low barriers to entry, where the competition is fierce. There is over supply. But you have nevertheless expanded aggressively. There are months, to be sure, when the cash flow looks good' – I groaned again as Truelove continued – 'but the infrastructure creaks, the supply chains are stretched and unreliable, while very soon your commercial credit is going to run out.'

'But why didn't you tell me this?'

'I did. Many times. But you did not want to listen. I grant you, a good retailer is not necessarily a good manager, but I am afraid that your retail genius seems to have abandoned you. Or maybe it has just gone into hiding while you pursue more important things. Like this ludicrous vanity project, the Factory. You have spent all the "profits" made by Bleu de Travail over the past five years on something that will yield no return.'

'For Christ's sake, Sylvester, you really do never think of anything other than fucking money, do you?'

Not meaning to be funny, Sylvester said, 'Well, sometimes I think about a new Porsche, but, in general, it is entirely fair to say that money is, luckily for you, what I think about all the time. Anyway, there are copycats out there. The novelty of Bleu de Travail is now as threadbare as one of your favourite antique Gujarat rugs. And its balance sheet looks just as thin.'

I poured more wine. Oh shit, I thought.

## morals and money

Back in London, a courier delivered a very stiff, cream-coloured envelope with the legend 'Royal Bachelors' Club Göteborg' die-stamped in blue on the flap. The address was handwritten in cheap blue biro. So too was the letter.

Arschloch wrote in fluent English.

*Like you, Eustace, I believe in skönhet für alle. Beauty for all. This is why I made the headquarters of LUXI in Sweden. I was inspired by*

*IKEA. We agree that it is more difficult to design a good chair for fifty krona than for one thousand. That is why design is interesting: it mingles morals with money. But unlike you, Eustace, I know how to control costs and to expand prudently. I greatly admire your sense of style and your energy. Perhaps, I sometimes think, too much energy. But I believe that simplicity and humility are the most important aspects of human relations. I, you see, ride the bus, not a German limousine. How would I dare to travel first class myself when I compel my managers to buy cheap tickets? I drive a second-hand Volvo.*

You tell me, sunshine, I thought to myself. Rich fucking hypocrite constipated bastard. Arschloch had actually lived in Switzerland for thirty years, where his real tastes might not be under scrutiny from an intrusive German press. All his money was in an ingenious financial vehicle designed, like the Porsche he really drove, to steer around obstacles, in this case taxmen.

Arschloch's letter ended with an invitation to meet urgently in Sweden.

I flew east to meet him. He chose Stockholm's Grand Hôtel since, Royal Bachelors' Club apart, Gothenburg, where LUXI was based, had few attractive options, if you did not have a Chekhovian cottage on the Kattegat which Arschloch, ever careful with money, did not. There was, I recalled, a restaurant in Gothenburg that always had bear's paw on the menu, but I was disappointed that bear's paw was always 'off'. Perhaps it was a metaphor of life in the city.

In the afternoon light, Arschloch was ostentatiously sipping water in the hotel's sumptuous Cadier Bar, looking across the water at the pretty Gamla Stan. There was no handshake, no small talk.

'My good friend Mr Truelove has explained the position, but if I may be honest with you, Eustace, it is a position which has been obvious to many of us for some time, if not to you. Bleu de Travail was a creation of genius, but it has become a mismanaged and money-losing embarrassment. You have, as your good countrymen say, taken your eye off the football. There are things about retailing that you do not appear to understand.'

I braced myself for a fairytale or a homily. I did not want either much and I got both.

'I know about the true value of things. I began buying matches in bulk, then moved on to fish. I am the world's richest ex-fishmonger! The expense of the stock you keep in-store is ruinous. It ties up what little capital you have. Truelove tells me you have failed to negotiate sensible banking covenants and that you risk losing the faith of your bankers. Your inner city sites were once charming and interesting, but they have become vulnerable. New inner-city parking laws have now made them totally inaccessible to the majority of your customers. You were slow into flatpack self-assembly, an area in which I have led the world.'

I grimaced and Arschloch continued: 'But it is only those who are asleep who never make mistakes. And I know you are alert. Perhaps always too alert with your new ventures here and there and all over the place that, I believe, distract you expensively from the real business of running a business.'

Used neither to being a supplicant nor to hearing criticism, I tried to manage an expression that showed concern balanced with curiosity. The atmosphere was somewhat like the headmaster's study.

'I do not have the numbers with me, but Mr Truelove and I have agreed a generous bid for your interest in Bleu de Travail. People say I am cheap and stingy, but I am not. I am simply a realist. Now, I say "generous", but this offer will remain generous for only so long as it is uncontested by you. I strongly suggest you accept my offer because, as Mr Truelove assures me, there are and will be no other offers on the table. In short, dear Eustace, you accept my offer or you are bankrupt.'

I nodded gravely, ordered another Macallan for myself and a

Klarvatten Morarp mineral water for Arschloch. You supercilious, graceless, joyless, sad, grim, grasping, pseudo-democratic-more-likely-Nazi, manipulative, sterile, disingenuous, mean-spirited Scandinavian shit, I thought. What do you know about *joie de vivre* with your awful fucking meatballs and your filthy low alcohol beer that looks and tastes like horse piss? Not to mention your ugly and ungracious furniture. Has anybody gone to bed tonight dreaming of the day they will buy a Billy bookcase? Has anyone been seduced by the gorgeousness of a fucking Ektorp sofa to make uninhibited, passionate love on after their undigestible meatballs? I don't think so.

And then I thought rather worse about Sylvester Truelove. Once a trusted intimate, now a betrayer to rival the Borgias in the cynical opportunism of his secret dealings with Arschloch. Never mind backstabbing, Truelove was now front-stabbing too. Truelove, I was certain, would be calculating the value of his new stake in Arschloch's holding company, a sweetener for bringing off this deal at such an attractive price to LUXI GmbH.

*The Times'* business pages soon led with the story, leaked, I imagined by Sylvester Truelove himself, who was proud to claim he knew the direct lines of all the City editors: 'Sir Eustace Dunne's dream is over', 'City tires of underperforming visionary'. I was now a 'so-called designer' who had 'failed the City' and 'lost his way'. 'LUXI GmbH flatpacks Dunne', 'Armin Arschloch makes meatballs of Sir Eustace', the *Sun* crowed, using a photograph of a naked twenty-three-year-old girl sitting on an Ektorp sofa to make its point.

Simultaneously, the professional design press weekly featured stories about how the Factory, still without a general manager, was adrift and lacking creative or intellectual credibility. A very expensive folly was the consensus. By Truelove's worrying calculations, I had spent nearly £60 million on the project, if you take into account loss of interest. That would be £600 million if you took into account the contamination of my brand.

Three months after the sale, half the Bleu de Travail shops were closed down and the remainder rebranded LUXI GmbH-Express.

> *Eustace Dunne made the British high street a place of cultural curiosity. He was the man who designed the world. But his influence is now disappearing from the urban landscape. This is a bitter and catastrophic humiliation. 'Vackrare vardagsvara' was the motto of the old Swedish designers. For all his vanity, greed and mendacity, Eustace had sincerely tried to offer these very same 'more beautiful everyday things' to his customers. And now they had rejected him. A place he had carefully designed for himself in the national imagination was now occupied by a boorish German resident in Sweden who shifted boxes and ate meatballs.*

Terri McGonagal, Protector, May 1992

And I did not disagree. I thought about the hellish Neasden LUXI GmbH, the North Circular Road, the toxic suburbs, a wobbling Billy bookcase, piss-awful beer, and wondered what that had to do with skönhet für fucking alle. Beauty for all, my arse.

In a life of easy style and great success, notions of betrayal and calamity were slowly gaining prominence in my view of things.

...........................................................................................................

® *Rollo Pinkie: All this is true, but Eustace, true to form, liked to present the humiliating LUXI GmbH fire-sale as a business initiative of (his) strategic genius.*

# 19

# 1996 – Tits up at the Negresco

*'I heard he sang a good song
I heard he had a style.'*

Charles Fox and Norman Gimbel, 'Killing Me
Softly', 1971, reissued by the Fugees, 1996

*The Promenade des Anglais en fête.*

I VISITED NICE OFTEN. SOMETIMES when I was happy, but always when I was sad. The Côte d'Azur is the Coast of the Blues, I liked to say, thinking it rather witty.

But it nevertheless always raised the spirits. There was always a sense of promise, sometimes unlocatable and hard to define, but present nonetheless. Even if on a bad day the Mediterranean looked dingy and the ochre tower blocks were reminders not of south Europe, but of south London, it was inspiring. You cannot understand Matisse unless you know the impossibly beautiful Bay of the Angels as seen from Mont Boron. In Nice, life followed art. Or was it the other way round?

And the Promenade des Anglais always offered a reliable shot of louche glamour, with its memories of Isadora Duncan and Grace Kelly, two-tone convertibles, dippy starlets and sea breezes. This 'English Promenade' was always so very foreign. Stepping out of the plane, there was – almost always – blue sky, warm air, blue sea, swaying palms and bougainvillea. The light was different, even erotic.

During the cab ride from the airport to the Negresco, I always wondered how many recently ravished naked odalisques were supine on *chaises longues* behind the mysterious shuttered windows of the grand villas along the Promenade, perhaps contemplating a bowl of tempting oranges that Matisse might have painted.

In Nice, the choices were always exciting. There was Italy in one direction, Provence in another, both prospects framed by the distant Alps. And always the opportunity everywhere and at all times of day to eat delicious food and drink quaffable wine served in the company of glamorous women, or so my theory went.

I loved Nice's mixture of sophistication and vulgarity, of luxury and dirt, strangeness and familiarity, sweetness and danger: my favourite restaurant on the Cours Saleya had a dish called *merda di can*. Or dog-shit pasta flecked with spinach. And surely Alziari was the best olive oil in the world, and who actually needed Dior's Eau Sauvage if you used Alziari's rough olive oil soap in the shower?

It was just outside Nice that, years before, I met Picasso, a present to myself for my fortieth birthday. Telexing Picasso's agent requesting a visit to the studio in Vallauris to buy some of his recent ceramics, I was surprised when a rendezvous was made with the artist himself at the old Hôtel les Arcades in Biot. Picasso arrived in the lovely, crumbling and pillared thirteenth-century square, driving himself in his extraordinary dark metallic green Facel Vega HK500, a car of such brutal refinement it suggested Emile Ruhlmann had designed a hot-rod. The artist was wearing his famous striped *pull marin*, rolled up workmen's shorts and faded pink espadrilles.

Picasso was as hard, wrinkled and brown as a walnut, but, settling at the table, the artist smiled and soon arranged the bread rolls to resemble the spread fingers of Robert Doisneau's portrait. Clearly, this was something he did often. Under hot sun, we shared the restaurant's *bourride* and several large carafes of pink wine. Holding his glass of rosé to catch the sun's rays, Picasso told me: '*Quand tu as soixante ans, tu peux redevenir jeune. Mais il est trop tard.*' And he laughed. He was always aware of age. And so too was I.

'When you are sixty, you can be young again. But it's too late.' And then I arranged to buy a series of Picasso's minotaur jugs, the ones showing the elderly man-bull copulating vigorously with teenage Cretan chorus girls. I also bought a Picasso rug whose decoration comprised an impressively engorged penis seeking one of several spectacularly hirsute and wrinkled vulvae which formed the carpet's central pattern. As I was saying, there is something erotic in the air.

I usually stayed at the Negresco, the very grand *belle époque* hotel on the Promenade des Anglais which Jeanne Augier had inherited in 1957. With her blind eye to the foibles of the famous and her very keen sense of personal publicity, Augier made the Negresco one of the most infamous hotels in the world: the Riviera in miniature with its easy access to sun, sex and sea. She said, 'Here everything is possible ... flamboyance served on a tray.' And, of course, flamboyance was not the only thing served on trays by dutifully bobbing waiters.

It had been a favourite of mine since my very first visit: an occasion, I noted with delight, when Salvador Dalí was also a guest. The Surrealist posed daily in the lobby, leading a lobster around the marble floors by a scarlet ribbon, which he insisted had once been part of the Queen of Sheba's underwear. It was a rare day when Jean Cocteau was not found in the bar. Although a lot of other stuff could be found in the bar as well.

In the Negresco, trays of champagne and blow were served to Romy Schneider and Alain Delon as they conducted their very public and artfully publicized affair. The hotel positively encouraged fornication, especially in public. Indeed, the hotel's reputation was established by its famous and outrageous pink domes, always said to be modelled on the breasts of the *demi-mondaine* dancer La Belle Otero, although the architectural features were as inhumanly symmetrical as moulds for blancmange. But an appetite for symmetry should never impede a good story. Nor, of course, a handsome *poitrine*.

The hotel's mood was infectious. I often pronounced on its merits, its libidinous associations and absolutely frank air of decadent luxury. I had even given Madame Augier a quote for the hotel's brochure: 'At the Negresco, style comes *en magnum*.'

Since the divorce from Beverley so many years ago, I had, like La Rochefoucauld, decided that marriage was possibly tolerable, but rarely delectable. And I could do without it. Of romance I had little need, while the more mechanical aspects of love could be handled by shepherdesses, Shanghai bar girls, opportunistic encounters in hotels, importuned staff, grateful acquaintances, careless wives, old-fashioned hookers or even, possibly, one day by Anika herself, although I had yet to find the keys to unlock the forbidding gates to her fortress.

This was scrolling through my mind as I swirled a whisky, sitting in the dark, wood-panelled bar, idly wondering about dinner, when I became aware someone was looking at me.

## telling detail

She was a black African with a profile like Nefertiti's: Cupid's-bow lips, a tumbling waterfall of curls and a clinging cocktail dress which I took to be Dior, or perhaps Saint Laurent. It was certainly a garment designed for a woman possessed of ample confidence, making few concessions to modesty. When observed, she slowly turned from staring at me to look down at her chest, whose defining features had not been disguised by the couturier's art.

I followed her gaze chestwards. Only a certain sort of woman, I knew, goes alone to the bar of the Negresco. 'Hooker' would be crass to say. But it was not a milieu where you would expect to find a novice nun or a sociology professor from a Grande Ecole. As breezes can make you catch a chill, the atmosphere at the Negresco has its own effect on wellbeing.

She returned to looking at me. Her stare was really quite intense and required a response.

I approached her table. 'I have a very good eye for telling detail,' I said as she adjusted her dress in a way intended to suggest modesty, but really, in fact, conveying the opposite.

'I suppose you know the story about La Belle Otero?' I said, in a style intended to sound didactic, while tossing my head upwards to indicate the presence of roseate *mamelles* pointed at paradise.

'Oh, yeah. Oh, yeah,' she said in a mid-Atlantic accent, smiling and flapping her hand while pushing her chest out. 'You mean that tits bullshit.' She giggled, theatrically offering me a hand as if she intended for me to kiss it. 'My name is Molly.'

Molly Mthembu came from the townships, but ambition and ability had won her a scholarship to South Africa's Roedean in Park-town, Johannesburg. Then to the University of Sussex where she met and briefly married the publicity-hound son of a borderline criminal casino-owner in London. Molly had soon come to a cer-tain sort of lewd prominence in the tabloids when she brought an action for libel against a Test cricketer, claiming to identify herself as a disguised character in his popular and salacious autobiography *You Need Leather Balls*.

The cricketer had written that, at a dinner party in Onslow Square, South Kensington, hosted by the German owner of a grand house full of over-restored and too-shiny Canalettos, he had had occasion to slip into the kitchen in the middle of the meal. Here he was followed by a woman who, to his great pleasure and sur-prise, but wholly uninvited, gave him a most satisfactory guerrilla blow-job while the unseeing maids were clearing and clattering the soup plates. 'From soup to nuts' was the way people sniggered about her.

Molly's grievance was that anybody in her party milieu would, on reading the cricketer's confessions, immediately identify her as the fellatrice, even though she was disguised by a *nom de plume*. In court the judge had said, 'So, Ms Mthembu, you readily accept that you might be identified as the sort of person who would *perform* – I think that is the word – "oral sex" on a complete stranger.' And promptly dismissed her case with a play on words about fellatio and fallacious which raised no laughs at all.

As we began to talk, I was playing with the nibbles on the bar: cured meats, vast green olives and cheese straws, the latter a talking point among the regulars who liked to debate whether Severin de Vauvenargues, the hotel's two-star chef, used Parmesan or Comté. I was piercing a slice of Jésus de Lyon with a cocktail stick when Molly explained: 'Personally, I never eat anything that has a face.'

'Personally, I don't think *saucisson* ever had a face.' I smiled, amused by my own wit.

Seeing no point in time-wasting reconnaissance, I speared another piece of *saucisson*, briefly put on a thoughtful expression and bluntly said, 'Would you like to come upstairs?'

She did not say no.

I chose not to use my own room, but a fifty pound note and a fraternal wink to the all-knowing, all-seeing concierge found us in a fine corner suite with an ocean – so dark it tempted similes – seen through palms and the shadows and reflections of the hotel's garish theatrical neon signage. Traffic noise and sea breezes came through the open windows. Eventually, she sighed. And I had the clear impression that Molly had, in every sense, been here before.

Contemplation and a smoke are conventional at these moments, but Molly was not the contemplative type and I had left the Havanas in my own room.

'I had a boob job in Mexico,' she said brightly. 'Did you notice? I'm really quite pleased with the effect, although the left one is a bit numb, to be honest. Still, that's a small price to pay for beauty, don't you think?'

I attempted a sad clown face and reached for the white bathrobe, noting with satisfaction that it was plush terry cotton by Frette. There was Alziari soap in the shower.

Two hours later, we were in La Petite Maison, Nice's restaurant-of-note, a ten minute stroll away in the old flower market. Fresh fruit and vegetables were always spread on the tables, an affectation which reminded me horribly of the dreadful Nightingale Hicks and his fucking awful tablescapes with onyx pyramids and ostrich eggs.

The restaurant (which liked to claim '*le monde entier est à la maison ici*') was run by an angry Provençal peasant woman, fat arms intimidatingly crossed over apron to meet and greet, whose great art was to distinguish between the merely prosperous and the very rich, the quite well-known and the supremely famous. This she did with a great deal of malice aforethought. Accordingly, people made exceptional efforts to ingratiate themselves to the grim old harridan who smelt of sweat, oil and oregano.

'Hi, Mick!' Molly shrieked and waved when she saw a miniature simian rockstar in a snakeskin jacket and astonishingly tight trousers sitting in a dark corner. 'I thought you were in Martinique.'

'Nah, Mols,' Mick said, 'Martinique's *le weekend*, love.'

Noting her first-name terms with a Rolling Stone, the angry peasant showed Molly and me to the second-best table in the house. After years of avoidance stratagems, prevarication and old-fashioned lies, I had avoided commitment for years, but I astonished myself by proposing to Molly at La Petite Maison, our very first dinner. Somewhere between the *omelette aux truffes* and the *rougets*, I found myself saying, with a mouthful of fish and perhaps a little too much local rosé, 'Would it be a good idea to get married?'

Again, she did not say no.

'I must be getting old,' I said to myself. 'Pushing sixty.' I thought of Picasso's swollen and deflating minotaurs.

French laws are very strict. To get married in the local *Mairie*, it is necessary to be a resident of the Commune for at least forty days.

But five hundred dollars to the same all-knowing concierge helped avoid strict French laws, putting us in the *Mairie* before the notary public early the next day. So now, to everyone's surprise, there was a new Lady Dunne.

I faxed Anika to explain and, knowing I would approve, she called the *Daily Post*. A splashily illustrated page three story duly appeared: 'A knight of love: Rushed Riviera Romance for Eustace Dunne'. An agency photographer had doorstepped us at the hotel and the paper had called me for comment. They used this as a pull-quote: 'If you are a designer, you always have a better idea. And I just had one! She's called Molly.'

## how rich am I, Sylvester?

While it was humiliating, the forced sale of Bleu de Travail had made me very rich. And I was ruefully pleased to have been enriched by that smug but joyless, Scandinavian flat-pack, screw-loose, cross-threaded huckster, Armin Arschloch. Sylvester Truelove, as if in a state of post-coital delirium after his deal had been done, had stopped wearing a tie, something I thought both significant and ridiculous. He actually looked half undressed.

But he had diligently done his sums about my new net worth.

'How rich am I, Sylvester?' I asked.

He ran a hand through his brilliantined permanent wave and said, 'Low hundreds, Eustace, low hundreds.'

I described the sale to Kevin – Chatty – Bumble of the *Daily Post* as 'a Napoleonic reversal', adding, 'but unlike Napoleon, I am not retreating, nor am I going into exile. I am most certainly coming back.' I didn't say to Kevin, but solemnly promised myself, that I would never open another shop, but I would open another restaurant. Possibly even one with Napoleonic ambition.

## *de luxe* fish soup

There was a standing invitation to visit the Ricard house in the Camargue, which, after a few calls, I was now able to redesign as an impromptu honeymoon.

It was Veuve Clicquot who had introduced me to Ludovic Ricard, the scion of the family firm that made *pastis*, the mother's ruin of France. Not one to miss an opportunity, I promptly made a slightly over-eager pitch to refresh the branding of Ricard's signature '51' *pastis*, a French national treasure of commercial art. This offer Ludovic wisely and politely ignored, but we had discovered a shared taste for tobacco and marc de Bourgogne, so made an amiable commitment to keep an open mind about other business opportunities. This I enthusiastically described to the business press as a 'long-term strategic alignment'.

With great French sophistication, Ricard had suggested that if this ever were to happen, it should be 'perhaps in London', since he wanted none of my interference in his family business, *pour être honnête*. But the arrangement was an equable one. To me, even vicarious contact with Ricard was to tap into the very essence of my beloved France. And, no matter how tentative the understanding, I felt able to add the splendid name of Ricard to our client list, to add lustre to some of the other fictions there. To Ludovic Ricard, who confused the crass English honours system with the noble peerage, as the French often do, contact with someone called Sir Eustace gave him valuable access to what he sweetly imagined was the aristocracy.

The Camargue is that vast, flat, salt-marshy area between Marseilles and the sea, an hour and a half's drive from Nice. Ricard's was not the typical Provençal *mas*, but a grander *manade*, meaning he kept cattle. More accurately, Spanish fighting bulls, the *toros bravos* bred for the *corrida* in Arles, Nîmes, Marseilles and Narbonne.

The *manade* was huge, low and rectangular. Protecting occupants from the mistral on the one hand and the cruel sun on the other, there were cypresses on one side, shady plane trees the other. Wisteria grew on the walls, the shutters were a nice, sun-bleached blue. It was surrounded by wild iris and daffodils, *étangs* and pink flamingos. Outside the *manade*: two dusty Citroën H-Type vans with Ricard livery, a picturesque restored Citroën 2cv and Ludovic Ricard's immaculate, pale yellow Rolls-Royce Corniche convertible with white-wall tyres and a white hood. Lost on most Frenchmen was Ricard's knowing reference to tragic Jay Gatsby's yellow Phantom.

Ricard had personally invested in Marcel Campo's new bistrot in Les Trois Mairies, the bleak main town of the Camargue. In only three years since opening, Le Gardian, named after the Camargue's cowboys, had already been enthusiastically noted by the Gault & Millau restaurant guide which gave Campo, a one-time Foreign Legionnaire from Corsica, a man with spectacular Russian criminal tattoos disguising even more spectacular scars, an encouraging 15 out of 20 score, with a clear suggestion that there was more to come.

And this was where the three of us, Ludovic being confirmed single, went for dinner. With great fanfare, we were trumpeted into the restaurant by sunburnt, smoking gypsy cowboys. Those who were not trumpeting were playing guitars. All were evidently very drunk. We ate Campo's superb *bouillabaisse* which was, Ricard explained, glass in hand, so much more than a *de luxe* fish soup, but a careful and extremely labour-intensive amalgamation of subtle flavours including *rascasse* and langoustine, fennel, saffron and *poissons de roche*. I said I knew a recipe that took thirteen pages.

We drank a local *gris de gris*, a wine of great minerality tinted a pink so fine and subtle it appeared to be grey. A wine influenced, perhaps, by the local flamingos themselves. We spoke of London's enlarging restaurant culture, Ludovic recalling that on his first visit as an exchange student, all he could find to eat was a Wimpy hamburger, all to drink sarsaparilla or disgusting warm bitter. I explained things were now getting very much better. Molly winked at me and, thinking I did not notice, put her hand on Ludovic's knee and squeezed hard.

Ignoring this provocation, I began to think how interesting, how extremely interesting, it would be to bring Marcel Campo and his *rascasse*, his fennel and his saffron to London.

# 1997 – A Celebrity Petting Zoo

*'I take a look at my life and realize there's nothin' left.'*

Wonder, Sanders, Ivey, Rasheed, 'Gangsta's Paradise', 1995

La Coupole, *Montparnasse*.

AFTER THE TAKEOVER OF BLEU de Travail and the troubles at the Factory, now that the fickle and pitiless scroungers of the City had tired of their clumsy flirtation with design, now that the papers mocked me, a new restaurant was to be a sort of redemption. The project was, it's true, almost Biblical in its symbolic value. It was an island paradise visible in the distance across dark, troubled waters populated by menacing creatures.

I did not need proof of my virility, but the hoo-hah about an ambitious new restaurant might helpfully restate to an increasingly sceptical – even sometimes critical – press my relevance, knack for reinvention, taste and style. It was, to continue a Biblical theme, truly to be a testament. Possibly even a resurrection.

It had always been like this. My concentration was powerful, like the beam of a lighthouse. But like the beam of a lighthouse, it came and went. My critics noticed and I quietly accepted its truth. My concentration was for a moment very bright indeed, but never stood still. It swept into and out of focus. When it was there, it was un-avoidable. When it was not there, it was forgotten.

But bringing Le Gardian to London was a project with excit-ing vectors of discovery and achievement. It might again supply the oxygen of publicity. It was no less than a reason to live. Le Gardian therefore received, for a long moment, my total concentration.

'The thing about success is this,' I told an interviewer from *The Caterer*. 'It's the ability to continue. To go from one mistake to the next with no loss of enthusiasm. Most of life is a mistake, a mess, an accident, a failure. What we call "success" is that tiny portion of life that is not a Royal Bengal, shot-peened, fuck-up. And besides, the greater the fall, the more impressive the ascent of recovery. As you will see.'

During this interview, I was doodling designs for cutlery and door-handles on a pad and added: 'The one thing that unites all truly successful people is their ability to forget their failures. It will be like a celebrity petting zoo,' I optimistically declared to the startled *Caterer* journalist. 'It will make La Coupole look like Mr Wimpy.'

*But while his concentration is fidgety and fugitive, when he decides on something, Eustace Dunne becomes unmovable and resolute. And he has decided to make no less than the best restaurant in the world. He has had his failures, but he declares them noble ones. He may not be a religious man, but this is a form of redemption. He may not be a religious man, but perhaps he will be crucified.*

*The Caterer*, September 1996

Molly and I soon returned to the Camargue.

From Nice to Marseilles we drove in a hire car on the old national roads through Vidauban, Gonfaron, Cuers and Solliès-Toucas itself, a place of earlier adventures with Richard Olney. We saw the plane trees, the faded Suze posters, the little cafes spilling out on to the road and I spoke, possibly even wistfully, of my first years travelling around France. The landscape was confirmation of the rightness of things. I thought of wild rabbit spit-roasted over a crackling blaze of olive branches, the smoke perfumed by the handfuls of wild oregano thrown on the fire.

'*Le bon goût? C'est normal ici,*' I suggested in stagily hesitant schoolboy French. Molly said nothing, and stared out of the window, tapping her fingers on her knees.

Arriving at Campo's restaurant, through swamps occupied by

flamingos and wild horses, through clouds of dust and a brittle pale sun, we were shown to the kitchen and invited to sit at a huge stainless-steel table while porters, with Gauloises irremovably attached to their lips, cursing under the uncharitable light, unloaded polystyrene boxes of fish and shellfish into the restaurant's cool store. You could actually hear the live crustacea-scratching at the plastic.

## killing the worm

Marcel Campo himself soon joined us. He presented himself as a corsair who had become a successful heavyweight boxer – two rings in one ear – and was carrying a bottle of rough brandy. It was ten in the morning.

'*Pour tuer le ver,*' he explained, offering shot glasses. Killing the worm was evidently a daily tradition each morning in his kitchen.

Campo, draining his glass immediately and wiping his mouth with the back of a tattooed arm, wanted to explain his *philosophie de la cuisine*. It was not mere cooking, it was a way of life, *un métier*. Wine alone cannot claim a *terroir*, food must have a place of origin too. The gods demand it. Another shot of brandy.

And food can have an entirely transformative effect not just on the appetite, but on life itself. He had told Gault & Millau: 'Your mouth is your hangman or your happiness.' In the past, you ate badly, you died. You ate well, it was a lasting pleasure. Even if you still, in any case, eventually died.

Then, after the worm had been most thoroughly killed, when I had retired to the terrace with my notebook for a cigarillo and some sketching and reflection, Molly accepted Marcel's invitation to look at his kitchen in more detail. The *commis* chefs all dispersed and I left Molly and Marcel alone with the Josper, walk-in fridge, steam-baths and the pathetically scratching *gambas*, yearning to be free.

Half an hour later, Molly and Marcel returned to the terrace where

I was still sketching, now in the company of a glass of pink wine, served from a handsome *carafe d'orangeade* bought from the *brocante* at Isle-sur-la-Sorgue, a little town near Daudet's famous Provençal windmill. Marcel was looking smug, possibly even elated, adjusting his chef's whites while Molly, a little flushed, dabbed her mouth with an Hermès scarf.

I had been sketching what I saw as the spirit of the Camargue. This I was going to bring to London: simple, elegant architecture, ample spaces defined by light and shadow alone. It was, like my inspiration here, to be called Le Gardian. And I had in mind two possible sites.

One was a landmark building off Soho Square, a London-French institution long since abandoned by its original tenants, the Little Sisters of Magdeleine de Jésus, and more recently decorated by the whimsical Jean Cocteau for a seriously boring French water utility company. The second was Ernö Goldfinger's office for Air France on Piccadilly, a building of Le Corbusian purity. Neither was actually on the market, but that was a stimulant, not a deterrent. Everything is always for sale, as poor Quentin Huskisson had taught me. It is just a matter of establishing the price.

We took a lease on the Goldfinger building. It was already a fine exercise in French *modernisme*, a double height space with impressive light, but we added an astonishing glass staircase with open treads supported on tensile steel wires. The customers' eyes were drawn to a vast seafood bar at the terminus of the vista, a recollection of Campo's *gambas*: mountains of crustaceans and lemons on ice were backed by a huge bevelled glass mirror with aircraft motifs.

The waiters' stations each had masterpiece Lalique glass and we installed Eileen Gray's Transat chairs in the lobby to emphasize the Frenchness of it all. Very much inspired by the china, glass and flat-ware Raymond Loewy had designed for the Air France Concorde, I drew a range myself.

'But one thing you will never find in Le Gardian,' I said to Terri

McGonagal of the *Protector*, 'is any fucking square plates!' Square plates were already becoming a lazy cliché of *nouvelle cuisine*.

I had the idea of all-day dining for Le Gardian. This was not merely an advance on the established all-day full English breakfast, not an institution I greatly admired; rather it was a unique experiment in what the smart arse critics were calling 'restauration'. Besides, it carried with it the advantage of maximizing profitability. Why have only lunch and dinner service when you could sell food around the clock?

Inadvertently, this had been Marcel Campo's idea. The chef had shown us records from an old Camarguais *mas* of the early nineteenth century when six meals were served every day. At sunrise there was *petit beurre*: anchovies, onions, radishes and wine. At nine-thirty, there was *grand beurre* with wine and cheese. Lunch was at midday and was a thick vegetable soup served with eggs. Again, there was wine, although sometimes it was diluted with water. At two in the afternoon was *le goûter*: a garlicky, oil-dressed mixed salad with cheese. This was followed at four by *la buvette* which was a slice of bread and a glass of wine. And, at sunset, a proper meal, the *gros repas*: soup, meat, vegetables and yet more wine. This seemed a very good way of life.

But I also introduced Camarguais staples: Campo's signature *bouillabaisse*, asparagus, *pâté de foie gras* in pots, *filet* cooked over open coals, *pommes sautées*, *petits pois*, *omelette aux herbes*, roast chicken or whatever fish fresh had escaped the hungry flamingos in the *étangs*.

'I have this idea for coffee service,' I said, to anybody who would listen. 'The waiter will weigh the beans at the table on a silver scale designed by Wilhelm Wagenfeld, a designer too austere for the Bauhaus. Then he will grind them by hand to the customer's preferred texture, while explaining the physics of pour-over filtration.'

And once again I hired Crisp Gascoyne, London's leading restaurant critic, as a consultant. Over a test lunch of that signature *bouillabaisse*, I said to her, 'Crisp, my love, would you help me out here? I need to get people to understand what we are doing. This is not chafing dishes, cloches and fucking *guéridons*. This is gutsy food. But it's also fine food. It's the food of French cowboys, not chain-smoking Marlboro men in gay leather chaps. It's simple yet sophisticated, but there's nothing bogus about it.'

Crisp picked a recalcitrant bone from her teeth. 'This is brilliant, Eustace. Of course I'll do it. But I'll need a budget.' She put her head down and her eyes up in a gesture internationally understood as, 'You know what I mean?'

'Of course, Crisp,' I said. 'I'll increase your retainer to forty thousand a year plus an open tab at Le Gardian. Would that be agreeable?'

We clinked glasses and planned to meet for breakfast the next day. She later wrote: 'Talking of revolutionizing British taste, Eustace Dunne has taught a nation to prefer anchovies to porridge. And to drink wine with toast at tea-time!'

Crisp used my line on her top *New York Times* contact and that paper duly declared Le Gardian 'The Best French Restaurant in the World', even if that was before the paper had actually sent a critic to Piccadilly. 'For real French food, go to London's Mayfield,' it said, making a notorious mistake about identifying Mayfair on a day when its normally very busy fact-checkers were asleep. Still, I enjoyed being quotable.

Marcel Campo was reverentially profiled in the *Times*' Saturday supplements, showing disgusted, but enthralled, Manhattanites how to bloodily gut a small fish using only thumb and forefinger. He reliably scandalized the readers, yet fascinated them by describing how you should bite the heads off the little *poissons de roche* and chew them, so as to enjoy the unique flavour of their brains, before spitting out the mess.

And I began enjoyably importing and bottling wine from the local co-op near Aix where Campo had long done business, meaning good terms were easily agreed. It arrived in London weekly by tanker, cost less than one pound for five litres and was undistinguished, in certain weeks almost undrinkable, but on the whole it was reliable.

I had asked the design studio to create some new labels for a wine that I had decided must be called Le Manadier, a name as grand as it was unspecific. Few customers caught the reference to a Camarguais *manade*, but the definite article gave a suggestion of authority and its association with Sir Eustace Dunne was surely enough, I felt, to dull the responses of the critical.

Disguised by our neat modern graphics, customers found this rough co-op wine very enjoyable, many of them comparing the red with the better sort of Châteauneuf-du-Pape and the whites and rosés to the elegant wines of Bandol. In this way, I reconfirmed a reputation for democratizing luxury. Even the austere and forbidding wine writer of the *Financial Times* was approving.

'Surely this *is* Châteauneuf-du-Pape?' she said, wrinkling a critical nose over a test lunch of braised civet and white asparagus I had served her during Le Gardian's soft opening. 'I'm getting *roussanne* and *cinsault*.'

I smiled mysteriously and pointed to the 'legs' of the wine, those trickles down the glass that indicate high alcohol content.

'Of course, you know about the Marangoni effect? It's the legs that suggest quality. A bit like a woman.'

She froze me.

## the history of stretching

I confess I was being a little deceitful about Le Manadier. But I also knew there was a long history of 'stretching' even the best wines. The great châteaux – unadvertised – often mix a little rough stuff with the proper vintage to give it more fruit, more sugar, more alcohol, or to correct any other unfortunate deficiency resulting from scrupulous and honest methods. In any case, it was not counterfeit. I was not *pretending* Le Manadier was anything it was not. I was just letting customers imagine it.

And the margin on Le Manadier was extremely attractive. Routinely marking up bottles by 300 per cent, restaurants make most of their profits on wine. But since I was buying in alcoholic co-op grape juice for a few pence a litre, Le Manadier was approaching 3000 per cent.

Inevitably, with a logic that Lucifer himself would recognize, it was only a very short step to buying a slightly better wine from the co-op and asking the London studio to design labels which said 'Gigondas' and 'Vacqueyras', the great, big reds of the Southern Rhône. At first, I did this to amuse my intimates, my *proches*.

'Tell me, Crisp, are you getting a Marangoni effect from this stonking huge Gigondas? This is a wine with legs. At 15 per cent, it should make your knees tremble. Then who knows what might happen?'

I had often wondered about the romantic mysteries beneath the layered and pleated folds of her sombre outfits, modelled apparently on a Meiji-era Japanese grandmother.

Crisp rolled her eyes.

For me, this wine business, this dance with the devil, was an amusing test for taste. Thus, like all my businesses. Offer the customer something better and they will want it. Even if it only *seems* to be better ...

How suggestible people were! Of course, there is a natural variation in all wines. And tasters often disagree, sometimes hilariously. Besides, it was very amusing to confuse ambitious billionaires. It was, of course, also an irresistible opportunity to enlarge Le Gardian's wine list in a most profitable way. Soon, Gigondas and Vacqueyras became Le Gardian's most popular wines.

Some experts wondered about provenance, since the modernist

labels the studio produced were designed more for effect than the transfer of precise or forensic information. But what do experts know? The customers loved these wines. I had a fantasy that one day I would go into the restaurant, arrive at a table and say: 'Do you know, you appalling tassel-loafered idiot, you have just paid £35 for something that cost me ten pence?'

But that was for another day.


## the screwing I am getting

While I was reading an extremely favourable review of Le Gardian's new southern Rhônes in *Decanter* magazine, written by one of Crisp Gascoyne's best friends after a big lunch, Anika came into my office holding a letter.

'I think you need to look at this,' she said, handing me a quivering letter while I was still re-reading *Decanter*'s rapt praise for my 'humungous' Vacqueyras and entering something of a reverie.

It was from Kevin – Chatty – Bumble who had now become the editor of the *Daily Post*.

> *My dear Eustace,*
>
> *I am so very sorry to write in these terms, but more than one source has provided us with astonishing information about Lady Dunne which we believe is in the public interest to publish.*
>
> *Before she became a popular figure, Molly Mthembu led a private life of what we might call uninhibited variety. It is not our intention to moralize about the now Lady Dunne's very vigorous expression of her liberal philosophy and free will, still less her prodigious appetite and impressively inclusive tastes, but we do wish to expose the hypocrisy at the centre of national life.*
>
> *It seems to us at the* Post *to be incompatible that Lady Dunne is a patron of Save the Children, the Women for Mosques*

*campaign, the Eat the Rich Foundation, a Trustee of the British Museum and of Greenpeace, not to mention a beneficiary of your own largesse, while leading an alternative personal life which our readers will feel borders on moral depravity.*

*Naturally, we would not wish to publish anything personally damaging to you and we do wish to give you the right of reply.*

*I am wondering if you might be able to meet me at White's to discuss this over a glass of vino.*

*Yours very truly,*
*Kevin – Chatty – Bumble*

I thought again of La Rochefoucauld: '*Il y a de bons mariages, mais il n'y en a point de délicieux.*'

Then, rather less finely, I thought about Kevin and said to myself, 'You righteous fucking twat.' If Quentin had not so selfishly died in the Paris canal, I would have sent him and his propellants to Derry Street to torch the newspaper HQ.

The confrontation with Molly was nasty, brutish and short.

'I would not do that, Eustace, if I were you. Put it down,' she said, making a disgusting mug of instant coffee and not apparently much worried that I was waving a Sabatier meat cleaver at her in the kitchen of our Belgravia *pied-à-terre.*

'Have you no idea, have you no fucking idea, what a terrible position this puts me in? You don't care, do you? You really don't!' I shouted.

'For once, you might be right. Just for once,' Molly said, dropping her sweetener in alarm as I thwacked the cleaver into the butcher's block with such force that the entire refectory table shook.

'I really think you should consider your position,' I said, adding, 'And I don't mean whether it's on your back, on your knees or on all fours. You may even have positions I can't even imagine. I am sure you do. But the positions I mean include: taste, good manners,

345

decorum, appropriateness, empathy, gratitude, common bloody sense. I thought you of all people would understand "common".'

The new Lady Dunne faked a yawn.

'I think you need to understand, Eustace, that Marcel is getting restless. He is just the latest talented person you are greedily exploiting. You're so mean that the kitchen in Le Gardian is impossibly cramped. Your ludicrous Camarguais all-day dining means impossible working hours. You have given him no share in the business. He has to turn down lucrative television contracts to work all the hours *le Bon Dieu* sends. And if I were you, I'd be very worried that he is going to grass you up about the wine fraud.'

'It is not wine fraud,' I said very slowly and with menacing coldness.

'Oh, but it is, Eustace, it is. And you know it,' were the last words Molly said to me.

## happiness and the hangman

I called the disgusting Bill Shein who spoke to his newspaper contacts, who reliably leaked diary stories that Marcel Campo was rumoured to be severely depressed. Adding, for extra flavour, that there was an internal investigation led by our extremely creative accountants into questions of the chef's mismanagement in the restaurant, including accepting backhanders from suppliers, skimming the tips and false accounting of petty cash. It was, Shein suggested, possible that Campo had, unknown to me, been complicit in a massive wine fraud.

The *Metro* was first with the story. And that was when Marcel Campo walked out ... taking Molly, so briefly Lady Dunne, with him.

She had written a letter, which I found beneath the Sabatier cleaver in the Belgravia kitchen. It was in green ink.

*My dearest Eustace,*

*Forgive me for walking out. But I never believed your heart
was in our relationship, even if your cock so very often was.*

*Marcel and I will find happiness. Or the hangman. Whichever
comes first. And you must believe me when I say I will never
betray our own secrets. No one is interested in the facts: that you
are a sadist, a psychopath, a fantasist, a swindler and a bully.
And we all found the wine fraud very amusing. I am as guilty as
you are, to be sure. Only pretentious fools were damaged by it.*

*But I do have to ask if you feel able to invest in Marcel's new
venture. Presently without a name, he plans to bring Niçoise
street food to London. Can you imagine stalls selling socca in
Southwark, pissaladière in Peckham, merda di can in Mortlake?*

*Marcel says five million pounds is sufficient investment to
allow him to acquire appropriate leases, train staff and bring it to
market. Of course, I will help him here.*

*And I feel this token investment from you will help make
public our lasting bond.*

*It might even make you money.*

*With love from
Molly*

And I thought, You horrible, ridiculous, predatory, arriviste, gagging-for-it, on-all-fours, Hottentot-arsed, over-perfumed, perspiring, under-dressed, mean, ungrateful, greedy, cheap, trashy, champagne-flavoured tart. I'd rather die than invest five *sous* in Marcel-up-your-arse-Campo.

So, having thrown it into the wood-burning stove, I ignored the implications of her letter.

Five days later, I received notice that the Masters of Wine were bringing a prosecution against me. I had, it was said, after their years of struggle to be accepted, brought British *sommeliers* into disrepute with artfully faked, but beautifully designed, labels. And there was, additionally, a collective claim, what Americans call a class action suit, from Le Gardian customers, hinting at the involvement of the Serious Fraud Office.

At Southwark Crown Court, the judge heard the conviction and granted me bail of half a million pounds. It was not a hangman, but it was close. I thought to myself, 'So long, Fifth and Park. So long, Avenue Montaigne.'

Reg was waiting for me. Reg, who had been my driver for ever. A gypsy from Gravesend who played country-and-western on the East Kent pub circuit, I found him a reassuring presence.

'Where to, guv?' Reg asked.

I replied, 'I'm afraid I really don't know.'

*The designer Sir Eustace Dunne yesterday appeared before a judge at Southwark Crown Court. Accused of conspiracy to defraud customers at his trendy restaurant in London's fashionable Chelsea, Sir Eustace was granted bail of £500,000. The case is expected to be heard in the autumn. Sir Eustace's fall from grace has been spectacular. Once considered an arbiter of taste to the ambitious consumer, he was the first man since French artist Marcel Duchamp to put his name on a urinal. These he sold to facilities managers around the world. Estimates say over 100,000 of Dunne's brightly coloured P-Loos have been sold to airports and stadiums from Boston to Bangalore. A crowd gathered outside the court to see Sir Eustace emerge dressed in his trademark French binman's jacket. Smoking a large cigarillo, the designer waved at the crowd and said, 'I hope you will give me the clap I so obviously deserve.' One protester was carrying a placard that said 'In vino duplicitas'. Sir Eustace blew a kiss to the elderly woman protester, later identified as his first wife, sixties dolly bird and art critic Beverley Grim. He then stepped into a black, chauffeur-driven Porsche and roared into the distance with two parking tickets under the windscreen wipers.*

Kevin – Chatty – Bumble, *Daily Post*, June 1997

# 21

# 2006 – Ripple Fade to Black

*'Nobody ever died of a feeling, he would say to himself, not believing a word of it, as he sweated his way through the feeling that he was dying of fear.'*

Edward St Aubyn, *Mother's Milk*, 2005

*The Getty Villa, Ladispoli.*

## Rollo Pinkie

THE ORIGIN OF EVERY BOOK is in the author's past.

And that applies to ghost writers too.

For several years, Eustace had been trying to buy Irish designer Eileen Gray's villa E-1027 at Roquebrune on the Côte d'Azur about twenty-five kilometres from Nice, to add to his peculiar portfolio of modernist properties.

Gray's supremely elegant seaside house had been the darling of the architectural press since it was finished in 1929, photographed lavishly and admired by everyone who had not had to experience its leaks, stains, rusted metal windows and disturbing acoustics.

As visually shocking as Le Corbusier, but at the same time more indulgent and luxurious, Gray's villa was a tectonic manifesto about *de luxe* modernism. Her own furniture – Transat and Bibendum chairs, geometrical rugs all inspired by ocean liners and Michelin tyres – animated every room.

Eustace liked them so much, he rather assumed they were his own intellectual property. This, of course, was always his way. Assimilation was second-best to inspiration. Gray's furniture often appeared in his restaurants. While he never actually claimed Eileen Gray's Transat and Bibendum chairs were his own designs, he never troubled over-zealously to dissuade anyone who made an innocent attribution to him.

Certainly, Eileen Gray anticipated Eustace and his very worldly tastes. Indeed, he was not afraid to cite E-1027 as a predecessor of his own style, in this way neatly, some said megalomaniacally, annexing the history of international early modernism into his own more local curriculum vitae.

He already owned an apartment in the Mies van der Rohe building on Lake Shore Drive in Chicago, a useful tax ruse when visiting NeoCon, that city's famous furniture fair. This apartment, when he inspected it, had a real Alexander Calder mobile hanging in the bathroom and a small Blue Period Picasso in the kitchenette, which the dim, clipboard-toting realtor did not seem to recognize. Eustace bought the lot and subsequent sales of the Calder and Picasso at Sotheby Parke Bernet in New York paid for the property many times over.

Eustace had even considered a new house proposed to him by the black-clad, *à la mode* French architect Jean Nouvel, whose ideas on building design, involving fractals, deconstruction, tarot, spirit visitors, feng shui, divination and parametric boundary layers were very much *dans le vent* circa 2000. I had recently introduced the two at a champagne breakfast for Timothy Clever in the Fondation Voltaire, on the occasion of the building's twenty-fifth birthday. I monitored their conversation.

In a comic French accent, Nouvel had said, 'Alors, Sir Dunne. You are, how you say, *le plus français*, the most French, Englishman I know. *Vachement chic.* I propose you a site I have found on the *plage* of Lac Léman. Is perfect. Is near the concrete *cabanon* Le Corbusier, *le plus français* of Swiss men, designed for his own mother near Vevey. *Bouf. Ça sera parfait pour un homme du monde, un homme du goût et du style. Ça sera parfait pour toi*, if I may *tutoyer vous*.' Nouvel produced Polaroids of the site from an inside pocket of his extravagant and billowing Yohji Yamamoto gown.

'*Je serai ravi d'être là*,' Eustace said in his atrocious French accent.

I could see that he was interested, partly because I knew he could never disguise his boredom – disingenuity was beyond the scope of his limited emotional range – and he briefly looked animated. But his world was becoming more one of problems than opportunities. Eustace's mood quickly changed from anticipation to resignation and he said to the black-clad architect with a shrug in his voice, '*On verra, on verra*,' and turned away.

I knew his thoughts were returning to the failing Factory, the LUXI GmbH takeover, a disgrace no matter how he argued the opposite, the Elysium extortion, Gary Knobber's crude assault on his reputation as designer, Molly's blackmail and the lingering threat of prosecution for wine fraud. We left the Voltaire and returned to London.

On the Eurostar, Eustace was unusually morose.

'Rollo, my dear, I have had it up to here,' he said as we passed Senlis, indicating the area beneath his chin with one hand while expertly pouring another glass of the Chablis we had bought at Hédiard – the world's greatest grocer – in the Place de la Madeleine with the other. Years before, during the *pissoir* adventure in Paris, Eustace had advised Hédiard about colour palettes, a modest and undemanding job which allowed him to add the magnificent sounding 'Hédiard, Paris' to his company's credentials and client list.

There was an additional bottle too, a specific against possible delays near Calais. Then Eustace offered me some of the caviar he had also bought at Hédiard. Even if Michelin's multiply starred Joël Robuchon was named executive chef of Eurostar, Eustace did not believe the great man actually was installed in the buffet car with his *toque*, skillet and spatula, so he always took precautionary measures with on-board gastronomy.

'There is so much fucking bollocks out there,' Eustace said. 'I trusted these people. I loved some of them. Some of them I still do. But every single person I invested trust in has betrayed me for their selfish ends. Knobber? What a toe-rag arse. Molly? What's that they say? You can take a whore to culture, but can't make her think. I'd rather have an honest kick in the balls than this ugly, dissimulating disloyalty.'

Thoughtful, then smiling, he said to me, 'Are you thinking of betraying me, Rollo?'

'Actually, no,' I replied. 'I'm thinking how I might be of some practical help.'

Eustace raised the Chablis in an ironic salute and said to a fussing steward that *le monde entier* could very well do without a '*sandwich jambon frappé du sac plastique Frigidaire*, thank you very much', then spooned a little more caviar on to the Hédiard blinis, dribbling a little down his chin as it was transported to his mouth.

Moments later, he spoke again. 'You know, Rollo, sometimes I wonder if I learnt more from my old dad than I ever realized. Isn't this whole design business really a sort of fraud? Haven't we been conning people all this time? I always told anybody who asked that "everything has been designed" and I thought that was a clever way of demonstrating the enormous scope of the subject. But if that's true, then everyone is a designer and there's really nothing very special about what we were doing. I do wish Charles Eames was here to make me more cheerful. Absent that possibility, I'm afraid my epitaph really might have to be "form follows fiction".'

Eustace, I could see, desperately needed to escape his own battle-fields, even if the conflicts fought there had been very much his own fault. He designed, it sometimes seemed, his own fate. And like many dispossessed emperors, he eventually found refuge on the outskirts of Rome. This was the help I arranged.

A Geneva *immobilier* who was always pestering me to feature his more absurd billionaire properties in my articles in *The Architectural Review*, *Country Life* and *Town & Country*, told me about a short lease on the old Getty Villa in Ladispoli.

This was the magnificent, but surely haunted, seventeenth-century house that John Paul Getty had acquired in 1960. He abandoned it thirteen years later, disillusioned with Italy after his grandson was very publicly kidnapped and tortured.

Even before Sardinian bandits cut off his grandson's ear, Getty was not a happy nor, by most accounts, a specially pleasant man. Demonstrably, great wealth did not bring great contentment, although it did bring great houses. The villa in Ladispoli was like a Hudson Valley mansion configured for the reincarnation of Nero or Tiberius. Whether its sepulchral gloom was a cause or an effect of a presence as melancholic as Getty, who can say? But the villa's situation was glorious, built upon a low embankment that dropped immediately into the Tyrrhenian Sea, always splashing outside.

I explained to Eustace that Ladispoli is a place with history, where the *genii locorum* assemble in swarms. It was the site of an Etruscan port and an Etruscan necropolis. Some Roman emperors favoured it as a resort. And it was here that they first spoke of *mal aria*, the airborne disease spread by the bad air of serpents in Africa. This bad air remained because there was not enough Christian breath in the area to disperse it, a theory not yet disproved.

For all its grandeur, Rome itself is melancholy: Alberto Moravia used to stop complete strangers and say, 'I am very bored. I want to die.' And Ladispoli was worse: it was suburban Rome.

The listless modern town was developed in the late nineteenth century by Principe Ladislao Odescalchi, hence its name: the *polis* of Ladislao. By the time Eustace arrived, Ladispoli had become a township of squalid social housing on malarial swamps, the former occupied by unhappy legal refugees from the *mezzogiorno*, the latter by the unhappy illegal sort from the Maghreb. If you want realism, go ride the bus. If you want a real version of Italy, visit Ladispoli. In an earlier stage of his career, when still bent on reform, Eustace would have called Ladispoli 'sad'. Now he just closed his eyes.

We had travelled from Fiumicino by boat, avoiding the ugliness of car paint-shops, big box stores, bike rentals and heartless cafes with rusted metal chairs that is the reality of a car journey through suburban Italy. Even an S-Class Mercedes with black-tinted, double-glazed windows cannot filter the whole of sad reality.

I had chartered a Chris-Craft Catalina to take us from the airport to the villa, but first there was a lunch at the famous Bastianello. This was a fine old fish restaurant, established in 1929, as the laminated menus declared. From here you could watch the Alitalia 747s lift off, optimistically, for the New World.

We were entirely alone except for dishes of *pesce spada, riso alla spigola*, a *zuppetta di pesce*, some rock hard bread rolls and plenty of good Soave. The tablecloths were coarse pink cloth with '1929' woven into the warp and weft as a decorative motif.

'Very nearly my birth year,' Eustace said wistfully.

I didn't answer.

'You know "*soave*" means "smooth", don't you?' he asked with raised eyebrows.

A beggar girl, a Roma, approached us literally with (baseball) cap in hand. Eustace astonished me by a fluent rush of Italian, which he later told me he had learnt at school, although I had no recollection of such a thing. It was something Byron had said to a beggar girl, probably another Roma, when riding through the Veneto: '*Cara, tu sei troppo bella e giovane per aver bisogno del soccorso mio.*'

Clever, patronizing, mean. Thus typical of the man. And then he returned, ruminatively, to the swordfish and the wine.

After coffee and three glasses of grappa by Jacopo Poli, his favourite maker after Nardini, unavailable here, the blue and white Chris-Craft under the command of a handsome, tanned scoundrel in an immaculately laundered striped shirt and aviator shades, bobbed, crashed and leapt like an oil-burning dolphin through the dark-grey Tyrrhenian sea.

An hour after leaving Bastianelli, Eustace and I, each feeling slightly sick, wobbled up the ladder to the Getty Villa's terrace where a small table had been set with a bottle of Frascati and a plate of honey biscuits with sesame seeds, a local speciality. We sat and breathed in the *mal aria* and the very good view. Invisible to us on the roadside of the villa, protected by an electric fence and foul barbed wire, some Senegalese entrepreneurs were stealing bicycles.

I had persuaded Eustace to take a three-month lease to write, with my assistance, his autobiography in seclusion. He told me it was to be an *apologia*, a *mea culpa*. I asked him, what mood did he want to strike? Did he know the painter Walter Sickert's observation: 'The only thing I cling to is my coolness and leisurely considered contemplation.'

Of course, he did not. But he sometimes had a rueful air. 'The sunnier the day, the more certain it is to rain,' he liked to say. And at this stage of his life, it was raining every day. But this was only after a long sunny spell.

Eustace took Getty's own bedroom, notably dark with a *seicento* Venetian *cassone*, canopies, magnificent brocade and antiqued mirrors which might very well have belonged once to Sforzas or Medicis. There was a writing desk before the shuttered windows through which light streamed like the sunshine in Hal Morey's photograph of Grand Central Station. Getty had insisted upon, and Eustace soon adopted for his own use, a preposterously ornate papal throne that also served as a commode. It was an environment Henry James might have appreciated.

Late that first night, we opened a bottle of Vecchia Romagna, that fine Roman brandy.

'Molly? What on earth happened there?' said Eustace. 'You know, I thought we'd actually go to Martha's Vineyard, buy a regulation white-with-green-shutters clapboard house and be looked after by a charming and obedient Mexican couple. I'd buy a Ford F-150 truck and learn to fish. Actually, rubbish. We would go to the Cotswolds to be near Carole Bamford and James Dyson. I'd buy a Range Rover, drive it myself and learn to fish. She would ...'

And he tailed off, in a *rallentando* not so much of regret as of boredom.

I had told him he must write a creative autobiography, perhaps in its way like Benvenuto Cellini's, still the ultimate account of an artist's life, but with a little more bruised irony and a lot less bombast.

'You know, it strikes me that for many creative people, certainly for me, a life which looks very successful is a failure as seen from within. Why? Because one knows there is still so very, very much left undone. But the rest of the world sees only the achievements. But the achievements of the past don't interest me. I'm only really interested in the achievements of the future, what you might, if you were disrespectful' – he wagged a finger at me – 'call the next new thing. Alas, we never see ourselves as we really are, do we? The outsider looking in can never understand the size and scale of all those unrealized ambitions. I still have them, you know.'

'So, Eustace, would you say you are a disappointed man?'

'I did the best I could with what I had,' Eustace began, a mite too coyly for my own taste. But then I had to remind him it was the boxer Joe Louis who said it.

'I am proud that my essential credo remains unchanged: it is simply too sad to think of getting up in the morning and going to an ugly kitchen or bathroom. And I am not at all sorry about family. If you are passionate about your work, you cannot make the commitment children demand.'

And here Eustace was at his most elegantly simple.

'Design wasn't just a fad, was it? The search for, enjoyment of and creation of beauty are, surely, the very point of existence. And isn't beauty perhaps evidence of the existence of God? And perhaps the opposite holds with ugliness? I sometimes wonder if that might be the justification of it all. Do you remember that Faust play we did at school? Doesn't Faust ask Mephistopheles how he got out of Hell and doesn't Mephistopheles say, "Why, this is Hell and nor am I out of it." Perhaps everyday life really is Hell and all we can do is glimpse possibilities of Heaven when we see something beautiful. Isn't that what we as designers were meant to do? I mean: design our way out of Hell.'

He lit a cigarillo and looked out to sea through narrowed eyes. And I asked myself: was he a dispossessed Roman emperor in this kingdom of gloom?

Actually, not at all. Eustace Dunne's resilience was astonishing. In fact, his spirits seemed raised by all his reversals. Never mind Faust: if anyone could intuit the meaning of C. S. Lewis's belief that Hell is a room whose doors have locks with keys on the inside, it was Eustace Dunne. Hell is a state of mind and Eustace had the keys to those locks. And he had his sharp pencils and his block of fine drawing paper from Marie Papier in Paris.

Not waiting to be asked, he turned his gaze from the Tyrrhenian to me and spoke. 'Yes. I do have one regret. Not enough sex. And I suppose I now realize that after seventy, every pound saved is a pound wasted. Still, I am slowly learning that nothing matters very much and very little matters at all. I have had fifteen Porsches and, as Her Majesty the Queen once told me, referring to something else, they do not, if I am honest, really help.'

This was our working method, our daily routine: On the enormous *pietre dure* table in the loggia, I arranged piles of papers with people's names on them: Ilona Jacobsen, Tony, Quentin Huskisson, John Davidson, Beverley, Kelly, Gary Knobber, Andy Warhol. We piled up notes there, like a memory palace. He remembered what he could, recorded it in scribble and added it to the pile. Passing backwards and forwards with a cigarillo, Eustace would add notes as they occurred to him.

Every day, there was breakfast and we shared the English papers delivered by motorbike from the airport. Recent press cuttings were in the same package and these would always command Eustace's total attention. His first cigarillo of the day would be lit after blood orange juice and coffee while he was scrutinizing a cutting from the *Metro* with the fanatical concentration Crick and Watson must have used while cracking the human genetic code.

Latterly, he had begun to use an illuminated looking glass, necessary in the Getty Villa's encompassing gloom, but I could see, unaided, that one morning his ferocious concentration was focused on a small paragraph from the *Metro*'s business pages:

LUXI GmbH has Dunne enough. The German megacompany announced at a press conference in Stockholm today that the three remaining stand-alone Bleu de Travail stores, acquired from Eustace Dunne in 1992, would either be shuttered or rebranded LUXI GmbH-Express. Armin Arschloch, LUXI GmbH's reclusive Chairman, made a rare appearance at the conference and said:

'Eustace Dunne's contribution to the modern growth and character of LUXI GmbH has been remarkable. The influential ideas and style of Bleu de Travail have now been fully absorbed into LUXI GmbH and we believe it is time to realign all our retail properties under the LUXI GmbH uber-brand. The LUXI GmbH-Express format allows our urban customers to buy our flat packs in attractive city-based stores without having to venture to big-box stores in the suburbs. So in this way, LUXI GmbH continues the design shopping revolution that Eustace Dunne began nearly fifty years ago.'

'Fucking Nazi,' Eustace said.

We would talk all morning until there was a lunch on terrace. Then we would doze in the sun, while the Senegalese continued their busy trade beneath the vacant gaze of the unmonitored CCTV. Then there would be more talk when we gathered again at cocktails.

Sometimes we drove into Rome for lunch or dinner at Piperno, a favourite place in the ghetto. Eustace often recalled Ilona and Beverley: something about Jewish women and Jewish food, never mind Jewish lightning, had always stayed with him.

It amused Eustace that the Chief Rabbi of Israel had declared the famous *carciofi alla giudia*, the artichokes deep-fried Jewish style, to be non-kosher since they might contain slugs and bugs, something very likely in both our experience. But that was of no matter. Piperno was a regular delight. In winter, a dark, panelled room rammed with Roman Jewish matrons in furs tucking into the *friggitorie*, the eclectic and sometimes disturbing fried offal. In summer, the focus of the restaurant shifted to a charming, scruffy little backyard with shady parasols in the very quiet Portico d'Ottavia.

One day, picking over the famous deep-fried *mammole*, the best of the local artichokes, Eustace started to talk about creativity as I began to scribble notes.

'One way of looking at it is to say that it's a need for urgency, a need for speed, a need for getting things done. What dull people might call "impulsive", I would call "motivated". And, of course, creative people never object to risk. In fact, they cultivate it. For me, busyness was always a form of relaxation. I mean to say: what would I do if I was not doing something?'

I nodded and wondered, What, indeed?

'And isn't that what art actually is? I mean, something new? Craft must always be the same, but art must always, always be different. And we must always, always invent. Don't you think? Tomorrow is surely more important than today and much more important than yesterday. Tradition is a matter of tending the flame, not worshipping the ashes.'

I told him to find the Scott Moncrieff edition of Proust, which I had noticed in the Getty *biblioteca*. I had no illusions about whether he would actually read it, he would not, but I was confident he would enjoy the pretty Enid Marx jacket, so similar in spirit to the London Transport Routemaster bus moquette upholstery she also designed. I had hoped he might be amused by the evident connection between the 88 from Clapham to Camden Town and the great *roman-fleuve*. To me, this was a nice demonstration of how the practical and the intellectual always have some common ground.

To my astonishment, the next morning Eustace appeared at breakfast holding the *Sodom and Gomorrah* volume. I imagined he had assumed it was pornography, when, apropos of nothing, he said: 'Did you ever know Rupert Murdoch? I was reminded of him by Baron de Charlus. Strange man, Rupert. He wore rings on every finger and only took them off when going on television. I'm going to speak to Rupert about the wine trial. See if we can get a little positive publicity for once.'

Proust had not been a stimulus. As another prompt for a day's conversation, I showed him a print of Albrecht Dürer's *Melencolia* engraving of 1514, whose mysterious, brooding allegorical subject is surrounded by abandoned devices, surely symbolic of something, but scholars could not decide what: a hand plane, a saw, a globe, a set of scales, an astrolabe.

'Could that be you, tragic with your butchers' blocks, workmen's jackets, counterfeit wine, superyachts, coffee pots and wooden spoons?' I asked.

To his credit, he laughed.

We continued in this fashion until there were nearly eighty thousand words. And as he talked and I wrote, there was a gathering of the famous ghosts themselves: Charles Eames, Elizabeth David, Philip Johnson. Quentin Huskisson, Gary Knobber and Marcel Campo would join later.

Then one day a jolly card arrived from Sven Roth. He had opened 21st Century Lox, a bagel-bookshop-gallery-performance space in Greenpoint, Brooklyn, not unlike the Factory. Eustace sighed and shook his head, but carefully put Roth's card (a Museum of Modern Art Rothko) on the travertine *mensola di caminetto* next to a carriage clock and a miniature of Giambologna's *Nettuno*.

And the next day, a summons arrived at the Getty Villa giving the date of Eustace's appearance at the Central Criminal Court in the matter of The Crown versus Eustace Dunne Restaurants Limited in a case of counterfeit wine. The Serious Fraud Office was, indeed, to be involved. Eustace groaned and put his gently shaking head in his hands.

It's a truth of aviation that when an aircraft crashes, there is rarely a single point of failure. It's a cumulative process, an aggregation of small errors which lead to catastrophe. That, it seemed to me, was what was happening to Eustace.

After a night disturbed by this summons, he told me the next day he had been standing at the stall in the Getty bedroom, a fine pink marble arrangement with *settecento* details, and staring in dismay at the pitiful, insignificant, withered thing he held in his hand.

'If your flow of urine can no longer push the inner of a match box across a polished floor, a helpful doctor told me once, you are, my dear Rollo, pretty much done for in that department. This may be how it ends,' he said dismally, but then made me smile by adding: 'Not with a bang, but a trickle. Certainly, I have observed that leaking and spillage of one sort or another seem to be characteristics of this stage of life.'

For the flight back to London, Eustace had borrowed the best business jet there is, a Bombardier Global Express belonging to Bernard Arnault, owner of Veuve Clicquot. The widow's orange so familiar from the champagne label dominated the interior design. Arnault had once said to Eustace at a luxury goods conference in St Moritz, 'Just say if you ever want to borrow the plane. *C'est facile.*' Eustace found the *décor* inelegant, but it was too *facile* an offer ever to decline. '*Grossière de refuser*', of course.

There was no Macallan on board, but Arnault owned Glenmorangie so an eighteen-year-old example of this whisky, aged in barrels of toasted Portuguese oak, had been set on the tray-table in front of the enormous cream leather captain's chairs on the aircraft. I occupied one chair, Eustace the other. He winced at the orange and gold trim.

'Tart's boudoir,' he said, not meaning to be kind.

But there was a personal note from Arnault underneath the bottle, as if he were the general manager of a luxury hotel with a *billet-doux* for a paying guest.

> *Mon cher ami. My plane is your plane. I hope when you get to London that the court's interpretation of* 'in vino veritas' *will work in your favour. You may count on me for support in any eventuality. Amicalement. Bernard.*

Eustace poured very generous measures of the Scotch and said to me, 'French luxury is feminine, but British luxury is masculine. You have gold and orange frou-frou or wet peat grouse moors. Bottoms up.'

The powerful BMW-Rolls-Royce BR710 turbo-fans lifted the small plane quickly to the cruise, where it levelled out at 45,000 feet and 900 kilometres per hour.

Eustace poured another large Scotch and said, after what was evidently some silent preparation, 'It is not, my dear, that I do not appreciate all the work you have been doing on my autobiography. Nor that I do not look forward to finishing it with you. And, indeed, in sharing the proceeds. I see it very much as your book as much as mine. And I want you to be very well rewarded indeed. Very well. But I feel it is presentationally important, indeed, it is presentationally essential, that it should appear to be all my own work. In fact, I am going to have to insist.'

'But, Eustace, that was not what we agreed. I want my name on it as well. Otherwise, I will walk away,' I said, dismayed beyond anger. 'I have been writing this book, one way or another, for nearly fifty years. You cannot keep exploiting people, Eustace. I'll do an awful lot for you, but just occasionally I also need to do things for myself.' I added, 'Be reasonable,' knowing that there was never any possibility of such a thing. His ego was not negotiable.

Then Eustace gave a terrible, jolting wince as the Bombardier hit a little ripple of turbulence, spilling some Glenmorangie over his pink cashmere sleeveless cardigan as his glass fell to the floor.

'Are you all right?' I asked.

'Not sure I am. My arms feel heavy. I can't lift them. I'd had a twinge yesterday, but this is much worse.' He spoke hoarsely and was evidently having difficulty breathing.

'And I have this fuck-awful pain in the chest.' He winced again, horribly, and tried to reach the attendant call button, but could not. There was a terrible convulsion and then he slumped in his beige, ruched leather captain's chair with its gold trim and fragrant memories of models' and starlets' bottoms.

Eustace never exercised himself. Nor any self-restraint. He would never walk if he could drive. And he would never drive himself if he could get someone to do it for him. He would never take a train if he could fly and he would never fly commercial if someone would lend him a bizjet. He ate, drank and smoked immoderately. He was a man of appetites. 'You know,' he liked to say with a glass of Scotch in one hand and a cigarillo in the other, 'alcohol preserves fruit and smoking preserves fish.'

But only for so long. Very Eustace Dunne to suffer a catastrophic myocardial infarction over the Alps, I thought. Monte Bianco slipped past below. Very smart. So typically Eustace, dying at an altitude inaccessible to most.

I was strangely unmoved at I looked at the dead body. *Was death*, I hastily scribbled in a Moleskine notebook, *another betrayer or a very rare friend?* The attendant, dressed in Christian Dior, respectfully put a tangerine-coloured Loro Piana throw over the inert remains of Sir Eustace Dunne, man of taste, as the plane began to descend. I remembered that line from Gibbon learnt at school: 'the melancholy calculation of human calamities'.

The pilot had radioed ahead to say he would make an emergency landing at Lyon-St Exupéry for a 'medical event'. The plane banked to the left and we began our steep descent.

And I thought how odd it was to name a major international airport after Antoine de St Exupéry, a fantasist-buccaneer who had crashed his plane into the Mediterranean.

*Ripple fade to black*, I wrote in the notebook, using the expression commercial directors use to describe the end effects of an advertisement. And what was that old line about advertising? The art of arresting the public's intelligence long enough to get money out of it. Dear Eustace, dear me, yes. Then I walked to the back of the plane and poured myself a glass of champagne. Vintage Krug, of course.

# 22

Obit

THE *PROTECTOR*'S OBITUARY EDITOR HAD his feet on the desk and was rolling a joint while he explained to me over the phone: 'The obituary is a minor art form, but nonetheless one with strict disciplines. While it is not a place of docile reverence, nor is it a place of frank hostility. There's really no point. We insist on good manners. Our weather is the light autumn mist of euphemism,' he inhaled deeply on his toke, getting carried away by his own eloquence, 'not the bright dawn of lacerating criticism.'

'By which you mean exactly what?' I asked, a little exasperated. 'You asked me to write this because I knew the man, didn't you?'

'Quite, but there are simple rules,' the editor explained and I could hear feet being rearranged on a hard surface beneath the sound of a deep exhalation. 'No one is ever a drunk, he is instead "convivial". Nor is anyone tight-fisted, he is economical, careful, fastidious or scrupulous about money. You may indicate that your subject is a groping, sexually incontinent, randy, fornicating gorilla by writing "he enjoyed the company of women".

'And a gay man is a "bachelor". A shrieking, howling, voracious, predatory old queen may be described as a "confirmed bachelor". A dyke is indicated by describing a woman as "handsome". Pederasts "enjoy the company of both old and young". A psychopath is "brilliantly persuasive". A cynic is "occasionally neglectful of banal niceties". A selfish shit is "vigilant in protecting his interests". Nor may your subject be described as a fraudster: instead, he will have had a "cavalier attitude to regulation".'

He went on. 'Recidivist criminals "occasionally run foul of the law" while habitual liars are "intrigued by fantasy". And our obituaries are never about stupefying bores, they are about fascinating individuals "who enjoy lengthy discussion and prolonged debate". Do you get it? Make sense?' He inhaled deeply again.

Everyone agreed that Eustace was difficult, reluctant to praise or apologize, self-aggrandizing, manipulative, pleased with himself, but rarely pleased with others, demanding attention, but unwilling ever to give it, better at selling than buying and as dispiritingly mean as he was unpredictably generous.

A sensitive man, he was brutally insensitive where others were concerned. And his own sensitivity was forever disguised by an easy arrogance that some found bracing, others repellent. To use an image or smutty innuendo which Eustace would have enjoyed, he was always coming into his own.

He left no one feeling indifferent. But it was certain, as Joe Louis had taught him, that he made the best of what he had. The very best. Other than neglecting to thank those who helped him, he neglected no opportunities for personal advancement that came his way. 'Greedy' was too crude a word to describe a man for whom style was paramount; it was more that he could not tolerate the waste of a neglected opportunity, a main chance missed. His achievements were obvious and benign, but they came at a great human cost. To himself and to others.

Yet his nose for what was confused, concessionary or secondhand was unerring; his instinct for the excellent was sure; somehow, by instinct and almost by gestures, he would nudge people into discovering it for themselves. His attraction was powerfully felt by all who knew him.

His powers of observation were superhuman, as was his obsession with detail. To the uncurious, this could appear to be snobbery, but it was much more complicated than that. He said to me once in real bewilderment, 'Did you know, there are people who think chunky cut marmalade is *posh*? I suppose they are the same people who order a *cappuccino* after midday and think chicken *lasagne* is an Italian dish.'

To work with him was to experience an educator of genius, and, indeed, someone who knew where to look for geniuses. And then how to wring them dry. For Eustace, anywhere, every day provided a lesson. He saw something and thought he could improve it. And was happy to tell you how.

In so many important ways, he enhanced the lives of everyone who passed through his intense, but ultimately fragile, aura. People who knew him never forgot him. Perhaps with his ramekins, he enhanced the lives of people who did not know him even more.

Like many successful people, Eustace was wary of, even sceptical of, his own success. For him, at least internally, I came to understand that existence seemed more like a succession of calamities than a catalogue of achievements. Indeed, to the very last I doubt that he ever felt successful, even as his popular image was of a man of great style and wealth, if not always of great intellectual or moral substance.

He was someone who stood with his Edward Green loafer on the throats of his various fallen adversaries. And he was lighting a cigarillo as he throttled these struggling weaklings. Here was a man who realized his moment to the full.

Yet to Eustace it did not feel like that. The houses and the cars, he found, cannot defend you against a sense of the imminent abyss. Irony was never a speciality, nor even a slight comfort: he could not take pleasure in the exquisite absurdities of life, nor of his own peculiar existence. Eustace took himself really very seriously.

But his was an existence – for all its symbols of success and impressive accumulation of goods – that was defined by continuous, nagging fears of betrayal and an enveloping atmosphere of distrust which never evaporated with the dawn. Maybe this was why Eustace was so reluctant to say please and thank you: they suggested a human obligation he was not prepared to make. Relationships diminished him.

What did Eustace think in those moments when all of us are left helplessly alone and vulnerable to our most disturbing thoughts? Those moments at four thirty in the morning when sleep is impossible and harrowing reflection unavoidable? The strange crépuscule of a long flight when the cabin lights are dimmed, the crew disappears and there is no one for company? The bathroom mirror? A birthday when your parents are dead? Did another new restaurant provide any comfort against an all-consuming dread of extinction? For someone so consumed by fear of betrayal and distrust in others, Eustace distrusted everyone and ruthlessly betrayed his closest collaborators with a predictable, metronomic consistency.

If you said 'a dish taken cold' to Eustace, he would immediately think of *vitello tonnato* or a chilled *vichyssoise*, perhaps a *semi-freddo* or a chilled *gazpacho*.

Perhaps, if feeling mellow, even of a Melton Mowbray pork pie. Of course he had never read Baltasar Gracián's classic on courtly manners with its wonderful observation that it is revenge which is best enjoyed when the heat has gone out of the inflammatory situation.

As we drifted apart some years ago, I had said I would write my own version of his life. He did not want that. He wanted a book with his own name on the cover. Not mine. But he promised we would *collaborate* on his autobiography, offering me exclusive access and an acknowledgement of my role as 'editor'. And he promised me £25 million in his will if I would sign a non-disclosure agreement that was binding even post-mortem. He wanted his autobiography to be his own design, even if the work was done by others.

I had quibbled and compromised. But then he died before it was finished. And, of course, he died intestate. That £25 million was as insubstantial as the *mal aria* of the Tyrrhenian coast.

One of the people Eustace Dunne betrayed was his old friend and ghost writer, whose revenge is the book you find now in your hands.

# New York Times obituary by Sam Kawasaki

*Eustace Wellbeloved Greville Dunne. b. Reigate, UK, 4 April, 1932.*
*d. Lyon, France, 15 August, 2006.*

The storied English designer, Eustace Dunne, had never drunk instant coffee in his life. He was bewildered by how shop-bought, chunky-cut marmalade could ever have acquired 'posh' status on anybody's breakfast table. Marmalade, he believed, should be homemade from oranges personally gathered in the Alcazar of Seville.

Yet this apparent social snobbism belied a true democrat and reformer, whose beneficial influence on British life was only matched by Terence Conran among his contemporaries.

Eustace Dunne was born in the comfortable 'stockbroker belt' of London. His father, Eustace Senior, had experienced rapid social promotion. From a Dickensian orphanage, he worked his way through humble jobs in the City of London to ownership of the newspaper that was to become the *Financial Times*. He became rich and then a Member of Parliament, but imprudent investments by this lawmaker found him accused of fraud and jailed for a five-year term. This stain both horrified and stimulated his son.

Although the beneficiary of an elite 'public' school education at the progressive Fraylings in Devon, where pupils were encouraged to play jazz and make bird tables, Eustace Dunne Junior was always uncomfortable in formal education. An exceptionally bright and motivated, if sometimes morose, boy, he moved into London's Lethaby Academy of Art and Design. Here he made few friends, but quickly made a reputation as a prodigally talented student, a brilliant aggregator of ideas, a tireless enthusiast for the next new thing. Offered a job as a designer by a leading London department store, Dunne left college before graduation.

The experience of America was formative. In an early visit to California, he met Charles Eames who became a mentor. Returning to London, he found work at the Festival of Britain of 1951, when only nineteen. With no formal qualifications, Dunne designed the furniture by which 1951 will always be remembered. Before he was twenty, British newspapers were describing Eustace Dunne as 'a man with a vision of the future'.

Whether by accident or design, he acquired some unique and significant foibles. Before the term was invented, he had become his own 'brand'. Eustace Dunne always carried an atomizer of Lalique crystal filled not with scent, but with vermouth, so dry martinis could be improvised anywhere gin was available.

He insisted on drinking champagne from goblets, not from flutes. And Burgundy from highballs. In his often-photographed garden, he wore Hungarian gaucho shirts with bespoke loafers from Edward Green of Jermyn Street. On occasions, he actually wore belt *and* braces, but insisted they were colour-matched. The perfumier Penhaligon's made a scent for him: he told them to be inspired by the smell of hot oil and burnt rubber. They called it Goodwood.

Dunne's reputation was based on the unique design consultancy he established in London during the fifties. Hitherto, 'design' had either been the province of artsy and craftsy artisans, or an inferior branch of architecture. But Dunne realized it was a discipline in its own right and many of Britain's leading businesses were transformed by his unique sense of style.

Then in the sixties, Dunne created a chain of furniture and homeware shops called Bleu de Travail, after a French workman's tunic, in frank acknowledgement of his ardent – if somewhat patronizing – Francophilia and his infatuation with the style and practice of the working man. Bleu de Travail became a Pop sensation, eventually bringing Swinging London to Manhattan with a store opening attended by every astonished gossip columnist as well as every admiring architectural critic.

His next venture was inspired by his friendship with Andy Warhol. This seemed an unlikely pairing, but each man appreciated the other's independent spirit and what, in an earlier age, would have been called crusading temperament. US *A La Mode* said, 'Eustace Dunne did to furniture what Andy Warhol did to gallery art.' However, many critics saw Dunne's version of Warhol's Factory that appeared in England as a misalliance, but its ambition was impressive, if overblown. A mixture of designers' atelier, recording studios and print workshops, it was intended to translate Warhol's boho collective to the commercial mainstream. But it was before its time and Dunne's Factory was damaged by internal disputes, acrimony, a faltering budget, press criticism and staff walking out of the door.

He recovered himself by reinvention as a restaurateur, since food and design were clearly linked in his imagination and his appetite at table as impressive as his taste for all of life's fine things. And this returned him to his workshop days in the fifties. His last London restaurant was described by the *New York Times* as 'the best restaurant in the world', but his first had been more modest, if astonishingly sophisticated for its day. When Londoners were still used to porridge and grey mutton, Dunne had given them *cuisine de grand-mère*.

But Eustace Dunne had no taste for affectation. One journalist visitor was invited into the kitchen to share a baguette ripped apart by hand, stuffed with roughly cut *rosette de Lyon* and to drink Beaujolais from the neck of the bottle.

But critics were circling, as they so often do in Britain. They said Dunne's new-found interest in restaurants was causing neglect of the core Bleu de Travail business. Imitators found it easy to copy 'Bleu', just as Dunne had himself earlier found design inspiration in the US and Milan. By the financial crisis of 1989, it was losing money and ignominiously sold to LUXI GmbH of Sweden whose founder, Armin Arschloch, Dunne had once described as 'an artless, joyless, mean-spirited, predatory, cynical, manipulative, failed Nazi.'

His powers of observation were phenomenal. His friend Rollo Pinkie, a leading art and design author, said: 'Eustace could always spot something you missed. And would never let you forget it! On a trip abroad, while I was admiring a conventional ochre façade, or a generous lunette window, he would, for example, point out some builder's netting in an unusual shade of green.'

He enjoyed fine cars, but they always remained exactly as they had left the factory. Even the driver's manuals were left untouched in their sealed packages. He bought yellow dusters obsessively and threw them away after one use. And as soon as he discovered aerosols of inert gas used by film-makers to remove hairs from the gate of movie cameras, he carried one with him always. And he was ruthless in its application, using his aerosol to disperse dust wherever it might be found – even once from the velvet collar of an astonished starlet he met at a charity reception.

Eustace Dunne's first marriage, to Beverley (Eshkenazi), ended in divorce. His second marriage to Molly (Mthembu) resulted in separation. There were no children, although he enjoyed a full social life, some said over full. He died on a private flight between Rome and London where he was summoned to attend a court to face trial for wine fraud.

Eustace Dunne divided opinion. A close associate wrote: 'For years I had known about Eustace's foibles and cruelties, but had always dismissed them as I had convinced myself there was a past when he was a true hero, when he was a man of dignity and principle. But ever so slowly I have come to the difficult realization that this was never actually the case. He had always been a selfish bastard, concerned with no one who would not advance his personal interests. Even that soft-spoken, reasonable and ever-so-middle-class voice was, in fact, a clever way of exerting control over his audience. Speaking softly was not deferential, but domineering, since it required an audience to shut up and listen. Still, I miss him terribly.'

Eustace Dunne was the author of many books, bringing new production standards to the mass-market. *In the L'Oignon Rouge*, an account of his pioneering discovery of French food, was published in 1960 and illustrated with his own drawings. Here Dunne made the connection between food and design that was to sustain him throughout an astonishing career. Food was always much more than mere nutrition. It had to be delicious and attractive, just as design, in his version, had to be beautiful and useful. And whether it was eating lunch or dinner, a meal was in every respect a performance where ideas, people and things jostled for position. It was at table that he demonstrated his commitment to 'the art of living', an art to be enjoyed at least twice a day.

On the opening of Bleu de Travail in 1964, Eustace Dunne was asked about his philosophy. He told the reporter: 'Why would anybody ever buy a lever-action corkscrew and a foil-cutter when an honest, decent waiter's friend and a sharp knife will do?' Nearly forty years later he told an English reporter that the one thing you would never find him using was 'fucking square plates'.

Later he said he would be happy with that as his epitaph.

# Acknowledgements

First, housekeeping. Bill Scott-Kerr is the unusually patient publisher. Our first conversation about this book was thirty years ago in La Famiglia, a Chelsea trattoria popular with footballers and ageing rock stars. In those days, Bill looked like a youthful rock star, a ruined cherub.

Eloisa Clegg has been the supremely diligent and exceptionally charming editor. She always has something helpful or cheerful to say, and there can be no better compliment. It's really quite something to *look forward* to an editor's messages. Charlie Brotherstone is my long-suffering agent, whose essential and very attractive optimism completely blinds him even to my obvious failings.

Second, apologia. It's agreed: all novels are memoirs, all memoirs are novels. The main characters in this satirical novel – which is also a lampoon, a send-up and a burlesque – are works of fiction: products of my imagination, informed by accumulated and compounded observations. In this case, observations made over the last forty years or so as a bit player in the antic malarkey of London's design culture.

Third, published sources. From before my time, I relied for period colour and bitchy asides on the diaries and memoirs of James Lees-Milne, especially *Another Self* (1970), *A Mingled Measure* (1994) and *Through Wood and Dale* (1998). Colin MacInnes's famous novel *Absolute Beginners* (1959) was also a useful source to help me catch the pre-Pop mood of London. But best of all was the painter Michael

Wishart's elegant and louche account of bohemia, *High Diver* (1977). Readers who know Lees-Milne, MacInnes and Wishart may recognize passages where my uninhibited and admiring post-modern sampling wanders into near plagiarism, just like my flawed hero, Eustace Dunne.

Fourth, what's really going on. The bulk of this book has been inspired by (almost) anything interesting that's been said to me since about 1980. Conversations, messages, postcards, scribbled notes, commonplace books, quotations half remembered and reinvented, witticisms digested and regurgitated. For example, the chapter title 'Spaghetti, gin and fucking the missus' was vouchsafed me by a peer of the realm who, competing in the London Marathon, had occasion to ask another runner, a postman from Glasgow, about his training regime. But, repurposed, it makes sense in another context.

# Picture Credits
## and Permissions

*Chapter 1*
Eric Gill © National Portrait Gallery, London

*Chapter 2*
Land Rover: National Motor Museum/Heritage Images via Getty Images

*Chapter 3*
Party on a seaplane: Loomis Dean/The LIFE Picture Collection via Getty Images

*Chapter 4*
Skylon, Festival of Britain: The National Archives/SSPL/Getty Images

*Chapter 5*
Elizabeth David: Picture Kitchen/Alamy stock photo

*Chapter 6*
Shabby chic interior: Avalon/Photoshot License/Alamy stock photo

*Chapter 7*
Jaguar E-type: Sjoerd van der Wal/Getty Images

*Chapter 8*
Guys 'n' Dolls in the Kings Road, Chelsea: Trinity Mirror/Mirrorpix/Alamy stock photo

*Chapter 9*
Splügen Bräu bar in Milan © Domus/Casali

*Chapter 10*
Semi-detached houses: L.V. Clark/Fox Photos/Getty Images

*Chapter 11*
Philip Johnson's house: Ramin Talaie/Corbis via Getty Images

*Chapter 12*
The AT&T Building, New York: Mauritius Images GmbH/Alamy stock photo

*Chapter 13*
Andy Warhol © Hulton-Deutsch Collection/Corbis via Getty Images

*Chapter 14*
Canal Saint-Martin: Keystone-France/Gamma-Rapho via Getty Images

*Chaper 15*
Superyacht: Peter John Moxham/Fairfax Media via Getty Images

*Chapter 16*
Interior of the Royal Train, 1928: Topical Press Agency/Getty Images

*Chapter 17*
The Pompidou Centre under construction: Daniele Dailloux/Gamma-Rapho via Getty Images

*Chapter 18*
IKEA store: Elizabeth Dobbie/Fairfax Media via Getty Images

*Chapter 19*
The Promenade des Anglais: Hulton Archive/Getty Images

*Chapter 20*
La Coupole: AFP via Getty Images

*Chapter 21*
The Getty Villa, Ladispoli: Elisabetta Villa/WireImage